THE GATEKEEPER'S NOTEBOOK

SAHAR ABDULAZIZ

DJARABI KITABS PUBLISHING
Dallas, Texas

THE GATEKEEPER'S NOTEBOOK

This book is a work of fiction. Names, characters, businesses, organizations, places, events and incidents either are the product of the author's imagination or are used fictitiously. Any resemblance to actual persons, living or dead, events, or locales is entirely coincidental.

For information contact:
DJARABI KITABS PUBLISHING
PO BOX 703733
DALLAS, TX 75370
www.djarabikitabs.com

Cover Design by Patrick Knowles
Interior Design by H.H
ISBN-10: 1-947148-26-5
ISBN-13: 978-1-947148-26-0
EPUB ISBN-10: 1-947148-27-3
EPUB ISBN-13: 978-1-947148-27-7
Library of Congress Control Number: 2019933665
First Edition: July 2019

10 9 8 7 6 5 4 3 2 1

CONTENTS

Also by Sahar Abdulaziz

Psychological/Suspense, Fiction

As One Door Closes

The Broken Half

Secrets That Find Us

Tight Rope

Expendable

Unlikely Friends

Non-Fiction

But You LOOK Just Fine, Unmasking Depression, Anxiety, Post-Traumatic Stress Disorder, Obsessive-Compulsive Disorder, Panic Disorder and Seasonal Affective Disorder

DEDICATION

This story is dedicated to authenticity, but especially to those who reject the cloak of sainthood and sanctimony.

"The more we learn, the less and less motive we find for suicide. But for murder, we begin to have a surprising collection of motives!"

—Agatha Christie, Hercule Poirot, The Complete Short Stories

PROLOGUE

A STUBBORN DENSE MIST lifted off the searing asphalt. Bashir switched on his fog lights—for all the good they did. High winds, each surge stronger than the next, triggered tree branches to whip and thrash, while mighty thunder rattled his car windows. Inside of a minute, lightning split the night sky, and the next round of torrential rains fractured the heavens, pelting the already saturated earth. Such a miserable night to be on the road.

Like many other misguided souls before him, Bashir forgot how deceptive the spectacular mountainous peaks and valleys of the Poconos could instantly become. Suffering under the false assumption that years of acquired skills attained from city driving could help a driver pilot through the vast rambling landscapes and unforeseen bends like a pro. But as stunning as the mountains admittedly are, they are also cunningly captivating. Lulling the senses and dulling the wits of the unsuspecting into a state of false complacency, particularly when Mother Nature resolves to throw her disruptive hat into the ring; when the many twisting, narrow streets, potholed roads, and highways converge as if the plug of equanimity had been pulled and discarded.

Travel outside the posh, gated community, with its fancy tree-lined sidewalks and quiet paved streets, had turned treacherous. Anybody else entertaining even a modicum of common sense would have traversed the slick curves this stormy evening with added caution, but not Bashir, who sped past turns and gunned inclines way too fast. Consumed by the heat of his emotions, he revved his gas and raced by rows of luxurious homes, all clustered in small, safeguarded enclaves.

Speeding on these mountains was pure idiocy, or what Bashir's wife called suicidal. Even on bright, calm days—when skies remained clear and the air tempered—one could never anticipate when roads would unexpectedly snake or dip.

"Would you *please* go slower," Kalila would snarl through clenched teeth from the front passenger side whenever they drove together. "You could have at least put your seatbelt on!" She stared ahead; her eyes transfixed in horror; her hand gripped the safety strap over the window for support. "I swear, one of these days you're either going to hurt somebody or get yourself killed."

But on this blustery, rainy night, Bashir suspended all logic. He drove by rote; alone, distracted, angry, speeding around sharp bends and hydroplaning along drenched backroads, seduced by the dangling promise of salvation he'd find within *her*.

Tonight's conversation hadn't gone as planned. Not even close, despite the countless hours he spent preparing to drop *the news*. As soon as the discussion began, warning bells assaulted his brain.

Stop.

Proceed with caution. Approaching the danger zone.

Tread with care.

Yet, instead of heeding, instead of taking his time to explain and to clarify—to convince—he rushed past his words, irascibly knocking the wind out of his wife's wall of resistance.

Instead of tenderness, Bashir ran slipshod over her raw, exposed emotions, blinded by an unreasonable hope against all the odds that perhaps this time they'd have an adult conversation. But no. He'd blown it and bad. Hurling at her what could only be described as a vulgar and cruel, subpar version of his overly-practiced speech, thus irrevocably breaking her heart.

"Please don't do this," Kalila had begged him, her beautiful face ravaged by agony. A part of Bashir still pained to see his wife's eyes inflamed and swollen from crying; tears he knowingly caused by his callous obstinateness. Nevertheless, nothing could make him concede nor stop. Not this time. Not about this.

"I'm not trying to hurt you," he told her, his voice sounding more irascible than intended. "You need to trust me. Haven't I always been here for you?" The portentous question lingered between the feuding pair. "All I'm asking you to do is support me in this one situation. Is that asking too much?" Bashir balled his hands in tight fists and flung his arms in the air, exasperated. Worn out from hours of arguing and name-calling, trading accusations and blame, pretending his other life didn't exist.

"I love you so much," his wife whimpered through heavy sobs, "and you, you said you loved me." Bare desperation peppered each of her exposed words. "And yet you expect me to accept this?"

"I do love you. That's never going to change."

"But how? How won't it change?" she had wailed, hands

pleading. "On the one hand, you say you love me, but then in your next breath admit to falling in love with somebody else. How the hell does this even make sense, Bashir? Tell me!" Splashes of tears fell from her eyes.

Bashir never meant to lose his temper. That had not been part of the plan either. For months leading up to tonight, he had sworn—no matter how many times his wife needed to hear him say it, no matter how many ways he needed to repeat it, no matter how many tears Kalila shed—he'd be there, by her side; confirming his love and devotion until no uncertainty dared linger.

But when the time finally arrived to step up to the plate and follow through; when the pressure of her accusations backed him to the wall, he caved, hiding behind pride. Reverting back to the confines of his own self-importance while running roughshod over hers.

"Enough!" Bashir had hollered, slamming a fist on the table. "We're just going in circles. At this point, I don't care whether you believe me or not." Inside he cringed. Appalled at the hateful words his mouth so easily spewed. Nothing but wretched, hurtful lies, but by then, Bashir couldn't rein it in. "I get it. You're upset, but enough already. Cry. Call me all the names in the book, but I'm not changing my mind. I won't give her up."

Kalila flung her body on top of their bed, pressing her face into her pillow. "Don't do this Bashir," she whimpered. "Please stop."

His words plummeted out; raw, cutting, slicing like a razor through the last vestiges of Kalila's vanishing courage. "No. You stop," he roared, his face twisted in rage. "I'll be damned if I'm going to beg you for approval for something I have a God-given right to do."

There.

Said.

And now, Bashir got to witness firsthand the absolute devastation he alone had caused, strained across her disbelieving face. He watched his wife's hopelessness melt first into despair, then transform into an unbridled, wretched fury.

"I won't let you do this," Kalila threatened, but her voice lacked true conviction.

Bashir sneered. "You won't *let* me?" he snorted, his vulgar arrogance asphyxiating the room. "I wasn't asking for your permission."

***

The increased fog had drastically reduced visibility, making it more difficult for Bashir to either judge distance or gain traction. An unexpected bend in the winding road caused him to swerve. He lifted his foot off the gas, sharply steering the wheel in the direction of the skid, but once righted, his wounded ego refused to allow him to slow down. Before long, the roadway again lulled his better judgment and opened another door for memories to intrude.

They had married young.

At that age, Bashir hadn't been entirely sure what to expect or what would be expected of him as a husband. With good intentions, he had done his best with the knowledge he possessed; working long, arduous hours to provide for all his wife's needs and most—if not all—her desires, loving nothing more than being the one responsible for putting a smile on her beautiful face. He remembered that time when…

Bashir slammed his fist on the horn. "Get out of the way!" he yelled at the frightened fawn skittering across the dark road. "*Astaghfirullah*. Damn deer."

The rain, like Bashir's intrusive memories, refused to relent. Recollections of the past, pouring in one after the next, like when his baby boy arrived on the scene.

How determined Bashir had been to channel his entire focus on strengthening their troubled marriage. And for the longest time, he believed he had done exactly that, until his path crossed with *her*, and overnight—*everything* changed. He changed. His energies shifted along with his desires. The ravenous promise of having it all became too much to either ignore or dismiss. With the right planning, Bashir knew he could make it work. He had what it took to love two women. All he needed was patience…ample time for his wife to process the change.

She loves me. I love her. It's not like Kalila's going to throw away the marriage we both worked so hard to grow.

Sure—she'll be upset for a time…

First wives always were.

Bashir figured eventually, she'd acquiesce. Accept the inevitable. It was, after all, his due—*his right*. In the interim, he prayed that whatever added risks he employed to conceal or justify his life of subterfuge, would ultimately prove well worth the gamble.

Bashir moaned. Almost laughable in hindsight. The way he foolishly had convinced himself that he, unlike other men, understood how to handle the pitfalls attached to merging two households. How childishly he tried to compartmentalize his duplicity. First, by priming his wife with expensive gifts, then bestowing on her lavish trips and added attention, while all along feeding her a trail of convoluted lies, all in some vain attempt to validate his dishonesty.

In truth, Bashir understood clearly his wife's resentment at being deceived, and her unhinged jealousy at the prospect of him marrying again. In hindsight, he should have listened to the advice from the brothers—the ones already knee-deep in the polygyny process when they forewarned him; explaining in detail how emotions concerning the heart could quickly escalate and implode.

But Bashir suffered from a false sense of security, refusing to listen to reason or advice from anyone. His arrogance led him to believe his wife would eventually consent as long as he did it *the right way*. Then he uttered the fatal words 'co-wife'—and nothing he'd ever done before or after mattered worth a damn. Last night had been no different.

"I trusted you," she had cried, her declaration splintering through thick, heavy sobs.

"But sweetheart, I didn't do anything to break your trust," he said, serving her another platter of convoluted lies.

"You just told me you want to marry another woman. That you've fallen in love—again. How is that not breaking my trust?"

"Because me taking on another wife isn't about not loving you or about distrust. It's about what I need as a man outside of us."

The unsheathed incredulity smeared across Kalila's tormented face infuriated him.

"Instead of telling me what I should be doing," spat Bashir, losing his cool, "why don't you remember your *deen*. The rewards from Allah for the wife who is patient and *obedie*—" But Bashir never got the opportunity to finish his sentence before a shoe came soaring in his direction.

"Well, that was mature," he hollered, head cocked to the side to avoid impact.

"Fuck you," she spat, hate resonating from her eyes.

Bashir knew he had breached his wife's trust, and while somewhat regretful for the hurt and pain caused to Kalila, the remorse and guilt hadn't been near enough of a deal breaker to change his mind; not if it meant losing *her.*

***

The oil on the roads rose to the top. "Damn it," he moaned, as his tires skidded and spun. "Come on, come on." The wipers barely moved fast enough to clear the windshield before another blinding coat of rainfall fell in their place.

I can't take much more of this.

He slammed his fist on the steering wheel.

It's not like I'm abandoning her or our son…

Outside, the rain poured down in a torrent, pelting the windows.

At some point, she's going to have to accept the inevitable.

Bashir switched the defogger on higher.

She needs to stop attacking me for a minute and listen—end the blame game already.

He swung a quick right around a sharp bend descending a steep incline. At the bottom of the narrow hill, a line of large, spaced boulders marked the makeshift curb, placed there by an owner apparently fed up with people driving too fast and running over his property.

Bashir's mobile rang.

"You have an incoming call from—" announced the automated voice filtering through his hands-free Bluetooth. Bashir leaned over to push accept, just as another vehicle barreled around the corner, seemingly out of nowhere and from the opposite direction—driving straight towards him with his brights on.

"Ah! You fucking idiot," he yelled, unable to see. His foot instinctively slammed on the brake, causing the steering wheel to lock and become unresponsive.

The other motorist, with more room to finagle than Bashir, somehow maintained enough space between the two cars to stay planted on his side of the road, gunning his gas as he plowed ahead. By some small miracle, the driver swerved out of Bashir's way, but once past, he accelerated to the top of the steep rise, skirting away from any further impending threat.

Terrified, Bashir gripped the steering wheel for dear life, bracing for impact. Water roared against the side of the vehicle's wheels as the car gained speed, lifting the car away as if by magic, sending it careening, spinning into a swirling metal missile off the mountain's edge, spiraling out of control and bashing full force into the largest boulder below. On impact, the vehicle flipped and soared clear over the rock, smashing sideways into the base of a thick oak tree.

Emergency responders found Bashir's unbelted, blood-soaked body protruding halfway through the demolished passenger's side window upside down. Eyes open. His neck crooked unnaturally to the side, snapped in half like a twig.

The other driver, with neither car nor person grazed, never bothered to stop.

CHAPTER 1

The Not So Young and Restless

TIME TO GO.

Kalila twisted her neck to peer over his shoulder, gauging what it would take to retrieve her things from the far corner of the room, get dressed and slip out. Eyeing the chaotic pile of clothes, she hoped the slacks and blouse she'd wore wouldn't be too wrinkled, but the condition of her attire wasn't her most pressing issue at the moment. She had maybe forty minutes until the school bus arrived, factoring in afternoon traffic and school buses, maybe closer to thirty-five. Either way, arriving late for pick-up for the second time in the same week could not happen. Not again, particularly not after the last humiliation.

The body hard-pressed next to her was sound asleep and apparently dreaming—if the rapid succession of eye flutters and soft moans were any indication. Kalila squinted and peered down. She hadn't noticed before, but his hairline seemed a bit off. Perhaps because it looked a little too perfect. She stared, fascinated. And then she saw it.

Hair plugs.

But of course.

The unwelcomed weight of his sleeping limb slung casually over hers made moving agonizingly tricky. It would take a feat of dexterity to successfully extricate her numbed leg from under his entangled embrace without awakening him.

For Kalila, leaving tended to become complicated when in the midst of conducting in trade. The prior flirtatious pretense which brought her to their beds became no longer a necessary requirement upon exiting. Instead, she retained a calculated and clear mindset; a crucial component to surviving this business intact.

Now, if she could only sneak out without disturbing him.

Then again, she considered, *he'll have to wake up to lock up after I leave.*

Kalila winced.

I'm doing it again. Always playing the mother, the nurturer, the fixer. What in the hell do I care what he does or doesn't do after I leave? Whether or not he locks up?

This wasn't her concern, or at least it shouldn't have been.

And wasn't this the same conversation she had only last week with her therapist; when she informed Kalila about her co-dependent personality?

"You focus on the needs of others as opposed to your own, Kalila, and to your own detriment," explained the doctor.

Apparently, some old habits were harder to break than others.

After a few painstaking moves, Kalila managed to wiggle her leg free; relieved when she could rise from the luxurious king-sized bed, tip-toe over to the chaotic heap of clothes amassed on the rich marble floors and get dressed without any further impediments blocking her. Kalila, conscious of time slipping away, fought down the anxiety kicking in.

What did Amara say the other day?

Ah, right. How could I forget—

"I don't mind holding onto your kid once in a while, but you're making this into a regular habit."

Funny, Kalila never recalled asking Amara to do any such thing and never would—not in this lifetime.

"What'll happen to your kid if I'm late or not here at all? Then what?" hammered Amara, her voice taking on that superior inflection of hers earmarked for lectures and public dressing downs.

Kalila moved faster, having already reached her fill of run-ins with this grating woman, not to want another repeat.

When Kalila and her husband had first decided to make Pennsylvania their home, she agreed thinking the change from busy city life to a quieter suburban environment would be the solution to temper Bashir's roving eye. In the city, there had been too much past history and too much future temptation. When Bashir's company offered him a new position for more money, they jumped at the chance for a fresh start; willing to try anything that would afford them a reprieve from their constant bickering. However, Kalila soon discovered how simple surface solutions and quick fixes only served to mask difficult underlying issues, which if left to fester, eventually usurped a marriage. Especially when one partner remained adamant in their refusal to acknowledge the problem in the first place.

She scrolled through her mobile a second time to check for any missed calls or messages, especially from the school; relieved to find nothing in her inbox which warranted immediate attention. Kalila felt immense guilt keeping her status on Do Not Disturb but had little choice when working. Bad for business. Clients did not appreciate interruptions, no less a reminder that their paid 'dates' have a real life.

The pressure on her bladder went ballistic the second Kalila slid her foot through her pant leg. Leaning forward on one foot she took in her surroundings, relieved to spot the bathroom, its door partially ajar.

For all his fancy marble floors, luxurious damask draperies and plush bed linens, the apartment still felt empty—lonely. It lacks a certain warmth, and—Shit!

Kalila checked the time.

What am I doing?

Bladder distress or not, she had no time to piss away—literally. Not with how her life kept nose-diving into the abyss of hell. Plus, there was only so much 'waterworks' and drama she could deal with in one day without losing her mind entirely.

Screw it. I'll hold it in.

Kalila crept around like a burglar. Anything to get out without having to contend with another long, drawn-out sendoff or an open-ended discussion about 'the next time'—lumbering through a bunch of contrived pleasantries like old lovers. Enough already with all the playacting, like this was some real date.

She rolled her slack socks into a ball, stuffing them in her bag. One less thing to juggle as she snagged her shoes and windbreaker with one arm while attempting to clutch her purse to her chest with the other. Bare-footed, Kalila tiptoed across the glossy, cold floor towards the door, stealing furtive glances his way…praying with each step the idiot would stay asleep. However, as soon as she twisted the bedroom doorknob, the loud click startled him awake, evidence that all her stealth attempts had been for naught.

"Leaving so soon?" he asked groggily, wiping real or imagined sleep from his eyes.

"Yes," she murmured, trying to hide her annoyance. She tucked an escaped wisp of hair behind her ear. "I have to run."

He tapped the now empty, still warm space next to him.

Here it comes.

"Are you sure you don't have time for a—" he said, more of a dare than invite. The arrogant smirk across his face said it all.

"Not today." Kalila bent over letting her shoes clatter noisily to the floor. Slipping her feet into her flats, she was grateful once again for having made the smart decision to wear this comfy pair as opposed to high heels.

The man sat up, squashed two pillows, and placed one behind his body. He folded the other one in half under his neck for support. "Shame."

Kalila clapped her hands. "Okay then…well, this was fun," she said, running the same lame stock line used on all her regulars.

"It was better than nice." His beady eyes never left her chest.

Kalila slid her arm through her jacket sleeve and feigned an ingratiating smile in return. It was the least she could do—part of the service.

"I'd like to see you again. The first girl they sent over, Tammy-Sammy—Cammy, something along those lines…she didn't do it for me. I found her a bit rough around the edges if you ask me."

Trust me, Champ, nobody's going to ask you.

Kalila mused but pretended to agree, discreetly masking the start of a snarl performing cartwheels on her lips. She loathed clients like this guy. So totally full of himself. Functioning under the false impression that money insulated him from using even common courtesy.

Besides getting to the bus stop on time, her bladder had started to protest. With only inches between her and freedom, Kalila needed this conversation to end.

"I think you and I got something special," he said.

Special? —as compared to what? Contracting typhoid?

He leaned further back onto the pillow with his hairy arms folded casually across his bare chest. His sneer made her uncomfortable. Kalila bit her bottom lip, a bad habit that surfaced whenever overly anxious.

I can do this.

She offered him her most practiced fawning smile. "I so agree," she purred.

Whatever. You're all just 'John' to me.

Kalila checked the time. She had to go. "Just let them know you want to book me when you call," she reminded him.

The man smiled smugly, apparently satisfied by her answer.

Resigned, Kalila stepped towards the bed, her bag still clenched. Ordinarily, she refrained from showing any intimate gestures to her customers but broke her rule and gave him a quick peck on the lips. A small price to pay to keep him satisfied…for now.

"Take care, Marie. I'll see you soon."

Fuckin A.

Once safely back in the confines of her car, Kalila stole a moment to check her face in the mirror.

Eww! Smear-proof my ass.

As suspected, she had mascara muddied under both eyes. All traces of her pearl-pink lipstick also long gone. However, the stubborn red pimple budding on the side of her cheek, cleverly concealed under dollar store concealer, now looked in rare form.

Kalila reached over and pulled out a travel size package of makeup remover along with a few personal care essentials from the glove compartment. She yanked out a sheet with lightning speed and began dabbing underneath her eyes. Then the rest of her face, attempting to remove all visible traces of the past two hours. Unfortunately, the wipes would do little to assuage the guilt or hide her shame.

She pinched a rather fancy hair clip found under the back seat from the middle console.

Hers—

And in all likelihood, a gift from Bashir. Not the first time she had discovered little souvenirs from her husband's duplicitous other life. But this latest aide-mémoire had long lost its power to produce the level of incredulity or disgust Kalila had once clung to. She had almost tossed it, but on second thought decided to add it to her growing collection of little bitch trinkets. Small, inconsequential items purposefully left around for the finding. Like the random slip of paper with the strange, flowery female handwriting on it—nothing more than a bulleted food list, but it had landed the same painful blow; innocuous and poisonous all at the same time. Then there were the menus shoved between maps in the side door pocket of the passenger side for restaurants never visited, or a bent up discarded ticket stub to a movie she'd never seen.

The last straw happened the day Kalila detected a whiff of fragrance sullying Bashir's discarded clothing. A vapid, cheap perfume and one Kalila would never have been caught dead wearing. Then to compound matters, she glimpsed a photo on his phone, and all hell broke loose. The arguments from that moment forward never stopped.

Kalila waved his phone close to his cheek. "Who is she, Bashir? And don't bother lying." A photo of her husband and his side chick filled the screen. "Don't you two look cozy."

Bashir reached to swipe the phone out of her hand but missed. "Give me that," he threatened.

"What's her name?" She swiped up. "Says here she—" But before Kalila could finish, Bashir had already snatched the phone back, blocking his wife's advances with his other extended arm.

Livid, Kalila fought back, flailing her hands, and clipping him on the side of his face. "I hate you!" she screamed, tears pouring down from her angry eyes. "You're a cheating son of a bitch." Kalila crumpled to her knees, her arms clenching her stomach. The bitter taste of his infidelity scorched her throat.

Bashir continued packing. "You need to get right with your Creator, Kalila."

"Shut up! Just shut up!"

"You've stopped me before, but not this time."

"Get out! I never want to see you again."

***

In a rush, Kalila decided to forgo a comb through or a quick pitstop home to pee. Instead, she swept back her longer than shoulder-length hair from her face with both hands, clipping it in a messy bun at the nape of her neck. From the passenger side, Kalila groped blindly around in search of her black scarf. After wrapping the cloth adeptly around her head and neck, she shoved the key into the ignition, turning to check for oncoming traffic before pulling out. Her bladder protested.

Damn! I knew I should have gone to the bathroom.

Too late now.

Stressed over being late again, Kalila threw caution along with common sense to the wind and drove, exceeding the speed limit the entire trip. Afternoon traffic during this hour could be gruesome but getting pulled over and ticketed would have been worse.

Taking a wide left turn, she pulled into The Royal Gates, the exclusive gated community located conveniently only minutes away from the Delaware Water Gap, and an easy drive into New Jersey. Kalila slowed to a complete stop just before the guard shack. Grabbing her bag, she searched for her gate pass, but as usual, it had dropped to the bottom. Behind her, driving away from the community mailboxes, was an expensive SUV sporting slightly tinted windows, honking its horn.

"All right already. Jeez, asshole," she grumbled, edging the car as close as possible to scan her pass. Kalila drove through, but not before stealing a quick peek into her rearview mirror to check out who in the hell felt the need to harass her. One glance told her all she needed to know.

With over half the week already shot, Kalila felt ready to pack it in, but she still needed to get home and make *ghusl*— anxious to scrub away the film of obscenity coating her body and catch up on her missed afternoon prayers.

She drove, concealing the humiliation, determined to ignore the glaring, despicable truth that she had just left yet another strange man's bed. Worn and exhausted, her entire being pleaded for a hot meal loaded with more carbs and calories than her thighs could possibly absorb, not to mention a few hours of uninterrupted sleep before facing the inevitable. Her soul, tattered and ashamed, begged for a few private moments alone with her Creator.

However, for the time being, Kalila granted herself a small reprieve in contrast to the usual self-reproach lap dancing around her life. This week alone she had earned enough to satisfy next month's hefty mortgage with some left over for groceries, as well as the fee to cover her son's upcoming field trip, *Insha'Allah*.

CHAPTER 2

Old life. New life. What life?

DESPITE THE AWKWARD ANGLE, Amara managed to stretch her flabby arm under the couch as far as she could, using her outstretched fingers to coax one chewed broken pencil, four coins of various denominations, an unidentifiable piece of plastic toy, and a somewhat still tacky food wrapper out of hiding. Not a bad haul. Continuing to grope blind, she yelped when her fingernail caught and tore on the rough under-couch fabric.

"Damn it to F-in Hell! That hurt."

Amara had a strict policy not to curse in front of the children, but there were times when only a strong, loud expletive would suffice. Besides, the boys weren't expected home for at least another thirty minutes, and Qasim practically lived at his job—*so fuck it.*

Just great.

Her nail looked as bad as it felt. She cautiously peeled the hanging piece off without ripping away new skin with it.

My fault for waiting this long to clean the place up.

This latest home-inspired combat injury throbbed. "Ouch!" she whined, flicking her finger in the air.

I do this to myself.

Truth was, Amara enjoyed running around and pretending to beat the clock while getting rid of clutter and chaos, comparing her blitz to actual cardio exercise. She had already tried her luck using exercise videos, with little success. Either her body flat-out refused to contort into the required positions, or she found them plain boring to do.

Too self-conscious to join a gym because of her weight, Amara searched for different ways to change up the pace and create a diversion for herself. Anything to stop from parking her fat ass on the couch and mindlessly marathon snacking herself into an early grave. At one point, she convinced herself to buy a rather expensive elliptical; one loaded with every bell and whistle known to mankind. However, after less than one flaky month of semi-use, the fancy machine got retired, dragged to the back corner of her kids' oversized playroom, and relegated to join the rest of the barely used discarded gym equipment.

Amara rummaged through the official family junk drawer.

Because like why keep medical supplies together?

She eventually found one barely sticking, highly questionable, bandage. "Much better," she grumbled after applying it.

Back to business. With an empty plastic laundry bin designated for crap retrieval firmly in hand, Amara began her daily purge. First, she dashed around the entire bottom floor of her house tossing in books, toys, stray socks, dirty cups, and even used tissues, but the collection was only half the battle. Disposal of said items took place on the second floor. Hiking up the stairs, she'd began her second line of attack, starting in the bedrooms. Sorting and putting everything back in its proper place until the rooms no longer resembled pure bedlam.

Amara never could figure out how her entire existence seemed to revolve around daily sock rescue or the dissemination of soiled clothing, but here she was, in all her glory and on her knees; searching under the bed for the partner of the stiff sock caked in dry mud clenched in her hand.

Before marriage, Amara, then referred to as *Amy* by family and friends, enjoyed quite the rowdy social life, having gained popularity more by default than likeability. Fairly well-feared, Amy knew who to cozy up to in the most popular crowds, casting herself in the highly-vetted position of everyone's trusted confidant and friend; and then hoarding any compromising information for later use. She attempted to employ the same questionable tactics far into adulthood, but with far fewer promising results.

During her youth, Amara's best asset was her solid, agile legs coupled with natural hand-eye coordination. In fact, she had been coveted by college scouts to play volleyball while still in high school. She fondly remembered how her parents had both wept the day the acceptance letter arrived in the mail, hugging their daughter with pride. With money tight, the offer had not only been a welcomed surprise but an embraced necessity.

Having earned a sports scholarship to attend a prestigious college only two hours' distance from home had been a dream come true. As expected, Amy fit in comfortably, enthralled with landing in the center of all the latest happenings. And while the team uniform–if you could even call it that–scarcely covered her butt cheeks, she hadn't minded. Not then. Not when her young, firm bosom perked to perfection and her bottom affably curved.

Amara and Qasim met on campus during the start of her third year. Both were studying accounting. The studious young man, nose deep within his textbooks, barely noticed the brash, pushy girl sitting next to him, much to Amy's chagrin. No matter how many times she tried to initiate a conversation, Qasim remained politely aloof. However, this did little to stop or discourage Amy, who thought him smart and sort of cute, although a bit on the slim side. However, she found Qasim's height, dark features, and square, prominent jaw immensely attractive. Not to mention his having the longest darn lashes she'd ever seen wasted on a man.

Amy, after practically stalking him for an entire semester, started to appreciate Qasim's reserved, well-mannered demeanor, especially in comparison to the guys she customarily gravitated toward.

***

"Ah Ha!" Amara declared. "Victory at last!" While Amara hadn't necessarily unearthed the MIA sock, she did discover something more valuable. Her son's retainer–misplaced for the umpteenth time. When the school called, claiming he lost it during lunch—*again*, she flat-out refused to help in the search, adamant that she breaks out in hives whenever reminded about the all-too-vivid nightmare of dumpster diving behind the school's cafeteria. Knee deep, standing in muck, while sifting through piles of some of the most highly questionable food trash, remained just as unappealing now as it did then. The fact her rotten kid outright lied to her through his formerly crooked teeth about where he said he misplaced it, paled under the weight of facing that mini-nightmare again. Nevertheless, Amara moved the little liar straight to the top of her revolving shit list.

Time to attack the bathrooms: spittle, hair on the sink, toothpaste slime, and a waste bin filled with more trash near it than in it. After a quick spritz here, a swipe or two there, she'd be finished for the day. Any of the more laborious scrubbing and scouring could wait for the maid's arrival. Although the weekly cleaning service made a valiant effort to restore her home to its magnificent showcase brilliance, it never lasted long enough to enjoy. By the next day, the kitchen would already be wrecked. The sink piled high with caked-on dirty dishes, the garbage pail overflowing, and the countertops littered with a heap of miscellaneous castoff household junk.

It never failed. Once the boys got home from school, they'd toss clothes, coats, backpacks, shoes…Within hours, a new set of toys or games, each owning a thousand pieces, would litter every available surface. Everything from poorly wiped spills to food crumbs, to the constant bickering and complaints—it never stopped. And all she had accomplished in their absence would vanish.

***

Back in the day—

Amy knew next to nothing about Muslims, except what she heard reported on the news or through passing conversations, and most of that was unhelpful, if not wholly inaccurate. It had surprised her how little the rigid conception she'd built in her head about Islam had matched up with the young, serious guy she'd come to like and admire. Curious to learn more, Amy tried thinking up stuff to say to Qasim to gauge his replies and measure his interest in her; a hit-miss proposition.

"After class, a few friends and I plan to grab a bite to eat," she announced one afternoon. Qasim half-smiled and went back to his writing.

"We're gonna try out that new brewery downtown. I hear they have amazing food and beer on the cheap." Qasim peered up. His expression seemed non-judgmental, which Amy of course, took as an invitation to continue. "Would you like to come?"

"Thanks, but I don't drink."

"Oh. Is that like a Muslim thing? Not drinking?"

Qasim snorted. "Yeah, it's a Muslim thing."

"Oh, wow, like, I'm sorry. I didn't mean any disrespect."

Qasim lowered his gaze.

"I mean, you can still come, right? It's not like you have to drink or anything, and like, the food is supposed to be seriously awesome."

Qasim dropped his pen in the crease of his open textbook. "Thanks, but I don't hang out at bars, even if I'm not drinking." He leaned back in his chair. "Not my 'Muslim thing,'" he said, simulating air quotes with his fingers.

Amy stared, unable to figure out if he was purposely being sarcastic or just plain, flat out rude. Either way, his flippancy made her uncomfortable. "Okay, well, if you change your mind," she mumbled, cheeks turning a crimson red. But Qasim never noticed, having already returned to his studies. Despite the apparent brush off, Amy swore never to bring up this touchy subject again.

Back in high school, Amy recalled a compulsory history class on world religions. Christianity, Judaism, and Islam were discussed and compared. The course also mentioned, however briefly, Hinduism, Buddhism, and Atheism, but only in passing.

Amy found the course fascinating. She found herself agreeing with many of the basic concepts of each belief, but for most of the female classmates, the hardest notion to wrap their head around was Islam's position on polygamy. For the teacher's part, he had tried to mention it with as little fanfare as possible; then tried moving on quickly. But as anticipated, the guys in the class favored the idea of polygamy. For Amy, the mere thought of sharing a husband with another wife—or three other women, seemed utterly bizarre. Almost barbaric. Something straight out of the middle ages—and against everything she'd been brought up to believe about the tenets of marriage.

"How in the world could that kind of thing work?" she had argued with her male classmates. "Even if everyone agrees to it. But what happens if let's say, one of the wives doesn't want it? Then what?" She could easily imagine the hurt and jealousy.

During her studies on Islam with Qasim, Amy's mind frequently wandered back to polygamy. She was dying to ask him his opinion but didn't know how to approach him without sounding like a total loser.

What if he wants more than one wife? Then what do I do?

Maybe he's already got a secret wife, or two stashed away somewhere...or another one waiting in the wings.

I never saw him wear a ring...

If he winds up marrying two or three–or gosh, even four wives, I wonder if he has to wear a wedding band for each?

Damn, she was so confused. Nevertheless, equally as eager to find out.

Boldly asking him out on a date had failed miserably, so she set out to grab Qasim's attention in other, more subtle ways, starting with the change of her appearance. Amy decided to try to dress more modestly, much like she'd seen the other Muslim girls on campus. Instead of relying on her usual tight jeans and fitted tops, worn to emphasize her more than ample cleavage, she shopped for a few less form-fitting garments; blouses with mid or long sleeves and longer, looser skirts.

Initially, the outward transition felt strange, but warmer weather allowed her to change styles, add long flowing skirts and peasant blouses without drawing further attention to herself.

Gradually, her strategy worked. Qasim not only noticed but began warming up to her. Instead of immediately averting his eyes when she said hello, he'd greet her. Nothing explicitly flirty or brash; that simply wasn't his way, but gentlemanly. As if genuinely happy to see her. Then, one day out of the blue, Qasim invited Amy to join him in the student lounge for lunch.

"So, what are you exactly?" Amy asked in the midst of devouring a plate of greasy fries swimming in ketchup.

"I assume you mean religiously?" said Qasim good-naturedly; his almond brown eyes burning into her ocean blues.

"No. I already know you're Islamic."

"Muslim," he corrected. "I am Muslim. My belief is Islam."

Her face grew hot under Qasim's baleful stare.

"Does it bother you I'm Muslim?" A faint trace of edginess tainted his question.

"Why should it?" Amy shot back, miffed. Ready to challenge Qasim's mistaken assumptions about her.

"These days, for most people it does."

"Well, for your information, I'm not most people," she answered spiritedly. And then, without missing a beat, she pointed to her plate. "French fry?"

***

Throughout the next two semesters, their frequent lunch dates consisted primarily of question and answer periods with Amy providing most, if not all, the questions. For Qasim's part, he patiently answered her, sometimes providing books or video suggestions, until finally, one afternoon before class, he presented Amy with a Quran.

"Here. This is for you," he mumbled, careful not to be overheard by the other students entering the classroom. "For the record, I'm not trying to convert you or anything, but since you're always asking me stuff, I thought it would give you way better answers than anything I can," he said, evidently uncomfortable.

Amy accepted the leather covered emerald green book with ornate gold lettering. "It's so beautiful," she said, touched by his gift. "Oh, good, there's English." Both English and Arabic adorned the pages.

Qasim grinned, pleased. "Yeah. The Quran's been translated into almost every language to make it easier for all people to read. It's not an exact translation of the Arabic, but close enough. The Arabic is much more precise."

Initially, Amy didn't know where to begin. Was this indeed a gift or just Qasim's way of getting her off his back? Unsure, she left the undisturbed book on her dorm desk. But after a week or so, she decided *what the hell* and began reading. Only a few pages at night, but after a while, she started jotting down a whole new slew of questions in a notebook, now prominently labeled 'Islamic Studies.' The more time she devoted to studying Islam under her new friend's tutelage, the more she became attracted to its principles—*and Qasim,* however, from the jump, he had made it clear why he didn't date.

"Never?" Amy asked stunned. "Like never-ever?"

"No. Never. Don't get me wrong, I'm not going to lie to you. It's hard, but I want to do this right. I want to get married like my parents did."

"And by 'right,' I assume you mean only to a Muslim girl?"

"That's my preference."

***

Up to this point, their casual lunches in the student lounge had been their only interactions, but instead of being discouraged, Amy became more determined. Having never met anyone like Qasim, she'd often tell her girlfriends she met a guy without baggage, and how she would never have thought they existed anymore.

"Be careful. The quiet ones are always the creepiest," one friend informed her over pizza.

"Qasim's not creepy—he's just, you know, shy," Amy explained.

"I don't know," piped up another friend, wiping her mouth with a napkin. "I remember watching this show where a girl was like, super into some dude, and he was like, super shy and all."

"What happened?" asked Amy.

"Well, once they got together, he was like some kind of closet psycho or something."

"You're making that up," countered Amy, miffed.

"Am not, I swear."

As the semesters rolled by, Amy's interest in her everyday extracurricular activities began to wane. Besides the change in her attire, she no longer attended off-campus keg parties, where she'd get drunk or laid. And although no one in her inner circle came right out and pressured her to join them; the truth was, she just didn't care.

After reading how Muslims didn't eat pork, Amy gave it up as well. However, the whole "*halal*" meat thing still confused her, so she opted to eat only chicken, beef, and occasionally lamb, hedging her bet Allah would be cool with that level of abstinence.

Eventually, Amy's grades improved, but the once oh-so-important volleyball team became irrelevant. She continued to show up for practice and games, knowing better than to ditch her scholarship entirely, but the required, skimpy uniform now felt strangely awkward and much too revealing.

Without disclosing to anyone, Amy took her *shahadah*. Her family and friends were alarmed, unable to fathom the drastic changes in her behavior, or her choice of religion, and certainly not with the strange clothing she now wore—the *hijab* in particular. Many of her old friends felt betrayed over what they saw as a duplicitous secret life.

"Over a guy?" accused her roommate and closest friend, Kerri. "Seriously? I thought you were smarter than this."

"No, not over *a guy*," said Amy, her arms crossed over her chest. "I believe in it."

"Sure, you do."

"I do."

"And I suppose that guy Qasim has nothing to do with this?" Kerri said, pointing at Amy's clothing. "You just woke up one day and decided, hey—you know what? Let's ditch everything. Old life, family, friends. Presto, I'm Islamic. Just like that," taunted Kerri, snapping her fingers in Amy's face.

"Hey!"

"Poof, old life gone. Flushed down the toilet, including your name and religion."

"Stop it."

"Why should I? It's exactly what you did, and you know it!"

"Only if you're judging me on the surface, but that's not what I'm doing."

Kerri's eyes widened. "Do tell."

"First off, I didn't presto-anything. I converted to Islam, not Islamic."

Not appreciating the correction, Kerri hurled a pillow at Amy's head. "Whatever."

"See, this is exactly why I never told you. It's not 'whatever.' This is important to me."

"No, it's not. Qasim is what's important to you."

"I knew you'd never get it."

"I get it all right. You dumped all your friends. All of a sudden, you're too good to hang with us lowlifes. Too perfect to eat our food, drink or party. Shit, even your volleyball game has crashed and burned."

Kerri's remarks cut deep. Apparently, she had become the topic of conversation among her so-called friends and teammates. Oh, how the tables had turned. Typically, Amy would be the one coveting the gossip, criticizing, backbiting, and finding fault in others. It was a known fact around campus nobody could tear a person apart like Amy. Being in the other shoe pinched.

"It is what it is," Amy countered, less emphatically.

"You're throwing your life away."

"No, I'm not. Qasim and I are in love."

Kerri laughed.

"You've got something you want to say?"

"Nope. I'm not saying anything else. You know everything."

"Say it!"

"Never mind."

"No, if you've got something to say, then say it, Kerri, or shut the hell up!"

"And there it is."

"What?"

"You. Amy. All of it. This stuff," Kerri waved her hands around the dorm room. "Your clothes, your new way of acting all high and mighty. You're so blinded by this guy that you can't even keep your lies straight anymore." Kerri grabbed her backpack. "I'm done," she hollered, stomping out of the dorm room, and slamming the door behind her.

A poster, a gift from Qasim taped precariously to the brick wall behind her made a loud snap as it whipped down and rolled across the floor, but Amy, now known as Amara, was too irritated to care. "Screw you, Kerri," she grumbled. "I don't care what any of you think."

But that was a lie. Amara did care, and she always would.

***

Amara hesitated at the top of the stairs. She couldn't help but feel a small glimmer of accomplishment wash over her as she glanced around at her freshly neatened home.

"Time to go." Amara darted to her room to change; running a mental checklist of everything that still needed to get done.

Bring garbage pail back, grab the mail, pick the boys up from the bus.

The utter meaninglessness of each day zapped so much of her energy. As much as Amara cooked and cleaned, doing what she could to keep the house and children in order, it never seemed enough to combat the loneliness and rejection she felt from being stuck in a loveless marriage to a man who barely cared, or remembered she existed.

CHAPTER 3

Another World

GENTLY STACKING HIS NEWEST, finished sketchbook on top of the already overly high pile, Melvin clicked his tongue three times. Never more, never less. His mother understood this gesture to indicate all was right in Melvin's World.

"Let's find you another notebook," she told him, leaning her small, frail frame against the doorway for support. "I think there's an extra one in the study. I'll go check," she mumbled, her statement clearly directed more to herself than to him.

Melvin's room boasted wall-to-wall shelving, meticulously lined with variously sized sketchbooks all in varying degrees of decay. Covers bent, frayed or yellowed over time, with some seemingly dustier than others. Those more recently completed were tucked flush to the back of the smallest ledge for easy access.

Excursions into habitual drawing began from the time Melvin could properly hold a pencil. Since then, decades of illustrations were accumulated into sketchbooks, sometimes one drawn right after the other, and each employing a voice distinctively its own. Detailed images showcasing a variable density of tones. Complicated scenes depicting love, disappointment, loss—hope—joy, sadness, and more recently—unspeakable grief. Upon each page, a distinctive story unfolded, sometimes accompanied by a simple scribbled comment or word.

Melvin preferred drawing outdoors whenever possible. Whether parked on his front porch, positioned on a step on the back deck or meandering around the neighborhood on his many strolls, he missed very little. These capsulated moments were sequenced, and when viewed together, they made for a rare chronological timeline, brought to fruition through the keen eye of their unique creator.

Without interference, Melvin watched, persistent…vigilant. His train of thought culminating into a minefield of precise visualizations. And while the tenor of his formidable drawings remained unquestionably exacting over the years, his observations were forever changing, evolving to the next level. Ironically, had anyone shown the slightest interest or requested a peek at his guarded pages, they would have been welcomed and left most certainly enthralled; awestruck at the treasure trove of hidden information embedded within about the comings and goings of an insulated community, which prided itself on privacy. However, to date, Melvin's notebooks had remained unvisited. Stacks of them. Out in the open and perched on their prospective shelves. And for now, their many secrets remained protected with nobody the wiser so far…

Melvin circled his bedroom, one arm extended out just far enough to allow his fingertips to brush past the outer binding of each housed sketchpad, the same ritual reenacted whenever another book joined the already impressive growing ranks.

"Look at those shelves, Melvin," said his mother. "Jam-packed. I'm surprised you can fit one more thing in."

Melvin tilted his head but continued pacing. He heard his mother's displeasure.

"One of these days your books are going to bust right out of this space," she said, eyeing what was for her a fire hazard. "And then what?" However, Melvin, engaged in his fixed routine, failed to see the problem; decades worth of filled sketchpads awaited his ceremonial christening.

While growing up, Melvin's parents, along with a host of teachers and doctors, and an extensive list of therapists had all endeavored to coach the young boy to verbally communicate. However, only after adolescence came and left did it become clear he'd probably never master a notable fluidity in speech.

Words frustrated Melvin. To him, people used way too many words. Sometimes bad words...hurtful words...sinister words which caused people to cry. Melvin didn't like when mean people called him naughty names. That hurt. But rather than engaging or taking the risk of further ridicule, he'd rely on a series of carefully orchestrated hand motions or sounds, like his three tongue clicks to describe his needs, clarify his wants or show his displeasures.

Mrs. Vine laid a new notebook on Melvin's desk blotter, putting it carefully down so as not to let it slip or fall. Melvin tended to become anxious and unduly upset if his notebooks weren't treated kindly.

"When you're finished, come to the kitchen. Lunch is ready," she said, but Melvin could not stop, even if he wanted to. The compulsion forced him to continue making his appointed rounds to precision.

Four steps, stop—three steps turn—touch, touch, touch.

"Melvin," called his mother from the kitchen. "Lunch."

Melvin scampered out of his bedroom to the front living room and pulled the curtain to the side just in time to catch pretty Kalila from next door backing her car out of her driveway. "Kalila gone," he said to no one.

Melvin remained at his post for a few minutes longer.

"What are you looking at, Melvin?" asked his mother.

Melvin, overly enthralled watching the mean lady from across the street angrily drag her garbage pail back didn't answer.

"Melvin, let's go. Your lunch is ready. Come, sit."

Melvin did as he was told, but his creative mind was already focused on capturing this moment in his next drawing.

Besides a bedroom, crammed with overstuffed bookshelves, Melvin collected an assortment of maps; an interest started when his father clipped a small diagram from the front of an old phone directory.

"Keep this handy, Melvin, just in case you should ever get lost," reminded his father. Before handing it off, Mr. Vine scribbled down their home address, drawing a pronounced red **X** specifically on their street. "All you gotta do is show this map to someone, and they'll be able to bring you back. Understand, son?"

Melvin tilted his head and sniffed the paper. Without offering any affirmation, he proceeded to fold the paper five times, creating the perfect sized square to fit securely in his shirt pocket. Funny enough, to date, the same neatly folded local map came along with him whenever he left the house—not because he needed it, Melvin had long since memorized the entire localized area, including every designated stop sign, road marker, and street name; but because his father told him to.

As Melvin's interest in maps grew, Mr. Vine made a point of clipping them from the town's free monthly newspaper or discarded circulars. Through a relatively arduous process of hit and miss, Mr. Vine soon figured out his son's preference centered around black and white drawings more so than the colorful variety often stamped on thick yellow tinted paper.

If Melvin ran across a map which interested him, he'd sniff the paper first. Once scent approved, he'd dash off, ready to cut and splice to perfection; then add it to the manila folder kept on his desk. However, should Melvin not approve, he'd show his displeasure by covering both his ears with his fists and shaking his head violently back and forth; moaning about the picture being "too loud."

The Gates—the nickname used by locals—is comprised of a stark mixture of older and newer homes. Many boasted spacious, multi-tiered decks with elaborate built-in BBQ pits and outdoor kitchens, for which their affluent owners paid extra so they could overlook sprawling lawns and gazebos facing the Appalachian Mountains or the closed community's golf course. Three-car garages were considered the standard, along with outdoor Jacuzzis and encased fire pits.

Sidewalks, a novelty in the Poconos, lined each property; lit up at night by classic black antique streetlamps, lending the neighborhood an air of sophistication and exclusivity. But for most residing families, The Gates represented their sanctuary…their oasis, a place to call home away from the hustle and bustle of an otherwise sprawling mountainous community. For Melvin, it described his entire existence.

Like most gated communities, The Gates expected their stringent rules to be observed. On any given day, a myriad of lawn service companies could be seen and heard, running mowers and blowers at rapid speeds across sprawling yards. Even without the help of a paid service, the Vines kept one of the best-manicured lawns in the area. Their glorious gardens and splendid flower beds attested to their prowess. A lush bed of elegant tulips—Mrs. Vine's darlings and the first flowers planted when they had purchased the house. A path of red and yellow lined the brick walkway leading up to the front stoop, boasting an unmistakable touch of Holland in the Poconos. However, the deer population, a constant menace, were notorious for consuming practically all foliage, especially flowerbeds and gardens, in a single evening's feeding. If the beasts caught wind of tulips, they'd go on the attack, eating like starving lumberjacks all the way down to the root.

For reasons nobody quite understood, the deer stayed clear away from the Vines' lawn, much to the resentment of their less than friendly neighbors—the Zubairi's, directly across the street, who paid through the nose for their chemically induced grass to grow. Whenever Mr. Zubairi chased the deer away, resorting to throwing pebbles or anything else quickly grabbed, Melvin would become frantic; stomping his feet and covering his ears to block out the cursing coming from across the street.

"No, no! Not nice," he'd yell in protest. Melvin had an entire shelf of notebooks dedicated to recording that family's antics.

Mrs. Vine, knowing how skittish deer behave, hung a series of wind chimes and other decorative ornaments made by Melvin and his dad. A whimsical collection of old keys or mixed-matched teacups tied together with fish wire to a shared branch, and then hung outside the house. It created a soft tinkling sound that even Melvin didn't complain about.

Melvin's daily chores also included collecting the home's area rugs for cleaning.

"Make sure to give them a good whacking this time," reminded his mother for the thirtieth year in a row. "Especially the one from the front hallway."

One by one, Melvin rolled, dragged, and threw each rug over the deck railing just as he'd been taught. Once sufficiently beaten with the broom, his mother would take over; vacuuming them just in case something got missed. Now that age and illness had caught up with her, a cleaning service came weekly, and while they did a reasonably adequate job, Mrs. Vine still trailed behind them, hovering close by to make sure they didn't miss a spot or fail to eradicate a stubborn stain.

A vast number of religious symbols adorned the Vine abode—all the ocular accouterments of a good Catholic home. Melvin didn't particularly care for those and found a few scary, especially the ornate crucifixes which hung over every bedroom door. In the family room, Bibles and other religious readings filled every available shelf space. Everything from *The Latin Vulgate Bible* to the *New Revised Standard Version, Catholic Edition.* Mrs. Vine was determined to make sure her son, despite his learning challenges, would be properly brought up within the fold. As far as she was concerned, if she couldn't protect Melvin's mind, she'd make sure as heck to save his soul.

"Come," she'd tell him, tapping the cushion next to her. "Sit with me, Melvin. Let me read you a story."

Melvin would join his mother for their daily supplications, although most of the time, he didn't understand what the heck she was talking about. For him, the biblical stories told by his father were the ones which really held his interest the most. His father would wave his hands and act out the various parts; creating tales mostly about angels and demons, saints and sinners, where he turned everyone into an action figure. And while his tales were shared verbatim, strewn together by a wild imagination and a faulty memory, they never failed to hold Melvin's rapt attention, much to Mrs. Vine's stern displeasure.

Melvin's favorite story was about Saint Bernadette of Lourdes, whose visions were said to give people the hope of a cure. To him, Saint Bernadette sounded beautiful and kind. Someone who would never call anyone a bad name or laugh uproariously after witnessing an unfortunate tumble or social blunder. Melvin thought it befitting that like him, Saint Bernadette could only read and write sparingly, due to her frequent illnesses. And while described as a woman small in stature, measuring only four feet, seven inches, he envisioned her larger than life; more like an angel-superhero than an agent for God.

Nonetheless, with each larger than life telling, a new host of evocative images summoned Melvin's process of reason and placement. While he may not have necessarily grasped the moral lessons each parable provided, or fully comprehended the concept of his mother's God, which remained forever ambiguous and omnipresent; he did fully comprehend the intent.

Angels were given messenger and superhero status and could be trusted, whereas demons were bad and dangerous—evil beings who should be avoided at all costs. Demons had the power to transform into human beings—mean people whose hearts were made of fire with souls of stone. And while Melvin couldn't necessarily apply the proposed instruction as his mother would have wished, he easily gleaned the difference between good or bad, even if in the most basic and human of terms.

Kalila, the nice lady from next door, reminded him of just such a superhero, an angel. The kind he could trust. She never spoke mean to him or called him any bad names. Pretty Kalila ... the lady with the happy hands that always waved nice. Melvin adored her flowery, long dresses and the many different colored scarfs worn on her head, sometimes wrapped high like a queen's crown. Melvin never saw Kalila get mad...only sad, but to him, she represented everything good.

"Morning, Melvin," Kalila yelled, waving from her driver's side window. "Where are you off to today?"

Melvin turned towards the familiar voice, "Hi," he answered holding his trusted notebook with one hand and waving back with the other. And although he didn't return the smile, on the inside his heart beamed.

"It's such a beautiful day today."

"Beautiful day," he repeated.

"Well, enjoy!" she called out before rolling up her window and driving away.

"Bye," said Melvin continuing to wave, eyes glued forlornly on the back of her car. His fingers itching to get back to drawing in his notebook.

The Vine's and Rahim's backyards were separated only by a low fence placed for aesthetics. Last fall, while Kalila gardened in her yard, she heard moaning and looked up in time to see how frustrated Melvin became when his pencil points broke. Later that day, she brought him over a set of new colored pencils, a small electric sharpener, and a large ream of crisp white paper; packed in a colorful gift bag with tissue paper. Although Melvin drew solely with graphite pencils, this generous and kind gesture planted Kalila forever in his heart and mind as the breathing embodiment of an angel. His very own superhero angel who happened to wear her cape on top of her head.

But Miss Kalila wasn't the only member of the Rahim family Melvin admired. He also liked her son, Hamza; one of the only children on the block who never teased or made fun of him. Hamza kept Melvin company on his deck when he drew, and spoke to him with nice words; like friends do. Hamza even once tussled with a few of the other neighborhood kids when they called Melvin names and threw acorns at him.

Hamza is nice. I like Hamza.

I don't like the mean lady. I don't like her naughty boys.

As his many drawings attested to, Melvin didn't like that family––not one tiny little bit.

***

Melvin lowered himself onto the deck stairs at the back of his house. Mesmerized by the symphony of noises emanating from the flock of unseen birds nesting high up in the oak tree's thick canopy; tweeting their call songs. He listened carefully, able to detect the subtle tone differences between their chirps—those of alarm and those of greeting.

A slight easterly breeze began to whip high through the overbrush; winds finding unimpeded passage echoed in a soft rustling fervor. Melvin relished how the gales caused the Pennsylvania forest to burst alive. Tall, massive trees gracefully swayed against the orchestrated flow.

Melvin, remaining perfectly still, watching a sprightly small chipmunk foraging on the ground by his feet, seemingly in a manic search for acorns or perhaps fungi. Oblivious to any impending danger, this scrupulous little fella kept stuffing its found tasty morsels into its already protruding cheek pouches, and with each new delectable addition it'd let out a satisfied clicking sound. Three to be exact. Melvin clicked his tongue three times in response.

The outdoors provided Melvin a safe space, his refuge. The place where he found solace when the world around him didn't care to understand or tolerate his existence. Here nobody questioned him. Neither the birds, the trees, the chipmunks or the other natural inhabitants. In this place and time, he was accepted just as he was—different and exquisitely beautiful, both in his equal and unequivocal reverence for their right to exist outside of him.

Melvin reached into his shirt pocket and drew out a newly sharpened pencil. On his lap rested his next sketchpad, wonderfully empty and inviting. Licking the tip, another habit of his, he began to fill the white space with lines. Many lines. Lines pushed hard and lines barely visible, all converging into shape and size, under his control and skill.

Melvin's drawings represented his world. They spoke for him, telling a story as discerning and sharp as if rendered by a bird's eye view. Within the assortment of lines, flourishes, and swirls, Melvin expressed a depth of perception beyond the ordinary. The accuracy of his connectivity to the chromatic was exceeded only by an actual photograph, but even then, the competition remained close. And although Melvin, now in his early thirties, commanded only a basic use of rudimentary vocabulary, his actual drawings were breathtakingly flawless and intricate in their eerie perfection.

Another stronger breeze blew past, this time slightly lifting the corner of the page, but not enough to impede progress. Once

Melvin began a drawing, little to nothing could stop him. Any interruption would send him into a full, uncontrollable fit.

Melvin peered up into the darkening sky. Thick gray clouds looming above blocked the sun's warm intensity. He sniffed. Tilting his head, he sniffed again. Rain. After a dry summer, the parched grass would relish the rainfall.

Although the winds caused quite the commotion, Melvin's pencil moved at a feverish pitch, coaxing forth a multitude of visualizations, many teetering on the edge of conception and awaiting permission to escape the sheltered caverns of his mind.

Off in the distance, a blaring high-pitched police siren rose over the birds' singing, and with each second the noise got louder and closer. Melvin gripped his sketchpad closer to his chest, whipping his head in search of an escape.

Thick raindrops fell, pelting the top of his head, but for him, the rain meant protecting his drawings at all cost. His stout body cowered, hunched over and vulnerable. There could be no mistaking the child trapped perpetually in a man's body. A man-child who unknowingly would soon be forced to face a different, unchartered hurdle—one that could possibly put his security in jeopardy.

Melvin sniffed the air.

Not good.

It was almost time for Hamza to come home from school. His foot bounced anxiously.

Hurry, Hamza.

The sirens disappeared, the birds continued to chirp undaunted by the rain, and the blustery winds rustled and roared.

Melvin shook his head.

Uh oh. Hamza is going to get wet.

CHAPTER 4

These are the Days of her Life

FIVE MINUTES. THAT'S all Amara had to spare before the kids' bus rolled in, and maybe not even that long before the grey sky, turning dark and gloomier by the minute—threatened to dump another torrential downpour.

Amara rushed to pin her *hijab* to the front of her *abaya* while shoving her swollen feet into a pair of worn flats. Although the bus stop was within walking distance from the house, she needed to pick up the mail, inconveniently located a driving distance away.

Most days, Amara opted to remain sequestered in her car during pick-up; away from the empty blatherings of the three musketeers–-Walaa Kamara, Nafiza Salaam, and the insufferable-two-faced Kalila Rahim. Since moving to the neighborhood, Kalila had been a constant thorn in Amara's side, but nobody but she seemed to understand why. Just the mere fact Kalila existed and looked—at least from the outside—to have it all, had been more than enough to make Amara despise her.

By the time Amara parked at the bus stop, the other mothers were already bunched in groups. All huddled together in their cliques.

She glanced around. "Well, at least that freak Melvin isn't here––the big dope." First chance she got, she planned to have a word with her neighbor, Felicia Vine, about her grown ass son and his obsession with minding everyone else's business. Just the other day Amara caught him standing like Lurch in his doorway, staring at her from across the street. Watching and writing a bunch of stupid stuff down in that ridiculous notebook of his like some degenerate spy.

Nafiza and Walaa offered their *salaams* to Amara from afar, while Kalila gave her a clipped, nondescript wave; then just as quickly diverted her eyes.

"You don't fool me," mumbled Amara, covertly watching as the three women laughed and exchanged stories; the way she had once done before that meddling Kalila Rahim moved into the neighborhood and ruined everything.

Walaa's having a good time.

A pang of jealousy gored Amara in the gut.

Hold up! Did Nafiza just give Kalila a fist bump?

Amara squinted, but couldn't get a good read on Nafiza since the darn woman insisted on wearing her blasted face veil all the time. "Turncoats," she seethed, but any further carping would have to wait as the school bus lumbered to a stop.

As soon as the doors swished open, a rush of neighborhood kids disembarked from their chariot. One after the next, barreling down steps, swinging book bags, and skipping to their chatting parents. One boy—probably no older than ten—walked with his head bowed, shuffling his feet as if his entire world had come to an abysmal end.

"You think you got troubles, kid," groaned Amara, her attention fixated on three young girls giggling ten octaves too loud.

By this time, all the children from this stop were off the bus, but Shirley—the bus driver—didn't close the doors and drive away. Instead, she signaled Kalila over with an angry crook of her finger and a flip-wave of her weighty arm. Then she craned her neck, apparently searching for another parent. Shirley cupped her hands around her mouth and shouted out a name.

"Who do you want?" shouted Walaa.

Shirley shouted again, pointing over to Amara, waving for her to walk over.

Ah—damn it.

Amara slammed the van's door and stomped the entire way over to the bus.

This had better be good.

"Shirley," she said.

"Amara," answered Shirley, equally as droll.

"Well? What is it now?" asked Amara.

Shirley jerked her chin towards the boys. "These three got into a physical altercation today," she explained. "I kept tellin' them to stop, but they wouldn't listen. Just kept on duking it out. Name-callin' and tossing each other around on the floor and all." Shirley blew a strand of hair out of her face. "Then the rest of them kids got in on it, screamin' and causin' a ruckus so loud, I had to pull over. Twice!"

Kalila, clearly upset, yanked her son's arm closer towards her, but Hamza managed to wiggle out of her grip. Undeterred, Kalila snatched him by the jacket collar. "Stand here and don't move," she warned him through lips drawn tight.

Shirley waited until she had Kalila's full and undivided attention again before continuing. "Like I was sayin'—I asked them what started the fight, but they wouldn't tell me. Even so, it makes no matter cause the school district has a zero-tolerance policy about fightin' on the bus. I hate to do it, but I'm gonna have to write them up—all of 'em."

Furious, Amara crooked her finger, motioning for Amir and Muhammad to stand next to her but they ignored her, preferring to keep a safe distance.

"It's likely they'll be suspended from the bus for at least a week," explained Shirley, coughing. "Pardon me." Her gravelly voice marked by the unmistakable sign of a chain smoker. "Where was I? Oh, right," she sighed. "Yeah, so the school should call or send somethin' home for you to sign."

Speech done, Shirley nodded to both mothers, saving a special sneer for the three boys. Pulling the bus doors closed, she drove off to finish making the last of her human deliveries.

By this time, Kalila had already hauled Hamza off to the side of the road; but this didn't stop Amara from trying to eavesdrop on what appeared to be quite the heated conversation. Unable to hear enough, she focused on her two offenders. "So? Which one of you wants to speak first?" Amara asked.

Amir, forever the self-anointed politician of the pair, stepped up to the plate. "Hamza started it," he declared.

"You got three whole seconds to do better than that, mister."

Amir knew his mother rarely bluffed. "Hamza said his mother was a better Muslim than you."

"No, he didn't," corrected Muhammad, smart enough to hedge his continued good health on lying less than his brother. "He said his mother was a good Muslim, too."

Amara rubbed her eyes. "Amir, keep your mouth shut. Muhammad, I want to hear what happened from you—and don't lie."

Muhammad kicked at a piece of gravel with the tip of his sneaker.

"Now, Muhammad—" Amara's patience was quickly waning thin.

Lips pursed, Muhammad appeared to be weighing his limited options, smart enough not to get on his mother's bad side. "We weren't even bothering Hamza or nothin'. Then Amir said something about fake Muslims and..." he paused, squinting, unsure how to continue without digging his brother's grave.

"And?" Amara repeated, her gaze fixed and hands aching to get busy.

"And then he said something like 'Hamza's mom.'"

Amara glared at Amir. "Is that true?" she asked, already knowing that sounded exactly like something he would say.

Amir stared down at the ground as if by avoiding eye contact he could ward off his mother's certain reproach.

"I asked you a question." Amara's voice rose, reaching full roar status and earning stern glances from the rest of the bus stop moms, but Amara neither noticed nor cared. "Did-you-say-*that*?" she repeated, stepping closer to Amir, nose-to-nose. "Well? Did you?"

"Yes," Amir grumbled.

"I didn't hear you. Speak louder."

"Yes," he said louder. "But it's because of what Hamza said first."

"Which was what?"

Amir rolled his sneaker over a pebble.

"Which was what, Amir?"

Shoulders slumped in defeat, Amir cocked his head and peered up. "—that at least my mother isn't a fat, mean, sloppy bitch."

Amara gasped.

From the mouths of babes.

"Let's go," she ordered," marching towards Kalila and her son. "You two will apologize for what you said," Amara ordered under her breath. "And if I ever catch either one of you two fools talking to Kalila's kid again or even so much as looking in his direction, I swear to Allah, I'll tear you a new one. Understood?"

"But, Ma," whined Amir.

"Shut your trap. It's bad enough I have to see that woman at the *masjid*, at the same bus stop, and across the street—and now because of your stupid behavior—" she shook her head in utter disgust. "Trust me when I tell you I've had enough."

"But what about Hamza?" complained Amir, not heeding his mother's warning. "He said a bunch of bad stuff, too."

Amara raised her hand in the air and lunged at Amir causing him to fall back and trip backward into his brother.

"Hey!" yelped Muhammad, hopping. "Get off my foot."

"Shut up."

"No, you shut up."

"Both of you, shut the hell up!"

With her boys in tow, Amara begrudgingly gave Kalila the *salaams*. "*As salaamu alaikum*."

"*Wa alaikum salaam*," responded Kalila and Hamza in unison, both visibly bracing for the onslaught.

Amara yanked both sons front and center. "Don't you two have something you want to say to Hamza?"

Amir sucked his teeth.

"Amir?" prodded Amara. "Suck those teeth again. I dare you."

Amir winced and cut his eyes at Hamza. "Sorry," he grumbled.

Amara jabbed Amir in the chest with her finger. "And…"

"—and for what I said," he muttered, hands dropped to his side.

"Muhammad?" Amara raised a brow expectantly at the boy. "You're up."

Muhammad stomped his foot. "Why do I have to say sorry? I didn't even do anything."

"*Muhammad!*" roared Amara, her hand back up in the air, at the ready.

"Fine," Muhammad whined. "I'm sorry, okay?" he mumbled half-heartedly, "even though I didn't do anything."

Kalila nodded. "Hamza?" she nudged her son. "What do you have to say to Amir and Muhammad?"

Hamza glowered first at Muhammad, then at Amir. Then he looked at his mother with eyes begging her not to force him to apologize, but Kalila merely motioned for him to continue.

"Sorry for saying what I said," Hamza muttered, resigned to the madness.

"That's it?" Amara interjected. "That's all you've got to say?"

Hamza shrugged, wearing a puzzled look across his face.

"Don't act confused. I think you owe me an apology as well," Amara demanded, "I don't appreciate what you called me."

Palms in the air, Hamza shot his mother another beseeching look, pleading for her to intervene in his favor.

"Go on," coached Kalila, oblivious. "Apologize."

"Sorry, Sister Amara for calling you the 'B' word," mumbled Hamza.

Kalila turned her head and glared expectantly at Amir, waiting for her apology, but nothing followed, which didn't go unnoticed.

"Amir should apologize to my mom, also!" insisted Hamza, demanding equal justice, but Amir merely smirked.

"Don't you tell me how to deal with my kids," Amara snapped at Hamza, before grudgingly prodding her son. "Well, go on. Apologize," but Amir refused. Amara nudged his shoulder to remind him she meant business. "I said apologize." But again, the boy stood mum.

In truth, Amara didn't give one fig if Amir apologized to Kalila, but she'd be damned to hell and back if this insolent child of hers would disrespect her in front of the entire neighborhood crew. "Apologize," she roared, eyes locked onto his.

All heads turned, young and old; snapping to attention—watching, waiting ...

"Why should I?" challenged Amir, his small chest puffed out. "You're the one who said she's nothin' but a two-bit, no good—" but before Amir could finish, Amara had already backslapped him hard across the mouth. Everyone within a mile radius gasped in unison.

Amara snatched her son by the arm. "Shut your mouth," she warned him, dragging him to the car.

"It's not fair," Amir kept yelling in protest. "You said she's a—" SLAP! Another crisp smack. This time Amir tried to block the blow but failed, but no number of whacks or threats would keep him from hollering.

Head bowed, Muhammad kept his eyes directed down to his feet and trailed behind, remaining at a safe distance. Smart enough not to volunteer as the next beneficiary of a mother's unhinged wrath. Everyone else dispersed equally as fast, including Walaa and Nafiza, who each bid Kalila a hasty, combined *salaam* and left.

"Let's go," said Kalila, putting a protective arm around her son's shoulder, but Hamza twisted his body out from his mother's range, fuming.

"Hamza!" Kalila scolded, but like Amir, Hamza no longer cared what his mother wanted. He stomped his way around to the passenger side of the car, ignoring his mother's pleas.

"Listen, okay, I'm sorry," she said, slapping the top of the car with her palm. "I shouldn't have made you apologize, but I didn't realize at the time that—"

Hamza smirked in disgust. "Right. So now you're sorry," he goaded, jerking the car door open. "That's all you ever are."

***

Amara

"Put your shoes on the shelf, hang up your backpacks, make your *salat* and then go straight to your rooms," Amara ordered. "And don't dare come out until I call—either one of you."

Amir, who lived life on the edge, continued to grumble, but Amara, more interested in the tempting aromas wafting from the kitchen, chose to ignore him. Grabbing her cell, she texted Walaa. "*As salaamu alaikum*. Can you talk?"

While waiting for a reply, Amara lifted the top of the crockpot. Inside, a delicious mixture of cubed beef, mixed vegetables, and wedged potatoes simmered and bubbled; her grandmother's no-fail beef stew recipe.

Thank Allah I started dinner ahead of time.

She didn't feel inclined to cook after this latest debacle. She checked her mobile; still no call or text. Amara stirred the pot and clamped the lid back on.

Qasim passed through the kitchen to grab something to drink when he noticed his wife's latest dinner preparations. His face said all that needed to be said. Disapproval.

Always disapproval.

It irritated Amara to no end how Qasim expected her to cook all his favorites, much like his mother did for her husband, and his mother did before that. If she dared apply her culinary skills in any other direction other than the one he expected, he'd refuse to eat. Pouting like a petulant child.

"I work hard all day. Customers, phone calls, meetings, you name it. I leave early and get home late. All I ask is that when I come home, I can expect to find a nice dinner waiting for me," he complained, slipping on his shoes.

"I made a nice dinner."

Qasim scrunched his nose taking an exaggerated sniff of air, "You made something. I'll give you that much."

"Your nose would know," came Amara's cutting retort. Qasim broke his nose back in high school and it never properly healed. While the slight curve didn't distract from his overall appearance, it was enough to make him feel self-conscious. He shot Amara a stern warning look.

"I have to go back to the office," he said, abruptly. "I'll be home late."

In fact, Qasim came home particularly late that night. Unable to sleep, Amara lay in the dark listening for his car to pull in the driveway. She must have dozed off, awakened by the familiar sound of his keys landing loudly in the shell tray kept by the front door. She heard his footsteps coming closer, but stopping in front of the hall closet instead, followed by a muffled swoosh, as if he were pulling something down from one of the higher shelves. From the sound of it, probably a pillow and blanket. Then another door opened—his office. Apparently, Qasim planned to sleep on the couch. Amara's punishment for contradicting *The King* in front of his subjects. Amara slunk under her blanket, consumed by loneliness.

It took a few more minutes of rustling from down the hall before the house fell noiseless again. Its slumbering inhabitants blissfully unaware of Amara's soft sobs, muffled by an already damp pillow.

***

A time before children. A time before Amy catapulted into Amara.

It had been roughly three months after graduation when she and Qasim decided to marry. They'd had a simple ceremony at a small *masjid*. Only a handful of his family members and a few of Qasim's friends attended. Amy's parents refused to come, taking the news of her conversion and pending nuptials as poorly as she expected. Most of her so-called friends also boycotted the event. No one except her new friend, Walaa, a lovely, young American Muslim woman, came to share in her excitement. Amara pretended not to care, putting up a strong front to hide the hurt.

The two friends had met at the weekly *masjid halaqah*—a Quranic study group Amara joined right after taking her *shahadah*. Their friendship blossomed quickly as all of Amy's relationships tended to do; steamrolling ahead.

Less than one month after the ceremony, Amara became pregnant. Despite her getting hit with a severe case of morning sickness, the young couple was elated. However, when the sonogram indicated twin boys, Qasim soared over the moon, doting on Amara day and night.

Amara basked in all the enthusiastic attention being bestowed upon her. As anticipated, her appetite during the pregnancy increased; as did her girth, but everyone, including Amara and Qasim, naturally assumed the additional weight was a result of having two babies, and certainly not the consequence of all the late-night snacks, pizzas, or the midnight ice cream runs.

To his credit, Qasim never made mention of Amara's added bulk during the pregnancy. However, his adoration towards his young wife came to a screeching halt. No longer bewitched by the pending births of his sons, his pretense of being a loving husband careened to a standstill with him often refusing to touch or embrace her for days at a time. And even when he did, only just barely. But his lack of attention never stopped Amara—desperate for his affection—from trying.

"Hon," Amara said one morning with a flirty lilt. "I was thinking..." Qasim squinted in her direction. "maybe after the boys go to bed tonight, you and I could have ourselves a date."

Qasim dropped his coffee mug in the sink and sneered at the woman standing before him clad in the same ugly sweatpants and stained tee shirt he'd seen her don a thousand times before. Her once luxurious long, curly mane was now pulled back severely off her face in a slapdash ponytail; tied with a regular office rubber band which did nothing but accentuate her round, puffy cheeks. "I'm working late tonight."

But Amara wouldn't take no for an answer. "Why can't you let Brian or maybe one of the other guys fill in for you? Just for tonight?"

Qasim grabbed his keys. "Not tonight."

"But you're their boss. You can—"

"I said, not tonight."

"But we're not done discussing this," she pleaded, her eyes welling up at his harsh brush off. Without thinking, she reached out to grab his arm, but then instantly jerked her hand away…remembering in agonizing detail what happened the last time she touched him without his consent.

"We're done."

Amara stepped back afraid. "Wouldn't you want to—" but her words fell on unresponsive ears. "Please Qasim, talk to me."

Pokerfaced, Qasim strode past Amara, stopping only to lean in to sniff her neck. "For God's sake, Amara, do something with yourself."

***

The more Qasim was made to wade through mounds of baby paraphernalia and dirty diapers littering his home, the more his silent disapproval switched into razor-sharp, pithy jabs and put-downs. Daily disagreements escalated into full-blown arguments until Qasim stopped talking to Amara altogether. The more distant and withdrawn he became, the more she self-soothed with food. And the more she ate, the crueler he became. His so-called pithy 'jokes' were nothing more than covert insults intended to hurt and belittle, and they did their job well. But for all his callousness and indifference, his lack of desire towards her hurt deeper.

Amara wanted to lose the added weight and tried every diet fad known to mankind. The cauliflower diet, the soup diet, the protein shake diet, all sorts of elimination diets, but so far, nothing worked. Food had become an addiction, her body size teetering on obese, and despite a drastic decrease in calorie intake, she had still been gaining weight. Desperate for answers, Amara made yet another appointment with the family physician.

"Your glucose count is almost as high as your weight," said Doctor Willis, clearly irritated. "You can't keep this up unless you're gunning for diabetes, and right now, I'd say you're borderline."

"I think it's my thyroid."

"Not this again." Doctor Willis ran his fingers through what little remained of his thinning hair.

"No, really. I read about it online, and I'm showing all the classic symptoms."

"Stop," he said, putting up a hand. "I'm looking at your blood tests results right here, and your thyroid is perfectly healthy."

"That can't be accurate."

Doctor Willis, apparently exasperated and no longer inclined to waste his time on her childishness, frowned. "I'll have my nurse make you a copy of the test results. Go home and study them if you want, but unless you adjust what you eat and start seriously exercising, I don't see a positive future for you, health-wise." He had known Amara since childhood; a patient of his from toddlerhood through her teenage years of self-loathing and self-deprecation, not to mention a severe case of acne. "See this number right here," he said, pointing to her blood pressure results with his thin, aging finger. "Look how high it is."

"I see it."

"All right. Now, if you were to lose some weight, it could either go back to normal or at least be manageable without medication."

Amara knew Doctor Willis meant well, but she despised him for it. "You act as if I'm purposely doing this to myself or something. I have twins," she reminded him for the millionth time. "I'm constantly running around behind those two all week long. Cooking, cleaning, picking them up and dropping them off here, there and everywhere—laundry, homework. And, as a matter of fact—"

"Here," he said, curtly interrupting her rant. "Take this." He handed her a pamphlet from the old oak bookcase situated behind his desk.

"What is it?"

"It's the number for a weight loss program in the area. I strongly suggest you give them a call."

Begrudgingly, Amara accepted the pamphlet. "And I suppose they charge to attend."

"They sure do. About the cost of two bags of potato chips and a liter of soda," he quipped back.

"That's not funny."

"Neither is diabetes."

CHAPTER 5

As Her World Turns

KALILA DIDN'T NEED THE added stress in her life right now. Shirley indicated a week, but who really knew how long Hamza would be suspended from the bus? And while dropping him off in the morning wouldn't be a big issue, picking him up after school would be. This added time constraint would reduce her work hours to rubble.

"I want the truth, Hamza," she said. "And don't bother skirting around it. Just tell me what happened."

"They were sitting in front of me, joking with their friends," said Hamza.

"Who was?"

"Amir and Muhammad."

"Okay, go on."

"Amir started it first by saying stuff."

"What kind of stuff?"

"Making fun of me."

"And that's what got you upset? His making fun of you?"

Hamza shook his head no, lowering his gaze. "No. Not exactly."

"Then what exactly? Just spit it out."

Hamza lowered his gaze. "I got mad when he started saying stuff about you."

"Me? Ah, I see. Then what happened?"

"I told him to shut his stupid mouth."

Kalila saw where this conversation was headed. "Listen," she said, coaxing him gently, "you can tell me whatever he said, all right?"

Hamza winced. "I don't want to say it."

"I appreciate you wanting to protect me, but I still need to know."

Hamza chewed on his bottom lip, clearly uncomfortable being forced to repeat what Amir called his mom. Eventually, under Kalila's stony glare, he gave in. "He said you weren't a real Muslim."

"Is that it?" Kalila suspected more to this story to make her son react so aggressively.

"No."

"It's okay, Hamza," Kalila prodded tenderly. "Just say it. I promise I won't be mad at you. I only want the truth."

Hamza tilted his head, resigned. "He said you were a fake…" Hamza turned away, unable to look his mother in the eyes. "and that's why dad didn't want you anymore."

Ouch.

"Then what happened?"

"I told him to take it back."

"Did he?"

"No. He laughed in my face."

"Is that when you hit him?"

"No. I said something to him first."

"Which was what?" Kalila saw Hamza's shoulders droop in embarrassment. "Just tell me. You're doing great."

"I told him that at least my mother wasn't a mean fat bitch." Kalila recoiled. "Then I sorta pushed him to get out of my face," continued Hamza. "And then he fell back into the aisle and starting crying like a baby."

"Do you think you were handling the situation in the right way by pushing him and calling his mother those terrible names?"

Hamza stared into his mother's eyes. Venom dilated each of his tiny pupils to pinpoint precision. "Yeah. I do."

***

That evening, positioned full frontal before her vanity mirror wearing nothing but a sheer nightgown, Kalila sighed.

Memories.

A house crammed with nothing but memories.

Her filigree number—a gift from…happier days.

Leaning closer toward the mirror, Kalila scrutinized the latest stress-induced damage holding council beneath her green, weary eyes. The pronounced discolored bags matched her splotchy cheeks and pale face. Thinking back, Kalila couldn't remember the last time the sun's warmth had touched her skin. On closer inspection, she cringed.

My poor lips.

Using the tip of her pointer finger, she lightly dabbed a bit of Vaseline, then chucked the appropriated hairclip off to the side and loosened her shoulder-length hair from her bun; running her fingers through the greasy strands.

Wash now or later?

More importantly, does it matter?

Tonight's dinner, minus the few overly polite requests to pass a bowl or a serving spoon, had turned into yet another arduous affair. Kalila missed the once lovely dinner spreads she had worked hard to assemble, all in the hope of impressing and spoiling Bashir. Now, most meals were replaced with a quick, simple assortment of ingredients that could be easily thrown together or found in the pantry in a pinch.

"How was your day in school?" she asked between mouthfuls, hoping to prompt a conversation.

Hamza shrugged, aloof. Chin down, he continued to chew, never once bothering to lift his eyes from his plate.

"Okay then. Any homework?"

This time he scarcely shook his head.

"I'll take that to mean *no*." She stared at her son in frustration. Since Bashir's funeral, Hamza's grades had plummeted. "You need to study your spelling and vocabulary words. Friday's the test."

Hamza's moods vacillated between snotty and full-blown rude since his father's death. The impact of such a loss left him sullen and short-tempered. More often than not, once home from school, he ate and then secluded himself in his bedroom, door locked and refusing to talk. With each passing day, the resentment grew deeper between them, with Hamza becoming harsher and crueler by the hour. Kalila always his target.

At one point, desperation set in. Somehow, Kalila needed to find a way to help her son cope and channel his anger. After many failed attempts, she eventually gave in and brought him to speak with a local grief counselor—despite his angry protests. Granted, in the beginning, the sessions did seem pointless. Especially because Hamza spent a good portion of the hour ignoring the counselor's questions and adamantly refusing to open up. However, despite the rocky start, there seemed to be some inkling of a headway. For the past few weeks, instead of automatically lashing out, he'd stop himself first, becoming pensive and more thoughtful with his responses; saying nothing or just abruptly leaving the room if he couldn't trust himself not to go on the attack.

Hamza wouldn't allow his mother to get close, recoiling whenever she reached out to comfort him; turning into the total opposite of the loving child he'd been not long ago. Back when he'd curl up in her lap to read a book or snuggle during movie night. Just the two of them…giggling through the funny parts and gripping one another tight through the scary ones. Now, things had become so bad that if Kalila dared touch his face or risked a rub on his head, he'd withdraw, wincing, quickly jerking his head or face away. To Hamza, his mother was a pariah.

Kalila desperately wanted her son back. She needed him in her corner or at least not plotting and scheming behind her back. Every day turned into a test of wits with her kid. One moment he'd be calm, then the next go full throttle on her. His mood swings were enough to drive her nuts.

Without replying, Hamza pushed his plate away. He loudly slid his chair back and stood, rebelliously slamming dishes in the name of clearing his spot. No thank you, no peck on the cheek, no nothing. If his juvenile plan included tormenting his mother—mission accomplished. Knowing Hamza wanted to make her suffer hurt deeply. She was suffering all right. Every single moment of every single day. More than this immature eleven-year-old mind would ever be able to comprehend fully.

"I said I'll do it," Hamza yelled. "Just get off my back already."

Just one good slap—

"Watch your mouth," she yelled back, appalled.

"Try taking your own advice."

The sass oozing out of those two teen lips caused Kalila to flinch.

Since when did he become so argumentative and rude? And why the hell to me?

It only had taken a few visits with the grief counselor to realize the sessions would not be an instant fix. Nothing, the counselor repeated, could be expected to change overnight.

"It takes time, Mrs. Rahim. Hamza is dealing with extreme grief. He's young, frightened—not entirely sure how to process all he is feeling proactively."

"He hates me."

"He doesn't hate you." She put her pen down on the mahogany desk. "What he is, is angry and you're available."

"But I don't get it. Why me?" said Kalila. "I'm the one trying to help him."

"I know this can be frustrating, but children are intuitive. They can sense when something is wrong, and become easily frightened by sudden changes, whether through an immediate life-altering upheaval in their daily routine, such as a death of a parent or in how they perceive the surviving parent is handling the situation. Sometimes, right or wrong, children blame themselves for what happened. They worry that somehow they caused the accident or the tragedy to occur."

"But that's ridiculous. Hamza didn't do anything. None of this is his fault."

"Nevertheless, this is how he feels." The counselor's eyes narrowed.

"But I never blamed him. How could I?" Kalila asked, arms out and palms forward.

"I understand what you're saying, I do, but for now, we aren't dealing with what actually happened. We are dealing with how your son perceives what happened. His response, his perceptions, his feelings. Quite often, during this phase, it's imperative you keep reassuring him that nothing he said, did, or even thought, had anything to do with his dad's accident."

***

Kalila remembered how heavily it had rained the night of the accident. The suffused fog combined with oil-slicked roads made driving a dangerous feat, but when Bashir fled the house, the last thing he'd cared about had been road conditions.

They had spent most of the day and clear into the evening battling. Malicious remarks and snippy comebacks turned into a barrage of horribly hurtful words. Words that could now never be taken back, justified or forgiven. Spiteful words overheard by a frightened, young, impressionable pair of listening ears pressed firmly to his closed bedroom door.

"Is that her?" Kalila cried, indicating the cellphone in Bashir's hand. The model-perfect photo popped up on Bashir's screen every time *she* called him, taunting Kalila. At least Bashir had been smart enough not to take those calls in front of her, although Kalila caught him returning texts when he thought she wasn't looking.

Bashir muted the sound and pocketed the phone; too drained for round three.

"Does *she* have a name or were you saving that for the big reveal also?" Kalila asked, wishing her legs would stop shaking.

"I haven't kept her a secret."

"Oh? That's rich." Kalila turned to face him, waiting for the comeback, but instead, he closed his eyes, refusing to meet her glare.

"Look at me!" Kalila screamed, snapping her finger angrily in his face. "You don't get to shut your eyes to the mess you created."

Jaw locked in protest, Bashir opened his eyes intentionally slow.

"You think I'm stupid? You think I didn't catch on to your girlfriend's trail of little hints purposely left in my car?"

"*My car*," interjected Bashir.

"*Our car*, Bashir!"

"You know what?" Bashir rose to his feet and headed straight into their bedroom. "I'm not doing this anymore."

"What does that mean?"

"It means I'm leaving."

"Where are you going?" Kalila scurried behind him, but Bashir didn't bother to respond. "We haven't finished discussing this."

"I think we need time apart to let cooler heads prevail."

"In other words, unless I give you the green light to do what you've already decided, we're done, right?"

"Your words, not mine, but eventually, you're going to have to come to grips with reality."

"Your reality. Not mine!"

"*Shush*. Lower your voice. You'll wake Hamza up." Bashir pulled a duffle bag down from the top shelf in the closet and filled it with his clothes and toiletries.

"Right. Far be it for our son to hear how his perfect father plans to abandon his family for a new piece of ass," Kalila crossed her arms combatively over her chest.

Bashir shot Kalila another sharp look but kept on packing.

"Just stop it," she pleaded. "Stop doing that," she begged, reaching into the duffle and yanking out his clothes almost as quickly as he stuffed them in.

Bashir snatched back his belongings. "Would you quit it, Kalila," he said, shoving them into the already over-stuffed duffle bag. "I'll collect the rest of my things later."

Somehow, whenever they argued, Bashir managed to regulate his temper; modulating his voice even when at his angriest. A fighting skill which drove Kalila batshit crazy.

"*Please*, listen," she pleaded. "You don't have to go. We can work this out."

"There nothing left to work out Kalila. Alexa—"

"A-lex-a? So, *she* does have a name."

"*Alexa* is going to be my wife."

"*Your wife?* And what about me? Who the hell am I?"

"Kalila—"

"So now I don't count for anything?"

"We're going in circles. For the last time, my relationship with Alexa has nothing to do with you or with us."

The room started to spin.

Bashir was slipping away, out of her grasp…

The man Kalila had once shared her dreams and aspirations with now wouldn't even stay to talk, to fight for his marriage. Instead, he packed as if desperate to get as far away from her as soon as possible.

"Obviously she doesn't care that you're already married."

"Alexa knows all about you. And Hamza. She accepts that she'll be my second wife."

Kalila sniffled. "Really *big* of her."

"Wife…"

Bashir's words crushed Kalila like never before. Any chance of salvaging their marriage was now shattered. These arguments were never about Bashir wanting to patch anything up. He wasn't here fighting to fix or save what they once had—that had all been a lie, a ruse…merely a way to ease his guilt and shirk his responsibility to the promises and commitments made to her.

Bashir was leaving. Off to start a new life and make a new family. In with the new, while kicking the old unceremoniously to the curb. Her anger boiled to the top at the stabbing realization that she no longer mattered to him.

"Fine!" she yelled through heavy sobs. "GO! Just get out of here." Kalila, barely able to catch her breath, stumbled around the bedroom tossing small items at Bashir. "Here, don't forget to take this, and this, and, oh—," she flung a photo taken of them on their honeymoon. "This should give your Alexa a big laugh."

"Nobody is laughing at you," Bashir said, his voice drifting off.

"Liar!"

After zipping his bag closed, Bashir threw the strap over his shoulder and turned to leave. Kalila tried to block the doorway using her body.

"If you dare take a single step out of this house, you had better never ask to come back!" she threatened, her voice trembling in a high-pitched shriek; fury clipping each enunciated word. "*Ya Allah*, Bashir, if you do this, you'll never be welcomed in my bed or in my life again."

"Move out of my way." Bashir's face registered nothing but long-suffering impatience.

"We don't need you," Kalila hollered after him, the words flying out of her mouth before she could stop them; the rage too powerful to control.

"We?"

"That's right, you heard me. WE-WE-WE!"

Bashir glared straight into his wife's eyes. "Don't play that game. Don't ever threaten to take my son away from me."

"It's not a threat."

"I mean it, Kalila. Don't do this."

"What will you do? Run off? Cry on Alexa's shoulder? Tell her how mean I am to you?" She reached out to grab Bashir's sleeve, but he was stronger and yanked it away. "Answer me!"

Bashir stood his ground. "Don't do this."

"Oh right. Don't do this. Don't do that. Don't do anything to interfere with *your life*."

Bashir hesitated.

"How dare I stand in your way," she snarled, her entire body shaking.

"Kalila—"

"Don't *ever* say my name again."

"*Kalila*—I never meant to hurt you. I thought you'd eventually understand." He pushed his way past, ducking under her extended arms.

"Eventually understand? Eventually understand *what*? That I've been lied to? Manipulated? Replaced? Exchanged? Cheated on? Betrayed?" Hysterical at this point, Kalila shadowed Bashir's every move, his every step; her arms waving erratically in every which direction. The urge to lash out, to make him feel her pain overtook her. She was out of control and knew it, but the fury imploding inside her now reigned, and she didn't know how to reel it in.

"*Wallahi.*" Bashir threw his hands up in surrender. "That's not what I am doing. This isn't the end of us."

"Oh, like hell it isn't!"

Bashir rolled his eyes towards the ceiling.

"You know what? Just get out!" screamed Kalila, growing madder as she watched Bashir cavalierly shoving his feet into his shoes.

Outside, the storm grew in intensity. Heavy rains continued to pelt the ground, coming down in sheets, whooshing against the home's window panes.

"Get out," Kalila sobbed, practically shoving Bashir out the front door before he could finish tying his laces; throwing whatever pairs of his shoes left on the shelf onto the wet, drenched lawn. Clipping him a few times on the back as he trotted down the porch towards his car, never once turning around.

"I *never* want to see you again," she yelled, shaking, and rattled to the core. Hurt tears trickled down her flushed cheeks.

Come back.

Kalila didn't want Bashir to leave, she loved him, but she couldn't coax the words out of her troubled heart to make herself say it.

Bashir popped his trunk open and tossed his bag in. "We'll talk soon," he countered, using that galling voice of reason of his.

"We have nothing left to talk about," she cried, wishing he'd turn around and come back inside.

Please don't leave me.

Once Bashir pulled out of the driveway, Kalila slammed the front door, practically heaving, unaware of being watched from across the street.

"I hate you!" she sobbed, her one fist pounding the door. "I hate you," she whimpered. "I hate you…I hate you…I hate you."

Without Bashir there to scream at, to fight with, Kalila took her frustration out on the remainder of his belongings. Marching erratically from room to room, back and forth and around the house, mumbling and cursing under her breath. Collecting the rest of his items and dumping them unceremoniously in a pile.

If she wants him, she can have him.

Back in the bedroom on the side of their bed, Kalila bent over and picked up Bashir's prayer mat, ready to toss it, when suddenly she clutched it tighter. A wave of something stronger than anger caused her to crash to her knees, overriding the blind fury that had controlled her only moments before. From within the deepest, darkest hole in her soul, she wailed. Pure unadulterated anguish filled the suffocating space surrounding her. Unable to stop, she crumpled the soft, well-used prayer rug and pressed it to her damp cheek. His lingering scent consumed every fragmented part left of her…

***

Kalila had just changed into a nightgown when her mobile rang. Diving for the cell, she half expected to hear Bashir's voice telling her he was sorry and that he was ready to talk. She prayed he'd ask to come home to work things out like before, but instead, a strange, unrecognizable, detached male voice sliced through the airway. In abrupt, proficient speech, the person on the other end just kept talking, asking Kalila a series of questions, which now, months later, she could barely recall. Only a few intermittent catch phrases cleared the fog controlling her brain. Expressions like 'extraordinary measures' 'airbags that failed to deploy' 'precarious road conditions' 'a car that careened'… 'accidents do happen.'

Shaken, Kalila darted around the bedroom scavenging through drawers, throwing on anything easily accessible. Somehow, between the rush and churn of panic, she remembered to phone Walaa to ask her to stay at the house with Hamza until she could return.

—from the hospital.

In the aftermath of the accident, Kalila recalled very little. Almost as if her body intuitively blocked the ability to reason. At the time, she had needed to act.

Thinking would have to come much later.

Mourning would last *forever*.

Most of all, Kalila remembered arriving at the hospital in a frenzy and a daze, practically running through the halls, her shoes clattering against the tiled floors. Bolting out of the elevator, all eyes fixated on her as she tried to make sense of the erudite voice resonating from the person wearing a long, white coat.

"I'm sorry, Mrs. Rahim. We did all we could do."

We did all we could do…

Kalila would never forget those words. How could she? Their very existence sealed her fate forever.

CHAPTER 6

A Guiding Light

STANDING OFF TO THE side of the road, Walaa and Nafiza moved a safe distance away from the fracas. This wasn't their first go around with Amara. Small, innocuous squabbles that most people could ignore, became bigger ordeals with Amara—and if tensions between Amara and Kalila weren't bad enough, now their petty squabbles had managed to trickle down to the children.

"It was bound to happen," whispered Nafiza, deliberately out of earshot of her kids. "I'm just sorry that it did, *astaghfirullah*."

"Me too," Walaa mouthed discreetly behind her hand.

"But let's be honest. Amara's and Kalila's boys aren't entirely to blame. Their mothers have instigated this food fight from the start."

"No, you're right."

"The kids are only repeating what they hear being said in the house, which isn't at all acceptable."

"I know, but what exactly is the problem between these two?" asked Walaa, and not for the first time. "I mean, obviously, they don't like each other—fine, that happens, but seriously? Why all the extra drama? What did Kalila do to make Amara so, I'm sorry but bitchy!"

"Or vice-a-versa. We shouldn't assume it's one or the other."

"True again."

"I just think that some sisters rub the others the wrong way, although, to be honest, Amara seems to have a particular penchant for ratcheting up any conversation to new levels of absurdity and making everything about her."

"You know, she always has to be right."

"—even when she's wrong."

"Especially when she's wrong."

"And she doesn't see it. Totally self-absorbed—"

"And because she doesn't care how she makes anyone else feel, as long as she gets her shit off." Nafiza took a deep breath. "Look, Amara lacks respect for other people's opinions unless they align with hers. That's why she name-calls, belittles people, questions their loyalty or friendship at the slightest hiccup. Poor Amara, everyone's always out to get her…yet she doesn't see how she pushes people out of her life; people who once really cared about her. And if you are her latest target, you either placate or agree with her because if not, get ready for the gaslighting to begin; which, by the way, are all signs of a toxic individual."

Walaa searched in her bag for car keys. "I hope this doesn't get any worse."

"We are talking about *Amara*, right?"

***

At times, it can be challenging to have a genuine friendship connection with some women, even with those who profess to share the same faith. Community acquaintances are common enough, and often friendly on the surface, but close, ride and die friendships? Not as often.

Walaa and Kalila hit it off instantly. Besides sharing the same warped sense of humor, a love for good food, and a passion for decorating, both women were expecting their first child reasonably close together. The doctor calculated Walaa's due date in late April, while Kalila expected her baby to arrive a little over a month later.

Undoubtedly, this commonality helped forge an even stronger bond and one that happily continued to grow past childbirth.

Although already renting in the nearby area, once the test confirmed Kalila's pregnancy, she and Bashir decided to make Pennsylvania their permanent residence. By happenstance, a lovely home down the block from Walaa in a quiet, gated community had gone up for sale the same week. A lovely brick colonial home sporting a tailored lawn, a cobblestone walkway, and a backyard already decked out with Amish wooden swings and a wooden play fort. The perfect place to raise a child. Two months after the first walk-through, Kalila and Bashir closed, moving in immediately afterward. To hear Kalila tell it, on the day of the move, Walaa had been almost as excited as she.

Because of Walaa's outstanding taste in fabrics, Kalila deferred to her new friend's palate without reserve, grateful for her help. Within months, the once lackluster shell of a home came together picture perfect. Sadly, the only thing left missing from the Rahim domicile was happiness. By then, small cracks in the marriage had started to show, but not nearly enough for either spouse to call it quits. Kalila just assumed the rocky start had more to do with Bashir's stress about becoming a father, the increasing responsibilities of being a new homeowner, and the stressful demands of a career with long hours.

Throughout the pregnancy, Kalila played her perky mother-to-be role to perfection. Never once letting on to anyone—including Bashir, how miserable and lonely she honestly felt; imagining that while she wallowed at home with swollen belly and feet, her husband was out and about, eyes on the hunt.

As close as Walaa was to Kalila, she never suspected anything wrong. Only a few years after Hamza's birth did the truth finally unveil itself, and even then, Walaa suspected her friend of holding back.

"I don't get it," said Walaa, honestly surprised. "All that time and you never said anything—even to me. Like why?"

Kalila poured her friend a cup of juice. "What should I have said? 'Hey Walaa, guess what? My marriage is a sham. My husband's a wanna-be polygamist. He'd decided to replace me with a newer model."

"Don't say it like that. You know Bashir loves you."

Kalila carried a cake stand filled with a wide assortment of baked goods to the table. "He's got a funny way of showing it."

"No. I just think he got caught up listening to those other brothers who've got him brainwashed into thinking he can pull it off." Walaa sipped her juice.

"I thought the same, but this time I think he's serious." Kalila took a bite out of a cookie. "Want one?"

"I shouldn't, but I will." Walaa bit into one. "Oh man, these are delicious. Homemade?"

"Bakery." Kalila refilled her own cup.

"When did you find out?"

"Bashir started dropping hints back when I was pregnant with Hamza."

"Seriously? While you were pregnant?"

"Yep. I didn't put two and two together at first, but you know what? I probably did but didn't want to believe it."

"Well, I never knew."

"I never told you."

"But why keep it all to yourself? You must have been so upset."

Kalila slumped in her chair. "You gotta understand. There I was pregnant, my body stretching in every direction, my emotions bouncing all over the place. But instead of empathy and compassion, Bashir started accusing me of not fulfilling his rights as a Muslim man. Everything I did suddenly wasn't good enough for him. It was as if he was looking for any excuse to make his move. After that, we just kept arguing, one fight after the next."

"That's so wrong." Walaa grabbed for another cookie. "That's not even the *sunnah*."

"Depends who you ask. As far as I know, he had the full support from the brothers."

Walaa looked shocked. "Even Imam Abdullah?"

"Him, I'm not sure about."

"Nafiza never gave me the impression he supports this kind of stuff. I mean, personally, I've never heard him speak about polygamy except to remind men to do the right thing."

Kalila shrugged. "Define 'doing the right thing.'"

Kalila had a point. There was no shortage of nightmare stories floating around about multiple households where equity hadn't been applied. "Then what happened?"

"We fought and fought," said Kalila. "Me crying all the time, him leaving rather than stay to argue. At one point, I even threatened to leave and take Hamza with me."

"Kalila! You didn't—"

"I sure did. And before you say it, I already know. I was wrong, out of control, but I was hurt. Angry. I wanted him to know how serious I was, but I wouldn't have actually done it."

Walaa wiped her lips with a napkin. "Then what did he do?"

"He ultimately dropped the subject, and everything went back to normal between us—for a while. Matter of fact, better than normal. The old Bashir returned. Loving, romantic…considerate again."

"For a while."

"Yes, exactly…for a short while. Then last year, out of nowhere, he started this polygamy nonsense all over again. The same madness, rinse and repeat. First by dropping innuendos and hints, then by complaining about everything I did. A broken record. Constantly criticizing and questioning my motives. Commenting on my looks. Little digs…you know the kind. When they say something about one thing, but really mean something entirely different."

Walaa didn't know. Talib had never treated her in this manner, but she nodded all the same. "And now?"

"And now, it feels different."

"Different how?"

"Because in the past, if I got upset enough, instead of arguing forever, Bashir would eventually give in and drop the subject. Sure, we may have stopped speaking for a few days—exchanging only civil banalities, but eventually, everything would go back to normal like before."

"But not this time?"

Kalila shrugged. "Nope."

"Do you think he already found somebody?"

Kalila guffawed. "He swears no, but he's lying."

Walaa stared pensively at her friend. In a lowered voice, she asked, "What will you do if he goes through with a second marriage? Would you consider being a co-wife?"

"Honestly?" Kalila pressed a hand to her throat. "I don't know. I love my husband, and I know he loves me. I don't want to lose him, but the thought of sharing Bashir with another woman…I can't even…the mere thought kills me."

Walaa's heart broke for her friend. While Kalila's situation sounded all too familiar and entirely predictable, she certainly wasn't alone. Quite a few community members appeared destined to board the runaway polygamy train.

"It could work for you," said Walaa. "I mean, I get that it's not what you want, but you may not have a choice if you want Bashir to remain in your life. And from what you're describing to me, he seems pretty determined."

Years back, tensions in their community had flared; this was before Kalila and Bashir moved in but over the same subject. At one point, a small but loud contingent of men had become so enthralled with the 'right' to take on another wife that the Imam felt obligated to offer a succession of Friday *khutbahs*, each expounding on the touchy subject in excruciating detail. The pros *and* cons. His fiery *khutbahs* generated so much interest on both sides of the disagreement that a call for additional discussions on the subject was announced. Meanwhile, the sudden clamor for speedy or 'secret' marriages performed at other more inclined *masjids* became the 'in' thing. One right after the other. Marriage—drama—community outrage—then divorce.

Most of the time, plural marriages took place without either the first wife's knowledge or blessing, which in turn prompted an upsurge in hysterical requests by irate first wives, demanding a speedy divorce. Some families tore apart under the pressure while others endured, but just barely. Only a select few survived and thrived.

Strangely, even couples avoiding the polygamy incursion had started to show signs of strain—Walaa and Talib included. She remembered clearly how she had begun to second guess her own husband's motives, their marriage. More than once suspecting him of plotting polygamy with the rest of the boy's club. Starting baseless arguments with Talib, stemming from nothing he did or said, and then throwing groundless accusations at him. Thankfully, Talib had been nobody's fool.

"You need to stop," he had told her emphatically. "I am not down with that mess, and I'm not in the market for anyone else. I love you, Walaa. Only you. I know you've been seeing some serious dysfunction go down with people you care about, but that's them––not us. I need you to trust me."

"But that's what Fatima's husband told her *before he—*"

"I don't care one iota what those other guys are doing or telling their wives. That's not me. You never have to worry."

Although Walaa had believed in Talib's sincerity, she also wasn't naïve enough to think in absolutes. She'd seen firsthand the fallout of those who became complacent. "Ah-huh. That's what they all say, but then look what happens."

Talib drew Walaa in closer, holding her tight. "*Wallahi*, I'm not going to hurt you."

But no matter how many which ways or times Talib tried to convince her, Walaa stayed on high alert. Keeping close tabs on her man. On the lookout for any eyelash fluttering, high heeled shoe ready to drop on her heart.

As quite a few marriages buckled and imploded, the women in the community began arguing vehemently amongst themselves. Qurans and *hadiths* were regrettably turned into useable props for debate. Catchphrases were bantered about.

"'Monogamy is the norm'... 'Polygyny is the Sunnah'... 'Want for your brother [sister] what you want for yourself'... 'Be grateful for what you have and build on that'... 'The Prophet ﷺ had more than one wife'... 'The Prophet ﷺ was madly in love with Khadijah'... 'You must follow the law of the land'... 'The law of the land doesn't supersede the law of Allah.'"

Overnight, everyone and their mother had become an armchair scholar.

During one particular sister's meeting, a heated debate ensued with women on opposing sides of the argument fiercely battling.

"So, let me get this straight, sister. What you're saying is that while it's normal to be jealous, feeling jealous doesn't equate to a valid reason to protest a second marriage?" countered one outspoken young woman, teetering on the cusp of losing her temper.

"That's what I meant," remarked the other sister, equally as determined. "Just because a wife is jealous, doesn't give her exclusive rights over her husband's choice to marry again or not. Remember, just because the husband decides to take on another wife, it doesn't mean he stops loving her. If she's jealous, she needs to handle it."

"Handle it? Okay, fine, I understand that, and I don't necessarily disagree. But besides feeling jealous, don't you think she may feel betrayed? Hurt because he might have broken their agreement—even if it was a verbal one? Maybe he told her when they first got married that he'd never take a second wife, or maybe she's just not into being a co-wife. Doesn't want the added family, financial burden or stress. I don't think her feelings should be casually dismissed. She's got just as much right to her feelings and wants as him."

"I agree, the first wife has a right to her feelings and wants, but at the same time, she doesn't have the right to try and force her husband into being monogamous just because she doesn't want polygamy—just because she doesn't want to be a co-wife. Allah made it permissible for men for a reason. The first wife can't make it *haram* just because of jealousy or because the husband has had a change of heart."

"Hold up—who said anything about *haram*? Just because the first wife doesn't want to be in a polygamous marriage doesn't mean she's saying it's forbidden. What she is saying is that it's not *for her*. It's not the way she wants or agreed to be married."

"She doesn't have that right if that's what her husband wants."

"Of course, she does. She can divorce."

"And what? Destroy a perfectly good marriage? Because of her issues? Her insecurities? Then what?"

"Are you kidding me right now?" The young woman scanned the room at the perplexed listening faces, gauging the level of support. "So, if I understand you correctly, you're saying that if the first wife doesn't go along with the husband's program, then she's the one to blame for their failed marriage. The husband gets off scot-free. He's just the innocent bystander in all this."

"If the first wife cannot accept Allah*'s* decree, then yes, she is to blame."

"No matter how much he's hurt or lied to her."

"It's not about her being hurt; it's about what is permissible."

"Oh right, sure, like you wouldn't care if your husband suddenly took on another wife without caring about how it made you feel."

The other sister's back stiffened, her voice turned curt. "My husband doesn't have to confer or ask my permission, sister. Neither does yours for that matter. Any insecurities I have are mine to work on—between me and Allah, not you, not his other potential wife, and not him. You sisters need to get your *deen* right."

"So nobly pretentious—until you're the one being forced to put it into practice."

"But that's on you then, isn't it?"

The young sister wasn't about to back down. "It's absolutely his problem. Remember, he made a commitment to his first family. He doesn't get to play *I changed my mind* after making a verbal agreement. He doesn't get to hide behind *halal* and *haram* to suit his *nafs*."

"How's he hiding by changing his mind?" snapped the older sister.

"How is he justifying destroying one healthy, already existing family unit to replace it with another all because of *his nafs*?"

"He's not the one destroying the marriage, his first wife is," countered the older sister, her eyes narrowed in fury.

"Like hell, he isn't. Just because he can take another wife—under extenuating circumstances I might add, doesn't mean he has to."

"And it doesn't mean he can't," retorted the other woman.

"Sisters, sisters," cried one of the other women present. "Control your tongues."

"This is the house of Allah," yelled another.

"You could have fooled me," snapped the younger woman before stomping out the door.

"And that's why men take on a second wife," whispered one sister conspiratorially to the other.

The women weren't the only ones weighing in, but the men in the community behaved entirely differently, albeit keeping two camps. Those who emphatically believed polygamy was a right to be enacted at will and those not so inclined. Those who endorsed polygamy tended to stick together, cheering one another on and unabashedly applauding those shared stories involving risk or presumed valor, while the others tried to avoid the conversation entirely, waiting for the day when the whole ordeal subsided once and for all.

Walaa could only remember a scant amount of polygamous relationships from back then having lasted. Those that did were undeniably strong and healthy. But if she remembered correctly, they were also the marriages where everyone had been on board, and nothing had been done deceitfully or underhanded. Just strictly and respectively by the *sunnah.*

But Walaa also remembered the fallout that had accompanied that time. How eventually most agreed to disagree. Divided camps with each side thinking they were right. Sadly, many lingering feelings of hurt, distrust, and resentment had produced enough internal damage to fracture a once cohesive community. Walaa feared round two fast approaching.

CHAPTER 7

A Mother's Broken Heart

THROUGH A SHEER CURTAINED window, Felicia Vine watched as her grown son sat on their back deck, drawing. One-minute relaxed—peaceful in his element, and the very next, frightened and reclusive. Felicia's heart broke when Melvin, jarred by the shrill of distant sirens, started to moan as if in pain.

"My poor boy," she whispered to the heavens. Melvin cowered; his arms wrapped around his head as if his very survival depended upon it. Perhaps, in some sad and prophetic way, it did.

Despite his many challenges, she and Bill had done all that they could to give Melvin a good life; providing him with a cloak of love and protection at least within the confines of their home. However, the outside world had proven to be an entirely more difficult environment to navigate, especially considering how difficult it was for Melvin to relate to other people.

"You've got nothing to be ashamed of, Melvin," Felicia would often remind him. "Friendship is based on trust and respect. Some kids aren't good at being friends yet. They haven't been taught how to deal with folks different than themselves. They don't mean to hurt your feelings, son. One day you'll meet the right people."

Once Melvin got older, Felicia assumed the bulk of his problems with bullies would be over after he got out of school, but sadly, the next generation of neighborhood tormenters began to hound him. Calling him names, throwing rocks, mocking him. However, the parents of some of these young tormenters were the absolute worst, particularly that horrible, vapid woman from across the street. Felicia had to deal with that piece of nasty work constantly.

"Amara," yelled Felicia marching to the edge of her lawn ready to battle. "Don't ever let me catch you calling my son that vile name again."

"First off, Felicia, before you go all politically correct on me, the word 'retarded' isn't that bad. It just means he's slow is all. What you overheard was me trying to explain that to my boys, and you jumped to conclusions. Secondly, I'm doing you a favor. Melvin's going to get treated far worse once he's on his own, and it's not like you'll be around to protect him forever. He might as well learn to defend himself now."

"Melvin doesn't need to be called a bunch of despicable names to get better equipped at being bullied by the likes of you or your kids," snapped Felicia. "The name calling stops now."

Amara crossed her arms over her chest, and stepped closer to Felicia, ready to interject, but Felicia beat her to it.

"And before you dare lecture me about how Melvin should adapt to your abuse, you should be spending your energy and time educating your children that what they're doing is unacceptable."

"That's what I was trying to do before you decided to butt in. Believe me, we all know Melvin's a bit off," said Amara, making the crazy sign with her finger around her temple. "Personally, I feel sorry for him."

"Save it. Melvin doesn't need your pity either."

"Fine. But since we're on the subject of Melvin and the need to educate our children, how about you take your own advice and teach your grown retarded son to stay away from the bus stop. He doesn't belong there, and you know it. Always gawking at everyone. It's plain weird." She said, her finger pointed at Felicia's face. "He's not a parent, and he's got no business showing his face, and scaring the kids."

"How dare you!" yelled Felicia.

Amara smirked. "You've been warned. If he shows up again, I'll call the cops."

"Melvin's never harmed a single soul in his life, no less scared children—and anybody who says different is a flat-out liar!" Felicia trembled, her anger turned her face a crimson red. "He's got as much right as anybody else to walk wherever he so chooses."

"Fine," snapped Amara, "Suit yourself, Felicia, but then don't get upset with me when somebody calls him a bunch of names you don't like." Amara spun on her back heel and headed across the street, mumbling loud enough for all to hear. "You know Felicia, if it quacks like a duck, it's a duck, and if it stalks like a stalker—"

"Go to hell!"

You Satan-spawned, evil, mean-spirited bitch.

But as furious as Felicia felt, she knew others in the neighborhood shared Amara's twisted mindset. They just weren't nearly as bold or rude to throw it in her face, but she'd caught their scowls and heard the vicious rumors.

Bill's death had been a devastating setback, especially for Melvin who folded into himself, not comprehending why his Daddy no longer lived at home. The frequency of his outbursts increased as did his tenacity for drawing, but at least his art provided Melvin a welcomed outlet, so she encouraged his creativity. Though, after a while, even Felicia found it near to impossible to keep her son supplied in sketchpads.

They had tried to safeguard their son from harm for over thirty-two years, fighting to keep him out of institutions and group homes, scrimping to save enough to financially fill all his immediate needs for the remainder of his life. Now, between continually battling with healthcare providers, doctors, insurance companies and nosy, cruel neighbors, Felicia faced another, more pressing obstacle: How to ensure Melvin's safety when she wouldn't be around and who would assume responsibility for his needs and wants. Who would understand Melvin's need to be alone? To draw? To touch? Who would advocate for him against an ever-changing health system? Know how to handle Melvin when he jerks away or clicks his tongue—or raises his hands in disapproval? Who would be able to decipher his many peculiarities and not be offended, or worse– attack him out of fear and ignorance?

While the prospect of her death didn't necessarily frighten Felicia, the uncertainty of what would happen to her beloved son without her there to protect him most certainly did.

***

Melvin had been Felicia's miracle baby.

After years of disappointment, Felicia and Bill went on with their lives, making peace with the knowledge that they'd never become parents. As a Ph.D., Bill taught history at the university while Felicia built up a small but profitable business medical coding from home. Their combined income provided a more than comfortable lifestyle in an up and coming neighborhood, until one particular routine gynecology visit.

"Pregnant?" Felicia repeated, mouth agape.

"Most definitely," said the doctor.

"But you said—I thought I couldn't—"

"It happens. The chances were slim, but it happens. Case in point."

"But all those tests?" Felicia wasn't sure if she should be happy or alarmed. "I need to tell Bill," she said pointing, indicating he was sitting for her in the waiting room. Bill typically didn't attend his wife's doctor visits; however, they had planned to go out for lunch afterward since he was off from work.

"That's fine. Get dressed and meet me in the office. I'll have the nurse call him back if you like."

Felicia agreed, but while dressing, her mind raced.

Pregnant? Me? How?

This has got to be a mistake!

The obstetrician cautioned Felicia and Bill that a first pregnancy so late in life could carry an increased risk of health issues, but the couple, enthralled with the possibility of becoming parents, believed their prayers had finally been answered.

Throughout the pregnancy, Felicia remained overly cautious. Close to forty years old when she conceived, her biggest concern centered around stillbirth, miscarriage or an ectopic pregnancy. However, once the prenatal tests came back negative, the couple rejoiced, anxious to hold their surprise bundle of joy.

"I read in a book that children born to older parents have certain advantages," said Bill one night as they cuddled together in bed.

"Such as?" Felicia rubbed her belly, trying to coax the baby growing inside her womb to awaken and kick for daddy.

"Well, for one, we old folks have better economics and can afford a heck of a lot more."

"What we lack in energy, we make up in money."

"That's one way of putting it."

Felicia laughed. "We're also more grounded. Have more experience and wisdom to impart."

"And we're a hell of a lot smarter than we were years ago."

"I know I am at least." Felicia playfully nudged her husband's shoulder. "Ah! I think he's finally awake. Put your hand here," she said, gently guiding Bill's palm over the baby bump to where an arm or a leg readily moved. "Feel him?"

Bill smiled. "Hey, little guy. It's Daddy," he whispered; lips pressed softly against Felicia's swollen belly.

"We're going to need to decide on a name for him soon," said Felicia.

"I'd like to name him after my father and give him your dad's name as his middle." Had it been a girl, the couple had already decided the opposite would have been true.

"Melvin Christopher Vine," she muttered. "It's got a nice ring to it."

"Then it's settled."

Melvin's birth couldn't have gone any smoother. Felicia's water broke mid-afternoon, and by midnight, a nurse announced to a dozing Bill that his beautiful baby boy with a full head of hair had entered the world. Elated, Bill leaped to his feet and began handing out cigars to the other dozing fathers.

Felicia doted on her baby boy, beside herself with joy, and for the first few weeks after the birth, everything seemed picture-perfect. It wasn't until around four months later when she began to grow concerned and wary that something had gone terribly wrong.

"I don't know what it is, but something's not right," she said one evening after putting the baby to bed. "Melvin should be doing certain things by now, and he's not."

Bill turned off the television. "What certain things?"

"For starters, he isn't trying to roll over or push himself up. He just lies there."

"All babies learn at a different pace. I don't think that means there's necessarily something wrong."

"He also makes no eye contact. Don't tell me you haven't noticed that no matter how much we talk to him, he never looks our way?"

Bill had noticed, but then again, he had never been around many babies, and didn't know what to expect; simply attributing Melvin's lack of interest as being new to the world. "Maybe we bore him," he offered lightly.

"That's not funny. I'm seriously worried. Dorothy Crammer's baby is about the same age as Melvin, and she's always reaching out to be picked up or smiling when Dorothy comes into the room. Melvin barely acknowledges me, as if I don't exist."

"What did the doctor say?"

"I'm taking him tomorrow."

Over the coming months, Felicia and Bill's concerns multiplied as Melvin continued to exhibit many, if not all the early indicators of autism: lack of smiling, poor eye contact, not following objects, disinterest in cuddling, not trying to crawl or roll over, an aversion to loud sounds, and totally unresponsive to his name.

As he got older, Melvin demonstrated a talent for drawing and mathematics—near genius level. However, the dichotomy of being extraordinarily talented yet unable to verbally communicate utterly confused his parents, and naturally alarmed healthcare providers. It also left Melvin frustrated; flying off into a rage and pounding his ears with his fists, almost as if the ideas locked up in his brain and the words he sought to speak repelled one another.

Now, with Bill long gone and her failing health, Felicia no longer had the emotional strength nor the willpower to protect Melvin—not only from strangers but also from himself. The many years of endless cruel taunts and ridicule had succeeded in ostracizing Melvin from the outside world, confining his feelings to his pictures. But even then, he only shared sparingly.

***

In a torrent, large raindrops fell from the sky, pounding the parched earth below. The air outside grew chilled and blustery, but Melvin, still sitting on the deck absorbed by his art, remained blissfully unaware as to the other looming storm threatening his existence and how soon everything in his microcosmic world would drastically change.

Felicia waited at the window. She wiped her eyes with the back of her sleeve. "Time to come inside," she said, tapping the glass with her knuckle twice.

Melvin lowered his head, pressing the sketchpad close to his chest, sheltering his treasures with the stout curve of his arms, protecting the contents from getting damaged. Without so much as a whisper, the curtain slid closed in more ways than one.

The winds picked up, and the clouds refused to hold back any longer. Massive raindrops pelted the sliding door at almost precisely the moment Melvin pulled it closed behind him.

"Perfect timing, son," said Felicia. "Put your things away while I get dinner on the table. Just has to warm up. Ruth prepared a nice meal for us today."

"Hamza will get wet."

"I know, dear, but his mother will pick him up in her car. He'll be okay."

Melvin tapped his foot, unhappy.

"Tomorrow's another day, Melvin. You can see Hamza tomorrow. Now don't forget to take your shoes off."

Melvin removed his shoes and lined them up neatly on the shelf.

"We're having spaghetti tonight. If you like, I can add the cheese you like to the meat sauce," said Felicia hoping to get Melvin's mind off Hamza, but Melvin had already grabbed his sketchpad and disappeared down the hall into his bedroom; making a faint clicking sound along the way.

***

Later in the evening after dinner, Melvin remained seated at the kitchen table, engrossed in his next drawing.

"Hey, Melvin." Ruth Epstein, the nice social worker assigned to Felicia's case entered the room. "I'm parched. Do you need anything?"

Melvin nodded. "Coldwater, please," he said without looking up. "Coldwater, please."

"Coming right up, buddy."

Melvin's tolerance for Ruth's constant presence in the house had increased since she first had started to come by. In the beginning, he'd either intensely stare at her when she spoke to him or refuse to answer her at all. But Ruth, conscious of his non-verbal cues, never took it personally. She understood Melvin's need to disengage emotionally and self-protect.

After about an hour, Melvin headed to bed. Felicia took his empty spot at the kitchen table. She had pushed her healthcare decisions to the back burner for far too long while concerns for Melvin's safety were pushed to the forefront.

Felicia spread the brochures and lists that Ruth brought to her months ago across the kitchen table. Caretakers, trust fund, an index of facilities to call. So much to decide and plan for. At least she still had a time left *before*—she'd have to use what little time she had left wisely, including preparing Melvin for her transition to hospice care.

Ruth sat across from Felicia at the table, pen and pad ready to take notes. "You need to be as clear and as precise as possible when explaining anything to a person with ASD," said Ruth, assigned to Felicia's case through the insurance's patient care program. Over the last year, the two women had developed a close relationship, more akin to a friendship. "Sending mixed messages will only confuse Melvin and cause him to become anxious. But whatever you do, hon, don't equate your death to sleep."

"Funny you should say that because that's what happened with Melvin when Bill died. In the beginning, I thought, okay. Fine. Let him think it, but then it turned into a mess."

"I bet."

"Poor thing became confused as heck, and it was mostly my fault."

Ruth got up from her seat. "Don't be so hard on yourself. It's not an easy conversation to have."

"It sure wasn't."

"Do you think Melvin understands the situation now? About Bill I mean?"

"It's hard to say. Melvin tends to have difficulty tolerating sudden change so who's to know?" Felicia winced. "I'm not sure how he's going to take this news."

Ruth lowered her voice. "Need another pillow?"

"No. I'm fine, thanks, but I wouldn't turn down a cup of water. This pain medication dries my mouth out."

Ruth fetched a cup. "I have the rest of the paperwork in my briefcase, but I will need you to sign-off on some of it."

"More?"

"I know, and there's still a few other issues we need to go over."

Felicia returned to reading the brochures. "So much to decide."

Ruth handed Felicia a cup. "Are you still concerned about the way Melvin might react when he visits you at the hospice?"

"Hospice—the funeral, and the memorial service, which is why I think Melvin should visit the hospice—" Felicia coughed hard, then cleared her throat, "before I go."

"Well, if you should decide to have him stay home, we'll need to include that in your directive and set up care. I hoped to have Melvin situated by then, wherever you decide."

Felicia sipped her water, already overwhelmed by the running list of decisions still needing to be addressed.

"Felicia, I can stay with Melvin to make his transition easier if you want."

"I know Ruth, thank you. I appreciate that." Felicia glanced down the hall at Melvin's room.

"I know this is hard, but he's going to be okay."

Felicia shivered and tugged her sweater tighter.

If only I knew that to be true…

CHAPTER 8

All My Children

"DO IT!" SNAPPED KALILA, sick and tired of having to repeat herself and way past hiding her annoyance. "Now!" She jumped to her feet, bracing for his next patronizing retort.

Hamza all but rolled his eyes. Swiping his jacket off the back of the chair—he made it his business to stomp up each individual step. "Dad wouldn't," he mumbled. "I don't have to…it's all your fault."

"What did you just say?" Kalila roared, chucking her plastic cup in the porcelain sink and taking off; hauling ass after the boy. "Answer me," she yelled, in an almost half run.

With lightning speed, Hamza's young body leaped up the last few stairs effortlessly, tearing down the long hall to his bedroom with ample time to slam the door and lock it behind him.

"Don't you run and hide on me, young man," yelled Kalila, banging the door with her fist. "You've got something to say, then say it to my face."

This whole *giving him time to work things out* had worn her last nerve.

Behind his door, Kalila heard the wood floors creaking slightly as Hamza climbed into bed. She had an overpowering urge to kick the door in, but instead, forced herself to leave. Disgusted that she had once again let him push her into losing her temper.

Since Bashir's death, Hamza's adoration for his father had turned into an unhealthy state of canonization. Somehow, all of Bashir's shortcomings had been granted an absolute and indisputable exoneration. Miraculously, all his faults disappeared, cast off into a world of obscurity. Neatly swept under the carpet, forever out of sight or reproach. But in contrast to Hamza's kid glove handling of his dad's memory, her failings were never spared his constant ridicule. In fact, her mistakes were fair game; paraded around on display and exposed for continuous rebuke.

In all fairness, Kalila had expected some of the son-father glorifying, but when Hamza shunned her support, she felt frustrated and confused. Ill-equipped to make him stop. With shock and grief obliterating her senses, Kalila had gone to seek advice.

"I didn't even know Hamza blamed himself," Kalila said, framing this half-truth in such a way as to dull the rawness ripping and stabbing at her gut. And although competent enough publicly, here, the weight of this world had once again come crashing straight into Kalila's already unhinged existence. The grieving that hid behind the demands of life but never dissipated came rushing to the surface. Fists clenched, she wanted desperately to lash out; to pound the wall or the door—kick the desk—anything to release the pain, but instead, she shut her eyes, vulnerable and alone.

The counselor, a sharp observer of human frailties, leaned back in her chair, clasping her hands on her lap. "Look—let's not get ahead of ourselves. All I am saying is that for right now, Hamza appears ill-equipped to channel these feelings. He's scared, anxious, and for whatever reason, unnecessarily guilty. He's also terribly confused. But as much as it hurts or how difficult it may be for you, he still needs to know you're on his side. That he can count on you to take care of him—that you will be there for him. But most of all, that you aren't going to go away as well."

Kalila rubbed her eyes with both hands. "I thought I was already doing all that," she murmured.

"You are, to some extent, but again, this takes time."

Time. Always time.

As days had turned into weeks and weeks had turned into months, the sizable rift and hostility between mother and son only seemed to magnify.

Kalila rose from her chair, ready to take her leave, but the counselor waved her to stay seated.

"Some children, like your son, sometimes find it difficult after a loss of a parent to put into words everything they're feeling, particularly when they think they haven't been told the entire truth."

Kalila's head snapped to attention. "What the hell are you implying?"

"You tell me, Mrs. Rahim. You tell me."

***

Upstairs, dresser drawers banged and slammed, but Kalila had no energy to prolong the fight. For tonight, Hamza had won.

***

As Kalila cleared the table, she couldn't help but reminisce. It was times like these that she missed Bashir the most, but not in the ways most people would have naturally assumed. She never really minded the random dirty dish left on the counter or his shoes that never entirely made it back on the shelf…or the keys strewn haphazardly on the counter instead of on the hook…or the discarded jacket left on the back of his chair...

The chair.

Bashir's chair.

Oh God, how could I have been so stupid?

The all-too-familiar sting of remorse rose hot in her chest.

The same chair Hamza keeps leaving his jacket on.

How could I have forgotten?

How could I have been so dense?

Kalila still kept a stack of Bashir's books from his To Be Read pile on the side of her bed. His extra-long plush bathrobe—the one he swore he never wanted, continued to hang on the bathroom hook. His wallet remained on the dresser. In many ways, like Hamza, Kalila also craved keeping a piece of his memory alive and unmoved.

Kalila gazed at the framed photo on the refrigerator showing the two of them cheesing it up for the camera the day Bashir, in his infinite wisdom, encouraged Kalila to try something new, "To let go for once and throw caution to the wind."

"Come on," Bashir said encouragingly. "It's easy, I swear." He held Kalila's elbow firmly. "Don't be scared."

On a whim, the two had decided to pack a picnic basket and drive to the county fair. And for some ungodly reason that Kalila to this day couldn't recall, they found themselves standing 300 feet above a river on a bridge, ready to take the plunge.

"I can't do this," Kalila whined, apparently unimpressed with the idea of leaping off a bridge with nothing more than some elastic rope between her and certain death. "I'm going to die," she said, despite wearing a full body harness.

Bashir laughed. "No, you're not."

Kalila ran her fingers over the braided shock cord, unconvinced.

"Come on Kalila—you just saw me do it and I'm still alive." Bashir kissed her neck.

"Stop, I'm serious!" She wasn't in the slightest mood for his antics. "What if the rope unhooks?"

"That's what the body harness is for," answered the overly tanned bungee jump operator. "We use that so jumpers won't get detached by the ankle."

"See?" said Bashir. "Nothing to worry about."

"Great. You guys think of everything," Kalila curtly mumbled back under her breath.

"I'll be right here, love," whispered Bashir.

"I can't." Kalila tried to shimmy away from the ledge, but there was nowhere to move but forward.

"Sure, you can," said Bashir. "I have faith in you."

"Oh really."

"Come on. Say *Bismillah* and jump."

Bashir made it sound so easy.

"On the count of three. One—"

"Wait!" Fear gripped Kalila's insides like a vice.

"Two—"

"Bashir! I can't—"

"Say it!"

Kalila closed her eyes, and Bashir pushed. Her *Bismillah* came out more like a trilled scream, but once airborne, the indescribable sensation of flying overtook her and Kalila began squealing with laughter. People awaiting their turn on the bridge clapped and yelled their support, hooting and hollering, and waving their hands. But out of all the clamor and excitement coming from high above, the single voice that resonated the loudest belonged to Bashir.

"That's my girl!" he yelled. "Did you see that?" shouted Bashir at the operator, already busy securing Kalila's retrieval. "I knew you could do it, baby!" he yelled over the railing. "*Alhamdulillah*, did you see that? My baby did it!"

My girl…

My baby…

Somehow, through his colossal belief in her, Bashir had uncovered a part of herself she never thought existed. At the time, she believed him when he had said she could do anything. Face anything. Be anything she wanted.

And she believed him.

Until his underhanded secret came out. After that, all her trust vanished. He had humiliated her, and he didn't care. Now all they did was argue.

"Where were you today?" Kalila had accused him, already assuming the answer.

"Why?" Bashir had countered back, his defensive tactic in full swing.

"What do you mean, why? I tried phoning you, but it kept going straight to voicemail." Kalila could see Bashir's mind working in overdrive, plotting his next two-faced answer.

"I turned off my mobile. I was in meetings all day."

"All day…"

"I texted you back."

"Three hours later?"

"I'm here now," he snapped. "What was so important?" Bashir's flippant retort stung.

"Why can't I even ask you where you've been or is that another covert mystery?"

"Either tell me your problem or stop hounding me." Bashir's hostility flared anytime she dared question his whereabouts. His elusive responses made her reluctant to probe, convinced that one day, she might not like what he had to say.

"You're the one losing his temper," she said.

"And you're creating problems that don't exist," he countered back. Defiant, mean.

Following her instincts, Kalila started to spy on him. One morning, she caught him on the phone, pacing the length of the driveway. As he spoke, she watched his demeanor change. Smiling and fully engaged with the caller. Kalila, nobody's fool, assumed it was a woman holding his attention on the other end. When he ended the call, she rushed downstairs when he came inside to grab his car keys, all ready to confront him.

"You're all dressed up," she said suspiciously. "Where are you going now?"

"I have a meeting."

"On a Sunday?"

"A brother from the *masjid* needs my assistance."

"Which brother?"

"You don't know him."

"That makes two of us."

"What the hell is that supposed to mean?"

"It means you're lying," accused Kalila.

"Then don't believe me," Bashir replied flippantly, barely registering her irritation.

"Who are you really meeting with?"

Bashir tried to leave.

"Answer me." Kalila's words trickled out in shallow pants, her desperation exposed.

Bashir sneered. "I'll answer when you have a question worth answering."

The more Kalila pushed, the more irritable and fidgety he became. Kalila wanted to scream. Fight it out, once and for all, but he didn't. Grabbing his keys off the counter, Bashir stormed past her, out of the house.

Kalila ran and pulled open the front door just in time to see Bashir peel out of the driveway, racing down their neighborhood block with no consideration for anyone else's life or safety. Overly caught up in his own world to care about anybody else's. Kalila plopped down on the stoop and cried. Her humiliation matched only by her indignation. Not wishing to be the neighborhood spectacle, she wiped her eyes on her sleeve and trudged back into the house, closing the front door swiftly behind her. Unaware of the fact that she had been watched, observed, and chronicled.

Defeated, Kalila curled up on the couch, drawing a lap blanket over her shoulders, but it was no use. She knew it.

No matter what I do, I won't measure up to his shiny new toy—

She knew that right now, Bashir viewed his world through narrow rose-colored glasses, consumed by an unrealistic and completely unsustainable obsession. Infused by waves of idealistic expectations that only new relationships could generate. Kalila hoped that once the novelty wore off, life would return to normal and his myopic inflated happiness would fade along with his oversized ego. But by then, would it be too late?

She heard a car pull back into the driveway. His. On first impulse, Kalila wanted to run to the door and plead with him to stay and work things out, but her mulishness kept her butt planted on the couch, her heart pounding in her throat.

The door pushed open in a flurry. "Kalila! Where's my wallet?"

Good for him.

Kalila snickered.

Serves him right.

"It was on the counter, and it's not here." Bashir lifted up a newspaper. "Damn it, where could I have put it?" Bashir mumbled, staring accusingly at Kalila. He began rifling through the chair cushions in the living room. Not finding it, he glared at her again. "Can you move?"

Kalila sluggishly slid off the couch, wrapping the blanket around her, claiming the chair previously accosted.

That's right… search for your precious wallet.

Bashir continued searching and then stiffened. "Kalila!" his voice boomed across the room. "Would you give me a hand, please? I'm running late."

Sure, I'll drop everything to help you.

Kalila didn't budge an inch.

Bashir shot Kalila a dagger-filled glance, slamming his fist onto the table. "Dammit."

Under Bashir's stony stare, Kalila leisurely sashayed over to the kitchen junk drawer to retrieve his wallet. With a theatrical thump, she dropped it onto the kitchen counter.

Bashir seethed.

She leered.

"Grow up," he snapped, playing the role of the offended victim like a pro, but when he left this time, Kalila's desire to follow and plead for his return had dissipated, replaced by a foreboding understanding that she been thrown under the bus. Tossed to the side.

Tired of constantly being forced to weigh Bashir's perception of the truth against his pathetic attempts at subterfuge made Kalila feel as if she were losing her mind. Yet, for all Bashir's so-called ultra-religiosity, his inability to keep his pants zipped eventually did him in. And when Bashir finally decided to grow a set and come clean, he couldn't just tell the truth. Instead, presenting the second wife topic as "a mere hypothetical situation" with "no one in particular in mind" —like that would make much of a difference.

"Absolutely not," said Kalila, pacing the living room floor, twisting her hands.

"You haven't even given me a chance to explain," complained Bashir.

"What's to explain? I know what polygamy is and I don't want it," she stammered.

"Can't we at least talk about it?"

"Why?"

"Because I need to know how you feel about it."

"Are you blind? Deaf? How do you think I feel about it?"

"Maybe if you'd just open your mind for a change without—"

"Why? Why do I need an open mind?" Kalila demanded, then stopped. "Oh wow," she groaned. "I can't believe this...you're asking me to let you take a second wife?"

"Islamically, I don't have to ask you at all."

POW!

The wind got knocked out of her. Kalila struggled to control her emotions. "I'd be careful, if I were you, Bashir," she roared, her eyes glaring. "Tread very carefully. What you assume is your right might be your final undoing."

"Then it's my undoing."

Kalila wanted to claw his eyes out. "That's the way you want to play this?" she asked.

Bashir leered. "I'm not trying to play you at all."

"And who do you have lined up to replace me?"

"Nobody is replacing you."

And there it was. She heard it crystal clear: The Non-Denial Denial. The NDD was the truth behind the lie. This wasn't about some hypothetical maybe. This was for real.

"Who is she, Bashir?" Kalila could barely breathe.

"You're putting words in my mouth."

"Put her name in your mouth and tell me who she is."

"There's nobody. I just wanted to see your reaction."

She stared in Bashir's face. He was so lying. "Well now you see it, and my answer is still no, and before you even try to give me your 'rights' speech again, know I also have rights."

"What are you saying?"

"Divorce. *Khula.* You can't force me to accept polygamy, you know."

"You'd seriously divorce me?" He asked, feigning shock. "Over this?"

"Try me." The words flew out of her mouth before she could stop them.

"I can't believe this—"

"Excuse me?" Kalila knew all of his gaslighting tricks, and this time she was ready.

"You'd actually destroy our marriage," he accused "Over a second wife? *Astaghfirullah*."

"I'm not the one destroying anything," she countered.

"We'll discuss this later when you're less irrational."

"No, we'll talk later when you're less of a self-serving, egotistical jerk."

And this same argument continued, all the way up to the night he died.

***

Kalila had made the fatal mistake of assuming that Bashir never had time to finalize his second marriage, but he left her little doubt that he would have. However, nothing could have prepared her for when his side chick showed up at the funeral *pregnant*, clad head to toe in black and lace like some mob Don's wife.

"Who's that?" Walaa had whispered, leaning into Kalila's shoulder.

"What?" Kalila replied, snappishly, losing her battle against the surge of dark thoughts thrashing wildly around in her head.

"The pregnant lady?" Walaa jutted her chin for emphasis. "The one standing by the tree."

"Probably one of Bashir's co-workers," said Kalila, barely managing to spit out the lie and working triply hard to feign disinterest.

Kalila veered her eyes, not wishing to look at the abomination standing in lace, rubbing both hands provocatively across her swollen belly. Alexa glared back with the same level of disdain.

"Well, considering her condition, it was nice of her to come," said Walaa, oblivious. "She looks ready to pop any minute."

Kalila had the overwhelming urge to punch the nervy bitch square in the jaw. "Ah huh," mumbled Kalila, reeling from shock, never believing that Bashir would have gone this far, but there the evidence stood, bulging in all her glory. The walking embodiment of every harbored fear, every self-doubt, and every nightmare. The tangible confirmation of her husband's infidelity.

Walaa squeezed Kalila's hand. "You know," she whispered, "this is going be a difficult time for you, but at least you can take comfort knowing you had a good man in your life."

Kalila snorted. Walaa mistook it for a sniffle.

"Bashir touched many hearts," said Walaa tenderly, sounding like a Hallmark card.

I guarantee Bashir touched more than that.

"—and by the turnout today, you can tell he was very loved."

Kalila's mind dredged up all the miserable conversations she and Bashir had before the accident, and only *now* did his callous behavior make perfect sense. All those arguments, traded barbs, insults, and quashing drivel, but they were *nothing* compared to what he really had in store for her.

CHAPTER 9

Allah is The Best of Planners

BACKPACKS FLUNG IN CORNERS, shoes kicked in the direction of the shoe shelf, and a pack of ravenous children rampaging towards the fridge in an endless pursuit of snacks ensued. All the markings of the usual after-school pandemonium Nafiza cherished and adored. While the kids did their thing, she seized a quiet moment to unwind.

Today's latest bus stop fiasco had been terribly disturbing, not because Nafiza considered Amara or Kalila to be close friends, but because theoretically, they were supposed to be sisters—not adversaries, not in competition, and certainly never enemies, questioning the validity of the other's *deen.*

A chair crashing to the floor startled Nafiza back to reality.

"*Umi!*" yelled Ra'id. "Munir took all the cookies and isn't sharing."

"I did too," shouted Munir.

"Stop your lying!"

"Munir's being selfish, *Umi,*" piped in Dalia, the family snitch and Nafiza's personal informer.

"All of you, just stop," yelled Nafiza, her nerves frayed. "I've had a long day. My head is pounding." Nafiza's cell vibrated on the counter.

Amara.

Most likely wanting to rehash the drama.

ASA. Can you talk?

Burr…

"Text me when you get this message.

Nafiza left the messages unopened. "I need to start dinner. Go do your homework. Now. Move it!"

After a bit of grumbling, a few covert kicks under the table, and some elbows to the shoulder outside their mother's direct line of vision, the three children settled down.

***

However, the temporary ceasefire skidded to a halt during dinner.

"So, what actually happened today on the bus?" inquired Nafiza.

Dalia raised her hand to speak first.

"Dalia, you don't have to do that at home," said her father gently. "Just speak."

Dalia, the family informant, also tended to exaggerate. Most of what she said had to be filtered through a truth cycle before any real facts could be assumed.

"Amir started it," Dalia declared most emphatically. "He's always messing with Hamza and saying mean things about his mother."

Nafiza glanced at her sons who surprisingly appeared in agreement. *So far—so good.*

"Then Hamza got really mad and called sister Amara the 'B' word, really loud." Dalia cupped her hands around her mouth to mouth the "B" —making extra sure her parents wouldn't blame the messenger. "The whole bus heard it, too."

The brothers exchanged smirks and giggled. Nafiza pointed and shushed the two of them, nodding for her daughter to continue.

"Then Amir tried to grab Hamza, but Hamza pushed him back first. Then they all started hitting, and everyone was screaming."

"I see," said Nafiza, shooting Abdullah a side-eye glance. "And what were the three of you doing?"

"Nothing," said Ra'id and Munir together.

"I couldn't see nothing," said Ra'id quickly.

"Anything," corrected his father.

"I sat in my seat like I'm supposed to," chimed Dalia.

"We were in the front of the bus," added Munir. "But Miss Shirley got mad," said Munir. "I mean like super mad."

"Who?" asked their father.

"The bus driver," clarified Nafiza.

"She—*I mean*, Miss Shirley, pulled the bus over two times," explained Ra'id. "That's what took us so long to get home. Can I have another roll?"

The bus hadn't been all that late, but Nafiza expected a bit of embellishing in the retelling. "Munir, you have Hamza and Amir in your class, right?"

"Yeah."

"Munir!" cautioned his father.

"Sorry. Yes," grumbled Munir, correcting himself.

Nafiza suspected this row to be only the tip of the iceberg where Amara's children were concerned. The tension between the mothers had brought everything to a head.

"They're getting suspended from the bus," said Munir.

"Is that true?" questioned his father.

"Yes. Zero-tolerance for fighting. School policy," replied Nafiza.

"They're so lucky," whined Amir. "I wish I could get driven to school."

"Enough," snapped Nafiza. "Clear your plate and get ready for bed."

"Can you drive us to school, too?" pleaded Dalia, always ready to take advantage from others' discomfort. "*Pretty please.*"

"Dalia!" her father warned.

"Okay…I'm going."

***

There had been a time when Nafiza and Abdullah thought they'd remain childless. Coming from a large family, infertility never crossed her mind, but after the first three years of trying with no pregnancy in sight, she'd almost lost hope. To Abdullah's credit, he never complained. Nor did he ever initiate a conversation about taking a second wife. But she did.

"I want to read you something," says Nafiza. "Allah *subhanahu wa ta ala* mentions in the Holy Quran:

> *'To Allah belongs the sovereignty of the heavens and the earth. He creates whatever He wills; He gives to whomever He wills, in the way of children, females, and He gives to whomever He wills, males. Or He combines them (or) He makes them, males and females; and He makes whomever He wills infertile. Surely, He is All Knowing, All Powerful.' (Surah As-Syuraa, verses 49 - 50)."*

Abdullah listened. "*Ameen*," he said, rubbing his wife's back. "And you are reading this to me why?"

"Three years, Abdullah? No pregnancy?" Faced with the anguish of not conceiving, Nafiza felt it was only right to open up the discussion about Abdullah taking on a second wife to have children.

"Three wonderful years spent with the woman of my dreams."

Nafiza smiled. She always appreciated the compassion her husband afforded to her whenever they spoke about difficult topics, going above and beyond to guard her heart. And although technically he had a right to take a second wife, the thought of him sharing that level of intimacy still hurt. Nafiza knew Abdullah loved her but wondered if that would change once another woman had his child.

"My turn," said Abdullah.

"Allah also relays the story of Zachariah, may Allah be pleased with him, who said, *'Oh My Lord! Bestow upon me from Thee a goodly offspring, verily, Thou are the Hearer, Answerer of supplication.'"*

Abdullah pulled his wife into his arms. "Listen…I know this has been hard on you, on us, but Allah is the Best of Planners. This is His will. If we get pregnant, *alhamdulillah*. If we don't, *mashaAllah*. I need you to stop looking at this as if it's your fault or problem. It's ours, and we will deal with it together."

"That's why I am saying you should consider taking on another wife."

"But I don't want another wife."

"But what if I don't conceive? Ever?"

"If *we* don't conceive, we'll find other ways to have children. Adoption, guardianship, fostering, there's a ton of other options, sweetheart."

Nafiza didn't look convinced.

"Look, maybe we won't conceive a child," he said. "I can accept that."

"Can you?" she asked. "Really? You won't wind up resenting me?"

"Resent you?" Abdullah laughed. "If we don't have kids, I promise to spend the rest of my life chasing after you without a bunch of crumb crushers fighting me for my time."

Nafiza wept. "I'm so sorry, Abdullah. You'd be a fabulous father…it's not fair."

Abdullah placed a kiss on the top of his wife's head and whispered. "This is Allah's decision. You have nothing to be sorry for. And concerning fault, it could be mine." He let that last comment linger in the air.

The couple discussed the possibility of fostering or perhaps down the road, adopting. Even going as far as taking the training which included filling out pages upon pages of lengthy, but necessary paperwork. Then, a month before their forms were finalized, Nafiza conceived. Her late period didn't trigger concern, in the beginning, having always been irregular. But after a few weeks without the slightest red drop present, she decided to go out on a limb and purchase an over-the-counter test, much like she had on numerous occasions in the past, only to pay the heavy emotional price tag of regret.

With only a small window of time home alone, she nervously unwrapped the plastic stick, deathly frightened to be thwarted yet again. *Bismillah,* she whispered. Minutes later, holding her breath, she carefully read the results.

This can't be right.

Heart racing, Nafiza grabbed the second test, destroying the wrapper while tearing it apart, convinced the first test had been a fluke.

Having already emptied her bladder, Nafiza strained and pushed. "Come on, just a few drops, something."

She couldn't stop staring at the first stick, half expecting it to change to a negative sign and start blinking, "Only kidding" or something.

Finally, enough dribbled out.

Nafiza closed her eyes scarcely able to contain her excitement, refusing to cheat or blink. Moments later, the truth revealed itself.

Ya Allah, Is this real?

Cupping the glorious news in her hands, Nafiza wasn't sure what to do next.

Call Abdullah at work? No, not a good idea.

After all the mishaps in the past, she couldn't bear to watch his hopes crumble or see disappointment smeared across his face if these were some cruel false readings.

And what if I miscarry?

Nafiza heard that happens more frequently than most people realize. No, she'd keep the news to herself, for the time being. Until it was safe to share.

At the end of her first trimester, her OBGYN doctor confirmed that she was, in fact, carrying a healthy fetus. All the blood tests had come back fantastically, miraculously normal. The baby's heartbeat stronger than ever. For Nafiza, those bleeps on the monitor were the loveliest sounds in the entire universe.

"Open it." Nafiza couldn't wait to see her husband's reaction.

"What is it?" Abdullah hated surprises.

"Stop being a party pooper and open it."

Abdullah smirked and began to unpeel the tape holding the small narrow shaped box.

"Just rip it off." Nafiza's leg bounced as she sat at the edge of the couch.

"Are you okay?"

"*Ya Allah*, Abdullah, if you don't open it up I am going to slay you."

"Opening, opening," he teased, no longer taking his time. "It's a box."

"Open the box!"

Abdullah went to lift the lid when Nafiza screamed, "STOP!"

"What? What's wrong?"

"Say *Bismillah* first."

"Oh man, you just gave me a heart attack."

"Yeah, sorry about that. Say it."

"*Bismillah*." Abdullah pushed out a deep breath. His eyes watered. "How did you…" He held in his hands a silver watch. A family heirloom of sorts. The same piece his mother gifted to his father the day she found out she was pregnant with him. "My dad's?"

"Yes." Nafiza held back the sniffles as she watched the man of her heart process the significance behind this gift.

"Does this mean?" His eyes lifted to hers.

"Yes."

"*Subhanallah*." Abdullah rubbed the watch with his thumb, the intricate etchings were as rich as he remembered. "I used to ask my mother about this. She told me it would be mine when the right time came. For my firstborn…" he voiced choked with emotion.

"Your *Umi* said to give it to you when I broke the news. That you'd know why."

Abdullah pinched his eyes. "Come here," he whispered, wrapping her protectively in his embrace. "Allah is The Best of Planners."

"*Ameen*." Nafiza felt the cool wetness of Abdullah's tear slide down her cheek.

From that moment forward, Nafiza's outlook on life took a gigantic U-turn. Where before she would have been willing to foster or stay a childless career woman, now she couldn't fathom life without this bundle of deliciousness forming in her womb.

From the tiniest morsel of food to every sip of drink, anything that crossed her lips had to be organically and nutritionally approved. Nafiza inundated herself with mothering articles and baby paraphernalia, spending hours in baby retail stores reading labels, writing out wish lists, and comparing her notes to those of more experienced parents in her circle. She even refused to watch television shows that could cause her to feel anxious, scared or upset, and that included the news.

"Aren't you taking this a tad bit too far?" teased Abdullah one evening when Nafiza abruptly turned off the TV after a show about the rise of home prices came on.

"It's a known fact that anxiety and stress can negatively affect a baby."

Abdullah nodded his head and chuckled behind his cupped hand.

"Laugh all you want, but my child is going to grow in a calm and soothing environment, at least for now, *inshaAllah*."

"And what about me? What do I do to survive this artificial utopia you have implemented? Do I have any say?"

She knew Abdullah was goading her, but she bit anyway. "None, and you'll be fine." Once Nafiza made up her mind, she went above and beyond. Nevertheless, at times, she could remain overly zealous and blindsided.

"I can't see how the housing market will have any bearing on our child's mental welfare," he said.

"It's not the information per se, but the way I react to the information that can affect the baby."

Abdullah chuckled.

"Stop teasing me," she said, poking him in the shoulder.

Abdullah drew nearer to his wife and wrapped his long, strong, and muscular arms around her expanding waistline. "You," he kissed her cheek, "are going to be amazing," he kissed her other cheek, "loving," he tenderly kissed her neck, "mother," he whispered ever-so-softly in her ear.

"*InshaAllah*…I hope so."

"I know so."

***

"Need help?" asked Abdullah. "The kids are upstairs, washed and ready for bed. I am at your disposal."

"I'm almost done," said Nafiza. "If you could take out the garbage."

"Sure thing." Abdullah pulled the bag out and tied the tabs. "So, what's really upsetting you?"

Nafiza grinned. "You know me so well."

"Did I do anything to upset you?"

"Oh, no, not at all, sweetheart. It's this thing between Kalila and Amara. It never ends. The two of them always at odds. More Amara than Kalila, it seems…not entirely sure, but it's infusing into everyone else. Even our kids. You heard them at dinner."

"What's their issue?"

"That's the thing. I don't know. Walaa doesn't know. And Kalila's not talking."

"I would assume Sister Kalila is just trying to cope after her husband's death. Have you reached out to her? Offered her assistance?"

"She hasn't mentioned anything specifically, but you have a point. Maybe there's something the community can help her with. She's closer to Walaa. I'll ask her to ask."

"If she needs *sadaqah,* let me know. I'll bring it up to the board and see what we can do."

"I should have thought of that. *Shukran* for the reminder." Nafiza silently thanked Allah for blessing her with a kind husband.

"No need to thank me. Just do me one favor."

"Anything. Just name it."

"Stay above the fray. I don't want you caught in the middle of anything."

"I will."

"I mean it. Domestic issues can turn dangerous—quick."

"*InshaAllah.*"

Later that evening, after Abdullah left for the *masjid* for *isha* prayer, and the kids were tucked in bed, Nafiza made a call. "*As salaamu alaikum*. Walaa? It's me, Nafiza. Do you have a minute?"

***

Nafiza typically didn't call anyone this late in the evening, but when she did, it was usually over something important. Wishing to converse unimpeded and out of ear range from the rest of her family, she grabbed a seat in her husband's office, mindful of closing the door behind her.

"I hope it's not too late. I wanted my kids to be in bed before chatting."

"Nope, it's fine. Talib's upstairs putting the kids to sleep. What's up?" asked Walaa.

"*Alhamdulillah*. Listen, before I say anything, I want to be clear; I'm not trying to backbite or anything, but I'm really upset about our regular Hatfield—McCoy situation at the bus stop.

Walaa rubbed her forehead. "I agree. This whole situation's getting out of control."

"Amara's been blowing up my phone since this afternoon, trying to get me to side with her."

"Mine as well."

"What did you tell her?" asked Nafiza.

"Nothing. I let it go to voicemail."

"Same here. I don't want to be dragged into this."

"I wish I knew what they were fighting about now. Do you know?"

"No, no clue."

Walaa knew from experience how ornery Amara could get. "Maybe something happened between them that we don't know about?"

"Maybe, but I've never heard Kalila rank on Amara. Have you?"

"No. But Kalila can get moody also," said Walaa, reaching for a bag of chips hidden in the back of the pantry.

"We all can, but Amara telling her sons that Kalila's not a real Muslim and questioning her *deen*—that's totally messed up."

"Yeah, that was a bit much," agreed Walaa.

Even for Amara.

"Besides the texting, has Amara tried to call you?"

"No," said Nafiza. "Why? She calls you?"

"Calls, texts. I assume it's about Kalila again, and I don't want to hear it."

"I don't blame you." Nafiza agreed. Something about this situation didn't sit right with her either.

"Maybe we can convince them to talk. Let them air out their grievances and make them agree to be civil."

Nafiza laughed, "Oh, sure."

"No, I mean it. Woman-to-woman, sister-to-sister."

"I get what you're saying, but keep in mind who we're talking about."

"True, but let's run it by Kalila first. See if she'd be willing to have a sit-down, and if she does, that might put enough pressure on Amara to agree. You know she's not going to want to be the one to look like the last holdout."

Nafiza thought about her promise to Abdullah. "All right. We'll ask them at Friday's community dinner. They usually both show up for those. We'll speak to Kalila and see if she's willing, and then approach Amara."

"Agreed."

"But if Kalila doesn't agree?"

"We leave it alone. Got it."

CHAPTER 10

The signs are there for those who know what to look for.

Tuesday Morning

"I'LL BE HERE to pick you up after school," reminded Kalila. "Depending on how crowded it gets, I might park in the second parking lot over there, so if you don't see me, head straight there."

With the morning rush in full swing, hordes of children noisily piled out of parked cars, one kid lining up behind the other, a few waving a parent a tentative goodbye. Some students, less than enthusiastic for their day to begin, dragged their backpacks and lunch boxes into the building. Hamza continued to gaze out of the car window. His fuming eyes and his adolescent pout spoke volumes.

"Did you hear me?" Kalila kept her eyes concentrated on the road, pulling behind another vehicle.

Hamza scowled in response.

Kalila slammed on the brake, gripping the steering wheel for dear life. "You really want to go there with me, son? Do you want to pretend to be Amir? I can play Amara's part, watch me," she said, daring him to reply. Kalila had never hit her son before, but his insufferable attitude had her getting precariously close. Little did he know the dangerous path he trampled, goading her every-single-Godforsaken day, pulling out the stoppers from his well-stocked juvenile arsenal and pushing every button known to mankind.

She had a good mind to—

Hamza suddenly unlocked the door, attempting to rush out.

"Hamza! I'm talking to you."

"I heard you," he screamed. "I heard you, already!" Hamza heaved his backpack over his shoulder and slammed the car door behind him, never bothering to glance back. Without the slightest hesitation, he immersed himself into the throng of students all heading into the building, never knowing or caring one iota about the heartbreak he had caused, again.

"*As salaamu alaikum* to you…*you little—*" Kalila pounded the steering wheel with her fists. "Damn it. Damn it—damn it all…" Sniffing back tears, she tried to compose herself.

A vehicle, this one directly behind her, impatiently tooted their horn. Kalila threw her hands up in surrender. "Everybody and their mother want to screw with me today," she grumbled, putting the car in drive. "Can't you wait a damn minute?"

Then another horn blasted, but this time from a few cars back. "I guess not."

The crossing guard, his mouth in a stern grimace, pointed and waved his hands wildly in her direction telling her to move on and drive.

"Yeah, yeah, to you, too," Kalila mouthed back, half-tempted to flip him the bird.

Five cars back, a red minivan with slightly tinted windows idled, waiting for her turn to pull up to the drop-off curb, pleased to no end about how well her darn horn worked.

***

When Kalila returned home, she had found that the realtor had called and left a message. Something about doing a walk-through and "crunching some numbers." "Crunching," *what a strange way of talking*, mused Kalila, deleting the message.

Since Bashir's death, Kalila had become quite fluent in a myriad of business vernaculars, learning rather quickly how each profession relied on a series of witty quipped shortcuts, acronyms, and labels for practically everything. Kalila initially found remembering all the shortened terms challenging, especially when discussing funeral arrangements. But now, that was behind her. She could concentrate on the latest of her long list of tasks, including, sadly, the selling of her house. Thanks to Bashir's oversight or self-centeredness, the life insurance policy she had counted on to help see her through the hard times now ceased to exist, much like the last year of her marriage.

"But there's got to be a mistake?" Kalila had complained into the phone, close to hyperventilating.

"I understand, Mrs. Rahim, but this is the last payment we received," explained the agent. "Dated back in February of last year. We sent you quite a few notifications."

Kalila barely registered the words. "Are you telling me we—I mean, I have nothing? No money? Nothing to take care of my child with? To pay my mortgage? To cover the funeral expenses?"

Damn you, Bashir! How could you do this?

"Please check again."

"I'm so sorry," said the agent soothingly, hearing Kalila begin to weep on the other end. "I truly am." In the face of rising costs, people did what they had to do to survive and make ends meet. When times get tough, many customers chose to stop payment on their life insurance, hedging their bets. Sometimes the gamble worked in their favor. Unfortunately, not always.

Kalila remembered pacing as she spoke, back and forth across the room repeatedly asking, "What am I supposed to do?"

With money being tight to non-existent, and as much as she didn't want to, selling the house became an immediate priority. No choice. Over the last few weeks, Kalila had started to box up many of their belongings to help stage the rooms for the open house next week.

What to keep, what to pack, and what to toss turned into a full-time vocation. Sifting through years' worth of stored memories needed time Kalila simply didn't have. A few times, she'd stopped altogether, her attention sidetracked after coming across a particular memento or photo. Kalila knew she shouldn't have opened her wedding album yesterday, but she did, and that brilliant decision sent her slinking back into her bedroom for a good marathon cry. Afterward, she'd admonish herself, mad that she had once again indulged in her misery.

Since the funeral, bills had been flying in faster than money going out with no letup in sight. Just opening the mailbox ignited a panic attack. Inundated and overwhelmed, Kalila stopped checking the mail altogether—out of sight, out of mind…until today when the overly kind mail lady took it upon herself to knock on the front door to offer unsolicited advice.

"I lost my Bernie fifteen years ago," she said, handing Kalila a large pile of accumulated mail. "And I did the same thing you did. Couldn't take another minute of folks bothering me for this and that. I even stopped answering the phone after a while. Couldn't take another conversation about how I was feeling—or if I needed anything. Anything I needed, even with the best of intentions, they couldn't provide."

"What did you do?" asked Kalila, kicking herself for giving in to her curiosity, but most of all embarrassed to find her just fine act wasn't holding up under public scrutiny.

"I turned into a hermit. Got to the point that even my folks accused me of giving up. Weirdly, I guess I did, at least in my head…yeah, those were rough days," she said wistfully. "And for a long time, I thought I'd never get through the grief. But I did, obviously, since I'm here pestering you." The woman smiled.

Kalila reached for the mail. "Thank you for bringing this to me," she said, slightly self-conscious. Never before had she shirked her responsibilities, no matter how hard times got, but now it seemed as if ducking and hiding were becoming a regular habit. "I'm sorry if I put you out."

"No, honey, no problem at all. I'd have left it in there and given you your privacy, 'cept there's no more room in there for anything else," she said, winking.

"I'm so sorry," Kalila repeated.

"Listen, it's not my place...I'm just your mail lady, right? But from one widow to another, you need to let people help you. Don't keep it all in like I did. I made it much harder on myself than I had to—too proud to accept any help. Thought I didn't need anybody...and wanted to prove that I could make it on my own. And I did...eventually, but not before practically starving to death, refusing to let anybody drop off even a damn box of mac and cheese."

Kalila chuckled, still struggling with how best to handle the outpouring of generosity. "How did you know? About me being a widow and all?"

The older woman smirked, taking a few steps closer almost as if to whisper. "I've been delivering mail for over thirty years," she said, leaning into Kalila. "Trust me when I tell you, I've seen it all. Everything from long-distance love letters, to foreclosure and divorce papers. Nothing gets past these two beauties." She pointed to her old, wise eyes. "The signs are there for those who know what to look for."

Kalila winced. Prophetically said and profoundly true.

"—not that I am prying or anything," added the mail lady, rubbing the back of her neck. "I wouldn't do that, but from the stack of mail, all the colorful envelopes with the loopy handwriting and fancy stamps, the car that's missing from the driveway...it all added up."

"You're quite observant."

"Part of doing my job." The mail lady turned to leave.

"If you don't mind me asking, how did you get through it?" asked Kalila, surprised how comfortable she felt opening up to a complete stranger.

"Time," promptly replied the woman, turning to face Kalila. "But whatever you decide to do, don't believe the mumbo-jumbo about time healing all because I can tell you from personal experience, that ain't entirely true. It does a good enough job, with most of it, and in the end, that's sometimes all you can count on."

Kalila nodded, somewhat deflated. Time being the last thing she had much of.

The woman grinned. "I best be going. I still have four more blocks to finish before I can call it quits. Take care of yourself."

"Same to you," said Kalila, anxious to close the door.

"Oh," called the mail lady, snapping her fingers. "I almost forgot, I also tried grief counseling. Just for a couple of months, but it helped. After a few weeks, I started feeling more like my old self again."

Kalila perked up. That was something she hadn't thought of doing. Maybe she and Hamza could do it together.

"That's an excellent idea," agreed Kalila, hopeful. "Maybe I'll do that. Look for someone to talk to." Kalila thanked the woman profusely and closed the door.

Sifting through the pile of bills and notices, she came across a card in a pale blue envelope. No return address or stamp, but her name prominently handwritten in a flowery, or as the mail lady dubbed, "loopy" feminine cursive across the front.

Strange.

Curious, Kalila tore the envelope open. An orange lily graced the front of the card. Written inside, in the same cursive script as the envelope, was an ominous curt message. "We need to talk. —*A*"

"Like hell we do," she roared; her blood pressure skyrocketing. Kalila tore the card up into tiny smithereens. "We have nothing to discuss."

All the pent-up resentment and fury Kalila had worked so hard to contain now erupted. Flying into an uncontrollable rage, she sought anything within reach to either break or throw. Snatching a sneaker from the floor, she hurled it across the living room, content when it made a satisfyingly loud thump on the far wall upon impact.

The doorbell rang again. "Now what!" she screamed in her most feral voice. Somebody pressed the bell again. "Oh, *my GOD*, make it stop," she muttered, trudging to the door. "I'm coming!"

For goodness sakes.

Kalila peeled back the side curtain to sneak a peek.

Oh shit! Bonnie—

She'd totally forgotten all about her appointment.

"Bonnie, hi!" she said, pulling the door open for the woman to enter. "Sorry! I was in the middle of–packing and stuff, and totally forgot the time."

If Bonnie noticed Kalila's disheveled appearance, she made no show of it. "Not a problem. I'm early. I think I told you I'd be around by one, right? But I had a cancellation in the area, so I swung by to see if could catch you in."

Kalila checked her watch. "I have to pick my son up at school by three-thirty. I can't be late."

"No worries. What I need to do won't take long. Do what you were doing, and I'll walk around taking notes and some measurements. Okay if I snap a few photos to upload for the web page?"

"Sure."

"Great. Then, if you have a spare minute, we'll talk about how we can make this process as easy as possible for you. Sounds good?"

"Sounds perfect."

***

True to her word, Bonnie did what she came for; ran the numbers, had Kalila finalize and sign the contract and promptly left. Efficient and pleasant. No prying, no redundant questions, and no pity party. Most of all, no recriminations. Kalila shuddered, taking a deep cleansing breath. Time to get moving.

Running ahead of schedule for once, she still had time to spare. Besides needing more boxes and packing tape, she needed to hit the food store. Rumor had it that eating wouldn't be a bad idea either.

Kalila tossed on some clothes, grabbed her keys, and took off downtown where everything needed was nearby, including Hamza's school, only five minutes further down the road.

"Darn it!" A quick glance indicated an almost empty gas tank. Kalila calculated how much money she had to spend to fill up. The prognosis of a big food shopping didn't look promising.

What had the mail lady said? —Mac and cheese? Ha! More like rice and beans.

The minute Kalila pulled into the gas station, she moaned, kicking herself for not waiting. Jam packed. Cars crammed everywhere. She checked in her rear-view mirror to see if she could back out but got thwarted when another vehicle pulled in right behind her. Now stuck, she had no other choice but to wait her turn.

Unfortunately, the owner of the pickup truck ahead of her appeared to be in no rush. Matter of fact, every move the old man made seemed a deliberate attempt to show how little he cared. Kalila smacked the steering wheel. "Ugh, fuck my life." With the weight of the world crashing in around her, she lowered her head, resting her forehead on the steering wheel. Kalila practically jumped out of skin when a loud rap at her passenger window nearly scared her to death.

"Oh, my God," she yelped, startled, her hands rising to block her face. "What the fu–?" For a spilled-second, she couldn't register the familiar face looming through the glass.

"Marie? Hey, it's me, Roger," he said, waving his hands at her. "I didn't mean to scare you."

Who the hell?

Roger?

Oh—Roger…Ah shit.

"Roger," she replied, barely recognizing him with his clothes on. "Hi," she said, making no move to lower the window, which in hindsight turned out to be her first major mistake.

"Yeah," he said. "Funny bumping into you here," he cracked himself up, repeating the word "bumping" over and over again, raising his voice louder to compensate for the glass between them. "I like your scarf, by the way. Very incognito," he said and winked. "Question—did you get my message? About Wednesday afternoon?"

Just go away…

"Wednesday?"

"I called like you told me to," said Roger. "Tina said she'd contact you. I guess you didn't get my—"

Reluctantly, Kalila rolled down the window, but only a smidgen; just enough to get him to stop yelling clear across the station.

Roger hunched over almost pressing his face to the glass. "Oh, that's better. Thanks. So, ah, Marie, we on for Wednesday or not?"

"I haven't had a chance to check," she answered curtly, wishing he'd lower his voice or better yet, go someplace else. Anyplace else.

"Hey, listen, Marie," he said, his voice somewhat modulated but not nearly enough to suit Kalila. "You and I can, you know, maybe we can come to an understanding," he said, leering. "Work around the system, if you get my drift." Roger winked, making Kalila's skin crawl. "No need for the middleman."

Kalila glanced up to find the old man done pumping his gas and moving onto a bit of housecleaning. Squeegee in hand, he endeavored to remove what looked like four seasons of grime from his truck windows. If she knew she wouldn't be sent to prison for the rest of her life, she'd have thrown her car into drive and run that old man over for taking his damn ass time. Anything to get away from this loud-mouthed scourge currently craning his neck through her cracked window in the middle of a small-town gas station. "Yes, well, the system is the system," she said airily, trying to blow him off.

"Here. Take my card in case you change your mind." Roger slipped a business card through the crack and wiggled it between his two fingers for her to take. "I gotta tell you, I really enjoyed our last time together," he said, grinning. "Both my heads couldn't think of anything else." He cracked up over his lame, tactless pun.

Kalila nodded, barely able to contain her disdain. She signaled for Roger to step away from the car and immediately rolled up her window.

"Take care and see you Wednesday," Roger called, puckering up and blowing Kalila a raunchy kiss. Then, under the spell of his own self-importance, slapped the roof of her car two times before swaggering back to his own vehicle, three lanes over.

Asshole.

How Roger ever spotted her, Kalila never knew. He must have glimpsed the car when she drove in. However, that idiot wasn't her biggest problem at the moment because at that same instant, another set of eyes were glued to Kalila from inside the red van parked directly on the driver's side.

You've got to be kidding me right now.

Of course, she'd have her window rolled completely down.

By the triumphant expression smeared across her face, Amara must have overheard everything.

The old man finally left.

About time.

Kalila squeezed her eyes closed, immersed in her misery, and mentally running over every word Roger had said, inferred, or spewed. Speculating on what—*if anything*—Amara could have heard.

Just then the car directly behind her laid on the horn.

"What is it with everybody and their damn horns today?" she groaned, pulling up to the pump.

Mustering up all the strength she didn't feel, Kalila stepped out of her car, ignoring all the looks, swiped her debit card to pay, and grabbed the nozzle to fill. While pumping, Kalila turned her head away to avoid Amara—who never once stopped gawking—staring. Closing her mouth, she inhaled through her nose and held her breath to the count of three. She could still feel Amara's eyes on her the whole time, clearly enjoying her discomfort.

I can never catch a freaking break, I swear—

Once finished, Kalila slipped into the car.

Drive away, Kalila… pretend for the watching audience how everything is just fine.

But as Kalila pulled away, her hands wouldn't stop trembling; deathly afraid at the thought of how everything that vapid woman just saw could come back to bite her in the ass.

CHAPTER 11

I See You

IT LOOKS LIKE SOMEBODY*'s guilty conscience is working overtime.*

Amara relished watching Little Miss Perfect's façade unravel—and in a gas station no less.

What did he call her again?

Amara swore she heard, "Marie."

And why did that guy look so familiar? I know I've seen him before, but where?

A car from behind her tapped his horn. Amara stuck her finger out the window and promptly pulled up to the pump.

From Bashir to this fool. How low will Kalila go?

Amara reached for her debit card to swipe.

I can only guess what those two have planned for Wednesday, but where?

***

Qasim

The boys were fast asleep. Amara and Qasim retired to the bedroom to discuss the bus stop situation in private.

"Granted, what the boys did wasn't right, but Hamza said a mouthful also." Amara slipped off her slippers.

Qasim unfolded the blanket from his side and slid in. "Let's assume his mother is dealing with him. I'd like to stay focused on what our sons did."

"Got *accused* of doing."

Amara … the living, breathing, reincarnation of Ma Barker.

"All right, Amara. It's obvious you've got something you want to add to this situation, so spill it." Qasim never understood why she insisted on making Kalila Rahim's life her undertaking. "Let's hear it, but it better be the truth," he cautioned.

"Oh, it's the truth. Heard with my own two ears and seen with my own two eyes."

Qasim sighed. Besides the embarrassment and unnecessary tension Amara's bickering and backbiting had caused, he just couldn't understand the preoccupation.

Amara continued talking, not paying Qasim's scowl any attention. "I saw Kalila with a man. He's either her steady boyfriend or a friend with benefits if you know what I'm saying."

"And why is this any of your business?" Qasim didn't know Kalila, having not shared anything except the occasional neighborly wave. She seemed pleasant enough. Certainly, stunning. Her beauty had caused him to consciously redirect his gaze on quite a few occasions.

"Because her behavior speaks volumes about her character," informed Amara, "She likes to pretend she's so virtuous. The perfect *muslimah*, the perfect mother, the perfect widow—"

"But we weren't talking about her, were we?"

"In a way, we were because again, her behavior dictates the values she raises her kid with."

Qasim let out a harsh breath.

"Go ahead, huff and puff all you want, but you know I'm right." Amara adjusted the blanket on her side. "And for the record, since when is having a boyfriend in Islam okay?"

"And where did you catch them rendezvousing?" he asked, playing along.

"At the gas station."

"Where?"

"He was talking to her through her window at the gas station."

"How romantic."

"I'm serious."

"Do you hear yourself right now?"

Amara frowned.

"We're supposed to be discussing our boys," he said curtly. "Not minding that sister's business or judging her by your estimation of her private life."

Amara gave a dismissive wave. "She's Hamza's mother. You should care about how her degenerate child keeps getting away with bothering our kids."

Qasim seriously doubted the accuracy of that jaded interpretation but kept that observation to himself. "Amara, my only concern right now is how our boys behaved, and from what I've gathered speaking to them, they instigated that entire thing. It's got to stop."

"But why is it okay for Hamza to get away with everything? Because his father died? All of a sudden, everyone has to walk around on eggshells? Poor little Hamza. He gets away with everything because she never disciplines him."

"How the hell do you know what she does or doesn't do? Have you got supernatural vision? Can you hear through brick walls?"

"You're not funny."

"I know! You're a secret double agent, and you've had her placed under surveillance."

Amara's lips protruded. "Why are you always defending her?"

It was like talking to a wall. "Nobody's defending her," he said, throwing his hands into the air.

"Sounds like it to me."

"I am *trying* to discuss *our* boys." Qasim shook his head. "Look, from now on, I'll drop them off at the bus stop and pick them up after school."

"That won't work."

"And why not?"

"They're suspended from the bus for a week, remember?"

"Fine, I'll bring and pick them up from school for this week as well. Problem solved."

"Pause," Amara said, her finger close to his face. "How do you plan to get them after school? What about work?"

"I'll figure something out."

"Oh, really," she snorted.

"What's the problem now?"

"I just find that amusing, is all."

"What are you talking about?"

"How you can suddenly change your entire schedule around to accommodate the boys, but when I need you to do something for me, there's always some issue that pops up."

Qasim cocked his head, confused. "I thought I was doing this for you."

Puckering her lips, Amara scowled.

"What more do you want?" Qasim massaged the strain building up in his neck.

"I want you to listen to what I'm telling you for once."

"I did listen—to every single solitary word. But did it ever occur to you that the sister's having a hard time since her husband died? Did you ever once think that she may be struggling? It can't be easy dealing with a preteen boy on your own. Look what ours are doing to us—and there are two of us to handle them."

"What's your point?"

"My point is that instead of you attacking the poor woman every chance you get, maybe for once in your miserable existence you could soften your heart. Offer to help. Be kind for a change. Otherwise, do the world and me a big favor and shut the hell up."

Amara's face turned a scarlet red; her fury boiled to the surface. "I wasn't even talking about her anymore, but fine. Glad we've established that *she's* your major concern. Good to know that another woman's feelings are more important than mine."

"I didn't even—," Qasim stopped. "You know what? Forget I said anything." Qasim turned, giving Amara his back. "I need to sleep," he grumbled, tugging the covers practically over his head.

Amara wasn't done. "I like how everyone bends over backward to come to her defense," carped Amara. Her bruised ego refused to let it go. "Just watch. You and all the rest of her admirers will see I was right all along about her."

Qasim remained silent.

"What then, Qasim? What are you gonna say then?"

"Go to bed, Amara," he grumbled, back turned.

"Poor Kalila...Qasim to the rescue."

"Enough already," he snapped, punching his pillow.

Like a petulant child, Amara flipped her husband's back the bird.

CHAPTER 12

Sleeping Forever

FROM HIS BEDROOM WINDOW facing the back of the house, Hamza noticed Melvin sitting on his back-porch drawing. He liked hanging out with Melvin even though he wound up doing most of the talking.

Hamza seized the opportunity to sneak downstairs while his mother showered; climbing over the small fence, straight into Melvin's backyard.

"Hey," Hamza greeted Melvin.

Melvin, absorbed by his sketching, remained quiet; but scooted over to give Hamza enough room to sit next to him on the step. Melvin continued sketching away, while Hamza picked at the cuticle on his thumb. The two friends compatibly silent, mutually sensitive to the other's need for a safe space to exist.

"What are you drawing?" asked Hamza, genuinely interested in Melvin's drawings.

Melvin stopped.

"Is that your mom?"

"Yes." This particular drawing depicted Melvin's mother wearing a bathrobe covered with large pastel flowers. He drew her sitting at the kitchen table, slumped over a cup of coffee with several various-shaped pill bottles, arranged in a line.

"Is she sick?"

Melvin tilted his head. "Yes." He placed his pad down and clicked his tongue three times. When Melvin's father died at home, the paramedics removed his body on the stretcher. All his father had on was an old bathrobe. Since then, Melvin has always associated bathrobes with illness and death.

"Why's your mom crying?" asked Hamza.

"Momma is sad."

Hamza bit his bottom lip. "I'm sorry."

Melvin paused, tilting his head to the side. "I'm sorry." Reaching down into his pocket, Melvin changed pencils. The point on the one he was using now had become dull. "Hamza sad." It wasn't a question.

"Yeah, kinda." Hamza drew his knees close to his chest to rest his forehead. "I miss my dad."

Melvin stopped drawing and flipped a few pages back in his sketchpad and pointed. "Look, Hamza."

Hamza peered over Melvin's shoulder. "Who's that?"

"My daddy sleeping."

Hamza squinted, confused. "But Melvin, he's in a coffin."

"Yes, daddy sleeping." Melvin had drawn his father laid out in his coffin with his mother standing over him. Her one hand rested on her husband's cheek, while the other gripped Melvin's adult hand for support. Melvin even included tears falling from her eyes.

"I understand," said Hamza, bowing his head slightly. "My dad is sleeping too. Forever."

Melvin clicked his tongue three times. "Yes. Sleeping forever."

Having long ago picked up on Melvin's non-verbal cues, Hamza understood Melvin. Over the years of friendship, they had formed an almost secret language. "You know, Melvin, you draw really good."

"Okay," said Melvin. Suddenly, he blurts out the same statement as before, but this time as a question. "Why Hamza sad?"

"I already told you. I miss my dad."

"I'm sorry."

"Thanks, but stop saying you're sorry. It's all my mom's fault. She's the reason why Dad's *dea-*," Hamza corrected himself, "sleeping."

Melvin shook his head briskly. "No, Hamza. No, no. Not nice."

"What? It's the truth."

"No, no, no." Melvin's rapidly tapped his foot on the step below.

"How would you know?"

Melvin stared forward and shut his book. Then he stood up and started walking into the house. "Come Hamza."

"Where ya going?"

"Come Hamza," Melvin repeated, waving his hand insistently.

"Fine." Hamza followed his friend inside. "Whatever."

"Hi, Mrs. Vine," greeted Hamza, following Melvin's lead and plunking his shoes on the shelf.

"Hello dear," replied Mrs. Vine, seated in her recliner in the living room. A lap blanket covered her from the just above the knee down to her feet, but there was no mistaking the bathrobe from Melvin's drawing.

"How's your Mom?" Mrs. Vine asked. "I haven't seen her for ages."

"She's good."

"Come Hamza," interjected Melvin, waving.

"Please make sure to give her my best," said Mrs. Vine.

"Come Hamza." Melvin tapped his foot impatiently.

"I better go," Hamza said, tipping his head in Melvin's direction.

"Yes, of course. Nice, seeing you again."

"You too," then for Melvin benefit, "—and before you say, "Come Hamza" again, I'm coming!"

"Come Hamza."

"Ugh," groaned Hamza.

Melvin dashed straight to his bedroom, seemingly heading towards one specific bookshelf.

"Wow." Hamza looked amazed at the sheer enormity of Melvin's collection. "You did all these?" He'd been inside the house before, but never in Melvin's bedroom. "Are these all filled with your drawings?"

Melvin wasn't listening. His eyes were busy scanning each book's spine, one almost identical to the next. Then he came to a sudden halt, pulling out a specific sketch pad from one of the lower shelves. Melvin handed it opened to the correct page to Hamza. "Look, Hamza."

Hamza accepted the pad, turning it right-side up. "Whoa," he said. "These are my parents—" Melvin had skillfully captured their likeness in uncanny detail.

"Yes."

The penciled sketch portrayed Hamza's father standing in their driveway, angrily pointing a finger at his mother. Her hands were over her eyes, crying. Something circular was drawn above her head.

"What's this?" Hamza asked, pointing.

"Angel," replied Melvin.

Hamza shrugged. "I don't get it," said Hamza, not entirely sure why had Melvin had insisted he see this particular drawing. "They were fighting. What of it?"

Melvin lowered his head, staring down at his feet. Then swiftly selected the next sketch pad. This one showed Kalila crying at her front door but at night. Her hands were cupped together as if pleading.

"No, this isn't right. Mom made Dad leave. I heard her."

Melvin anxiously paced around his bedroom, extending a finger far enough to reach the spines of his other shelved books all neatly arranged by date of completion.

"What are you doing now?" asked Hamza, but Melvin kept circling. After a few moments, he stopped. With pinpoint precision, Melvin chose another sketch pad.

"Look, Hamza," Melvin ordered, his stocky finger pointing impatiently and tapping the page. This time, the drawing showed Hamza's father's funeral.

Hamza's eyes watered. Memories from this excruciating day surged through his protective veneer all at once, latching onto a cache of disjointed memories. Images of how hot the sun had felt beating down on his head as he mourned by the grave…how his mother's pale, sickly face and red-rimmed eyes kept imploring him to stay close as she gripped his clammy hand in hers. He remembered how badly he just wanted to pull away and run. Go anywhere to hide and think, but in the end, he stayed, hoping his knees wouldn't buckle from underneath him as he accompanied his father's simple, unpretentious pine coffin to its final resting place. Most of all, Hamza remembered holding back tears, refusing to weep publicly; in full denial of the inevitable.

Hamza studied the picture. On closer inspection, it sorta reminded him of a penciled photograph. Mesmerizing clarity, almost as if Melvin could snap a photo with his eyes and physically transfer what he saw precisely onto paper.

Hamza wiped away a tear forming in the corner of his eye as he noticed how the drawing had his mother sitting on a concrete bench next to sister Walaa, him on his mother's other side. Melvin drew him scowling. He had worn the same expression through most of the service, despite everyone's effort to provide him comfort.

Hamza squinted and looked closer.

Why's mom's head turned in a different direction?

Hamza searched his memory but couldn't recall his mom doing that. Then again, he had been too busy being angry to have noticed.

"Look Hamza." Melvin pointed to his drawing at a woman solicitously cupping her belly.

Hamza didn't recognize the pregnant woman dressed in black standing off by a tree, but by his mother's expression, she had been definitely throwing some serious daggers. "Man, my mom looks really mad at her," said Hamza, thinking aloud.

Melvin clicked his tongue three times. "Really mad. Really mad."

CHAPTER 13

Taking it to The Grave

Alexa

LEAVING THE CARD IN *Kalila's mailbox had been so dumb.*

Nothing more than a pathetic, last-ditch attempt to appeal to a co-wife's humanity—a pretty hard sell considering that Alexa hadn't shown the slightest hint of hesitation in upending Kalila's marriage. Funny how people forget that what they reap, they sow.

Curled in a fetal position on a small car blanket, Alexa laid her head down on the balled-up sweater she'd rolled into a make-shift pillow. "I miss you so much," she whispered into the wind. Resting her face on her extended arm, she used her one free hand to brush against the engraved lettering of Bashir's name. There was no avoiding the stone's macabre, cold smoothness.

"I wish you could have been here to see Safa. She's so beautiful. I think she has your eyes, my lips, and your dark hair." With each gentle stroke, another small whimper escaped her lips.

A slight breeze coupled with the sun's warm-filled rays made for a beautiful day, but Alexa, too heartbroken to notice, couldn't appreciate much if any of it. Too consumed by the grief that held her hostage to the recent past; her heart in a vice which refused to let go. One minute she'd be fine, going through the motions.

Perhaps to the store; her baby in tow. Yet, without warning, at even the slightest provocation, a memory could still blindside her, leaving her on her knees in a parking lot, crying behind somebody's car. It was this level of desolation, this overwhelming emptiness that now defined her entire existence and she didn't know how to make it stop. A young life earmarked solely by diaper changes, bottles, bills, and despair.

The baby.

For the next two hours in the temporary care of Alexa's less than enthusiastic mother.

"Go, but don't be long," reminded her mother, a cigarette dangling from the corner of her mouth. "My shift starts at four."

"I know." Alexa leaned over the crib and softly kissed her sleeping baby on the forehead.

"Don't keep me waiting, Lexi. My job keeps a roof over you and your kid's head."

How could I ever forget?

"Go. Say what you need to. Get it all out of your system. Cry as much as you like but move on for Christ's sake. Close the door on that hell of a mistake you made and join the living."

Alexa could always count on her mother to make her feel worse, but her own consuming grief had overridden any ability she had to respond effectively to the craggy old woman's coldhearted volley.

"Three-thirty—the latest," Alexa promised. "Be a good girl for Grandma," she whispered. "I'll be back soon."

"Lexi," called her mother, already planted on the sofa in front of the television. "On your way back, stop at Karl's Shop & Mart, and pick up diapers and wipes. You're running low."

"Okay," replied Alexa, yanking the front door shut; listening to make sure the temperamental lock on the mobile home's door clicked closed.

Diapers. Wipes.

With what money?

Alexa hadn't thought through about all of the ramifications surrounding becoming a second wife—and not even a legal second wife. More of a wife in spirit, at least as far as the law was concerned. But now that Bashir was gone, the mounting complications glared her in the face tenfold—and in neon lettering.

I've been such a fool.

Their clandestine wedding ceremony left her with a piece of worthless paper, unprotected. As far as anybody else was concerned, she had been nothing more than Bashir's fling—and now his baby mama. Certainly not a wife…not *his* wife. Why she had agreed to such a stupid setup, she couldn't say.

Love?

That's what she told herself at the time.

Romance?

That had played a big role in their sneaky relationship. All the little love messages. His extravagant gifts. His stolen attention all for her. For once she had been made to feel so special by a man. Wanted. Cherished. The possibility of a real future had been too much to pass up.

Perhaps, in the end, their relationship had been a delusion. Two desperate people playing a dangerous, hurtful game just as worthless as the piece of paper hidden in her dresser drawer declaring her his wife.

The shame of having to return to her mother's dilapidated hovel pregnant, with no money, no job, and no husband had been humiliating enough, but as miserable as she felt, she'd have to stay put; the target of her mother's constant snide jibs delivered in ample supply.

***

"*Alhamdullilah,*" Bashir had said, running his large, strong hand over her flat belly, overjoyed at the news of her pregnancy.

"I wanted to make sure before I told you," Alexa said, her cheeks blushing with excitement.

"How pregnant?" he asked, his eyes moist.

"Nine weeks or so. The doctor said we'd know for sure after I had a sonogram."

Bashir lifted her hand, brushing his lips against each finger tenderly.

The last thing Alexa wanted to do was spoil the moment, but she had to know— "Did you tell Kalila?" She caught Bashir flinch. "Bashir! You said you'd tell her!" Alexa moaned, disappointed.

"I know, I know," said Bashir. "I will. Soon. I promise. *Wallahi*."

"This isn't fair," Alexa pouted. She remembered the first time Bashir had approached her about plural marriage; how upset she got.

"I don't understand why you can't just divorce her?" she had said, still warm from his lovemaking.

"I'm never going to divorce Kalila. She's the mother of my son. I can't just abandon her like that."

"Do you still love her?"

"I do love her, but I'm *in love* with you."

At the time, that had been enough for Alexa, eager to get away from her mother and her going-no-where-life, and throw her whole future in what she thought were Bashir's capable hands.

After countless hours of discussion, uncertainties and tears, Alexa grudgingly agreed to at least read about it.

Initially, Alexa gleaned whatever she could from various books and pamphlets given to her by Bashir, of course, not realizing at the time the absolute misogynistic slant of the information being explicitly gifted to her. Then she joined an online group chat to read numerous posts left by second wives. Some seemed genuinely happy—content. She learned about the complaints of dealing with the emotional baggage of the first wife, but that, they had said, was to be expected.

Others she met online were less enthralled with their situation, and their complaints seemed endless, but she did her best to learn about some of the touchier aspects of polygamy from them. Stuff like how to manage the husband's time equally amongst his wives as well as his obligation to be financially equitable. Alexa also learned that at least religiously, Bashir wasn't required to ask Kalila for permission to marry again.

So, if that's true, then what exactly was his problem in telling Kalila, then?

"Are you embarrassed of me?" Alexa asked him, long suspecting that Bashir felt ashamed of her because unlike Kalila, she wasn't Muslim and didn't cover.

"No. It's nothing like that," he had told her. "To be honest, I'm having a hard time finding a way to break the news to Kalila without her destroying everything else—including us." Bashir drew in a reluctant breath, "and now the baby."

"But we love each other, and we have the right to be together." Alexa refused to allow anything—*especially Kalila*—from blocking her from the man she wanted. "And even Allah says so," Alexa added, pulling out all the stops.

She remembered how Bashir had kissed her hungrily, wrapping his strong arms around her shoulders and gently squeezing. "I promise. I'll tell Kalila tonight."

Alexa rested her head on her arm. The grass tickled her nose. "I miss you so much," she whimpered, sobbing harder than ever before. Trembling, she draped the bulky sweater around her chilled arms and shoulders, no longer caring who saw or overheard. But Alexa needn't have worried for today, only the dead were listening.

***

Bashir's last day alive.

Alexa had worn out the floor pacing, expecting him to arrive any minute, anxious to hear how the conversation between him and Kalila had gone.

Bashir had called over an hour before. From the sound of his strained voice, she assumed their conversation hadn't gone well, but at this point, with the baby only weeks away from being born, Alexa didn't care. No matter what Kalila tried to do to prevent or block them from being together, Kalila didn't have the power to stop the little baby growing inside Alexa's womb. But Alexa sorely underestimated Kalila's hold over Bashir, and now bigger problems had come home to roost.

***

Kalila

The uniformed cut of the green grass swayed soothingly in the gentle breeze. The narrow footpath should have led her to Bashir's marker, but somehow, Kalila must have taken a wrong turn somewhere. She stopped walking, uncertain where she got turned around. If her memory served her correctly, there should have been a cement bench, the same one she had sat on the day of the funeral, under a willow tree off to the side, only a few more yards away.

Kalila dreaded being here and hadn't been back since the funeral. She paced her stride to the sudden rush of memories flooding her senses, each one leaving behind a trail of polarized feelings that had plagued her for months. Everything—from grief to sadness, anger to hurt, and heaps of resentment all competed for attention while circumventing the truth at the cost of her sanity. Today's visit was about putting some of that to rest…closing the door on the feeling of being crazy and lost at the same time.

Relieved to spot the familiar bench, Kalila almost broke out into a run, but instead, stopped dead in her tracks staring at what appeared to be a young woman curled up on a blanket by Bashir's marker, crying.

What the hell?

Kalila made a beeline over to the grave toward the woman, outraged to the core that even in a damn cemetery she couldn't escape the legacy of the bullshit Bashir had saddled her with.

"Excuse me," said Kalila curtly, raising her hand over her eyes to block out the sun. "Oh, for fuck's sake."

Alexa peered up sniffling back tears, trying to focus on the looming voice standing over her. "Can I help you?" she asked meekly.

In no mood for banalities, Kalila stood menacingly over Alexa. "What in the hell do you think you're doing?"

Alexa sat up, frightened. "Who—"

"Don't play stupid with me. I'm Bashir's wife and I sure as shit know who you are. What are you doing here?"

The two women sized up one another.

Kalila scowled. "I asked you a question. What the hell are you doing here?"

"*As salaamu alaikum,*" replied Alexa, standing to brush herself off.

Kalila seethed.

Oh, right. Now she thinks she can pull the Muslim card out of her ass. I don't think so.

"How did you find me?" asked Alexa timidly, clearly out of her depth.

Refusing to get baited into some frivolous, stupid conversation with this half pint, Kalila cut to the chase. "I got your card. You said we needed to talk. So—talk."

Although intimidated, Alexa didn't back down. "Bashir is the father of my baby."

"Goody for you." Bile burned the back of Kalila's throat.

"But—"

"Bashir is dead," Kalila blurted out, interrupting anything Alexa was about to say. "Your kid is not my problem."

"Your son and my daughter are brother and sister."

"Shut your mouth."

"I have as much right to Bashir's name and inheritance as you do."

"How dare you! You were nothing but a fling. Not even Bashir's first attempt."

"I wasn't a fling," yelled Alexa. "I was Bashir's wife too."

BOOM!

Blindsided.

Just when Kalila felt safe from the possibility of any more surprise attacks, there waiting in the wings, straight from the grave came round-two. "Are you telling me he married you?"

"Yes." Alexa nodded.

"Legally?"

"Islamically."

Kalila laughed. "So that would be a big-fat-*no* —according to the law of the land."

"I need help."

"You haven't been listening. It's not my problem."

"But I need money—for the baby," stammered Alexa. "Bashir's baby."

Kalila's hand recoiled, fully prepared to punch Alexa six-feet into the ground so she could join her man. "Then ask him for it," screamed Kalila, pointing down at Bashir's grave. "Not me." Kalila turned to leave.

"Wait!" Desperate, Alexa called after Kalila. "Bashir loved me."

Now Kalila stopped. "Stop it."

"No! I won't. If you hadn't been so selfish, Bashir wouldn't have been driving so upset that night—"

"Shut up!"

"We didn't do anything wrong. We just wanted to be together."

"Shut up, shut up, shut up!" Kalila shouted, covering her ears to block Alexa's words out.

"I loved him, and he loved me."

Kalila lunged for Alexa, but Alexa moved out of the way, practically tripping over another marker.

"No!" Alexa screamed hysterically. "I won't, and you can't make me. You didn't deserve Bashir. He was the kindest, most decent man I have ever met. We could have had a life together. We could have been happy."

"He was married legally and Islamically to me!"

"I know that, and I'm sorry, but you have to understand. I thought that after you got to know me, that you'd stop being so mad."

Incensed and unable to process the absurdity, Kalila's eyes grew big. "You're delusional—you know that?" she said disgusted, shaking her head. "Now, if you don't mind, I'd like a word with *my husband*—in private."

Alexa tucked her sweater into her bag, then gathered the folded blanket and held it close to her chest. "We never meant to hurt you," Alexa said somberly.

Kalila stepped closer to the younger woman; her hands balled into tight fists. "You're full of shit. You meant it—he meant it. All of it. You two carried on behind my back never once showing one iota of compassion for me or my son. We didn't matter as long as you and Bashir got to play house." Kalila couldn't stop her body from shaking. Jabbing a finger in Alexa's face, she yelled, "You stand there so full of yourself, but because of you and your duplicitous, selfish bullshit, my entire world came crashing down around me."

Alexa neither budged nor made any move to walk away. Kalila, squared her shoulders bracing for a fight.

"You think I wanted to be a co-wife?"

Eyebrows raised a notch, Kalila's mouth dropped open.

The nerve.

"I admit it. After I got to know Bashir better, I didn't care that he had another wife. It didn't matter to me anymore."

"It didn't matter?" Kalila turned away. "It didn't matter? My God, what the *hell* is wrong with you?"

"I'm sorry, okay? But I loved him!"

"So did I!"

"But Bashir promised you'd eventually understand."

"Oh, did he now?"

"He also said that you'd accept us once the baby came."

That sounded just like something Bashir would have said. "Get out of my way."

"I'm sorry," Alexa blurted out.

"You're sorry? *You're sorry.*" Kalila aped, refusing to comply. "And what about your card?" Her words came out clipped and strained. "Sent that to gloat, did you? Rub it in that he knocked you up?"

"No, not to gloat," Alexa bowed her head, embarrassed. "Desperation. I told you, we need money."

Hands on hips, Kalila shook her head, staring at the sky.

"I just thought that if we could talk—you know, face to face, that I could appeal to you for help."

"From me?" yelled Kalila. "You want *me* to help *you*?"

Ain't this a bitch.

Alexa dropped her bag on the ground along with the blanket and sat, wrapping her thin arms around her legs. "Ever since I agreed to marry Bashir, most of my family won't talk to me—all except my mother, and believe me, whatever she has to say is pretty awful. I've lost my job, my apartment. Most of my money's gone. I've got hospital bills galore, and now a baby with no father." Alexa put her hand up. "I know…I have nobody to blame but myself." She began to weep. "I really am sorry."

Kalila paced back and forth, not knowing whether to walk away or punch Alexa in the jaw. "I'm only going to say this once, so pay very close attention. Bashir's no longer here to protect you, so I strongly suggest you never make the mistake of contacting me again."

No more words were necessary to address the tragedy of losing a man they both had loved. There they both convened, two women, two mothers, two wives, vulnerable and exposed, and facing the overwhelming responsibility of putting the wreckage of their devastated worlds back together, one painful broken piece at a time. The casualties of one man's callous, self-serving desires.

***

Kalila stayed behind after Alexa left to make her peace with Bashir.

"Well, I hope you're happy," she said, tugging at the weeds sprouting around his marker. "My therapist tells me that I'm supposed to make peace with you." Kalila pulled a stubborn plant by its roots. "She also said I need to tell you how much you hurt me." Kalila threw her head back, her face to the sky. "A bit hard to do since you're dead and all."

Fury tore through Kalila's heart. Pounding the cushioned earth with her fists, "You hurt me so bad," she cried out. "How the hell am I supposed to pull my life together after what you did?" Kalila sobbed. "*Ya Allah*—look at me. I'm pathetic. I'm on my knees pulling out your weeds—still cleaning up after your messes." Kalila tugged at anything within her reach. "I'm-so-angry at you right now," she stammered. "I-I can't believe you did this, after everything we've been through." Tears gushed and slid down her cheeks. "How could you leave me like this—in this-this—hell, alone? Every day another struggle, and now I come to find out that you have another wife—and a baby." Kalila flung the newly collected weeds at his marker.

"That's it," she said, rising to her feet, "I'm done." Kalila brushed the dirt off her pants and hands. The indelible fury that had controlled her up to this point had all but evaporated, replaced by an almost cold cynicism. "Listen up, dead man," she said. "Before you died, you kept demanding that I make a decision." Kalila inhaled. "Well, today's your lucky day."

Kalila flung her handbag over her shoulder and marched away. Unlike the day of the funeral when she cowered in fear, afraid about what others would think of her; today she left with her head held high, infused with a renewed purpose—furious that she had wasted so much of her life mourning a relationship lost long ago.

The time to begin anew had arrived, but this time Kalila was determined to find a way to live on her terms no matter who she had to shove out of her way—starting with Amara.

CHAPTER 14

I SPY

AMARA CHECKED THE TIME.

What the hell is taking this woman so long?

Having already finished pulverizing the few stale chips found in an open bag left behind from one of her kids' lunches the day before, she searched for things to do to fight the boredom. She had already cleaned out her pocketbook and taken a bunch of old paper napkins saved from one of her many quick pitstops to various fast food joints, to clean her dusty dashboard.

Watching from a comfortable distance, Amara noticed that the only other person in the last half-hour to leave the cemetery so far was a young woman bawling her eyes out.

Why does she look familiar?

Amara knew the face but couldn't place her.

So far, her plan had been simple enough. Follow Kalila around until she led her to wherever she prearranged to meet with that guy from the gas station. Snap a couple of pictures, take a few notes, and collect as much intel on this two-faced double-dealing witch as she could.

Not even twenty minutes later, Amara spotted Kalila darting across the parking lot towards her car. Thankfully, Kalila drove out through the main gates.

Here we go.

Amara started her engine, maintaining a respectful distance. Kalila's blinkers indicated she intended to turn left towards downtown. At this time of day, traffic tended to be exceptionally light so Amara would have to be extra careful not to get caught. Once in downtown, amongst the hustle and bustle, she'd probably be able to ease up on all the covert intelligence tactics enough to get in real close.

Kalila made another turn, but this time taking a right.

The highway?

Amara did the same.

Kalila turned off at the next exit, entering a small, but quaint suburban Main Street. Then unexpectedly, made a sharp left turn as opposed to the right.

Where is she going?

Annoyed, Amara slowed down to make an equally sharp turn, following Kalila down the road for about a quarter of a mile more until she made a soft right turn into a reasonably upscale hotel parking lot, driving like she'd been there before. Kalila parked around the back to the far side, furthest away from the public's eye, and right next to a silver Mercedes with an estate decal on the license plate.

"Yes!" yelled Amara, slapping her wheel. "I got you now, bitch."

Amara's elation turned short-lived as she quickly realized she didn't know what to do next, so she hung back, preferring to park inconspicuously, all the way at the other end of the lot.

Kalila lingered in her car for about five minutes. Then she stepped out of her vehicle, searching for someone or something. Amara quickly crouched below the steering wheel, which thankfully, provided enough space to still peek out and steal a better look while not being detected.

Unaware of the eyes burrowing into her, Kalila brushed off her outfit, then got back into the car and began fixing herself up in the car mirror. When she finally emerged, she no longer had her *hijab* on. Her hair floated stylishly down around her slender shoulders. She tucked her shirt into her slacks and left her neck seductively opened. Amara watched Kalila spritz herself with perfume on both wrists and neck, casually tossing the bottle in the front seat before slamming the car door shut. As Kalila pulled the side door of the hotel open, she stopped and stepped back, turning around again.

"Shit!" yelped Amara, quickly ducking below the steering wheel, scared silly she'd been scoped out. After a second, she inched her way back up, catching Kalila lingering over something on her phone. Even from a distance, Amara could tell the bitch was upset.

Kalila squared her shoulders, pocketed her phone, and entered the building. She didn't reappear until way over an hour later.

Clutching an assignment pad, an extra from the pack purchased early in the year for the boys, Amara began making notes.

- 1pm-? K rendezvous at gas station.
- Mercedes, guy driving to hotel off Main Street.
- Slut dressed to kill.

Reaching into the glove compartment, Amara snatched a bag of pretzels stashed from the other day. "Damn. I should have brought something to drink," she muttered, annoyed she hadn't thought far enough ahead. Then another, more calculating idea popped into her conniving head.

Glancing around to make sure nobody was looking, Amara gradually pulled out of her space, driving unhurriedly past the parked cars. She stopped only long enough to snap one photo of the guy's license plate, and then another picture of their cars parked next to each other.

Try explaining this.

Although unable to run the plate like some TV detective, Amara still felt rather proud. Re-parking, she leaned back in the seat to wait, celebrating her accomplishments with a bag of dry, salty pretzels, stuffing a few in her mouth at a time.

***

Meanwhile, inside the hotel…

Seductively poised in silk lace undergarments, Kalila moved to the edge of the bed as Roger ran his thick but soft fingers across her hips. His tongue buried just above the band of her thong.

"I've missed you, Marie," he said softly, cupping each of her ass cheeks and pressing her closer to his expanding chest. "Why are you tensing? Loosen up." He pulled her on top of him as he leaned back onto the bed.

Kalila despised the warmup routine. The fake romance Roger insisted on acting out each time she serviced him. She preferred the raunchy old men who got down to business before the Viagra wore off. But bills had to get paid. Food needed buying.

Kalila bent forward and kissed his forehead, allowing her breasts to sway teasingly in his face. "I'm fine," she pretend-moaned.

"You certainly are."

Lifting herself up, she huddled forward straddling his face. Roger panted, his chest rising and falling with rapid breaths; hands clung to her hips as his tongue worked furtively in and out, drinking her up in chaotic swallows. Reaching back, Kalila gripped and worked him into a fevered passion, while Roger's tongue twitched and flicked inside of her, begging her to come.

It won't be much longer now.

His breaths quickened as his legs stretched and flared, heels digging wildly into the bed, begging for release.

Outside, a massive torrent of wind pelted the hotel windows with a deluge of rain. Kalila silently thanked Allah for the much-needed distraction. Since childhood, wind and rain storms had brought her comfort and a sense of security, helping her to vacate her body, while directing her mind safely elsewhere whenever she had to do—*this*.

"Now," Roger moaned, pushing her body to receive him, forcibly manipulating her hips around his pounding without reserve. Faster and faster, he rode her until he groaned in ecstasy.

Rolling off of him, Kalila laid on her back, staring up at the ceiling to calm herself down. Listening to the rain's steady patter

"I gotta run today," Roger said as if she cared. "Short lunch break."

Lumbering across the room, he headed straight into the bathroom to shower, but first picked up his wallet and tossed an extra hundred-dollar bill at her, cracking up when it landed on her belly. "You earned it."

Fighting back the humiliation, Kalila crumbled the bill in her fist. "Thanks," she replied, wearing a facade of appreciation when in reality, had she not been so desperate for money, she would have spit in his stupid face.

"Same time, same place next week?" he asked, oblivious to her loathing.

"You bet," she called back, swinging her legs over the bed, reaching down to grab a towel left on the side of the bed. The faster she dressed, the quicker she'd be out of here.

Kalila poked her head into the bathroom to bid Roger a final goodbye. Pulling back the curtain he placed a wet, soapy kiss on her lips. "Wait up. I'm almost done. I'll walk you out."

Thanks, but no thanks.

Besides not wanting to take the chance of getting caught, Kalila refused to encourage any informal behavior. Strictly business.

"I need to run, but I'll see you next week." Then as an afterthought, she added, "I'll take care of letting the office know we have a standing weekly appointment, so you don't have to keep calling," she offered, using her pleasant, approachable voice.

"Okay, great. Appreciate it." Roger shouted from behind the curtain. "Take care of yourself, Marie," he said, peeking out and giving her wink.

"You too."

"Oh—"

Kalila stopped.

Now what?

"How about the next time, we do it with you wearing that scarf thing on your head, the one you wore the other day. I think you looked hot in it."

If skin truly had the ability to crawl off of one's body, then this would have certainly been the perfect opportunity for it to make its great escape once and for all.

***

About time.

Slightly disheveled, Kalila rushed out the side door holding her pocketbook over her head to protect her hair from the downpour.

Over the next five minutes, she lingered inside her vehicle without starting the engine. Then, when she finally turned the car on, she drove right past Amara none the wiser; her *hijab* once again fastened back on and eyes focused straight ahead. This time, Amara didn't bother to duck out of sight. Too busy snapping as many incriminating photos as she could muster, and unfazed by the fact that they would most likely turn out blurry.

Instead of following Kalila, Amara decided to hang around…see if Kalila's boyfriend made an appearance.

When Roger emerged a few minutes later, he appeared euphoric…light on his feet.

"Would you look at this mess," Amara mumbled, watching the guy toss, what appeared to be some sort of duffle bag into his trunk.

Expensive suit. Expensive ride. Expensive tastes…and not hard on the eyes.

So where exactly does the two-faced-Kalila fall into this guy's life?

***

Back home, Amara puttered around the house, pleased with the way today's mission had gone. Ecstatic over how deliciously scandalous it all felt.

Who knows, I may have stumbled on a new career, she pondered.

Sleuthing—The Under-Covered Detective.

She couldn't help but chuckle at her play on words.

Time to get dinner started.

It would be nice to have my own income.

While Qasim never denied Amara money, it was still his to give, which in her opinion, gave him the upper hand. An income of her own would suit her fine. Plus, it might be fun to start her own detective agency. She could follow cheating spouses during school hours using her minivan, catching the double-dealers doing the dirty deed when least expected.

Besides, what else is there to do all day? Wait for Qasim to come home? Laundry? Watch TV, catching reruns of Law and Order?

Peeling then dicing an onion to throw in the sauce, she contemplated all the dirt she had collected on most of the people she knew. Stuff they didn't even know she had. Take Walaa for example, who, while considered a friend, still had made the fateful mistake of revealing her true feelings one day about turning up pregnant again. At the time, suffering from postpartum depression, Walaa let it slip about how much she resented being a mother; how she prayed for a miscarriage this time.

Amara tugged a large stockpot out of the cabinet and filled it halfway full of water.

Bet her picture-perfect marriage wouldn't be so perfect if Talib found out how his lovey-dovey wife really felt about him and his offspring.

Amara grabbed a jar of tomato sauce and a box of spaghetti from the cabinet. Qasim despised pasta, but she didn't feel like making anything else tonight. Besides, knowing her husband, he'd more than likely eat out again. Amara threw a handful of salt into the water, and set it on the stove.

I'm pretty good at detecting stuff.

Her memory latched onto Nafiza.

Miss Religious. Always correcting everyone about their deen. Thinks that just because her husband is the Imam, she can go around schooling the rest of us in her perfect Arabic. Miss Holier than thou, covered to the tens, except when she's busy making—

"Ma! We're home!" shouted Amir, racing his brother to the kitchen.

"*As salaamu alaikum.* How was school?" she hollered, as they barreled in and attacked the snacks.

"Boring," answered Muhammad.

"I hate school," said Amir, rummaging through the pantry.

"Where's your dad?" Amara reached for a frying pan.

"At Hamza's house talking to his mother," offered up Muhammad. "Can I have a soda?"

Amara practically dropped the pan. "Why's he over there?"

"Can I have soda? Muhammad has a soda."

"No!" snapped Amara, madder than she had meant to sound. "No soda before dinner. Put it back. Both of you."

Briskly wiping her hands on her apron, she rushed into the dining room where she could spy easier. As she peeped through the curtain, her rage grew. Fuming, Amara cracked her knuckles.

Just what in hell do you think you're up to now?

CHAPTER 15

Brief Encounter, one hour earlier

QASIM PULLED BEHIND A long line of other parents already assembled in front of the school, waiting for child pick-up. Some parents were busy looking around, while others took advantage of the small reprieve to rest, enjoying their last precious minutes of heavenly solitude before the school doors burst open, and released their little cherubs back into the wild.

Behind him, a familiar car pulled in. Kalila Rahim. The last person on the planet he wished to bump into. For months, his guilty conscience had punished him, robbing him of everything from sleep to his appetite. Nothing had been spared, including the shame he masked by wearing a perpetual frown. He prayed Kalila wouldn't notice him.

Qasim popped his fourth antacid into his mouth. A regular habit since the night he hurled his manhood into the gutter and drove away like a coward. The night he left a man to die, alone.

Why hadn't he stopped? He played the same nagging question over and over in his head, and each time drew a blank. Despite the anonymity behind tinted windows, Qasim's cheeks colored.

From his rearview mirror, he watched Kalila dab her eyes with a tissue. Had she been crying? More guilt washed over him. Had he just fessed up that night…taken responsibility. Done anything but what he did, he wouldn't now be consumed by remorse.

Inside the building, a bell rang.

Only a few more minutes to go.

Qasim picked up his phone and began to scroll. Reading the news helped keep his mind off his personal troubles. Peering up, he noticed Kalila just sitting in her car not doing much of anything.

Glad she can be calm.

Suddenly, Kalila peered up, looking straight at him, or at least it felt that way. Qasim quickly skirted his eyes, pretending he hadn't noticed. A moment later when he got the nerve to peek up, he found Kalila on her phone seemingly upset about something.

The school doors flew open, and the first group of students piled out of the building, dragging their feet and book bags. With their kids in tow, a few cars and minivans started pulling away, making room for the next batch of anxious parents ready to take their place.

Organized bedlam. My tax dollars at work.

A few more kids came out, one of them Kalila's son, Hamza. Head hung low, he shuffled his feet, taking all the time in the world to reach his waiting mother.

"Hey Hamza!" called a fellow student rushing past, but Hamza did little more than give a slight head bob of acknowledgment.

What's that all about?

Qasim wondered, curious as to why the boy looked so miserable. Just then Qasim's own back door whooshed open, startling him.

"Hey Dad," said Amir.

"*As salaamu alaikum.*"

"*Wa alaikum salaam.*" Amir tossed his backpack in the back and buckled up. "Where's Mom?"

"Home. Where's your brother?"

"He should be here soon. He had gym."

Qasim nodded, feeling clearly out of his realm. In the rearview mirror, he saw Kalila's indicator on. She was ready to pull out. Thankfully, she never turned in his direction as she drove right past him. Hamza, on the other hand, shoulders slumped and leaning his head on the window of the front passenger seat, wore an irritated frown across his preteen face.

Qasim winced as another pang of guilt stabbed his stomach.

Probably another ulcer.

Qasim had named the last one Amara. At the time, she hadn't found him funny, which was more than fine since he hadn't been making a joke. Qasim popped two more antacids.

"Can I have one?" asked Amir.

"How do you ask for something when you don't even know what it is?" replied his father, perplexed.

"Gum?"

"No."

"Sucking candy?"

"I wish."

Muhammad opened the door and slid in.

"Finally," said Amir, annoyed. "What took you so long?"

"The turd hid my backpack."

"Patrick Sweeny?"

"Yeah."

"Is he the one whose nose is always full of snot?"

"Yeah, him." Muhammad closed the door.

"That guy always sounds like he's talking underwater."

"Amir!" chastised Qasim. "Give it a break."

"Oh, hey, dad," said Muhammad, fidgeting with his seatbelt.

"*As salaamu alaikum*. You two ready?"

"Yeah," the boys chorused together.

Qasim started the engine.

"Where's mom?" asked Muhammad.

"Home," said Amir.

"I wasn't asking you."

"So? The answer's still gonna be the same, pimple face, right Dad?"

"At least my face doesn't look like dog poop."

"Boys—," admonished Qasim. "Enough already, sheesh."

Why did I ever agree to do this?

"Your mother is home."

"See!" Amir grinned, vindicated.

"Why are you picking us up?" asked Muhammad, ignoring his brother's smirk.

"Because I am helping mom."

Both boys looked questionably at the other, not remembering the last time their father had been at the school, no less there to pick them up.

"Where are we going?" asked Amir, ready for an adventure.

"Home."

"Oh..." chorused the twins, clearly disappointed.

Qasim, drove with one hand, using the other to massage his throbbing forehead.

"Are you okay, Dad?" asked Muhammad.

"I'm fine." Once Qasim dropped the boys at the house, he'd have to head straight back to work. There was a slew of outstanding phone calls to make and some paperwork that needed finishing before tomorrow's board meeting. "Thanks for asking, Muhammad."

"Well, you look kinda weird," replied the human pit bull. Once an idea got stuck in Muhammad's head, he wouldn't leave it alone.

"Dad's sick," informed Amir. "He's popping pills."

Qasim winced. "Antacids, Amir—not pills."

"Why're you popping pills?" asked Muhammad, sounding genuinely concerned.

"I bet it's Viagra," said Amir, smirking.

Qasim braked hard, almost driving through a stop sign. Unlike his brother, Amir always aimed for a person's Achilles' heel. "What do you know about Viagra?" he roared.

"Chill, Dad—commercials." Both boys giggled hysterically, pretending to kiss and hug each other like star-crossed lovers.

Clowns.

Qasim pursed his lips, annoyed. He really needed to speak to Amara about how much time those two spent in front of the boob tube.

"What are they, then?" asked Muhammad slyly, and under his brother's winking approval.

Qasim thought for a second, not exactly sure how to answer. "They're medicine for parents whose kids are a pain in the ass."

With that, the boys cracked up again, loving the fact their dad used the 'a' word. But unfortunately, their blissful hilarity lasted only long enough for the incessant sibling bickering to wedge its way back in.

***

In many ways, marrying Amara had been one of Qasim's biggest mistakes, but by the time he had realized it, the relationship had been solidified. Impossible to back out of without causing his family undue hardship and shame.

Back in college, Amara had led him to believe they shared the same goals and interests, like faith, values, and morals. At the time, Qasim thought he had found in Amara a friend, a lover, companionship…intimacy; someone to share his dreams and aspirations with, but that had been a terrible ruse. One of Amara's many deceptions.

Back then, Qasim remembered when Amara walked across the campus, laughing with her friends. She'd been so attractive, always taking extra care with her clothes and hair. A cute shape as well, but pregnant, she began eating non-stop and blew up like a blowfish—which during the pregnancy had been perfectly fine, except the woman never stopped. Now bordering on obese and facing lifelong diabetes.

"Don't give me that look." Amara had told him. "It's a small piece," she said, cupping a rather hefty slice of chocolate double fudge cake from his reach.

Qasim, tired of fighting, shrugged and left her to her sugar. If Amara didn't care enough about her health, why should he?

Amara hated her body. Always complaining about how fat she felt, how much weight she gained. Wearing long large caftans and overgarments to hide herself in, and not just for modesty's sake either. Food, the boys, even interfering in other people's lives all reigned supreme in Amara's life, but not him. She had stopped putting him or their marriage first a long time ago.

In bed, Qasim had to make sure all lights were turned off before Amara would agree to strip down. And during sex, he always had to be the one on top. No passionate caressing, no hungry fumbling. For a long time, Qasim wished things between them could be different. Then one day, he came across an article about how men like him can be reconditioned to sexually bond to whatever they are looking at—if the man has a sexual release at the same time. The psychologist went on to say that if a man kept his eyes open during sexual intimacy and released, he would bond with his wife again, regardless of the way she looked now. Qasim decided to give it a shot the first chance he had.

The next night while busy doing the do, Qasim's cell phone on his night table lit up, enough to illuminate the bedroom. Qasim opened his eyes as planned, but instead of passion or intimacy, he caught the most irked expression plastered across Amara's face. Almost as if she was bored out of her mind. From that moment on, Qasim despised his wife, and any desire or passion left—vanished, never to return.

Now, whenever needing release, he'd pound into his wife with cold, unfeeling savagery. Once done, he'd roll off her round, flabby body without the slightest concern for either her or her feelings.

Qasim also equated food with love. His mother always cooked for his father, and at the start of their marriage, Amara prepared just for him. She'd made him the most delicious meals. A bed of rice with sautéed meat and vegetables…soups that simmered on the stovetop for hours, loaves of bread that melted in his mouth. Now Qasim would be lucky to get a plate of tater-tots and a leg or two of dry, overcooked chicken with canned corn slopped on a paper plate.

People keep asking if I'm all right. No, I'm not all right. I'm empty. Alone.

No, not alone—lonely.

Qasim felt lonely. Going through each day with no immediate reprieve in sight. He despised his wife and could scarcely stand to look at her, let alone touch her, but what could he do? Divorce? Never. His parents, both still alive, would never forgive him.

And what would happen to the boys if he left Amara? His wild brats?

Qasim would never admit it aloud, much too ashamed, but he never really wanted children. Sure, he loved his sons, but since their birth, all his dreams and wishes had gotten sidelined; forced to work at a job he despised to make money for a family who acted like they could barely tolerate him.

I'm ashamed.

There it was again. Shame. The emotion that followed and mocked his very existence. The constant and irritating reminder of his many failings. If Qasim were to be honest with himself, which he rarely was, he would have to admit that most—if not all—of his decisions were based off of shame, guilt, or misplaced loyalty. Now, after what happened with Bashir, shame and guilt seemed to have partnered, stalking him for eternity and doing a fine job of it.

Qasim thought about the recent bus incident and the reason behind why he was now stuck transporting these two kids back and forth while his exorbitant taxes paid for bus transportation. From the start, he had assumed his sons were the problem—the instigators. He knew how those two liked needling kids, especially the ones who appeared shy or vulnerable.

Just like their mother.

And Amara—she'd never heard one word against her two progenies, defending them to the bitter end like a real-life Ma Barker. Forever ready to confront or condemn anyone, including him, who tried to intercede. Ole Amara, swooping in on her broomstick to save the day. And no matter how many times the school called, no matter how many times the Imam complained, no matter how many times a parent cornered Qasim to "discuss his sons" —she'd butt in and go on the attack, viciously. Coming up with some of the wackiest excuses in an attempt to shield the boys from taking accountability for their actions.

Of all people, Qasim sneered at the sheer and utter audacity of him expecting two young boys to be held accountable for their poor behavior was rich, especially considering his recent track record.

Qasim pulled into The Royal Gates, easing off the gas when he saw one of the security cars driving deliberately past, eyeing him up and waiting for the first opportunity to hand him a hefty fine.

Swinging onto his block, he drove past Kalila who was fumbling with her garbage can; trying unsuccessfully to tug it from behind a lawnmower. Qasim quickly parked his car.

"Go inside," he told the boys. "I'll be right back."

Jogging across the street, Qasim approached the garage, but without stepping inside.

"*As salaamu alaikum*, sister. Need help with that?"

Kalila glanced up, surprised to see Qasim standing in her driveway, and automatically assuming he wanted to speak to her about the bus incident. "*Wa alaikum salaam.* Sure, I'd appreciate that. I can't get the mower's wheels to move back. I think there might be a twig stuck or something."

Qasim doubted a twig could cause the issue but proceeded to lift the machine up, leaning it over enough to push it out of the way. Then he pulled the drive control lever to check for a broken or disconnected drive cable. Releasing the mower handle, he lowered the machine to an upright position. "Ah, I see now."

"You know what's wrong?"

"I believe I do." Qasim removed the mounted screws to discharge the height adjuster lever just enough to pull the drive cover off.

"How do you know what to do?" Kalila asked, sounding impressed.

"I used to fiddle with these things as a kid. Ours was forever breaking down, and we couldn't afford to replace it."

Kalila nodded and smiled appreciatively, noticeably grateful for the help.

"You see this piece here," Qasim asked, pointing. "You're lucky it isn't broken, or you'd need to get the deck tray replaced." Kalila leaned over his shoulder to take a closer look. He tried to ignore her sweet, alluring scent.

"Excuse me." Qasim bent lower to reconnect the drive cable to the anchor post. "There you go. Should be good as new."

"Thank you so much, brother Qasim."

"My pleasure." Without waiting for a reply, he walked over to the garbage and recycling bins and started dragging them to the curb.

"Oh, you don't have to do that," Kalila said, appearing somewhat uncomfortable.

"Not a problem," Qasim called over his shoulder, entirely unaware of the pissed off pair of beady eyes aiming daggers at him from across the street.

Once he had the cans properly situated, Qasim headed home but stopped. "You're not planning on doing the lawn yourself, are you?" he asked Kalila, back at the mower attempting to start it. "You have a pretty big patch of land here."

"No choice. If I don't, I'll get fined for being the block eyesore." Kalila shrugged. "Besides, I could use the exercise."

Qasim only believed half that excuse. Not an ounce of anything extra graced those svelte bones. "Don't you use the same lawn service we do?"

"We did—I mean, I did," she quickly corrected herself, "but I had to cancel them. Their rates were getting a bit steep, and with hospital bills, funeral costs, and the open house this weekend, I can't exactly splurge on their service. Not when I can just as easily do it myself."

It never occurred to Qasim that Kalila would be struggling financially. He had assumed, probably like everyone else, that Bashir had left her life insurance and money in the bank. His shame and guilt once again resurfaced and intensified, creeping up his throat, raging. Qasim hoped she hadn't noticed.

"Look, put that thing away. The guy who owns the company, Rich Townsend? He owes me a big favor. I'll give him a call and see what I can work out." Reaching into his pocket, Qasim pulled out his wallet. "Here's my business card," he said, tapping his shirt pocket. "Do you have a pen or pencil?"

Kalila put her *give me a second* finger up and rushed inside, emerging seconds later holding a pen.

"Thanks." Qasim turned over the card and started writing on the back. "This is my work number, and this," he said, pointing to what he just wrote, "is my personal cell number if you need to contact me right away."

"I appreciate that," said Kalila.

"Just call or text. Either one."

"That's really kind of you, but I can't let you do that." Kalila tried her hand at starting the mower again but with little success.

Proud and beautiful.

"Well, then at least let me do the lawn for you." Qasim caught Kalila wince. "Just this one time. Your grass is kind of—" He searched for a diplomatic way of putting it, "long right now. It won't be easy for the machine to cut."

Kalila blushed. *Long* wasn't the word for it. She hesitated. "Are you sure?"

"It would be my pleasure, sister."

Please let me at least do this for you.

Kalila glanced around the lawn.

"A fresh cut could make a big difference as to whether or not the house sells and at what price," he added to sway her in his favor.

Kalila wrung her hands. "I mean, it is a big lawn, and I do have the open house this weekend...but I wouldn't want to put you out."

"It's not a big deal. Give me a few minutes to change out of my suit, and I'll be right over. Just leave the machine right there; I'll take care of it." Qasim spun around and jogged off in the direction of his house.

Kalila gave him the thumbs up.

"Oh," he called out, snapping his fingers, turning to face her. "You wouldn't happen to know if the mower has gas?"

This time Kalila genuinely smiled and laughed. "Maybe?" she admitted, palms up to the sky.

Qasim laughed. "Okay, I'll be right back."

She's gorgeous.

Qasim sprinted home, a big smile plastered across his face.

***

Meanwhile, the furious face pressed smack against the window across the street seethed long heated breaths. Each exhale left huge watermarks and smudges on the glass.

Since when did his lazy ass start jogging?

"Ma! Can I have cereal?" shouted Amir from the kitchen.

"No," snapped Amara, reluctant to leave her post.

"How about pretzels?"

Ya Allah. Why won't these kids leave me alone for one damn freakin' minute?

"Take an apple, Amir."

What the heck did Qasim just hand that viper?

"I don't want an apple."

"I want an apple," countered Muhammad.

"Shut up," snapped Amir. "I'm trying to talk to mom."

"Mom! Amir just told me to shut up."

"Tattletale."

"Snitch."

Allah, kill me now.

"Amir, leave your brother alone," shouted Amara.

"He started it."

"Both of you—take a damn apple." Amara pressed her face to the glass.

What's he all smiles about?

"Can I have pretzels and an apple?" asked Amir.

"Would you two leave me alone for one freaking minute!" roared Amara. "Take one or the other. Apple or pretzels. I don't care which but eat it and shut the hell up!"

The front door flew open. Qasim barreled inside, kicking off his shoes and taking the stairs two at a time. His grand entrance only served to make Amara seethe even harder. Trailing after him, she had a few questions that needed answering.

Qasim peeled off his suit and flung it across the bed. Just as he stepped into a pair of jeans, he caught Amara standing in the doorway, face patchy pink and fuming.

"What were you doing at her house?" she asked, eyes squinting mad.

"The sister had a problem with her lawn mower." Qasim knew from past experience that adding details to his answers would only open him up to further interrogation. "Where's my gray sweatshirt?"

"Second drawer from the top, right side," snapped Amara curtly. "What are you all in a rush about? And why are you getting changed? I thought you had to go straight back to work."

"I don't want my suit getting messed up."

Amara scowled. "And why pray tell, would your suit get messed up?" She only used "pray tell" when zeroing in for the kill.

"Because I'm going to mow the lawn." Qasim stiffened, waiting for the inevitable explosion.

"Whose lawn? Our lawn?" Amara gripped her waist with both hands, shaking her head in disbelief. "Oh, I get it now. You mean *her* lawn."

"She needs help, Amara."

"And you've decided to play her knight in shining armor."

"It's a lawn, Amara. That's all. Just a lawn."

"You don't even do our lawn and all of a sudden you can't wait to do hers."

"She can't afford the service," he interjected. "Times are tough for her."

"Times are tough *for her*," repeated Amara, belligerently, but Qasim refused to take the bait, knowing full well that the minute he got drawn into a justification—he lost. She'd have to be mad because he sure as shit would never admit how his guilt and debilitating shame were the key motivators in his making the offer. Nor was Qasim ready to admit how desire had also decided to show up in the mix. Rushing, he tugged his dresser drawer open. "It's not here," he said as he sifted wildly through the clothes. "My sweatshirt isn't here."

Amara sneered. "Try checking in Kalila's garbage can."

CHAPTER 16

Neighbors, Friends & Foes

Walaa

"HOLD UP. THIS CAN'T be right," murmured Walaa as she drove past Kalila's house, practically twisting in a neck-breaking double take. "Well I'll be—" she mumbled, mind-blown after realizing the identity of the guy mowing Kalila's lawn.

No way…

Walaa peered into her rearview mirror to confirm that Amara's van was, in fact, parked in her driveway.

I'm so confused.

Walaa had been on her way to go food shopping, but now she was half-tempted to drive past Kalila's house again for a better look-see. On second thought, she pulled over to the mailboxes near the front gate and parked, fumbling in her bag for her phone.

> *As salaamu alaikum. You won't believe what I just saw or rather who.*
>
> Dots moved in the message bar, indicating Nafiza was responding. *Wa alaikum salaam. Who?*
>
> Walaa typed back. *r u sitting? u have to be sitting for this.*
>
> *LOL, ok—lay it on me.*

I just drove by Kalila's house. Brother Qasim is mowing her lawn.

A moment went by. The moving dots in the message bar indicated typing. Then it stopped. Then it started again and then stopped. Apparently, Nafiza was at a loss for words. A one-word response came a minute later. *Wallahi?*

Yes! By Allah, I just saw him.
Amara's Qasim?
Yes!
No words. Thoroughly confused. Does Amara know?
Walaa wiggled her finger over the keys, unsure of how to answer. *No clue, but A's van is in the driveway. Maybe A & K made peace?*

Nafiza sent back a thinking emoji face, then a laughing hysterically emoji with tears springing from the eyes. Then typed, *Yeah, ok…*
What do you mean?

A few seconds went by before Nafiza answered. *I mean it could be the exact opposite.*
—*I don't understand,* Walaa typed back, then quickly followed it up with, *OH! Wait–r-u-saying?*
Another short pause. *Just saying don't assume anything.*
Walaa sighed. *Amara will lose her mind.*
I think that's a given, replied Nafiza.
I'm not joking. This could start a war.
A moment later, Nafiza responded. *Do NOT get involved.*
Walaa swallowed hard. *Gotta go. TTYL. ASA.*

Walaa tossed her phone onto the passenger seat like it was a hot coal. Exhaling, she closed her eyes to absorb the enormity of what Nafiza just implied.

If Nafiza's right—and I'm not saying she is, but if—

Walaa groaned, unable to imagine the level of toxic fallout this could produce. Reaching into the glove compartment, she grabbed another bag of salty chips from her stash and started shoving them in her mouth by the handful, not sure who or what to blame for her nausea this time.

***

Nafiza

Nafiza pocketed her phone. *Ya Allah.* She'd been an Imam's wife long enough to know the signs of impending disaster when she saw them, but honestly, who in their right mind could have predicted this match made in hell?

Over a third cup of decaf coffee, she mulled over what to do next with this new information. Whether or not to warn Abdullah about what he could expect as the Imam. Nafiza knew already how carefully she'd have to tread. She felt protective, wanting to make sure her husband had a heads up to give him ample time to prepare for the onslaught that would inevitably follow once this news broke.

She weighed her options.

If I go ahead and tell him something of this magnitude and it turns out not to be true, besides feeling like a fool, he'll automatically assume I engage in gossip. Then he'll never trust my instincts or confide in me in the future.

No, I better wait, just to make sure.

She hoped she wasn't barking up the wrong tree. Nafiza mindlessly tapped her manicured nail on the table.

Then again, what if I'm right and some crazy stuff pops off before I get the chance to tell Abdullah? I can't let him get cornered by Amara—

Nafiza reached out for her mobile.

I'll just ask Kalila straight out.

Nafiza almost pressed the number for Kalila's phone, but stopped.

What do I say? How do I word it?

"Hey, Kalila? It's me, Nafiza. Just curious, you wouldn't be currently in hot pursuit of Amara's husband, would you?"

Ugh.

Nafiza pushed the cell away.

This is stupid. Kalila would never be interested in Qasim.

Would she?

Nafiza counted back the months on her fingers since Bashir died. One-two-three—over six months ago, almost seven now. Maybe closer to eight. With Kalila's *iddah* more than satisfied, she could marry again without worrying about anyone criticizing her for remarrying too quickly after her husband's death. Kalila certainly wouldn't be pregnant...not after this length of time, *unless...*

Nafiza leaned back in her chair, eyes up to the ceiling, unable for the life of her to picture Kalila and Qasim as a couple. Then again, she remembered Kalila's meltdown after finding out that Bashir stopped paying on his life insurance. Nafiza had witnessed firsthand the fear splattered across many a widow's face. Without that money to count on to get through the rough patches, Kalila could be feeling desperate and vulnerable; willing to make choices she might not have ever entertained before.

"Damn it!" Nafiza moaned, thumping her fist on the table. Circumstances like Kalila's had become the norm, with a surprising number of men flagrantly ignoring the guidance provided to them, not just from the leadership, but from within the Quran as well.

How many lengthy, detailed *khutbahs*, expounding about the need for all husbands to make a will in favor of their wives had Abdullah given over the years? Repeatedly emphasizing the obligation all husbands—*and fathers*—had to leave the proper provisions in case of an unexpected death or illness. Yet still, despite all of Abdullah's reminders and guidance, his words fell on deaf and arrogant ears—bullish men more than willing to play Russian roulette with their family's security.

Then of course, when something catastrophic happens, and it always does, it wasn't these guys left to suffer, but their families! Hysterical widows calling on my husband to save the day.

Without much recourse, people had begun to rely on social media as a way to generate funds to collect additional money as a means to cover exorbitant funeral costs or to help the surviving children with future college expenses. During Friday prayers, the collection basket got passed around on a regular basis, but in a time of crisis, more often than not, the bake sales and fundraisers were left to the sisters; many of whom knew that it could have been any one of them left destitute. It was only by the Grace of God, that they had been spared.

This all made absolutely no sense to Nafiza, who felt this was basically, a preventable issue. Yet hardheaded men continued to do it and often.

One thing's for sure, decided Nafiza; *No matter what Kalila thinks she has up her sleeve, if any of her plans include Qasim Zubairi in any shape or form, then guaranteed, Amara will be on the warpath.*

And that, Kalila could take to the bank.

CHAPTER 17

Paper Trail

Melvin

MELVIN COULDN'T FALL ASLEEP, too wound up to rest. His anxiety often betrayed and trapped him beneath the weight of a thousand jumbled images all competing for his attention; forever engaging him in an unrelenting desire for repetitive and obsessive behaviors. With only a limited ability to communicate his feelings, he relied primarily on his tools—paper and pencil—to do the talking for him. To liberate the pictures and thoughts trapped inside his brain, and in doing so, make space available for the next wave of exhaustive images to arrive in an already co-opted sphere.

Melvin leaned on the sink brushing his teeth for precisely two minutes straight; reciting the alphabet precisely three times. When done, he banged his toothbrush against the sink three times before placing it back in the jar. Once finished scrubbing his face and hands, Melvin combed through his thinning hair before switching the bathroom light off. Never a deviation.

Earlier in the evening, as Melvin sat in the kitchen sketching, he heard his mother's slippers clack down the hall as she scrambled to the bathroom. Melvin started to moan. He quickly covered his ears to block out the retching noises, all while rocking back and forth.

Although Melvin often resisted most outward signs of affection, he accepted the occasional hug or kiss from his mother. "Mama," he called, knocking on the door. "Mama. Mama. Mama." He repeated; his voice devoid of emotion.

"I'm okay, Melvin," came the hoarse, garbled reply. "Just a little bellyache. Nothing to worry about, son."

But Melvin wasn't worried so much as frightened. Sounds, particularly those that were loud, scared him. Every time Mama ran to the bathroom, he'd become nervous and disappear into his bedroom, safely out of earshot.

Melvin usually went to bed at the same time every evening, but when his anxiety loomed, he preferred staying awake to draw. Letting his thoughts expel themselves on paper; discharged permanently from his head. Tonight, would be that kind of night. Melvin returned to his bedroom and closed the door.

He hung his bathrobe on the door hook, then slipped off his slippers at the side of his bed and propped the pillows behind his back and neck for adequate support. Once comfortable, he tucked the blanket around his legs, and reached for his pad and pencil, ready and waiting on his night table.

And then, seemingly with a mind of their own, his fingers took over, turning lines, swirls, squiggles, and circles into clear and concise images. The pencil became his microphone. A living extension of his biological digits. Casual loops, dashes, and dots melded together into an exquisite picture. Depending on his mood, the figures he drew could be either light and blithe, giving off an almost impressionistic air—or dark and looming—and exacting in their appearance. This evening, Melvin's characters would lean towards the latter as he penciled what he had seen but not understood.

Melvin began by sketching two full figures. Once done, he then added a third, a more ominous figure who stood in the shadows, half-hidden by a curtain. A silhouette with mostly angry, mean eyes full of rage and hate. Melvin knew those eyes, and they had frightened him.

Melvin heard his mother's soft, familiar steps pass by his door, on her way to the kitchen. Mama often woke up throughout the night, unable to sleep the entire way through. He'd awaken hearing her turn on the faucet to fill her glass. She'd swallow tiny medicine pills before retiring in her recliner.

Melvin had begun to notice the frequency of Ruth's visits but made no further connection as to why. She smiled a lot. Melvin liked people who smiled a lot.

"I like your drawings, Melvin," said Ruth that evening, standing a bit too close for Melvin's tastes. The longer she stayed over his shoulder, the harder he tapped in his shoe under the table.

Ruth sat across from Melvin. "Melvin, do your drawings tell a story?" she asked, holding a big manila envelope.

Melvin tilted his head.

"I mean, are they pictures of what you see happening around you? Like here in the house…with your mom for instance."

Melvin put his pencil down and flipped through a few pages of his sketch pad before coming to one of Ruth, and his mother huddled together, teacups in hand, having a serious discussion.

"Ah! That's me and your mom," Ruth said, delighted. "From the other day! That's incredible. And look, you even made sure to include the broach I wore on my lapel."

Melvin's foot stopped tapping.

"That's incredible, Melvin. Thank you for sharing." Ruth slid the book back. Her smile slipped away, and her tone of voice turned thoughtful.

"Melvin? Have you noticed recently how sick your mom has been feeling?" Ruth stared at Melvin's face.

Melvin bowed his head as if in prayer.

Ruth couldn't see his leg bouncing under the table but noticed his shoulders slump. "Melvin…your mom is very sick."

"Mama takes medicine for her tummy."

"Yes, you're right. She does."

"The doctor said."

Ruth's head tilted in sorrow. "Yes. The doctor told her to do that. You're right." Then Ruth folded her hands and leaned in as if she were about to share a secret. "But sometimes Melvin, the medicine doesn't do a good job. It doesn't work. Even though the doctors want the medicine to work, sometimes it doesn't. Do you understand?"

Melvin clicked his tongue three times.

"The medicine isn't working for your mother." She waited. "Do you understand what I'm saying?"

Melvin clicked his tongue three times again. Both legs bounced rapidly under the table. Wringing his hands, he looked up into Ruth's sad face.

"Mama is going to go to sleep like daddy," he said, matter-of-factly.

"Yes, Melvin, you're right." Ruth almost reached over to touch Melvin's hand but stopped herself. "And like your daddy, she's not going to wake back up."

Melvin snatched his pencil and pad and walked off to his room.

"Melvin!" called Ruth, rising to her feet to give chase.

"Let him go," said Felicia, who had been standing in the doorway listening. Wrapped in her pink bathrobe, she looked exhausted but resigned. "He understands more than you think."

Ruth sat back down. "He needed to be told, Felicia. We discussed this."

"I know."

"Melvin's got the right to be prepared."

"I wish you would have let me do it."

"I have, for weeks now, but making sure Melvin's needs are met, including emotional, are also my responsibility. As the family social worker, it's my job to get him prepared for the changes heading his way."

"I don't want him to leave the only home he's known. It just feels wrong."

"I know, but what choice do you have? Unless someone steps up and is willing to take responsibility for him, Melvin will be an adult ward of the state. At least the place he's going to is nice."

Felicia had difficulty accepting the truth.

"I'll be back around tomorrow to help you start sorting and packing. I also want to take Melvin over to visit the hospice, so when the time comes, he won't be afraid to visit you."

Felicia raised her hand. She desperately wanted Ruth to stop talking.

Ruth stood. "Right, well, did the office call you with the arrangements and dates for the rest of your household items?"

"They did. All taken care of."

Ruth walked over and placed a supportive arm around Felicia's shoulders. "We'll get Melvin through this—you and me, together."

Felicia nodded.

"I promise, I won't let him or you down."

Felicia felt eternally grateful for all of Ruth's help and compassion. She couldn't have done it without her, but that didn't prevent her from praying for a miracle.

***

In his bedroom down the hall, Melvin sat hunched over a sketchpad, refusing to close his eyes until he completed the drawing.

CHAPTER 18

What Lies Beneath

Monday Morning

"I CAN'T. I ALREADY told you, I have to be at the school…to pick up my son. No later than three-thirty…" Kalila kept her voice controlled to a whisper. "I understand that, but if he can't be there by one, then get somebody else to service him…" The pressure behind her eyes ached. She wasn't sure how much more of this nonsense she could take. "Fine. Two 'clock, but whether he's late or not, I am out of there by three and not a minute later." She tossed the phone onto the bed.

PING.

"What now?" Kalila retrieved the phone, relieved it was only a text from the realtor confirming for Saturday.

> *Everything's ready. Signs are up, and photos are uploaded to the website.*
>
> Kalila sighed, saddened she needed to sell the house. *Appreciated. Thank you.*
>
> Another message followed. *All good on your end?*
>
> Kalila rolled her eyes.
>
> "Yup, the house is spotless, and the lawn looks marvelous, however, my life sucks, but hey—thanks for asking,

Bonnie," grumbled Kalila. She waited a moment before typing back.

Yes. Everything's fantastic.

Awesome. See you Saturday!

The sooner the house sold, the better. With a mortgage this high, Kalila was barely treading water. Trying to maintain the expenses on her own left her drained and financially depleted. The only solution was to find a smaller, more manageable place. Something within her now limited budget and preferably in the same school district so Hamza wouldn't have to change schools mid-year.

During the ride home from school, Hamza had been notably quiet. Either he had a miserable day and didn't want to talk about it, or he was saving up his usual barbed retorts for later. Either way, he barely acknowledged her during dinner.

"It was nice of brother Qasim to mow our lawn," she'd said.

Hamza continued to eat.

"The realtor said curb appeal is really critical when selling a house." Kalila pecked at her plate. "People want to see a home with a well-manicured lawn." She glanced up. Nothing.

"I'm going to need you to make sure your room is clean by Friday and no later. That means pristine. Everything, books, clothes, all of it, away. The Open House starts by nine a.m."

Kalila waited.

Hamza spooned his last mouthful.

"And don't forget, Friday night is the community dinner," she told him. "I promised we would be there."

Hamza wiped his mouth, picked up his dish, utensils, and glass. "May I be excused?" he asked, not looking at her as much as through her.

"Fine," answered Kalila, heartsick. "I'll see you in the morning." She could have sworn her ears caught a muttered, "Whatever."

***

Kalila pulled a leg out of her pants, remembering Qasim's business card in her pocket. "Won't be needing this," she said, tossing it in the small trash pail by the vanity.

As the days went on, she had an increasingly difficult time picturing the details of Bashir's face. It felt like a different lifetime. None of it felt real anymore. Even the anger she felt towards him had begun to quiet.

And then there was Qasim.

What in the world could have possessed him to help her? Even when Bashir was alive, the two men hardly exchanged anything more than a *salaam*, no less any friendly conversations. Kalila had to admit; he did help—*a lot*—but nothing comes without a cost, especially when it comes to the male species. Nor did she believe for one hot minute that Amara endorsed her husband's generosity towards her. So, what gives?

Kalila shut the light off. For now, there were more pressing matters to deal with, starting with the Open House on Saturday. The community dinner she'd promised Walaa she'd attend…her pain in the ass clients—not to mention living with a rude, impertinent, cheeky adolescent. "Anything else?" she implored to the heavens, before smooshing a pillow over her face to hide.

Her phone buzzed again. Kalila lobbed the pillow to the side and sat up. Grumbling, she read the message. "Are we serious right now?"

The message screen showed a photo of a stunningly beautiful, smiling baby, less than a year old. The brief caption read, "For Hamza. His sister, Safa."

Didn't I warn her?

Kalila deleted the photo, flailed her arms wide and flung herself back on the bed, too livid to cry anymore.

***

Wednesday morning

After dropping the less than congenial Hamza off at school, Kalila did the mad rush back to the house to stage another room before meeting her client. As instructed by the realtor, this meant removing most of her personal effects, packing up all the extras, ridding the place of clutter, and cleaning every nook and cranny. Kalila had attempted to make the house appear inviting by storing the majority of her furniture and playing musical chairs with the remainder.

The place desperately needed a bright splash of color, especially something to soften up the high-end utilitarian kitchen. Kalila made a mental note to raid her backyard to clip a few fern fronds or a couple of marigolds to throw in a vase.

After successfully straightening all the bedding, fluffing pillows on the den's overstuffed sofa and comfortable armchairs, not to mention filling three hefty garbage bags for charity, Kalila permitted herself a moment to rest. Hands on hips, she looked around, admiring how much emptier the space that she once called home felt. A blank canvas for the next homeowner to claim and cherish.

If the house sold well, she'd be able to support her and Hamza with a regular job's income. Instead of having sex with strange, lascivious men.

Just a few more weeks and I'm done, she promised herself.

Living a double life meant living a lie, and while everyone had their versions of the truth, not everyone was forced to live their deceptions as their truths.

Body perfumed, lotioned, hair straightened, makeup meticulously complete. Lace panties—check, push-up bra and diaphragm in place—double check. Kalila unwrapped a slice of spearmint gum, ready to flick the wrapper into the can when her eye caught Qasim's card lying on top.

On second thought.

She reached in and grabbed it.

This might come in handy.

She tucked it into her handbag for safe keeping. One more peek.

Good.

Twelve-thirty.

Gotta go.

***

Amara dragged her garbage cans back from the curb just as Kalila pulled out of her driveway. She would have jumped in the van to follow hadn't Qasim made a big deal about her sticking around to sign for a delivery. At least she had received a text from the carrier letting her know he was only minutes away, still giving Amara enough time to do a bit of sleuthing.

Why Qasim couldn't have had his stupid package delivered to the office was beyond her.

I mean, what the hell does his stupid receptionist do all day other than parade around scantily dressed, making coffee, and answering a goddamn telephone? Idiot.

Unfortunately, not being able to follow her left her with only one alternative–checking the hotel—a hit or miss proposition.

She hadn't slept well, overly consumed with holding in her anger, not mildly entertained by Qasim's rooster parade. After completing Kalila's lawn, he had returned home stomping around the place like some big guy rescuer—sweat pouring from his dirty face down his grimy neck, and all too proud of himself—the first real physical work done in ages.

What a joke.

She didn't see him rushing off to drag her overstuffed garbage cans to the curb. Most of the time, he made the boys to do it.

Now, dressed in one of his best suits, he had the utter audacity to swig juice straight out of the bottle like some he-man, much to her disdain, and to the delight of his two young spawns.

"It's not funny," Amara snapped at Amir, his beady eyes bugging out of his face.

"Hey Dad, you picking us up today?" asked Muhammad, busy on his second bowl of cereal.

"I am, so get out on time," Qasim said pointedly to Muhammad. "Don't keep me waiting. I have to get right back to work today. Got a big board meeting and I can't be late."

Amira gave an amused snort. "What, you're not doing any more landscaping jobs?" she quipped standing in front of the sink, her back turned to her husband.

"Let's go, boys. In the car," instructed Qasim ignoring her. "Make sure you have everything you need because I'm not your mother. I won't turn around. You'll be flat out of luck." His dig landed.

Amara flinched and pursed her lips, but when she turned around, her face wore nothing but an empty smile. "That's right boys, do as your father says. Get a move on," she said wickedly sweet, watching his face and daring him to say something.

Qasim shot Amara the side-eye and belched. The boys cracked up laughing again, and Amara cringed, seething. Mission accomplished.

***

True to her word, Kalila parked in her usual spot next to Roger's ridiculous change of life car and headed directly to their designated room, committed to being in and out on time.

"Marie," Roger popped his head around the door, "Come in," he said with his salesman's coated smile, motioning for her to step inside quickly.

"Roger," she said, pecking him on the cheek; completely unfazed by his being buck naked. "How are you?"

Roger closed and locked the door. Turning around, he wore the biggest shit-eating grin. "Marie," he said, grabbing his cock. "Can't you tell how happy Big Roger is to see you?"

Kalila swallowed, digging her nail into her palm to keep calm.

One hour… and not one freaking second longer.

***

Qasim picked up his mobile even though he knew full well how stupid he'd have to be to expect Kalila to call or leave a message. Yet, here he was, for the umpteenth time, checking anyway. Each time more disappointed than the last.

Realizing it was almost time to pick up the boys, Qasim straightened up his desk. "Darlene?" he said, popping his head out of the office. "While I'm gone, would you mind getting the conference room ready? There will be eight of us attending."

"Sure thing," she said. "Did you want bottled water or glasses?"

"Surprise me. Oh, and make sure every member has a folder with copies of the proposal."

"The proposal?" Darlene looked at Qasim puzzled. "But I don't have it. Remember? You brought it home. You said you wanted to add to it or edit it."

Qasim gave an apologetic shrug. "Damn, you're right. It's at home." He tapped his pen on his palm a few times. "Okay. Here's what I'll do. I'm going to swing by there now and grab it. I'll drop it back off here so you can make copies while I get my boys. Damn, I can't believe I did that." Qasim rubbed his eyes. "I might need you to stay late today. Is that going to be a problem?"

"Not at all."

"Thanks," Qasim snatched his briefcase, threw his coat over his shoulder, and pulled the office door shut. "Be back soon," he said, mumbling to himself. "A quick stop at home—grab folder. Drop-off with Darlene. Pick boys up and drop them off at home. Go straight back to work. Sounds like a plan."

***

"That was great," murmured Roger, rather satisfied. "You're something else. You know that?"

Wisps of hair escaped her bun, delicately falling curvaceously around her flushed face. Stretching her neck, Kalila was aware of how Roger's eyes were sliding across her breasts. "I have to go," she blurted out, not meaning to sound as abrupt as she did.

"Just a few more minutes," he moaned, ready to mount her again.

"I can't. I've gotta go."

Tired of her pulling this routine, Roger snatched Kalila's wrist, unwilling to be brushed off that easy.

To the untrained eye, Roger would have appeared merely exasperated, but to a professional like her, his mannerisms revealed so much more. Kalila couldn't afford to lose him as a client. Not yet anyway.

But what about Hamza?

Then she remembered Qasim's offer.

"You know what? Give me a minute. Let me see if I can get somebody to, um, cover for me so that I can stay longer with you," she said, practically in a purr.

Almost appeased, Roger released his grip on her wrist, but never took his eyes off her. "Go ahead."

Kalila dug in her bag for the card and moved next to the bed, giving Roger a twitch of a playful grin, but careful to hide her phone from his scrutinizing gaze.

> *As salaamu alaikum Brother Qasim. I hate to bother you like this, but I'm in the middle of a job interview and won't be done in time to pick up Hamza. Would you mind picking him up and dropping him off at my house?*

"I should hear something back soon," she said, not entirely confident that would be the case, but willing to play it off. Thankfully, she didn't have to wait long for a single word response: *Okay.*

Thank you, Qasim.

"See? All done," she said, allowing Roger, more than ready and now standing behind her, to pull her closer.

"Bend over," Roger groaned, gripping her hips to straddling her from behind. Spreading her legs apart with his knee he thrust himself into her. "Oh, Marie," he moaned. "Make big Roger happy."

***

Turning onto his block, Qasim spotted Kalila's car missing, and it strangely irked him even with what she told him earlier.

I wonder where she is…

With no time to waste, he yelled, "*As salaamu alaikum*," as he opened the front door so as not to startle Amara.

"*Wa alaikum salaam*," she answered, coming out from the kitchen, wiping her hands on a dish towel. "What are you doing home?"

I forgot a file for the board meeting," he said, dropping his keys and phone on the hall table, then rushing up the stairs.

Amara heard him sprinting around his office, opening and closing a drawer. Before she knew it, he was back downstairs, file in hand, sitting on the step, putting his shoes back on.

"Will you be home for dinner?"

"No. I'll catch something while I'm out."

Amara glared at her husband, this man she shared a house and bed with, but apparently little else. Out of habit, she picked up his keys and phone to give him when the phone buzzed in her hand. Qasim's head snapped up, and quickly reached over to swipe the phone away, but not before gleaning the name plastered across the screen.

Qasim eyes rapidly perused the message. Under Amara's seething stare he typed back a single word response, eager to get away.

"You gave her your phone number?" Mad didn't begin to describe Amara's face. "Give me that phone."

Phone in another hand, Qasim extended an arm to keep her at a safe distance. "It's not what you're thinking."

"Don't tell me what I'm thinking."

"All I'm saying is—"

"I can't believe you gave her your phone number."

Qasim's shoulders tensed, waiting for the next question.

"Why is she texting you?"

And there it was.

"Amara, I—"

"Don't lie, Qasim, why is that woman texting *my* husband?"

"You're getting upset for no reason. If you'd let me *expl*—"

"Answer me!" she yelled, hysterical.

"I'm trying to," he yelled back. "If you'd give me a damn minute."

Amara crossed her arms, blinking rapidly.

As calmly as he could, he spoke, modulating each word to convey his innocence. "I gave it to her in case of emergency."

"What's her emergency then? Come on, let me see your phone."

Qasim adamantly refused to hand over his phone, practically hiding it behind his back.

"Show me this so-called emergency."

"—or if she needed help," he added since Kalila's request fell well below emergency status. "See." Qasim held up the phone for Amara but held it tight enough so she wouldn't be able to swipe it away. "Like I said, just being a good neighbor. That's all."

"I bet."

"What should I have done? I felt bad for her."

"Bad for her?" Amara screwed her face in a grimace that could melt metal. "You felt bad for her," she mimicked, the vehemence resurfacing. "Ain't that something…"

"I was just trying to be nice."

"Just trying to be nice. My husband, Mr. Nice Guy…"

"I better get going."

No use arguing with her when she gets like this.

Qasim hurried out the door; smart enough not to turn around or show fear, praying he had nothing aimed at his back.

CHAPTER 19

How I Met Your Mother

HAMZA WAITED OUTSIDE THE school for his mother to arrive when he heard his name.

"Hamza!" shouted the somewhat familiar male voice. "Hamza, over here." Mr. Zubairi waved his arm through the open passenger side window, trying to catch Hamza's attention.

Confused, Hamza, his gaze unfocused, stared at the man before eventually registering where the demand came from. Inhaling a deep breath, he lumbered over to the car, mind racing over a plethora of possibilities as to why.

"*As salaamu alaikum*, Hamza."

"*Wa alaikum salaam.*" Hamza bent his body slightly, cocking his head to the side to peer into the car window.

"Listen, your mom's running late. She asked me to pick you up from school. Hop in."

"She called you?"

"Texted. Here, sit in the front," he said, opening the door from inside. "Muhammad and Amir should be out any minute."

Hamza followed Qasim's instructions begrudgingly, but once inside the car he checked his cell phone for any missed messages from his mother. Nothing—*whatever.*

Amir and Muhammad came swooping out of the school building, swinging backpacks and pushing one another. Qasim laid on the horn a few times and the two brothers, whooping it up, waved, then jogged over to the car. Still loud and goofing around, they stopped abruptly when they saw who inhabited the front seat.

"What's he doing here?" asked Amir.

Hamza didn't bother to comment but instead glared out the front window wishing this day over, and madder than hell at his mother for subjecting him to these two miscreants from the netherworld.

"I'm driving Hamza home today," explained Qasim impatiently. "Now both of you, get in already, I'm running late." Qasim started the engine.

The usual repartee from the back remained shockingly silent; each passenger lost in their private set of contemplations, but for Hamza, the ride felt as if it would never end. When Qasim pulled up in front of his house, he couldn't jump out of the vehicle fast enough, mumbling a barely audible thank you, then slamming the door to take off.

"What a jerk," muttered Amir, giving his brother a mischievous slant-side eye.

Hamza took off. His legs barely taking him away fast enough as he ran towards the back of the house, over the fence, and straight to Melvin, who was already sitting on his back deck patiently waiting for his arrival. A standard ritual which had become Hamza's mainstay. His safe place. His refuge. In the past, Melvin used to wait for him at the top of the road where the bus stopped or on his front stoop, but since Hamza's bus suspension and Amara's intrusion, their location for their daily meet and greet had changed. And remarkably enough, without much if any discussion.

"I hate her," Hamza yelled, slamming his backpack on the step.

Melvin, never one to handle displayed anger or impatience from people well, made an exception for Hamza, whose adolescent mood swings could change quicker than the direction of the wind.

Melvin wasn't scared or put-off by Hamza's outburst and accepted his behavior with neither judgment nor fear.

"Hi, Hamza," said Melvin, his voice imperceptibly lifting.

"Hi, Melvin." Hamza paced on the grass too upset to sit.

"Why are you mad, Hamza?"

"It's all my mom's fault."

Melvin cocked his head, waiting for his little buddy to explain.

Hamza stopped in front of Melvin. "You'll never guess who just drove me home from school."

Melvin tipped his head to project curiosity. A little gesture he'd picked up from studying Hamza's body language.

"Go on," prompted Hamza. "Guess."

Melvin shrugged.

"Come on."

Melvin shrugged again.

"Mr. Zubairi."

Melvin stared.

Hamza pointed. "From across the street?"

Melvin's expression never changed.

"The father of those two jerks always messing with you."

Melvin's eyes widened. He looked almost comical while trying to render an expression of astonishment. Yet, it was another one of his practiced mannerisms awkwardly executed.

"Exactly!" bellowed Hamza, finally satisfied Melvin got his point.

Melvin clicked his tongue; happy Hamza was pleased.

Bending over, Hamza tore a nice handful of grass out of the ground and flung it in the air. "I can't stand Amir and Muhammad, for real."

"Bad boys." Melvin tapped his foot. His recurrent run-ins with those two had left an indelible mark on his psyche. Rotten children, who liked nothing better than to call him "retard" or "perv." And the main reason why he now waited at the top of the bus stop hill for Hamza as opposed to down below where the other parents waited. Because of them and their cruel mother, who had taken it upon herself to make a big stink with the bus lady about him, rallying the other mothers into a frenzy and insinuated his purpose for being there stemmed from lechery, and not friendship. “Bad, bad boys,” repeated Melvin.

“Tell me about it,” agreed Hamza. “They're the reason I got into trouble in the first place.”

“Not nice.”

“My mother's always late.”

Melvin continued tapping his foot.

“““I'm sorry, Hamza,””” Hamza mocked, doing his mother's voice impersonation. Hamza picked up an acorn, chocking it at a nearby tree. “I'm sick of it. Why him? Why'd she have to ask that guy to drive me home?”

“Hamza—” Melvin's attention had already drifted elsewhere.

“I can't believe she's doing this.”

“Hamza—”

“Ever since my dad died, she's been acting all weird …always making up excuses…”

“Hamza—”

“She doesn't even care about me anymore.”

“Hamza—”

“What already?” snapped Hamza, plopping down next to his friend. “What?”

“Look.” Melvin pointed. “Bunny rabbit.”

There, on a small patch of grass, behind a scraggly shrub hid a brown rabbit, popping his head out only quick enough to scurry to-and-fro, ears twitching and confused as to which way to turn next. The two friends watched, breaking up into fits of shared laughter when the rabbit, startled by something it must have heard, suddenly hopped away, falling freefall into a small grassy pit, then bouncing back up to dart away, no worse for the wear.

“I wish I were a rabbit,” grumbled Hamza.

“Me too,” said Melvin.

“I'd hop the hell away from here.”

Without comment, Melvin abruptly stood and walked away.

“Hey! Where're you going?”

“Come Hamza.” Melvin slid open the deck door. “Snack time.”

With no penchant to protest, Hamza complied, snatching his backpack off the deck floor to follow his friend inside.

"Oh, hello," greeted a small, handsome woman busy at the kitchen sink. "I'm Ruth, Felicia and Melvin's friend."

"Hi," said Hamza, offering her a warm smile. "I'm Hamza."

"Ruth is Mama's friend," corrected Melvin, walking to the cabinet door to fetch a bag of cookies.

"That's right," said Ruth, still graciously smiling at Hamza.

A wide selection of pill bottles of all various shapes and sizes cluttered the counter. More medicine than Hamza had ever seen amassed in one place at one time. Although many of the bottles looked the same to him, Ruth apparently had no problem making a distinction between them. She placed a few of the bottles on a small metal tray along with a glass of cold tap water. Ruth spotted Hamza studying her.

"Yes, well, I had better get these to Felicia," she said. "You boys enjoy yourselves."

Melvin placed a bag of cookies on the table and handed Hamza a napkin. Then he filled two glasses with milk almost touching the rim.

"Is she a nurse?" asked Hamza, biting into his cookie.

"Ruth is Mama's friend," answered Melvin dunking his cookie in his glass, meticulously cautious not to push too deep.

Unsure of what else to say, Hamza sipped his milk before dunking his cookie in.

"Mama's going to sleep soon," said Melvin flatly, never looking at Hamza, "but Ruth said she won't wake up."

Hamza stopped chewing, caught entirely off guard by Melvin's bluntness. "You mean?"

"Mama's going to go to sleep," Melvin repeated, again dunking his cookie in his milk, unaware of the gravity of his statements. "Like Daddy," he added.

By this time, Ruth had joined them, still carrying the tray; catching enough of the conversation to ascertain what had just transpired. Frowning, she solemnly nodded her head at Hamza, confirmation of Melvin's recent assertion. Ruth, her back to the guys, placed the tray on the counter and began reorganizing the bottles.

Finished with his three allotted cookies and milk, Melvin crumpled his napkin and put his cup in the sink. "Be right back, Hamza."

A million questions erupted in Hamza's head, but unsure of how to proceed, he remained quiet, grateful when Ruth interjected.

"May I join you?" she asked, indicating she'd like to sit down. Her face lit up upon spotting the bag of cookies. "Oh, chocolate chip! One of my favorites." She picked out one and bit—releasing a small satisfied moan. "So, good. I haven't indulged in one of these beauties for a long time."

Hamza thought Ruth had a kind face.

Ruth grabbed a napkin and wiped her mouth, her mood turning somber. "Look, Hamza," she said, voice low. "I'm going to be honest with you, Felicia—uh, I mean Mrs. Vine—has told me how much Melvin likes and trusts you."

Hamza shrugged. "He's my friend."

"I know, and he's very fortunate to have someone like you in his life."

Hamza bit into another cookie, staring, waiting, knowing that most adults liked to preface difficult information with a bunch of sweet, mushy junk before slamming you in the gut with the bad stuff. His mother did it all the time.

Ruth inhaled before continuing.

Here it comes.

Hamza braced himself.

"Melvin's going to be facing many—" She searched for the right way to say it. Never a good sign. "—changes soon."

"What kind of changes?"

Ruth paused, pursed her lips, again treading ultra-carefully.

"Is Mrs. Vine dying?" he asked.

A small, sad titter escaped her lips. "Yes. She is."

Hamza always liked Mrs. Vine, so this news hit hard. He'd known from Melvin that she'd been sick recently, and she was old and all…

But dying?

"But what'll happen to Melvin?" he asked.

"Ah, yes, well, Melvin will be very well cared for," she said softly as if she were attempting to convince herself of this statement more than Hamza. "His mother has made arrangements for him."

"What do you mean arrangements?"

"Unfortunately, I'm not at liberty to disclose that information right now, but I assure you, the new home has a great staff, full of caring people who will look after him."

"Staff? But Melvin doesn't like strangers," said Hamza, getting worked up.

"I know, but there's little choice. I think you know, Melvin needs people around him to…" again, she stopped, grappling with safe words, "…stay safe."

"But why? He loves living here."

"I know."

"Why can't he stay here?" Hamza never meant to sound so whiny, but the thought of his best friend in some strange place with people he didn't know sliced deep.

Ruth folded her hands together and leaned forward. "It's complicated."

"Complicated? What's complicated about him living in his own house."

"Well, first off, that would mean that extra helpers would need to live here as well. That's extremely costly."

"But he's not alone," he fussed. "I live right next door. I'll come over every day."

Ruth smiled. "That is very kind of you, but Melvin needs much more supervision than you can provide."

"But it's not fair. You're making Melvin move from the only home he knows." Hamza's eyes watered, his anger growing.

Ruth's eyes lowered, giving Hamza the privacy to calm down.

Hamza wiped his eyes with the back of his sleeve. "Does he even know he's moving to a new place?"

"No. Not yet," Ruth whispered. "His mother plans on speaking to him soon, but I hope you will be here to support him when the time comes." She smiled at him. "As his best friend."

Hamza shrugged, mad at a world callously ripping the people he cared most about out of his life for good.

What does she expect me to do? I'm just a kid…

As if she could read his mind, she interjected. "I don't expect you to do anything different than you are doing now, Hamza. Just be his friend."

He nodded to appease, much as he did with most adults, but inwardly he wanted to scream, curse, throw things. Fed up with how presumptuous adults explained difficult problems, and then laced them with stupid and dismissive platitudes. As if because of his age, he somehow couldn't comprehend the complexities of what she implied.

Melvin returned, sketchbook and pencil in hand. "All done, Hamza." Slipping on his shoes, Melvin pulled the sliding door open and stepped outside, resuming his favored place on the deck. Hamza reached over to clear his spot.

"Leave it. I got it," instructed Ruth. "Go on."

Gathering his backpack and sneakers, Hamza dutifully followed Melvin outside taking his place next to his best friend, conscious that this small reprieve would soon end, leaving an even emptier hole in his heart.

Hamza leaned over to check out Melvin's drawing, surprised at what he saw, but he shouldn't have been. Melvin knew way more than he let on.

"Hamza is my best friend," said Melvin, busy sketching, unperturbed.

Hamza wiped away a lone tear, mournfully lowering his head as if in prayer. "You're my best friend, too," he said.

Melvin, out of character, patted Hamza lightly on the shoulder. "I know."

***

Ruth

Ruth dropped the curtain, wandering away from the living room window, her heart breaking at the thought of snatching Melvin away from the only home and friend he ever had.

Why is life so cruel?

"Ruth?" called Felicia from her bedroom. "I need your help."

Ruth snapped to attention, practically sprinting down the hall. She found Felicia bent over her vanity, her face concealed by an amassed clump of blood-soaked tissues.

"It's happening again," shrugged Felicia, as if commenting on a change of temperature.

"Here, let me get you cleaned up." Ruth gently held Felicia under the elbow to guide her carefully to a hard seat. Once situated, she traded the wet tissues for a warm wet washcloth. "I want you to sit straight up and lean slightly forward." Felicia leaned way over. "No, not that much. I don't want you to choke."

Ruth pinched Felicia's nose using her thumb and first finger to hold the pressure. "Can you hold the washcloth?"

Felicia nodded from underneath the cloth.

"Good. I'm going to get some ice. Be right back."

"Take your time. I'm not going anywhere."

Ruth smirked but rushed into the kitchen anyway. Once back, she held the cold compress up to Felicia's face. "How often is this happening now?" She asked.

Felicia squinted, pondering the question. Her advanced-stage cancer had left her deteriorated, drained, and increasingly weak. The time for the hospice had arrived.

"You need more around the clock assistance, Felicia. Much more than I can provide."

"I know, but Melvin?"

"He understands more than you're giving him credit for."

"You think so, do you." Felicia highly doubted Ruth's assessment. While Melvin may appear to understand parts of the issue, she didn't believe he fully grasped the difficulties soon facing him.

"I hate to be the bearer of bad news, but you need to finalize the paperwork."

"I know."

"You haven't signed it."

"I will. I will." Felicia clasped her trembling hands. "Tonight."

Ruth gently lifted the towel from Felicia's nose. "There, I think that did the trick."

Felicia shifted her body weight. The muscles in her back and neck ached from forcing her body to sit unnaturally erect. "Until the next time."

Ruth massaged Felicia's lower back. "Yes, until the next time."

***

Kalila

Outside the sun dipped behind an army of clouds, ready to set. Hamza saw that his mother had pulled in, but took his time going home, dragging his feet to the back door. Before stepping inside, he stopped to give Melvin a half-wave.

"Hamza?" called his mother. "Is that you?"

Hamza tossed his backpack and jacket defiantly over the kitchen chair. "Yeah, it's me."

Kalila rushed into the kitchen. "I'm so," she almost said *sorry* but hesitated under his glare. "The job interview lasted longer than anticipated." Hamza's lip curled, but Kalila chose to ignore it. "I picked up takeout on my way home." She pulled a few plastic and cardboard containers from the brown paper bag. "Chinese food—from that new *halal* spot on Main Street. It smells so good." Kalila smiled. Hamza loved Chinese food, and she had purposely used this as a peace offering.

Hamza helped set the table begrudgingly, his hunger propelling more than a willingness to forgive and forget. Then an idea popped into his head.

"Ma?" he asked, his voice devoid of sarcasm.

Kalila's head whipped around. She hadn't heard her baby boy call her that in months. "Yes, Hamza," she answered, holding her breath.

"I need to talk to you about something important."

"Of course." Kalila patted the chair. "Let's eat, and you can tell me what's going on."

Hamza grabbed a spoon and scooped a nice portion of Beef Lo Mein onto his plate. Kalila placed a shrimp roll on the side. Then she served herself.

"I'm all yours," she said, trying to hide the sheer relief bubbling up inside of her. Kalila reached over and tapped the table with her nail, close to his dish. "Whatever it is, I'm here for you," she said, meaning it.

Hamza bit into his shrimp roll, stalling. Kalila waited, her eyes never leaving his face, watching him self-consciously wipe his mouth, before beginning to speak.

"I found out today that Mrs. Vine is dying," he mumbled. Hamza lifted his fork, twirling a few noodles. "Melvin's gonna get taken away forever. They're going to force him to live someplace else—someplace where nobody knows him."

"How do you know this?"

"The nurse told me."

"The who?"

"The nurse, Miss Ruth. She's at the house helping Mrs. Vine."

Kalila nodded, thinking. "I'm sorry. I know how much you like Melvin."

"Can he live with us?"

Kalila blinked. "Wait—what?"

"He can have my bedroom. I'll move into the guest room."

"Hamza, it's not that simple."

"Please, Mom. Melvin doesn't have anybody else but me. I can't let him go to some strange place. He'll get so scared."

Kalila dropped her fork, pushed her plate away, no longer hungry. Never would she have anticipated this conversation and appeared lost for words. "I'm trying to sell the house," she mumbled, drawn to the hope in her son's eyes. "We're barely making it as is."

"I'll eat less."

Kalila laughed. "How do you even know Melvin would want to be with us?" she asked earnestly.

"I know he would."

"But he's a grown man."

"He needs us, Mom."

"But you said his mother already decided where she wants him to live…"

"I know, but can't you just talk to her? Just ask her?"

"I don't know..."

"Mom, *please.*"

Kalila hadn't seen Hamza this animated since...well, for a long time. He'd be devastated if she didn't at least say she'd try.

"Okay, fine. I'll speak to Mrs. Vine, but—" She barely finished her sentence before Hamza jumped from his chair, flinging his arms around her neck.

"Thank you, Mom, thank you."

"Wait, wait, wait, don't start thanking me yet," she said, trying to get him to hear her. "His mother could say no." But even as she uttered those words, she couldn't help but bask in the return of her son's embrace, cherishing the closeness, and willing to do whatever it took never to lose him again.

CHAPTER 20

Cries and Whispers

Felicia

WITH THE NOON LUNCH rush over, for the most part, traffic on the roads should be minimal. Nevertheless, Melvin's trip downtown presented an uncomfortable sense of urgency—at least for Felicia.

"Run a comb through your hair, Melvin," reminded his mother, stepping aside in the hall to make room for Ruth, arms weighed down with a load of folded towels and sheets.

"I'm good," Ruth replied, smoothly squeezing past Felicia, balancing a stack of towels precariously under her chin.

Standing in front of the mirror, Melvin did as he was told, systematically running a comb through his short hair; his concentration solely focused on a single, stubborn, shock standing at attention.

"You may want to wet that part down a bit," instructed Felicia, stopping herself from further intervening. Melvin listened but could also become quite irritated if anybody interrupted his flow. Because of his sensitivity to touch, Felicia held back from rubbing his back, even in encouragement.

He has to do for himself now.

Her thoughts journeyed back to a time when Melvin stood at the same mirror but as a small child, barely tall enough to peer over the counter, combing through a head full of soft, unruly auburn curls. She recalled the despair and heartache knowing—even back then—how Melvin's ability to communicate had failed to develop fully, separating him from a world of social relationships. Most of all, she recollected standing in this same exact place looking at the same pair of eyes with the same precise vacant intense stare; thoroughly engaged with the repetitive movements, whose appeal rested within following the rigidly familiar pattern.

Once satisfied, Melvin exited the bathroom wearing a pair of casual slacks and a button-down shirt tucked into his pants.

"Put a belt on, Melvin," reminded Felicia.

"I'll be with you in a minute," called Ruth, still busy zipping around the house, putting laundry away.

"Now remember, Melvin. This is just a quick visit to see where I will be staying," she explained, following him into his bedroom. Ruth had been encouraging Felicia not to rely on euphemisms when discussing her situation.

"Don't underestimate Melvin's ability to comprehend what's going on," repeated Ruth. "Speak directly to him; be clear, and don't beat around the bush trying to protect his feelings. There's no need to gloss over anything."

"I've always been the one advocating for him to have home-based options, and now that I'm dying, he might wind up living in one of those places anyway." Felicia's voice trailed off. As a toddler, Melvin had started off like all other children, but by the time he reached twenty-one months, his differences became glaringly apparent with him suddenly acting strangely, rejecting her or his father's touch, and losing many of the social skills he had already acquired. His obsession with order intensified and consumed him. He'd walk around the house straightening chairs or shoes. Books and pencils also had to be lined up in size order; his toothbrush and comb placed in the same position as he found them. Instead of playing outside or riding a bike, he preferred sitting in front of the kitchen pantry cabinet fixated on lining up the same cans and boxes for hours, and if—*God forbid*—she dared move a single can before he completed his task, he would throw a terrible tantrum. Stomping his feet, scratching at her or throwing whatever he could find nearby.

How will anybody understand his need for structure?

Will they realize how loud noises jar him, causing him to become upset or anxious?

What will happen when they find out how aggressive he can become if frightened?

"There's an enormous amount of stuff on your plate right now," said Ruth gently. "All we can do is tackle each issue as it arises, one at a time. Let me first bring him to where you'll be staying. I'll show him around for a bit, introduce him to the staff and volunteers…demystify the process enough for him to feel comfortable visiting you."

Once done putting on his belt, Melvin grabbed a freshly sharpened pencil and his sketch pad. Trudging into the kitchen, he resumed his place at the table and waited.

"All ready to go?" asked Ruth, finishing up making a tray of items Felicia may need in her absence.

"Ready to go," said Melvin, placing his pencil in his shirt pocket.

"I want you to listen to Ruth," said Felicia, accepting a cup of water and a pill from Ruth.

"I will," said Melvin, good-naturedly.

"He'll be fine, right, Melvin?" asked Ruth, winking, another subtle social clue that held no meaning for Melvin.

"Right," said Melvin, flatly.

Adult or not, man or child, Felicia wanted to reach over and throw her bony arms tightly around her son. She tried to cocoon him in her love, protect him forever and keep him out of harm's way, but that, regrettably, wasn't realistic. Instead, she did as always, holding enough of a physical distance between them until he gave her some indication that more would be tolerated.

Felicia sighed, attempting to mask a ragged sob. "I'm going to lay down for a bit to rest. I'll see you both when you get back."

Ruth grabbed her bag and keys. "We'll be back soon. If you need anything, I left the number for—"

Felicia pulled a tissue from her pocket blowing her nose loudly. "I know, I know," she interrupted. "Stop fussing all the time. Just go."

Ruth didn't seem the slightest bit jarred by Felicia's dismissive attitude. She'd been a caseworker long enough to understand how sick or terminal clients could react under stress, sometimes turning curt or outright abrasive; often masking their fear and apprehension behind a brusque persona.

"Let's go, Melvin," said Ruth.

Melvin rose from his chair. After slipping on his loafers, he followed Ruth out the front door. "Bye, Mama," he said waving, avoiding eye contact.

Hearing her name, Felicia swung her head around in time to catch Melvin leaving. "Bye, dear," she said, forlornly watching the door close behind him.

As she toddled down the hall, an intense weariness stretched over her. With each subsequent step forward, her legs grew heavy and uncooperative. "It won't be long now," she muttered, her body aching in places she didn't know existed. Feeling dizzy, she used the wall to steady herself. "Thank God for that."

***

Ruth

Determined to find a closer parking space, Ruth took yet another spin around the block, hoping her patience would eventually pay off. Not that she had anything against walking. Matter of fact, when given the opportunity she preferred to stretch her legs, but not with Melvin in her charge. He needed to see the place and gain a familiarity with this new environment.

Driving slower than usual caused an impatient truck driver behind them to lay on his horn, blasting it three times long. The loud, jarring noise caused Melvin to yell in alarm covering his ears in a panic. Stuck in the car and unable to escape, he started rocking back and forth to simulate escape and to self-soothe.

Ruth didn't yell back, refusing to set Melvin off any further. Instead, she pulled her car to the side as far as she could to give the irate driver enough room to go around her, while purposely snubbing the flipped bird heralded in her direction. Gripping the steering wheel, and more concerned for Melvin's emotional welfare, Ruth declined to satisfy the moron's base infantile behavior. As soon as she saw an opening, she pulled back into traffic. "Sorry about all that," she said, modulating her voice almost to a stage whisper.

Rounding the corner, Ruth glimpsed a gray sedan pulling away from the curb. "Yes," she declared relieved, happy to snap up a space almost directly in front of the hospice. "This will do perfectly."

Unaffected, Melvin sat calmly, no longer rocking, moaning, or holding his ears. Staring out the passenger side window, fixated on something across the street.

Too busy to notice, Ruth parked leaving ample room for Melvin to get out. "Stay inside until I come around and open the door for you," she instructed, peering over her shoulder, timing a break between oncoming traffic long enough to step safely outside.

Once securely on the other side, she bent over to pull open his door. "Give me one more minute," she said, pointer finger in the air. "I need to feed the meter." But before she could close his door again, Melvin had already released his seatbelt.

Unflustered, Ruth stepped back to give him room. "Watch your step, Melvin."

"Watch your step, Melvin," he repeated, watching his step.

Ruth smiled. "Just stay put while I feed the meter," she explained.

Melvin tilted his head but didn't budge from where he waited.

Ruth fed enough coins in the meter to cover the two hours she allotted for the visit. When she glanced up, she found Melvin waving.

"Do you see somebody you know?" she asked, curiously following the direction of his stare, but Melvin only clicked his tongue three times in response.

Ruth looked left, then right, and even spun her head entirely around, trying to figure out who the heck Melvin was waving to, but after a moment gave up.

"Melvin," she signaled, trying to get his attention, but Melvin continued to wave, thoroughly fixated and unable to grasp Ruth's growing frustration.

"Come on, Melvin. It's not waving time. Only walking time." She reached out to tap him on the shoulder, but he promptly jerked away. "Sorry! Sorry! I forgot," she said, shifting impatiently from one foot to the other.

In the distance, behind the bank and off to the far left in another adjacent parking lot, a silhouette of a lone familiar figure discreetly entered a building. Melvin abruptly stopped waving.

Ruth peered up from her watch and noticed. "Good. You're done," she said relieved, "'cause we gotta go."

Out of nowhere, Melvin started violently shaking his head and tapping his foot.

"What happened? What's the matter?" Ruth asked concerned, again searching in every direction but still unable to see the problem. "Let's just go inside," she pleaded, completely misreading his reactions. "I promise, it's going to be okay."

Distressed, but no longer frozen in place, Melvin bowed his head, gripped his notebook to his chest, and scurried after Ruth. However, before entering the building, he stopped for one last cautious peep over his shoulder.

A second passed and then Ruth watched his shoulders relax. Whatever had scared him was now long gone.

"See? This isn't so bad," soothed Ruth, grateful when Melvin finally decided to step inside.

The reception area, behind glass panels, gave the appearance of a medical office. But the painted cream and earthy terracotta color walls and tall ceilings made the place feel homey and pleasant. Instead of a typical waiting area with uniformed chairs lining the walls, this common room sported a comfy couch, a coffee table and a few wing-back winged chairs, a television, kitchenette, a desk with a leather chair, and even a small play area.

Melvin frowned. He sniffed the air a few times and scrunched his shoulders, apparently bothered by the fusion of antiseptic, bleach, and illness wafting through the air.

Ruth had also noticed the strong odor when she first walked in. Perhaps something had happened recently requiring a vigorous cleaning. Nonetheless, she tactfully covered her nose with her hand.

Unfazed by decorum, Melvin slapped his hand over his nose.

"Yes," snuffled Ruth. "The smell in here does take some getting used to."

***

Melvin

Later that evening behind closed doors, Melvin leaned over his bedroom desk intently drawing. Chronicling the many new faces and places he saw this afternoon. Drawing helped him navigate through the newness and strangeness of it all.

After arriving home, his mother had been anxious to talk, but Melvin wouldn't cooperate. Instead, he ate at the kitchen table, scoffing down his sandwich and chips as quickly as possible.

"Slow down, Melvin. Take human bites," admonished his mother, only half joking, but Melvin neither slowed down nor took different sized bites. On overload from a day of peopling, his mind needed more than anything to be alone, space to process all he had witnessed, time to think and reconnoiter. But most of all, time to properly compartmentalize.

As planned, Ruth had taken him around the building, pointing out various rooms and areas, filling the airwaves with bothersome idle chitter chatter. Redundant comments about different wall art or the big windows with the "lovely view." All stuff Melvin had no use for. Nothing that he cared about until they arrived at the one place Melvin would never forget.

"This will be the room your mother will be in when she comes to stay," Ruth said reassuringly, permitting Melvin time to enter at his own pace. "Each room is private, and there's even extra space for when you want to visit."

Melvin stood upright, not touching a thing. Once inside, he barely moved a muscle, but that didn't prevent his eyes from darting back and forth, soaking up and absorbing every last detail, nook, and cranny. He missed nothing.

Although Ruth couldn't tell for sure whether or not Melvin liked the place, at least he didn't appear overly anxious or withdrawn.

"Where I walked, he walked. Where I pointed, he pointed," Ruth told Felicia later on that evening. "I took that as a positive sign."

Tonight, Melvin sketched the many corridors and halls. He drew the faces of the palliative care physicians, nurses, and a couple of the specially trained support volunteers Ruth had introduced him to. All of whom had treated him kindly.

Melvin sketched his mother's room. The empty bed with the green and gold quilt and a few toss pillows to match. The warm wood floors and light buttercream walls…two mustard yellow chairs, a love seat, and a round wooden table with a slight chip on one corner. The room had large French doors which opened onto a small patio. He drew the high ceiling fan which also functioned as soft lighting. Melvin even included every switch plate and call button; everything down to the last tastefully placed machine.

Another drawing showed the common room where Ruth allowed him to watch television and drink hot cocoa before leaving. However, Melvin still had one more scene rumbling around in his head that he had to get down on paper. That drawing he saved for last.

CHAPTER 21

Say a Little Prayer for Me

Late Tuesday Evening

QASIM PARKED HIS CAR and rushed into the *masjid* for *isha salat* feeling hyped after another successful, if not too long of a meeting. With the prospect of a lucrative contract in the wings, not only would Qasim's income increase, but also his standing as a successful business owner in the community.

Nevertheless, tonight's meeting had been especially difficult for him personally. While intuitively understanding the need to be present and act sharp, Qasim's mind strayed, failing to cooperate as less than tasteful visions of Kalila took over, front and center. Everything from her walk to her smile reeked of womanliness. Not the smartest thing to do with a room full of potential investors.

To hell with everyone else.

With Bashir permanently out of the picture, Qasim felt entitled to pursue Kalila and make her his forever.

The men lined up with the call to prayer, shoulder to shoulder, foot to foot. Imam Abdullah led the *salat*. Afterward, Qasim relaxed, chatting with a few of the brothers, and enjoying an offered cup of tea.

Somewhat off to the side, the Imam appeared engrossed in a private conversation with a younger brother, Saif Kazmi; a local tax accountant who Qasim had dealt with on occasion when helping with the *masjid*'s finances.

Nice enough guy.

After a few minutes of conversation, the Imam scanned the room, searching for someone. Catching Qasim's eye, he waved him over.

"*As salaamu alaikum*, Brother Qasim," greeted the Imam, still sitting, offering Qasim a warm handshake. "You know brother Saif?"

"I do," he said, extending his hand. Saif rose to his feet to give Qasim a warm embrace and *salaam*.

"We've worked together before," explained Saif, smiling.

"Please join us for a moment if you can," motioned the Imam. "I need your assistance in a private matter."

Qasim obliged, lowering himself onto the rug.

"Brother Saif is looking to marry," proclaimed the Imam.

Qasim beamed at Saif, clapping him on the back. "*Alhamdulillah!* So, you're ready to make the big plunge, huh?"

"*InshaAllah*," answered Saif, reserved.

"Good for you."

"Yes," replied the Imam, "He's ready to join the rest of us old married guys."

The trio shared a friendly laugh.

"Well, I'm happy for you brother," said Qasim. "What can I do to help?"

The Imam leaned in, lowering his voice. "The brother is interested in your neighbor—sister Kalila."

"Kalila Rahim?" Qasim's stomach lurched. Up to that moment, he'd conceitedly never contemplated Kalila having other suitors. The thought had never crossed his mind. "What can I help you with?" he asked, sporting a fake smile plastered across his face.

Now Saif piped in. "I know she's a widow with a young son, but I couldn't remember exactly how long ago her husband died and if her waiting period was over," he said. "I didn't want to offend her by approaching too early."

Qasim nodded, distraught about this young man wanting to approach her at all.

"You wouldn't happen to recall when Brother Bashir died?" asked the Imam. "I have it in my records, I could check, but I'm thinking over six months ago at least, right?"

The date of Bashir's death would be forever charred into Qasim's memory, haunting him for the remainder of his days. Qasim needed to tread carefully, not wishing to give himself away. "Over seven months now," he said nonchalantly. "Probably closer to eight." He knew for a fact Kalila had finished her waiting period months ago, and was free to marry again without anyone's interference or disapproval.

Saif beamed, satisfied with the answer. "*Shukran*, brother. That's great news."

Qasim fought the urge to reach over and choke the damn smile out of him, but forced a tight grin in return.

The Imam thanked Qasim as well, politely signaling his help no longer necessary.

Just as well.

Qasim, ready to withdraw, felt utterly perplexed by how panicked he had suddenly become by the mere prospect of anyone but him having access to Kalila. He reached into his pocket for his keys, and unlocked the car. He turned the engine on and left the parking lot, not to go home, but to Kalila's house. He had to speak with her before the inquiry from the Imam came. He needed to make his intentions clear—and first.

But what exactly are my intentions?

Before the pressure from somebody else honing in on his action, Qasim had been perfectly content to take his time, enjoying Kalila at a comfortable arm's length, while he figured out a way to claim her heart and bed. But hearing that another guy wanted her knocked that strategy off the table.

Qasim's chest tightened. What he planned reeked of dishonesty and deceit, and while admittedly a bit underhanded—*even for him*—he decided to pitch caution to the wind and make his move before Saif or any other guy thought they had the slightest chance in hell to usurp him for what rightfully belonged to him.

I have to, he told himself. *I just have to.*

***

Amara

Agitated, Amara couldn't sleep. There were too many conflicting thoughts racing through her mind. After hours of tossing and turning, she finally gave up and headed downstairs to make herself a cup of warm milk. She'd never gotten used to Qasim's late hours, and while they recently hadn't had much cause to revel in one another's affection, she still undeniably missed having his body resting close to hers.

Where is he?

The carefully crafted wall of protection Amara had used in the past to safeguard herself against Qasim's lack of affection no longer existed. That fortification had since come crashing down, propelling her ruthlessly through a maze of existing fissures, leaving her to wallow in a pit of self-pity. Whatever this thing was that had transpired between her husband and Kalila had her ready to pull out the stoppers—willing to go for the attack head-on.

"I'll make that bitch pay," she muttered, drawing back the curtain for the hundredth time, inexplicably anxious for Qasim to get home. She checked the hour. No board meeting lasted this late.

What could he be doing?

Amara stared across the street. All but the front porch lights were on at Kalila's. She stood there glaring, lost in thought until the unmistakable hiss of milk boiling over caught her attention.

"Damn it."

Amara rushed to the kitchen. Propping the pot of scalded milk on a trivet, she started scrubbing the mess away before it had a chance to cake on and dry. As she scoured, a band of sweat formed at the top of her hairline, trickling alongside the folds on her neck, saturating the collar of her tee-shirt.

Mindlessly lost in the task, she failed to notice when her husband's car pulled in and parked. Never caught him jogging across the street or knocking at Kalila's door. Nor did she see when he rung her doorbell or how he nervously bounced from foot to foot while waiting on her porch. But when Kalila's house lit up bright as day, the light reflected through Amara's living room enough to catch her attention. Amara dropped the pot in the sink and rushed into the living room. She jerked the curtain to the side in time to see Kalila's front door opening a crack, then wide enough to allow a man to step inside.

Ha! Booty call, huh—

Then Amara gasped. "Hold up. That's *my* man!"

Eyes bulging, she didn't know what to do first.

Do I run over and confront them—or stay put and punch him square in the jaw the minute he steps inside...

With the boys sound asleep upstairs, she hesitated. Gripping the curtain, she tugged it clear to the side for a better view. "I'll strangle him," she mumbled repeatedly, the adrenaline coursing through her veins. "No, I'll destroy her first—then strangle him."

Amara squeezed her arm, shaking mad. "I wonder what excuse he'll use this time?" she muttered, straining her neck to make out what the shadows moving about were doing. "You are so dead Kalila. Wait till he knows..."

For a good long while, the figures seemed to remain still. Then just as abruptly, the front door swung open and out stepped Qasim. She watched him turn and give Kalila a slight wave. Then, hands shoved in his pockets, he leisurely ambled towards home, his head dropped, staring down at his feet. Just when he hit their curb, something made him glance up. That's when Qasim noticed Amara standing at their window, glowering. By the way he stumbled, it was clear to her the warning bell of detection had finally gone off in that stupid head of his like a siren.

Disheveled and madder than hell, Amara glared at Qasim as he pushed their door open and sat on the stair to remove his shoes. She scrutinized his tired face for any sign that he was about to come clean; give her some excuse for his sneaky behavior—*anything*— but instead Qasim remained silent for a good long while. Fuming, Amara finally broke the ice.

"What the hell do you think you're playing at?" she demanded, but Qasim stayed quiet. He hung up his jacket, keeping his back faced toward her the entire time.

"I asked you a question!" she snapped.

Qasim sneered. "I saw that fat face of yours plastered at the window from all the way across the street," he shot back, then snickered.

She gasped, stunned, never expecting such a vicious response.

"Look at you," he said, apparently not finished. "Do something with yourself. Comb your hair, take a shower once in a while."

"That's not funny."

"You're right. It's not funny. It's pathetic. You're pathetic. The thing is, if you spent half as much time on the elliptical as you do spying on me, we might not be in the position we're in now."

Amara clasped her neck. "Which is what?" she murmured, unable to move. The aftertaste of mortification stung the back of her throat.

"Go to bed, Amara."

"You can't treat me like this."

Qasim reached for the banister. His legs heavy, his body past exhaustion. "Whatever you think you have to say—save it. I'm not interested."

"Kalila—"

Before Amara finished belting out her grievance, Qasim spun around, ready to pounce, his face bursting with unbridled rage. "Keep Kalila's name out of your filthy mouth," he threatened, stabbing a finger in her chest. "You hear me? I won't tell you again."

Bleary-eyed and frightened, Amara winced with each jab but refused to back down. "You'll be sorry you did this," she sobbed. "I swear."

Qasim let out a curdling, sardonic laugh. "Oh, trust me. From the day I first married you, I've been sorry."

CHAPTER 22

Indecent Proposal

Kalila

KALILA FLIPPED OFF THE front and living room lights once more, grateful the unexpected doorbell ring hadn't awakened Hamza. They had just started patching up whatever fell between them. Kalila wasn't prepared to have her efforts to regain her son's affection thwarted by the likes of Qasim.

Leaning back on the closed front door, Kalila gave herself a minute to fully comprehend the enormity of what had just transpired. Hand pressed against the door, she attempted to match her breaths to a count of twenty, hoping to dissipate her anxiety enough to function again.

Without a doubt, Qasim's unanticipated stopover had winded her. His visit seemed almost illusory, perhaps a delusion. Maybe a nighttime hallucination brought on by mounting stress. But despite all the weirdness and surprise of what had just occurred, it had felt unnervingly real…hurtling her once again from one unimagined bizarre series of events to the next with no foreseeable end in sight. Confounded and at a loss for words she wanted to wake up and see it was all a big mistake.

Kalila trudged forward, shoulders slumped. Slipping off the one-piece *hijab*, she crumpled it into a ball, tossing it hastily into the hall basket. A slight chill bristled up her spine. Tugging her bathrobe cord tighter around her waist, she proceeded to pad her way upstairs to bed, feeling alone and more confused than ever.

Never, ever, in a thousand-million years—could she have anticipated Qasim dropping by unannounced, close to midnight to propose marriage, which seemed utterly bizarre the more Kalila recounted the limited totality of their past interactions—consisting mostly of ordinary, sporadic conversations between neighbors. Indeed, *nothing to suggest this*—

The arrogant way the man just showed up on her doorstep out of nowhere…his litany of outlandish reasons why she should agree to his proposal—and then selectively spouting off a series of rehearsed religiosity seemed comical at best. Pitiful at worst.

"*As salaamu alaikum.* I'm sorry to bother you so late, but I needed to speak with you," he said, his whole demeanor somewhat staid.

"*Wa alaikum salaam.* Of course," Kalila opened the door wider. "Would you like to come inside?"

"Thank you." Qasim stepped in and placed his shoes on the mat, following Kalila into her living room.

"Please, take a seat," she said, totally self-conscious about her rushed getup and fussing with her robe; adjusting the fabric to make sure her bare legs stayed sufficiently covered.

"I didn't mean to disturb you," he said, staring at the rug, attempting to divert his eyes from her curves.

He appeared jumpy, uneasy. "Is everything okay?" She wasn't sure what else to say.

Qasim lowered himself onto the edge of the seat, propping both elbows on his knees, clasping his hands. "I've been giving your situation a lot of thought," he began, the lies coming easy.

"My situation?" Kalila pressed a hand to her throat.

"Yes, about how I can help you—and your son now that Brother Bashir is no longer with us." He caught her flinch at the mere mention of her husband's name. "It can't be easy dealing with all this," he said, waving a hand indicating the house.

"No. Not at all," she said, unconsciously twisting the wedding band she still wore on her finger—not sure where this odd conversation was headed. "It's been one of the most difficult times of my life, to be honest."

Qasim paused. "I can only imagine."

Her eyes kept darting to the stairs as if at any moment, Hamza would be standing there, judging her, a look of suspicion smeared across his condemnatory face. She wished Qasim would say what he had to and leave.

"Sister—I'm a wealthy man," he said, fidgeting. "I own my own business, my home…I have no debt, *alhamdulillah*."

Why is he saying this stuff?

Kalila squinted, perplexed.

It's not like I asked him for money.

"I'm a fair man," he continued, "and if given the opportunity, I could make this burden you are facing go away or at the least, be easier, *inshaAllah*."

"I'm sorry?" she asked, perplexed.

What burden? The lawn?

"I'm not following you." Kalila self-consciously tugged on the hem of her *hijab*, twisting it between her fingers.

"I'm asking you to marry me."

"Excuse me?" Kalila struggled to hide the shock.

"I know this is sudden, but now that your *iddah* is completed, you'll need to make some difficult decisions about your future."

"My future?" she repeated guardedly; her eyes shifting toward the stairs.

"I mean your well-being. Your security."

"Oh…well, I see, but for the moment—" Kalila swallowed rapidly.

"Plus, with Bashir gone," Qasim interjected, "Hamza's going to need a strong male model."

"Ah huh." Kalila gazed down at her hands, folded on her lap.

"You're a young woman, he said. "Too young to be a widow, but *Allahu alim*. You shouldn't have to be struggling as hard as you are to make ends meet."

That much was true.

"As my wife, I can support you. Take that burden off your shoulders. Provide the kind of life a woman like you deserves."

"That's very kind of you," she said, trying to find a way to let him down easy. "But how? You're already married."

"Can I be honest with you?" he asked, rubbing his hands together.

"Yes, of course."

"My marriage to Amara isn't the greatest."

Oh, here we go…

"We married young. Both of us probably weren't ready to enter into such a serious commitment, but we did. We've stayed together because of the children, at least that's why I have."

"I see."

"The boys need me in their life."

"Absolutely."

"I'm not looking to get a divorce."

"So, you're asking me to be your—"

"Second wife. Correct."

Polygamy? Oh, the irony.

Kalila had heard enough. "Pause," she said, raising a finger in the air before he continued rambling on. "I thank you for your kind and thoughtful, and um…generous—very generous offer, brother Qasim—but I'm still in the midst of sorting my life out. So many things to deal with. Difficult things, like you already mentioned, so I'm going to have to say—"

Qasim lifted his hands. "You don't need to give me an answer right away," he said quickly. "Just think about it. That's all I ask."

Just think about it? Like we're playing "Let's Make a Deal."

She really wished he'd go home already, back to his nutty wife. "Okay, I can do that," she conceded, saying anything to get him to leave. Kalila pulled her robe tighter around her waist. "I'll think about it."

Taking his cue, Qasim got to his feet and *salaamed* her, moving towards his shoes but not nearly as briskly as when he arrived.

I can't believe this…

Kalila followed him to the door, glancing over her shoulder, praying Hamza stayed asleep.

I should have been sharper.

I should have known Qasim's sudden urge to be Mr. Helpful would come at a price.

How did I miss the signs?

From time to time, she'd catch Qasim from his driveway checking her out, stealing an admiring glance or two. She remembered that time over a year ago when she had elicited a slight blush from him when they had exchanged a polite *salaam* at the food store, but that was it. Nothing ever much else happened that she could recall, and if it did, it was always at a respectable distance.

So back to the question—why now?

Kalila shook her head, honestly stumped. Face growing hot, she rubbed her clammy palms together and began to pace; trudging impatiently up and down the rugged hall.

Amara would lose her mind if she found out her husband came here and asked me to marry him.

That thought alone made her stomach churn.

Co-wife.

Qasim must be insane.

That made her giggle, but then just as fast, her eyes welled up in tears.

This is crazy, she shuddered, wiping her face on her sleeve, overcome by the murky sea of conflicting emotions all hitting her at once.

God Almighty, co-wife…

—with Amara—the original queen of bat-shit crazy and the absolute worst neighbor from hell.

Like I'd agree to be her or anybody else's co-wife——

Kalila softly closed her bedroom door.

It's not my fault if Qasim has a thing for me…

I didn't cause this to happen.

She hung her robe on the back hook and plopped on the bed; drawing the blanket up to her chin.

What are we talking about? A lawn? A few garbage cans? A school pick-up?

She huddled under the covers. "This is ridiculous..." she mumbled, slapping the pillow until it fit comfortably under her neck and head.

And why the sudden rush?

And for that matter, the cloak and dagger late-night visit?

Amara must not know what he's up to.

Pressing on her temples, Kalila couldn't rein in her frustration nor quiet the pounding in her head.

For someone who makes her living fucking strange men, you'd think I'd be smarter than this by now.

Kalila struck the mattress with her fists. A mad gush of tears stung her eyes, slipping out the corners, and sliding down her neck only to drop randomly onto her pillow. Unable to fall asleep, she opted to lie still in the dark, nursing her fears.

I should have thrown him out—kicked his arrogant ass to the curb; coming here in the dead of night like some thief...

... or better yet, I should have dragged his ass home and let his shrew of a wife deal with him.

Kalila lurched forward only to let her body free fall back onto her pillow; arms splayed to the side. "I give up!" she grumbled.

Qasim and his stupid visit...

—as if my life wasn't already complicated enough.

As to Qasim's real intent, who knew? Kalila had been around enough men to read between the lines, and Qasim, who wore his intentions plainly on his sleeve—was apparently no different—despite all his well-timed precipitous religiosity. *Sister* this and *sister* that.

What a cruel joke.

But Kalila did have to hand it to him, though. She would never have thought he'd try to slide under Amara's radar the way he had. Sneaking over and then summoning up a list of well-timed *hadiths* to support his cause; as if his sole desire in broaching her with his proposal stemmed from a deep-seated desire to serve humanity.

Still, something about this visit wasn't adding up. Kalila rolled on her side.

And seriously? What in the world would make him think for one minute his throwing his wife under the bus would be the least bit appealing to me?

Kalila rolled on her back, putting her hands behind her head for support. "Guys kill me," she grumbled.

As much as I despise that woman, if he's willing to do this to her, the mother of his children, and behind her back... How would he treat me?

Kalila yawned, becoming drowsy; her exhaustion finally winning the uphill battle against the ever-present adrenaline.

Why do all men think every woman wants to be married?

Kalila stretched her arms. Her eyelids grew heavy.

It's partly my fault.

I'm the dumbbell who let him know money is tight, but still...

I can't let this divert me. I'm moving on...starting over—away from this crazy place and haunting memories. I'll find a new home where Hamza and I will have a chance to reclaim our lives.

Mentally ripped and too bushed to speculate any further, Kalila decided to leave the whole sordid situation alone for now; content to give it a sufficient amount of time before slamming the door permanently shut.

Then another, more pressing thought shoved it way through her subconscious.

Melvin.

She'd made a promise to look into helping him. Hamza counted on her keeping to it, but how could a child begin to understand the level of commitment necessary to bring a grown man with learning challenges into their lives? He only saw his friend, his pal, and not the work involved, and although she liked Melvin, Hamza needed friends his own age.

No, she'd follow through, like she said she would. She'd call Felicia as promised, get a few details, express her sympathy and call it a day. The only consolation, once done, she'd be at least able to legitimately tell Hamza that there was nothing they could do to help Melvin. Of course, Hamza would be disappointed, that's only natural, but for once, not with her. He'll have to move on and get over it.

Kalila winced, hating how callous she'd become, but truthfully, was she being that coldhearted? Uncaring? Or just realistically dealing with life the same way it dealt with her—one taciturn slap in the face after the other.

Move on and get over it, her new and improved *modus operandi.*

CHAPTER 23

Love Story

Abdullah

THE CONVERSATION WITH THE brother had lasted longer than anticipated. By the time Abdullah returned home, the house was dark. Only a single light shone over the kitchen sink, thoughtfully left on for his benefit. Abdullah found a plate of dinner waiting for him in the fridge; a heart scribbled thoughtfully on a sticky note taped to the foil, ready to be popped in the oven. Exhausted and too worn-out to eat, he left the plate undisturbed, dragging his feet upstairs, determined to dive into bed. Upon opening the bedroom door, much to his surprise, he found his lovely wife propped up on two pillows, reading in bed, wearing his old college tee-shirt. Nafiza had her reading glasses perched seductively on the bridge of her nose. Wisps of hair escaped her messy bun piled adorably high on her head.

Cute as all hell.

Leaning over, he placed a single kiss softly on her lips.

"I didn't think you'd still be up," he whispered, running his hand beneath the blanket, pleased to feel nothing but warm, soft skin.

"*Wa alaikum salaam,*" she purred tenderly, giving him a jolt. "Just getting some reading in while the inmates are asleep."

Abdullah's mouth laughed, but his attention focused solely on the way her slender hand fidgeted with the blanket, slipping the corner between her thin, delicate, fingers.

Oh man.

Abdullah cleared his throat. "Rough day?" he asked, turning towards the bathroom, removing his clothes, anxious to join her in bed.

"Not more than usual. Just our typical shenanigans at dinner."

Abdullah popped his head out of the bathroom and smacked his forehead. "Before I forget," he said, wearing nothing but a towel knotted around his tight, lean waist. "There's a brother who wants to talk to your friend," he said, leaning against the door frame.

"My friend? Which one?" inquired Nafiza, her light chestnut eyes glued to her paperback; the same exact one she started and stopped for the last few weeks, but never seemed able to complete.

"Kalila."

Nafiza jolted upright, "Oh?" she asked, no longer engrossed by her book.

"About her *iddah*. It's been over three months, probably closer to six, correct?"

"Eight."

"Eight. So, it's finished," he said, exiting the bathroom, and drying his face with a hand towel. "Still not the longest time, but I told the brother I spoke to tonight that I'd inquire as to whether or not she's prepared to get married again."

"Or wanting to," Nafiza immediately corrected.

"Yes, or wanting to. You're absolutely right. In my defense, that's why I am bringing this to you." Abdullah casually tossed the hand cloth over his narrow shoulder. "I was hoping you could give me some insight."

"Like?"

"Like whether I should tell him to proceed or tell him to wait. Maybe she needs more time?"

Nafiza's expression hardened. "I'm not sure, to be honest," she answered, giving Abdullah a non-committal half shrug.

"I think I understand," he said judiciously, unwilling to make Nafiza feel as if she had to impede on the boundaries of her friendship for his sake. "I guess I just thought the sister might have mentioned something in passing."

"Yeah, I know what you mean. I get that, but these past few months have been rough for Kalila. There's a lot to digest, work through. It's not easy picking up the pieces after losing a spouse."

Abdullah listened, remaining quiet.

"Kalila may put up a good front, but she's struggling." Nafiza removed her glasses and rubbed her tired eyes. "Plus, she's not the type to broadcast her problems or even ask for help." Nafiza tucked a lock of fallen hair behind her ear. "Between you and me, I'm not sure how she's making ends meet."

"Didn't she get an insurance payout?" asked Abdullah.

"No. Bashir let his policy lapse and left their bank account drained."

"I didn't know that." Abdullah stroked his beard. This situation was quickly becoming more complicated than initially anticipated, but from experience, he knew nothing was as it appeared. This news gave him a lot to think about.

Nafiza shrugged. "Now you see what I mean, right? Kalila may not be ready to deal with another man right now or…or she might. I can't make that call for her." She opened her mouth as if to say more, then stopped.

"Where are you?" Abdullah asked Nafiza, before scooting underneath the blanket to join her, playfully tapping the bed as if she had disappeared. "Maybe a man in her life would be a positive thing. Marriage could take away some of the financial pressure, and perhaps the brother could be a father figure for Hamza."

"Agreed, but not just any guy—the right guy." Nafiza slipped the bookmarker between the pages before leaving the book on the night table. "What makes you think this brother has what it takes to marry a widow with a son?"

"Good question." Abdullah kissed her shoulder. "For one, he's gainfully employed."

"That's not what I meant," she chastised. "Money isn't everything, although that's in his favor. What else?"

"Two," Abdullah said breathily into Nafiza's ear, his hands exploring underneath her tee-shirt, "He's got no issue with the fact she's a widow with a child."

"That's big of him," Nafiza snorted, removing his hand currently creeping under her shirt.

"And three, and probably most importantly, he seems sincere." Abdullah gently removed his wife's glasses. "Take your hair down," he whispered.

Nafiza coyly complied, unclipping her bun. Her hair cascaded down around her shoulders, framing her pretty face.

Abdullah smiled. "You're gorgeous."

"You're horny."

"I am, but you're still gorgeous."

"Stop changing the subject."

Abdullah cleared his throat again. "Where were we? Ah, right—so, if I understand you—your opinion is she's not ready?" he asked, wishing to Allah he never brought this topic up in the first place. Playing with the edge of Nafiza's shirt, his fingers lightly brushed along the inside of her thigh. The heat of her body called to him.

Flushed, Nafiza placed her hand over Abdullah's, attempting to redirect his fingers to a safer, less sensitive zone. "Not exactly. I'm just saying that Kalila's struggling, especially with Hamza. He's not taking Bashir's passing well at all."

"That's understandable." Abdullah nuzzled his wife's neck. "That must be really," kiss, "really," kiss, "really hard," he mumbled.

"Jerk!" Nafiza laughed, attempting to push his face away.

"What did I do?" he asked, letting out a mirthless laugh, one hand still cupping her ample hip. Pulling his head back, he stared into her eyes. "Honestly, from what I hear and know, he's a good brother."

"Ah huh."

"No, seriously, he seems genuine." Abdullah caressed Nafiza's face and neck, raking his fingers through her strands, working his lips down the nape of her neck.

"You're terrible," she murmured, her breath quickening. "You need to stop," she moaned, playfully elbowing him, her eyes locked onto his. "And I suppose you want me to ask her?" Nafiza pursed her lips; something Abdullah found irresistible.

Abdullah pulled his curvaceous wife closer, no longer willing to sacrifice his night for anybody else. "I'd appreciate it," he said, nibbling her ear, savoring her sweet taste. His chest rose and fell with rapid breaths. "Let me show you how much."

Nafiza gasped as his hands ran down her thighs. "Fine," she moaned, goosebumps rising on her arms. Tilting her head back, she stretched her slender neck, toying with him. "You missed a spot."

That's all he needed to hear. Abdullah covered her body with his, licking and kissing, lost in the sensation of feeling her under him.

"I'll-speak-to-her-tomorrow," Nafiza whimpered; her every word breathlessly abrupt.

Abdullah extended his arm, stretching his fingers to flip off the light. Tugging the blanket over them both, he moaned. "Take your time…there's no rush."

***

The morning arrived quickly.

Abdullah heard the shower running upstairs. A surge of delicious images of his wife's delicate curves and the touch of her silken skin came careening into his mind…especially when she—

"Dad!" shouted Ra'id. "It's gonna spill!"

"Sorry, sorry." *Damn.*

Dalia giggled. "Daddy's funny."

Mornings were hectic for Nafiza. Abdullah tried to lend a hand before hurrying out the door to his day job, but between working full time and being an assistant Imam, time with the family had unacceptably dwindled.

"I can't have *reg-ala* milk," wailed Dalia. "Mommy said."

"Re-gu-lar," corrected her father. "Okay, switch bowls with Munir. I didn't pour any milk in his yet."

"I'm not eating out of a pink bowl," whined Munir, none too happy about the change.

"Cut me some slack, son," teased Abdullah. "Give your old dad a break—just for today."

Munir grumbled but obliged, sliding his sister's bowl his way.

"Daddy? Are you gonna bring us to the bus stop today?" asked Dalia.

"No, honey. I have to get a move on."

"Aw…" complained Dalia.

"I know, but I'm running late as is."

"Morning, Mommy," chorused the children.

Nafiza entered the kitchen looking refreshed. "Morning, people," she sang out making her rounds; inspecting each child's attire. Abdullah watched as she adjusted collars, re-pined Dalia's *hijab*, and gave each child an approving peck on the top of their heads.

I am indeed blessed.

Abdullah held out his arms, waiting for his hug.

Nafiza seductively pressed her body into his. "Good morning, sir," she said, arching her back and lifting her face; saving a tender kiss just for him.

"Eww," moaned Munir.

"How do you think you got here, boy?" teased Abdullah, winking at Nafiza who, although shooting him a disapproving eye roll, still seemed powerless to stop herself from laughing.

"Ra'id," Nafiza barked, attempting to go back to business. "I need you to make sure you hand the teacher the note today. No more goofing around or you won't be able to be dismissed early for your dental appointment tomorrow."

Ra'id, mouth jam-packed, gave a quick confirming nod.

Standing at the counter with his back facing the family, Abdullah finished prepping his travel mug of coffee, admiring his wife's ability to implement an orderly system in an otherwise chaotic existence.

"Dalia, here." Nafiza handed her a lunch bag. "And eat all of it, including your carrots."

"Do I have to?" Dalia grumbled, hands crossed over her chest in her typical bratty sulk mode.

"Dalia," chastised her father.

"Okay," she pouted, shoving the lunch into her backpack.

"Munir, don't forget to go to the Lost and Found about your jacket," said Nafiza.

"Another one?" asked Abdullah.

"Third time this year," answered his wife, adjusting his collar. Mutually drained from the parent struggle they both shared a longsuffering laugh.

"I gotta go," announced Abdullah, grabbing his mug. "Kids, listen to your mother. Do well in school. Dalia, eat your carrots. And Munir—"

"I know…my jacket."

"Excellent." Abdullah ruffled his son's hair. Tilting his head, Abdullah planted a kiss on his wife's cheek. "I'll be thinking about last night all day," he whispered, smirking. "Any chance you'll be wearing that tee-shirt again tonight?" he teased.

Nafiza pushed him playfully away. "Go to work."

Abdullah had only been half-joking. The time spent together the evening before had been incredible. Then again, most nights were. "Fine. I'm off. *As salaamu alaikum* everybody."

"*Wa alaikum salaam,*" his family chorused in return.

Before stepping out of the kitchen, Abdullah stole one long look at the family Allah had blessed him with; marveling over the love he felt for each one. He glanced over at his wife…his friend and his heart. The mere thought of losing either Nafiza or his children scared him senseless.

Nafiza

With everyone gone, Nafiza had a small window of time to take a breather before diving head first to tackle the endless homes chores that seemed to multiply while she slept. She considered the quiet of the morning her time to rejuvenate…pay homage to her thoughts without battling the constant intrusion of little voices demanding the next *this* or *that.* Needling her, making deals or outright begging, anything to satisfy their every last whim. Skillfully manipulating her for the next treat or indulgence, all while using that grating high-pitched whiny voice infused with the power to cause the nerves of all human mothers to stand on edge.

Nafiza wiped the crumbs off the kitchen table, waiting for the kettle to boil.

How is it possible that I already miss Abdullah? My rock. My partner.

The man who knocked her socks off and kept her smiling.

I'm so proud of him.

Each morning, as he walks out the door to provide for his family, a portion of her heart leaves along with him.

He's such a good man. Honest… trustworthy.

Nafiza could never get her fill of her husband's affection; his warm embraces, the long, lingering kisses.

Even after all these years, the kids, the mortgage, the septic tank, the car payments—you name it, and yet she still longed to hear his voice on the other end of the phone. Because of his love, affection, and devotion, Nafiza considered herself to be the most blessed person on earth. Sometimes she found it burdensome having to share Abdullah with a community who sometimes treated him more like an appendage than a source of knowledge; habitually ungrateful for his efforts.

Not only does he provide sound counsel to anyone who seeks his help, but he takes his obligations to the community seriously.

I don't understand how he does it. Listening to people's problems all the time. It would have driven me crazy a long time ago.

"Being the Imam is a big responsibility," he'd remind Nafiza when she got upset. "I offer counsel to people who are dealing with major life issues sometimes. Not only do they want my help or advice, but they want me to protect their secrets and agreements as well. Sometimes I'm privy to information that I never thought I'd ever hear—private, intimate issues on often difficult, painful topics."

Ya Allah, if Abdullah isn't careful, he's going to get burnt dealing with these flaky folks.

Women from the community naturally assumed that since Nafiza was the Imam's wife, that somehow made her their second choice to confide in, but unlike Abdullah, Nafiza never made the same commitment and couldn't be bothered getting entangled in people's drama, until now.

Nafiza drummed her fingers on the table.

What if Kalila is just toying with Amara's husband to mess with her?

As vengeful and as irritating as Amara could get, she's not someone to randomly piss off. Not the type to hesitate; just go for the attack whether right or wrong. And when she did, there would be nowhere to hide from the wrath of that unbalanced, scornful woman if she felt impeded upon.

Kalila's playing with fire. Maybe I should warn her…

Then again, sometimes the best course of action with the unhinged is to accept that they won't likely change and then detach. Stay as polite as possible to avoid future dramatic scenes, and slip far, far away. Unfortunately, that tactic hadn't worked for Kalila.

It had taken everything Nafiza had to feign indifference when Abdullah first broached the topic of Kalila. However, directing her husband's attention elsewhere, to a more pleasurable wavelength hadn't been difficult at all.

CHAPTER 24

Surprise Visitor

KALILA STOOD ON FELICIA's porch feeling like an imbecilic interloper, but a promise was a promise.

Why did I agree to this?

Her shoe scraped the cement step.

What do I say? "Hi! Heard you were dying... how about if Melvin stays with us?"

Yup, that sounds just as ludicrous as I feel.

Misery bore through her insides like a tsunami.

A handsome, middle-aged woman, Kalila assumed to be Ruth, Felicia's nurse by Hamza's description, opened the door after the third knock. "Can I help you?" she asked kindly.

"Hi. I'm Kalila Rahim from next door," she said, pointing to her house. "I'm Hamza's mom?" Kalila hated that her voice got that annoying question lilt to it whenever she got nervous.

"Oh, yes," Ruth smiled. "Nice of you to stop by. I'm Ruth," she said, reaching out to shake Kalila's hand. For a small woman, she had an impressive, firm grip.

"I should have called in advance, but I just wanted to pop in to say hello to Felicia to see how she's doing." Kalila practically shoved the box of cookies she brought at Ruth like some sweepstake door prize.

"Oh, how lovely!" Ruth stepped to the side. "Why don't you come in and wait here. I'll go see if Felicia's feeling up to a short visit."

Kalila picked up on Ruth's subtle reference to the word *short.* "That would be great, thanks. I won't keep her long," Kalila added, hoping her *not too long* comment would sway in her favor, but just as Ruth turned to leave, a voice called out from a room somewhere inside.

"Ruth?" said the voice, presumably Felicia, "is someone here?"

"Yes. Your neighbor," called Ruth. "Hamza's mom."

"Kalila," prompted Kalila, silently mouthing her name.

"Kalila," added Ruth, winking her thanks.

"Oh, how nice," called Felicia. "Come in, Kalila."

Shutting the door behind Kalila, Ruth leaned in and whispered, "Felicia loves visitors."

Kalila followed Ruth down the long corridor, past the kitchen where she saw Melvin at the table.

"Morning Melvin," Kalila waved.

Melvin peered up from his bowl; his eyes clouding over in confusion. Tilting his head to the side, he tentatively waved back.

"This way," said Ruth.

"See you later, Melvin," called Kalila, smiling and waving back.

Melvin clicked his tongue three times. "See you later," he repeated flatly and resumed eating.

"Morning!" greeted Felicia, stretched out on a recliner. A small pillow supported her head while the lower half of her body remained hidden under a lap blanket. "I'd get up, but Ruth's got me bundled up like a chrysalis. I've got to be the oldest damn butterfly on the planet," she jested.

"No need," laughed Kalila, making her way over to the chair to give Felicia a slight peck on the cheek. "I come bearing cookies."

"Oh. How lovely," said Felicia. Kalila opened the box for Felicia to peek inside. "My favorite."

Kalila somehow doubted that but beamed anyway.

"Sit anywhere," Felicia pointed around the room. "Usually, it's standing room only," she teased again.

Kalila chose the chair closest to Felicia. "Sorry I haven't been here before now," she said, "but things have gotten hectic since Bashir's—" She didn't feel right saying *the funeral*, so she opted to breeze right past it. "Everything's been hitting me all at once, and to be honest, I'm still trying to pick up all the pieces."

"Please, no need to explain," said Felicia warmly. "I understand. Most of my days were spent in a perpetual state of blur after Bill died."

"I can so relate."

Felicia nodded. "But I will say this; that experience taught me an invaluable lesson."

"Which was?"

"That time is a great equalizer. It waits for nobody. You go through life plodding along, thinking that you'll always have time to accomplish what you've put on the back burner except that before you know it, time slips out of control and speeds ahead just when you least expect it, and by then," Felicia sighed. "By then, you're stuck on the ride from hell with no way of getting off." Her words trickled into nothingness as she stared dreamily off into the distance.

"Felicia?" whispered Ruth, observing the conversation while standing quietly off to the side.

"Huh? Oh, I'm so sorry, Kalila. I tend to get morose sometimes."

"You're fine," assured Kalila.

Ruth gently patted Felicia's shoulder. "I'll leave you two alone to catch up," she said, then asked, "Tea, Kalila?"

"Thank you. I'd love some."

"Do you prefer herb? Black? Decaf?" Ruth asked, her hand resting protectively on Felicia's shoulder. "And how do you take it?"

"Plain—no sugar or milk, and either herbal or black. No decaf. Thanks."

"You got it." Ruth crooked her head toward Felicia, still nursing her mug of tea. "How are you doing? Want a top-off?"

"No, no," said Felicia, cupping the top of her mug. "I'm still good." Felicia's eyes drifted down. "Oh! Did you see what Kalila brought us?" she asked, pointing to the box of cookies resting on her lap.

"I certainly did." Ruth slightly lifted the corner top to steal a quick peek. "Oh, I love these. May I?"

"Please," encouraged Kalila, relieved she'd selected the right ones. "I brought enough for everyone."

Ruth raised the box to her face and took a whiff. Her eyes fluttered to the ceiling. "That smell. I wish they could bottle it," she said, making her selection. "I'll ask Melvin if he wants some." Ruth placed the opened box on the coffee table and left the two women alone. Felicia, never one to mince words, seized the moment. "So, I assume Hamza told you?"

Kalila shrank back in her chair some, sighing. "Only bits and pieces, but enough to know it's extremely dire." Kalila, also not one to mince her words, continued. "He also told me that when the time comes, you intend on going to—Hamza called it *a place*, but I'm assuming hospice care?"

"I prefer Hamza's word 'place' better, but yes, hospice. It seems checkout time is around the corner. Time to skedaddle." Felicia cleared her throat, pointing to the cookie box. "Would you mind handing me one of those? The chocolate rainbow kind. I love 'em."

Leaning forward, Kalila held the box open for Felicia so she could select the cookie she wanted. Kalila recalled, just before her own mother passed, how important it had been for her to retain the dignity of making even the smallest of decisions.

"Here," Kalila said, placing the cookie on the extra wax paper the bakery had laid on top.

"Ah, thank you." Felicia opened her mouth but only wide enough to manage a small nibble. "Perfect," she mumbled, winking appreciatively. "Big bites cause me horrendous coughing fits," she said, noticing Kalila's disconcerted expression. "The chocolate is the best part." Closing her eyes, Felicia nodded her approval. "Delicious," she moaned in delight.

Kalila picked out a cookie for herself and bit down. "Hmm. You're right. They are pretty good."

"The best." Felicia dabbed her lips with her napkin. "Now, where were we?"

"The hospice."

"Ah yes, how could I forget?" Felicia's face saddened. "It's the building directly across from that new smoothie bar on Main Street."

Kalila furrowed her brow, trying to place it.

"I'm sure you've seen it a hundred times but never noticed it before. It's been there for years."

Kalila still looked puzzled.

"It's got a donut shop on the corner—what's it called? Some silly name. Ah!" Felicia snapped her fingers. "I remember now. *A Hole in One*. There's a stupid guy on the sign golfing using a donut instead of a ball. Dumbest thing ever."

Kalila laughed.

"There's also a small hotel clear on the other side and a dry cleaner. Sam's, I think."

Kalila nodded. "Okay, I know where you mean. A newish looking brick building."

"Yep. A nice enough place to croak in." Felicia lifted the cookie to her lips for another nibble; her demeanor somber. "They gave me the royal tour. The place has great windows."

"Would you rather stay here?" asked Kalila, ignoring the sardonic witticisms.

"Here? At the house?"

"Sure. We were able to keep my mom home. Actually, at my sister's place."

"Did hospice help you?"

"Don't quote me, but if I'm correct, while hospice isn't around the clock care, I'm pretty sure their services are 24/7 if you need them. But again, this was a while ago."

"Interesting."

"You know what? I do remember my mother's caseworker at the house a lot. There were actually two—one spotted the other."

Felicia stopped nibbling and placed the remainder of her barely eaten cookie on the wax paper. "In hindsight, do you think your mother's decision to stay home was the best for everyone or would you have preferred the hospice?"

"Everyone's needs are different," explained Kalila. "But yes, in hindsight, I think for my mom at least, being home was the best choice. Besides my siblings, my dad was there round-the-clock. Of course, we tried taking turns spotting him whenever we could to give him time to rest."

Kalila had been close to her mother and had taken her death extremely hard. For quite some time afterward, depression had set in, accompanied by a series of risky life choices; many of which merged into dangerous results.

"Her team—I include her doctors and nurses—they were all great," confided Kalila. "Incredibly supportive. They taught us what we needed to know to take care of mom and keep her as comfortable as possible. They were even with us when she—" again, Kalila felt compelled to search for another word in place of dying. "Passed."

"Ah, yes, well, I'm afraid any extended family is either long gone or far away, and Melvin isn't exactly equipped to carry that load on his own."

"I understand," Kalila nodded, but her mind had already begun formulating another idea. But she'd wait to speak with Ruth first, not wanting to get Felicia's hopes high if she couldn't come through. "Does Melvin understand what's going on?"

"To some extent. Ruth's been explaining it to him a little at a time. I tried to but couldn't figure out a way to explain it without scaring him to death. He just doesn't do well with change." Feeling mildly winded, Felicia gasped, trying to catch her breath.

Kalila gripped the chair arm, remembering how her mother had also strained taking her last breaths. Each one harder than the last.

"I'm not sure Melvin understands even now," said Felicia. "I didn't know how to explain it to him, so I let him keep using the sleep analogy. Not the brightest move, trust me. For weeks, he just kept asking over and over again when his father would wake up. Broke my heart. I sure dropped the ball on that one big time."

"It's not easy to describe. I know I haven't done the greatest job explaining everything to Hamza."

"I assume he's still taking his dad's death pretty hard?"

"Oh, for sure. For a while, he barely spoke to me. I think my son blames me."

"Oh, I doubt that. Children just need time to process."

Kalila hoped so. "I have to tell you; I'm truly delighted Hamza and Melvin are friends. Melvin's had a real calming effect on Hamza. More than me."

Felicia chuckled. "Well, Melvin, as you probably know, doesn't just march to the tune of his own drum. No, that boy of mine has an entire damn band," she winced from the pain. "Hold on—give me a second. Ruth!" Felicia called. "Can you come here a minute, please? I need some assistance."

"Can I help?" asked Kalila.

"No, don't be silly. Stay put. Ruth!"

"Coming," Ruth answered from somewhere in the house.

Felicia shifted slightly in her chair. Scooting her frail body under the comforter.

"Is there anything I can do or get you?"

"No dear. Ruth's got a system. She'll be here lickety-split." After fussing with the pillow, Felicia leaned back. "Ah, that's better. Sometimes the old bones complain too much," she said, slapping her palms on her lap. "Now what was I saying? —Ah yes," Felicia said, lifting a long bony finger in the air. "Melvin. Personally, I think those two get along as well as they do because Hamza has always accepted Melvin in the package he came in. And Melvin? He accepts everyone's packages; makes him no mind. I'll tell you, Kalila, I wish more people understood that about him instead of teasing and calling him names. I hate when they make him feel like he's some kind of freak." Felicia's eyes shifted towards the front window of the house directly across from hers.

"Has that happened a lot?"

"Sure has. Some people aren't right. Just mean to the core. Accusing Melvin of stuff—terrible, terrible stuff he never did or would never think of ever doing." Felicia's gazed rested on Kalila. "Not like your son. Hamza's a gem. He's got a good heart, that kid of yours," she added.

Kalila beamed. "He actually came home pretty upset last night when he found out Melvin won't be able to stay here after—"

"Yes," Felicia interjected, saving Kalila from her obviously uncomfortable word search again. "Well, I'm afraid that's true. While Melvin is independent in so many ways, he still needs supervision. He knows how to make his meals, does his own laundry, and nobody can clean up like him, but shopping—paying bills, doctor appointments, and whatnot—he can't do that on his own. Somebody will need to be around to keep an eye out on him, at least for part of the day, but especially during the night time." Felicia wrung the tissue still clenched in her other hand.

"Here we go," Ruth said, placing a small tray of tea on the table. "Kalila?" she offered. "It's hot." Ruth pulled a medicine bottle out of her sweater pocket and popped it open, handing Felicia two tiny tablets and a half-full cup of water. A straw was already propped inside. "When you're ready," she reminded Felicia.

"Come, sit with us, Ruth," instructed Felicia after chugging down the meds. "We were just discussing Melvin."

"Ah." Ruth sat on the couch across from both women.

"By the way, asked Felicia conspiratorially. "Where is he? I don't want him hearing us discuss him."

"In his room making his bed when I last checked, but his door's closed."

"You see?" Felicia winked at Kalila. "Independent. Always was."

Kalila smiled and faced Ruth. "I was just telling Felicia how upset Hamza was last night about Melvin not being able to live here anymore." Kalila decided not to specifically mention Ruth's talk with Hamza, although she hadn't appreciated Ruth taking the liberty of speaking to Hamza without her prior consent. "They've been best buds for like—" Kalila glanced at Felicia and shrugged, "since we moved here, right?"

"Yes," agreed Felicia. "Just about. They act more like brothers than friends."

Ruth smiled. "Anyone watching them together would have come to the same conclusion."

"Which is kind of another reason for my visit." Kalila's heart raced. She shifted in her seat. "I wanted to talk to you, well, actually, I wanted to run something by you."

Both women waited, watching Kalila continue to fidget and fret.

"Just spit it out dear," prodded Felicia. "I'm on a time clock over here."

Ruth smirked, apparently much more accustomed to Felicia's gallows humor than Kalila, who appeared slightly uncomfortable. "You really need to stop doing that, Felicia," Ruth admonished Felicia goodheartedly, her chin jutting toward Kalila. "Look at what you did to the poor girl."

Kalila chuckled, rubbing her clammy palms on her lap, all while nervously hooking her feet around the spindly leg of the chair. "To be honest, I feel incredibly stupid right now even bothering you about this, but I promised Hamza I'd ask. I'm not even sure I have what it takes to make it happen."

"Bothering me about what? Make what happen?" asked Felicia, shooting Ruth a raised eyebrow. Ruth shrugged, offering up an equally as bewildered shoulder-shrug in return.

Kalila smoothed down her already flat skirt, regretting that she had agreed to this—and acutely aware of how easily what she proposed could be misconstrued as a vulgar intrusion. Nevertheless, she continued, heart racing. "I know I have no right to ask this, and please, if you think I'm being presumptuous, tell me to shut up and leave." Kalila's stomach clenched. "But would you consider allowing Melvin to stay with us? To live, I mean. Not now but afterward, of course."

Way to go.

Kalila's cheeks flushed.

Brilliant delivery.

Felicia's gaping puzzled look matched Ruth's astonishment. The two women swapped a series of furtive glances between them before staring at Kalila together.

"You would really take Melvin on?" asked Ruth calmly. "Into your home to live?"

"Yes." Kalila nodded. "It's just Hamza and me now. We talked it over and agreed that we'd love for Melvin to join our family—only if you're okay with it, Felicia."

Felicia's eyes softened, radiating high spirits. "That's quite a generous offer," she said, tempering her obvious enthusiasm against reality. "Melvin's a wonderful son, but it's only fair to tell you, he's no kid despite, well, you know. Let's just say he's set in his ways and doesn't always do well with change."

"I understand," agreed Kalila.

Felicia stared at Ruth, still somewhat reserved.

"Are you sure you understand what this would entail?" asked Ruth, blown away by Kalila's generosity.

"Not really," admitted Kalila, "but we adore Melvin. Hamza loves him. The thought of Melvin living far away with a bunch of strangers is—" she cringed, "upsetting."

"I can certainly agree with that," said Felicia. "I've been dreading sending him to one of those places his entire life."

Kalila glanced from Ruth to Felicia. "I don't expect an answer right away," she said. "I know this all came out of left field and honestly, who am I to throw a monkey wrench into the mix so late in the decision-making process. Please don't feel pressured to agree. My feelings won't be hurt. And no matter what you ultimately decide, Hamza and I will always look out for Melvin."

Felicia dabbed her cheek with a tissue. "This is one of the kindest things anybody has ever offered to do for us. For him," she murmured, eyes glistening with tears.

Ruth, whose cheeks were equally as moist, swooped to Felicia's side and hugged her, handing Felicia a fresh tissue from the box, before retrieving one for herself. "I agree. This is beyond kind," she added.

Kalila rose to her feet. "I promised I'd only stay for a short time," she said, winking at Ruth. "I better get going."

"Kalila." Felicia reached out to hold Kalila's hand. "Let me discuss this with Melvin, and see what he wants to do." She choked up. "I'm just grateful my son now has a choice."

Kalila squeezed Felicia's hand gently before leaning over to kiss her cheek.

"Let me walk you to the door," offered Ruth.

"That's okay. I can find my way out."

***

Ruth

After the door closed, Felicia turned to Ruth, eyes wide, wet, and glistening with the prospect of hope. "Tell me, what do you think," she asked Ruth, her voice quivering despite the optimism.

"I'm not sure, to tell you the truth. I don't know Kalila—or Hamza for that matter. Not like you do. The better question is, what do you think? Is this something you believe Melvin would embrace, and if so, do you think they could make it work?"

Felicia grinned. "I think you already know my answer," she said. "Heck, I've been praying for an alternative to sending him off to that place, for months. I'd almost given up hope, God forgive me."

"I know."

"Can we make it happen? I mean legally—if Melvin chooses to live with them?"

"That's up to you and Melvin," explained Ruth. "Undoubtedly, it will require extensive paperwork, a bunch of legal stuff, securing Melvin's financial support from the state and with what you and your husband have entrusted for him. It's a lot, and to be honest, I'm not sure where to begin."

Felicia's excitement started to crumble.

"No, don't do that!" Ruth admonished. "I said it's a lot, I didn't say it was impossible. If this is something you and Melvin want, then I'll advocate for you both to make it happen. Whatever it takes."

"Thank you, my friend," said Felicia, who hadn't looked this happy in months. "You're a Godsend."

Ruth gently hugged her friend, sniffling back her own tears.

"And I promise not to rub it in your face," teased Felicia.

"Rub what in my face?" Ruth asked.

"How I told you miracles existed." There was no hiding the self-satisfied grin spreading ear to ear across Felicia's face.

Ruth smirked. "Yes. You certainly did indeed," she agreed. While not nearly as persuaded as her friend that the Rahims would be the best choice for Melvin, she was committed to moving mountains to make it happen if that's what Melvin wanted.

CHAPTER 25

Deranged

Friday Evening

ANY *MASJID* COMMUNITY GATHERING where the consumption of food is involved is always packed to the rafters. By the size of the crowd, tonight would be no different. The parking lot overflowed with cars, many of which were jammed into every conceivable space, legally or not.

As soon as Kalila parked, teenage boys surrounded her car, tapping and waving through the glass. Hamza's crew, anxious for him to hang out.

"Go ahead, but stay inside or over there," Kalila pointed. "Don't go anywhere else."

Hamza readily agreed and bolted. The comradery and loud laughter emanating from their small group made Kalila smile. Seeing Hamza behaving carefree, joking around with his friends had also improved her spirits, but in many ways, she had Melvin to thank for the change.

Her first clue arrived earlier in the day when she picked Hamza up from school.

"Did you speak to Mrs. Vine yet?" her son asked as soon as he got in the car. Hamza kept wiggling in his seat, apparently unable to sit still. His voice held no mockery or pending sarcasm. Nor did his face, usually set in a permanent scowl.

"*As salaamu alaikum* son," cautioned Kalila, more as a reminder than greeting.

"Sorry. *Wa alaikum salaam*, Mom."

"Close the door before the cars behind me lose it."

Hamza did as he was told.

"How was your day?" she asked, taking her time to answer him and having a little fun at his expense.

"All right."

"Homework?"

"Just history. I have to write a stupid, two-page paper about the three branches of government," he complained, "but it's not due until next Thursday."

"That doesn't sound stupid to me."

"But I already know this stuff, like since third grade."

"Then you shouldn't have a problem writing the paper," Kalila shot Hamza a smirk, prompting an indulgent chuckle in return.

"Well?" he said, buckling into his seatbelt.

"Well what?" she asked, feigning dipsy ignorance.

"Come on, Ma, stop playing. Did you speak to Mrs. Vine yet?"

"I did."

Hamza's eyes grew wide with anticipation. "And? What did she say?"

"We had a lovely talk."

"Ma!" yelped Hamza, lips pouting.

"Okay, fine," she laughed. "Mrs. Vine said she'd discuss our proposal with Melvin.

"Yes!" shouted Hamza, awkwardly stretching to throw his arms around his mother's neck.

"Hamza! Stop! I'm driving," she chastised, but only half meaning it. "And please remember, this is an important decision. His mother wants to give him an opportunity to decide what he wants to do."

"Thank you so much, Ma," he said, rubbing his hands together.

"Hold up. That wasn't a yes or a no."

"I know."

"And don't forget about what we agreed to. This is Melvin's choice. If he decides not to live with us—for whatever the reason–
–you promised not to get mad or upset with him, or anybody else."

Especially me.

"I know—I won't."

"I'm serious, honey. I know Melvin's your friend; I like him as well, but he's also a grown adult who has the right to make his own decisions."

"I know, but he's going to pick us. I'm sure of it."

Kalila, not nearly as convinced of the outcome as her son, would be damned to be the one to extinguish his hopes, at least not until she had to. "Well, let's see what happens first, but at least now Melvin has a choice." Kalila smiled when she repeated Felicia's comment. Felicia had been right. For many people, having choices were the norm, something they anticipated, while for others like Melvin, options remain an enigma, often out of reach and expectation.

Kalila pulled into the driveway. After getting stuck in afternoon traffic, the pair had to dash around only to head right back out. "Hurry up. Go get washed so we can get over to the *masjid*," Kalila said, rushed.

"Okay!" Hamza scrambled up the stairs two at a time. "Can I bring my football?" he shouted from the top step.

"No!"

"Aw…"

***

Despite being a relatively small Muslim community, they were indeed an affluent one, able to afford a lovely building equipped with many extra amenities, including a modern cafeteria which seated everyone comfortably.

Bidding Hamza and his friends goodbye, Kalila wound her way through a crowd of folks going in and out of the building. Upon entering the cafeteria, she immediately caught sight of Walaa and Nafiza, already indulging in a plate of food. She waved.

"*As salaamu alaikum!*" They both mouthed back, gesturing her to join them. Nafiza lifted her bag off the chair next to hers, so Kalila had someplace to sit.

"That looks so good," said Kalila eyeing their plates, famished. The incredible aroma emanating from the kitchen made her stomach growl in protest. "I'll be right back," she told them. "Can I leave this here?" she asked, indicating her bag.

Once gone, Nafiza leaned over to whisper to Walaa, "Are we still going through with this?" she asked, taking another forkful. She sat up straighter. "Oh man, this really is delicious." She mumbled, thoroughly relishing her meal.

"You bet we are," confirmed Walaa, picking up a piece of chicken daintily with two fingers. Lips parted in a half-smile, she asked, "Have I ever told you how much I love BBQ chicken?"

"Once or twice," chuckled Nafiza, mouth bursting. "Try the rice. It's to die for."

"Oh wow," Walaa moaned. "You're right. *MashaAllah*, this food is so, so good." Dabbing the corners of her mouth with a napkin, she rested her chin on her elbow and cleared her throat. In a lowered, tempered voice she whispered, "Personally, I think Kalila's going to be cool with what we propose. I'm more worried about how Amara's gonna take it."

Nafiza nodded. "Speaking of which…"

From the side entrance, carrying a large tray of food stood Amara, scanning the room like a sniper on a reconnaissance mission, looking ready to pick a fight.

"Take this," she ordered, pawning off the food on the first unsuspecting person walking past. "Bring it to the kitchen," she barked, shoving the tray into the reluctant girl's arms. No please…no thank you…no nothing.

"Did you see that?" prodded Nafiza, her chin jutted in Amara's direction. "She's unbelievable."

"Never fails to disappoint, does she?" mumbled Walaa, lips twisted, equally as appalled.

From across the room, Amara—apparently beyond livid about something—caught Walaa's attention and scowled. Walaa's half-hearted wave was met by Amara first holding up a finger indicating she needed a minute, and then with her taking off in a heated march, huffing past the entryway into the women's prayer area. She even dared to slam the door behind her.

"Whoa," said Walaa, smacking her forehead. "What the heck was that all about?" she asked, munching on few salty chips.

"I have no idea, but if looks could kill, she'd be runner-up for Lizzie Borden's stand-in. Wait—are you eating chips?"

Walaa shouldn't have, but she laughed. "Yup."

"Are you?"

"I think so."

"Does Talib know?"

"Not yet."

"Walaa!"

Walaa laughed again. "I plan on telling him later tonight." Walaa rubbed her belly protectively. "You know, on second thought, we may not want to broach Amara with this tonight. It may not be safe."

"If you want, I'll keep her busy if she decides to come over, or I'll speak to Kalila while you keep Amara busy. Pick your poison."

"I'll take Kalila over Amara any day," said Walaa emphatically.

"As you wish, but truthfully, it makes me no mind."

"Why is that?"

"Because I don't think either one is ready to make peace."

"Then why are we going through with this?" Walaa blurted out, eyeing Nafiza up and down. "I thought you agreed this was a good idea."

"I did, in the beginning, but to be honest, after watching those two go at it, I'm not entirely sure we should interfere."

"We could at least try."

"Why? So they can both be mad at us?"

Just then, Kalila returned to the table victorious, coddling a full plate of food and a bottle of water. "This looks delicious," she cooed, plopping down in the chair next to Nafiza, ready to dig in.

Walaa raised an eyebrow at Nafiza, who in turn, shot her a double eyebrow raise along with a quick—*not yet* head shake.

Walaa upped Nafiza's—*not yet* head shake by rapidly nodding, *yes*.

"Okay you two, what's going on," Kalila asked. Her eyes darting between the two women as she cautiously nibbled her naan.

Nafiza, lips pursed, crossed her arms over her chest. "Well, you might as well," she said, her comment directed at Walaa.

"Might as well what?" asked Kalila, amid a mid-chew. "Okay. What's happened now?" Kalila's shoulders tensed, stiffening in full panic mode.

"No, no. Relax. Nothing's happened," comforted Walaa, quick to rub Kalila's back assuredly, cutting Nafiza a sneer with her eyes. "I just wanted to talk to you about—"

Kalila's brows furrowed waiting for the next shoe to drop. when she noticed the two-empty bag of chips. "Are you?"

"What is it with you two? Can't a girl eat a darn chip unless she's pregnant?" joked Walaa.

"She is," confirmed Nafiza, winking.

"*Alhamdulillah!*" shouted Kalila. "That's wonderful news!"

Walaa grinned. "Thanks, but that's not exactly what I wanted to talk to you about, thank you, Nafiza."

Kalila looked sufficiently confused.

"Here's the thing. We wanted to know if there is anything we can do to help put this—what would you call this thing between Kalila and Amara?" Walaa asked Nafiza, "A fight? An argument? Dispute? Quarrel?"

"How about feud?" blurted Nafiza.

Walaa indulgently nodded along.

"*Feud* works for me," interjected Kalila, chewing.

"Fine, feud it is." Walaa conceded. "Call it anything you two want, but it's gone on for too long."

"I agree," admitted Kalila, dabbing her mouth with a napkin. "Honestly, I'm at a loss. Amara's had it out for me since the day I moved here."

"She's got it out for everybody," piped in Nafiza. "You're just her latest target."

"She's like a viper on steroids," jested Kalila, feigning fangs. Nafiza laughed. Walaa did not.

"Regardless, you two," interrupted Walaa taking on her mother hen intonation. "Now the kids are involved. It's got to stop."

Kalila and Nafiza stopped giggling and fixed their faces.

"You're right. I agree. What do you propose?" asked Kalila.

Walaa shifted slightly in her chair. "We thought that—"

"Mostly her," quipped Nafiza, nudging Kalila with an elbow.

"Fine, mostly *me*," corrected Walaa dramatically, "that perhaps we could hold an intervention."

"Intervention?" echoed Kalila, perplexed.

"More like an incursion," quipped Nafiza.

"No! More like a conversation—" Walaa huffed to clear the air, reaching for another bag of chips.

"With who?" asked Kalila. "The Imam?"

"No, the four of us. You, me, Nafiza and Amara." Walaa chewed. "Throw everything on the table and end this—um…"

"Feud," interjected Nafiza.

"Feud. Yes, thank you." Walaa bowed her head majestically toward Nafiza.

Kalila looked at the two women who seemed genuinely sincere to help. Although she hadn't shared her plans to move, she had to admit, it would be nice not having to go head-to-toe with Amara all the time.

"I'm in," Kalila said. "Let me know when and where, although I'd prefer not here. I'd like to keep this as private as possible. Plus, you know how loud Amara gets."

"Fine," agreed Walaa. "We could do it at my house while the kids and hubby are out. Keep it in a neutral place."

"That works for me." Kalila bit into her bread.

"And me," agreed Nafiza just as something caught her attention. "Uh oh," she muttered, jutting her chin to the doorway.

"What?" chorused Kalila and Walaa, following Nafiza's line of sight.

"Here she comes." Nafiza braced herself for the onslaught.

"*As salaamu alaikum,*" greeted Amara, blatantly ignoring Kalila. Without asking, she commandeered a chair from another table and slid it over, but inexplicably chose to remain standing. "Kalila, I'm surprised you've decided to show your face," she goaded.

Kalila, refusing to take the bait, continued eating.

The tension around the table rose, "It's sure packed tonight," Amara said, pretending to glance around. "Is your boyfriend here, too?" she taunted, glaring directly down at Kalila.

Kalila put her fork down. Then, with the corner of her napkin, dabbed her lips, staring challengingly at Amara. "And who said he wasn't?"

That's all it took.

"You manipulative—lowlife—scheming *bitch*!" accused Amara, yelling at the top of her lungs, and not caring who heard her.

Within seconds, the entire cafeteria fell dead silent. All eyes zeroed in on the mayhem about to be unleashed.

"I am *so* going to kick your ass," threatened Amara, jaw clenched, shoving the table forward and knocking Kalila's water bottle over.

Walaa leaped to her feet trying to grab hold of it before it spilled and splashed across the floor, but missed.

Nafiza rose, placing her body between Amara and Kalila. "Don't do this," she warned.

Kalila rose from her seat, brandishing her plastic fork like a sword. "Leave me alone. I swear it."

Amara kicked a chair over. "Don't you dare tell me what to do."

Nafiza threw her hands up to block Amara from being able to push forward.

"Get out of my way, Nafiza," Amara threatened, "or I'll beat your ass, next."

Bystanders at the far side of the room stretched their necks to search for those responsible for causing the racket.

"Uh, Qasim," nudged a guy nearby. "I think it's your wife."

Qasim muttered something unintelligible as he hightailed it across the room to rein his wife in.

Hamza, about to make his plate, realized his mother was under attack and came sprinting from the opposite direction.

Imam Abdullah, currently enjoying a meal and conversation with brother Talib, jumped to his feet, furious when he saw Nafiza waving her hands in the air, attempting to fend off an attack. "*Astaghfirullah.*"

"Walaa," muttered Talib at the same time. The two men darted across the cafeteria to break up the fight.

Blinking back angry tears, Kalila faced Amara, reluctant to say or do anything else to egg the crazy woman on, but then again, Amara didn't need provocation.

"I know all about you," seethed Amara, flicking her pointer finger in Kalila's face. "No use pretending. I saw you and your *boyfriend…*" She made sure to enunciate the word, *boyfriend*, so the entire room heard. "I saw you two at the—"

But before Amara had a chance to finish, Qasim grabbed her arm from behind. "Enough!"

"Leave me alone!"

"Stop this."

Amara tried tugging her wrist from her husband's firm grip. "Why should I?" she screamed, turning her unbridled fury on him. Slapping and pushing him with both hands; pelting him on the shoulder, the face—anywhere she could land a blow.

Ducking and bobbing, Qasim somehow managed to snatch Amara by both wrists. "Just stop it," he ordered, his stern face already sporting a few red welts from where a couple of his wife's wallops landed. But Amara refused to stop.

Hamza wedged himself between his mother and Amara. "Leave her alone," he screamed bravely, but his shouts were all but drowned out by Amara's hysteria.

"Move out of the way little boy," Amara threatened.

Kalila snatched Hamza by the shoulders and shoved him protectively behind her.

Qasim shook Amara by the wrists. "Would you calm down!"

"Let go of me," Amara shrieked, trying to bite Qasim's hand. "I'm not stupid," she snarled. "I know what you two are up to."

Hamza's head recoiled, but Kalila wouldn't take her eyes off her attacker, and failed to notice.

"Come on." Walaa tugged Kalila by the arm. "Let's get out of here," she coaxed, trying to drag her away, but Kalila refused to budge.

"Run you, sneaky little bitch," taunted Amara, unable to jerk her wrists free from Qasim's tight grip. "Go on—listen to Walaa," she ridiculed. "Go hide. Slither back under your rock. Nobody wants you here."

"Stop this, Amara. You're making a fool of yourself," said Qasim, but his wife refused to comply.

Somehow, Qasim managed to yank Amara forward, but when he pulled, she let her legs go limp, sending the two of them plummeting to the floor in a heap.

"Damn it!" he blurted out, stepping on Amara's hand.

Amara yelped, and struggled to stand, but wound up sliding on spilled water instead. Then she tripped backward over a chair, bouncing off Qasim, which caused her to land flat on her back with her thick legs sprawled wide open. By this point, her black overgarment somehow managed to bunch up around her waist, exposing what could only be described as a less than attractive pair of granny panties, complimented by a pair of ratty white, red-rimmed tube socks.

Most of the room either collectively gasped in horror or turned their faces away in disbelief. A group of giggling, persnickety teenagers, thoroughly entertained by the Keystone Cop madness, attempted to move in closer with their phones. Busy recording the entire, humiliating debacle, while others gleefully snapped photo after photo, anxious to be the first to upload the hilarity on social media.

"Stand up," Qasim demanded, now squarely on his feet, fuming. "I mean it. Now!"

"No!" screamed Amara back, drool running down her chin. "She's ruining our lives!"

"Let's go!" Qasim yelled, dragging his combative wife out by the arm.

Everyone else pretty much lingered off to the side out of the way. Some chose to move in closer to gawk, but Amara didn't care, nor would she stop shouting.

"Play as innocent and helpless as you want, Kalila," Amara yelled over her shoulder, "but you're nothing but a two-bit whore and I got the proof!"

Kalila's cheeks turned scarlet red. Glancing around the stunned room, she saw how the younger children huddled close to their mothers, while the amused teens milled about—making hushed snide comments. A few of the families clustered together appeared uncertain whether to stay or leave.

Humilated and overwhelmed, Kalila remained frozen in place, unable to move until she heard what sounded like high-pitched laughter coming from a group of women.

Amara's friends.

"You find this funny?" she screamed at the brash of gaggling offenders.

"Take Kalila out," order Imam Abdullah to Nafiza.

"Shut your stupid mouths," Kalila yelled at the women. "All of you!"

"Take her to my office," barked the Imam at Nafiza. "Drag her if you have to. I'll be there in a minute."

Abdullah leaned into Nafiza as she brushed past him. "Is this what you think *staying above the fray* means?"

"I—"

"I asked you for one favor. Just one," he muttered.

"I know." Nafiza lowered her gaze, regretful.

"You could have gotten hurt," he said, frowning.

"But I can explain—" But Abdullah wasn't listening, turning his attention to the uproar. "Not now. I need to get this mess under control first. Now go," he snapped.

Talib, equally as exasperated, pointed at his wife. "Go with Nafiza," he told an already guilt-ridden Walaa.

Nafiza snatched her and Kalila's bags and joined Walaa, already clutching one of Kalila's elbows. The women led her forward, straight out of the cafeteria and away from the gawking crowd. They could still hear Amara yelling, while bracing her body in the door frame, refusing to be huddled out of the side exit before she got in one last condemnation.

"You're a whore!" Amara yelled, screaming at the top of her lungs. "And now everybody knows it!"

What a scene. Many families had already begun to pack up their belongings and collect their children, ready to call it a night. A couple of Amara's groupies, the same ones laughing a moment before, shot Kalila malicious daggers as she passed.

"Just ignore them and keep walking," ordered Walaa, guiding Kalila out of the room.

As the three women pressed through the crowd, Kalila caught sight of Hamza off to the side, and sandwiched between a few of his friends. His face a mixture of concern and embarrassment.

"Meet me at the car," Kalila ordered. "I'll be there in a minute."

Nafiza followed the women in and slammed the office door closed.

Kalila snatched her arm out of Walaa's grip. "You all saw that, right! I didn't do a damn thing to that crazy bitch and look what she did."

Walaa sat down and pushed an empty chair over.

"No. I'm not staying," roared Kalila, refusing the offered seat. "I've had enough of her and this place."

But Walaa couldn't leave well enough alone. "Why did she do that?"

"How the hell would I know?" screamed Kalila.

"You've got no idea why she turned on you like that?"

"None," Kalila snapped back, pacing.

Nafiza, standing to the side rolled her eyes, seriously doubting that.

Kalila moved towards the door. "But for the record, I would have tried to work things out with her, but you can forget it now. All bets off. I don't want to hear another thing about making peace with my fellow Muslim sister bullshit. Not after that scene."

"*Kalila—*"

"No, Walaa. Save it. I don't want to hear it from you," she yelled. "Or you," Kalila said pointing a finger at Nafiza, already backing out of the way with her hands thrown up in the air in surrender. "And certainly, *nothing* from you!" Kalila roared at the Imam who had just managed to step inside the office. "I'm done playing nice." She snatched her bag from Nafiza. "Amara's going to be sorry she ever decided to screw with me," she sputtered, pushing past the Imam, and out the door.

Walaa stared down at her feet, powerless to offer a retort.

Furious, Imam Abdullah stared at his wife.

Nafiza, unable to stop herself, shrugged. "Well, that certainly didn't go as planned."

***

Barely able to contain her rage, Kalila ordered Hamza into the car. "Get in and don't you dare open your mouth."

Hamza slid into the seat. He buckled up, too embarrassed to say a word.

"I've had it with that nutcase," Kalila hissed. "Always something. I'm going to make her regret she ever fucked with me."

Eyes watering, Hamza looked away, spending the remainder of the ride home leaning on the window, staring off into space.

Once home, the two parted to their separate corners of the house. Hamza darted up to his bedroom and locked the door behind him, while Kalila, in a fit of rage, stormed into the house muttering—beyond pissed off.

"Every single damn time," Kalila grumbled, "Without fail. That stupid bitch starts some shit with me." Her mouth twisted into a scowl. Adrenaline kept her moving, clomping from room to room with no mission except to rant.

"She's so demented, I swear!" Kalila chucked a wet dishrag at the sink. "If only she knew her husband asked me to marry him, she'd really lose her shit—"

Kalila stopped-full brake-midsentence, allowing that thought to sink in. Then she pulled her phone out of her pocket and began texting.

> *As salaamu alaikum Brother Qasim. Sorry to contact you so late, especially after what happened tonight, but I've been giving your proposal a lot of thought. I'll be home tomorrow for the Open House. If you're still interested and you have time, I'd like you to stop by so we can discuss it further. Salaams, Kalila.*

"You should have left me alone, Amara," she muttered bitterly, right before pushing SEND.

CHAPTER 26

Trading Places

Kalila

KALILA MADE ONE FINAL walkthrough. The house looked perfectly staged and ready to present, as per Bonnie's instructions.

Kalila nervously restraightened a vase, fluffed an already fluffy pillow, and put a new bag in the garbage pail under the sink even though the old one was practically empty. As a final touch, she lit a vanilla candle on the stove to add a homey aroma to the place.

Bonnie had called earlier that morning, letting Kalila know to expect an excellent turnout. Quite a few promising inquiries from off the website had made appointments, making for a high probability of finding a buyer by the end of the day. Kalila hoped Bonnie's prediction came to fruition. Anything to get as far away as humanly possible from that nutcase across the street.

Hamza planned on spending the day hanging out with Melvin, but Kalila heard him upstairs taking his time, despite being explicitly told to be done and out.

A knock at the door caused Kalila's heart to jump.

Here we go—

Qasim tensed, clearly as nervous as her. Maybe more so.

Kalila opened the door. *"As salaamu alaikum."*

"*Wa alaikum salaam.*" Qasim's arms remained stoically at his side.

Kalila stepped out and closed the front door behind her. "Let's talk outside in the garage where we can't be overheard."

"I'm assuming you've asked me here to decline my offer of marriage," Qasim shrugged, defeated. "I fully understand, especially after what Amara pulled. I'm truly sorry about that, by the way."

"Please, don't apologize. That wasn't your fault, although I do have a question." Kalila tilted her head demurely, looking at Qasim expectantly.

"Ah, sure—"

"Did you tell Amara about your proposal?"

"Not at all. Not a word, which made her outburst last night all the more unexpected."

This pleased Kalila, but for all the morally reprehensible reasons.

Payback's a bitch.

Kalila only hoped she'd be around when Amara heard the bombshell news, but for now, she had to play her role.

"I'm so sorry sister Amara got upset yesterday," she said. "I'll keep her in my prayers. I'll ask Allah, The Most Merciful to soften her heart, so she'll eventually accept me into her life—not only as her sister but as her co-wife." Kalila gazed into Qasim's eyes, gauging his response.

Qasim leaned against the wall. "I'm sorry, what?" He looked downright confused.

Kalila feigned bashfulness. "Oh wow…did I misread you? I'm so embarrassed," she said, turning her face away. "I was under the impression that you still wanted to marry me." Kalila lowered her eyes. "Or did last night change your mind?"

"No! I didn't change *my* mind. I thought you did." Qasim's entire demeanor changed in a flash. "When you texted me, I didn't think, you know, that you'd say yes."

Kalila gave him her warmest, most ingratiating smile.

No longer crushed, Qasim stood tall, grinning like a man who had just been thrown a life jacket.

"No…I didn't change my mind at all. *Alhamdulillah,"* she smiled. "I guess we should discuss our future then?" Kalila said, ready to implement the next phase of her plan.

"Kalila!"

"Oh, my realtor is here. I should go speak to her." Kalila greeted Bonnie like a long-lost friend, then waved Qasim over. "Qasim, this is Bonnie, my realtor. Bonnie, this is my fiancé, Qasim."

Bonnie, the ever-consummate businesswoman, hid her surprise nicely. "Nice to meet you," she said, grinning like a Cheshire Cat. Turning to Kalila. "If all goes as well as I'm anticipating, I think we'll get this house off the market by the end of the day."

"That's fantastic!" said Kalila who could see Qasim's wheels turning…

"Excuse me, but can I talk to you for a minute," Qasim asked Kalila. "I just need to speak to my fiancé for a second," he said politely to Bonnie, who responded with a gracious smile in return.

"What's up?" whispered Kalila, hoping to hear what she prayed he'd say.

"Listen, I'm not sure what you owe on the house, but moving forward, you and Hamza will be my responsibility. How would you feel if I take the house off the market, and take over the bills, whatever they are? At least until we decide what we want to do."

BINGO!

"Really?" Kalila's voice overflowed with appreciation. "Do you mean it?" she asked with just enough lilt to parody a Southern Belle, but Qasim, her Knight in Shining Bank Accounts, neither noticed nor cared; undoubtedly starving for some show of gratitude after living with that ungrateful wench of a wife.

"Let me speak to Bonnie," said Qasim helpfully. "I'll make sure she's adequately compensated for her time, so there's no hard feelings."

"But I feel so bad, though."

"Not to worry." Then an idea flashed across Qasim's face. "You know what? I've got a building I've been meaning to put on the market for the longest," he said. "I'm sure Bonnie's just the person to handle that for me," said Qasim, always the consummate businessman. "I'll go talk to her, but first, let's get that sign off the lawn."

One down. One more to go. Kalila only hoped Hamza would take the news as well.

CHAPTER 27

What If

Qasim

IT'S STRANGE HOW LIFE *changes minute by minute.*

Qasim went to bed last night convinced beyond a shadow of a doubt that Kalila would never speak to him again, no less accept his marriage proposal.

The argument with Amara on the way home after the *masjid* fiasco, had been yet another disaster. One curt retort after the next.

"Stop accusing me of lying," snapped Amara, "or backbiting. I have proof, but as usual, Sir Knight Qasim, you refuse to hear or believe it. And why you ask? Because you're a pathetic sycophant!"

Qasim's hands gripped the wheel. "You and your so-called proof. What did you do to get it? Hide in garbage cans? Sneak behind mailboxes?"

"Actually, I didn't have to do much since Kalila likes to spread her business as far and wide as her legs will go."

"You're disgusting."

"I'm disgusting?" she hissed. "I'm not the whore."

Shut up, Amara!"

"Why should I? She's destroying our marriage, and unlike you, I'm not going to help her."

Qasim had a good mind to drop Amara off at the side of the road and let her take her tirade out on the bears. "I don't care what proof you think you have. You made a fool out of yourself tonight. Shit, you made a fool out of me, and for what? To get your rocks off on Kalila? To make people dislike her? What did you think you gained by this embarrassing display except earning everyone's contempt?" His white knuckles gripped the steering wheel harder. Mind racing, he couldn't get past the level of disgrace this woman had brought to his good name. Reaching home, he swerved into their driveway and slammed on the brakes.

If she doesn't shut up—

"Not everybody's a dupe like you," she said, "you just make it look easy." Amara tore out of the car and ran into the house, leaving Qasim to face the boys.

"Well?" Qasim barked. "What are you two waiting for? Get out!" he yelled. "Go to bed. And don't let me hear either one of you tonight."

The boys didn't have to be told twice.

Qasim, still in his car fuming, tried to calm down. In his rearview mirror, he saw Kalila pulling in, and by how she and Hamza both stormed out of the car and slammed their doors, he knew their evening wasn't faring any better than his. Qasim watched Kalila stomp up the steps, practically kicking in her door.

She'll never talk to me again.

Once inside, he decided to sleep in the guest room. Qasim reached for a blanket from the bedroom closet. As he padded down the hall to the guest room, he passed his boys' room, dead silent. Amara, still in full fight mode trailed after him, tossing a notebook at his head.

"What the hell?" he yelled, catching it. "What is this?"

"The truth," she answered curtly. "Try it sometime. Let me know when you get to the part with Kalila and that guy at the hotel room."

Qasim chewed his lip, astounded by how low and vindictive Amara had become to compile such a pack of disgusting lies. Shaking his head in disgust, he tossed the book at her feet. "Save it. I'm not interested in your imaginary world."

"Suit yourself, sheep."

As Qasim slammed the office door behind her, his mobile vibrated.

Who would be messaging me this late?

Kalila.

Qasim anxiously scanned her message reading it over and over, and with each pass, his hopes sank that much further.

I hate you, Amara. I really do.

Qasim went to bed more miserable and alone than he had ever thought possible. He reluctantly texted Kalila back, agreeing to stop by in the morning to talk, dreading what he believed she had to say to him.

And then not one full day later, everything in Qasim's life changed.

***

The marriage conversation had gone surprisingly smooth. Talking with Kalila didn't cause Qasim the same level of anxiety and dread the way speaking to Amara did.

"So, you don't mind?" Kalila asked him sweetly, considerately.

Qasim appreciated how Kalila respected his feelings—a welcomed change. "Not at all. I'd prefer getting married outside of our community. It gives me time to speak with Amara before she pulls everyone into our business."

Kalila grinned.

"I know another *masjid*, not far from here where we can get married," he said. "I know the Imam."

"How do you know he'd be willing to perform our marriage?"

"He's got three wives himself."

"Ah," Kalila said, absently twisting the wedding band still worn on her finger.

Qasim peered down at her ring. "Are you sure you're ready?" he asked. "We can wait if you want to."

"What? Oh, this?" Kalila slid the band off her finger and stuck it into her pocket. "I'm fine."

They discussed a few more issues, with Kalila, in the end, volunteering to type up everything they had agreed to.

"Email me anything else you want to include in the contract before Monday," she said. "If I have anything else to discuss, can I text you or should I just wait? I don't want to cause you any more trouble with your wife."

"*You* haven't caused anything, but if you need to contact me, text me." He would guard his phone with his life if he had to.

"And you don't mind putting the honeymoon off for a while?" Kalila asked, reaching over to move a small cardboard box to the other side of the garage.

"Here, let me get that for you," offered Qasim, lifting it out of her hands. "Where do you want it?"

"Over here, please." Kalila pointed to the shelf holding other packed memories from a life she no longer recognized. "I appreciate your patience. This is going to be hard enough on Hamza without throwing that into the mix."

"What will be hard enough?" asked Hamza, standing by the garage door that led inside the house. They'd been so engrossed in their plans, neither Qasim nor Kalila had heard him enter.

Qasim shot Kalila a look of concern, not sure how much the boy had heard. "I better get going. I have a lot to get done today."

"I'll call you later," Kalila muttered. "*As salaamu alaikum*."

Qasim *salaamed* them both and left.

***

Hamza glared at his mother.

"We need to talk," she said to Hamza. "Let's go inside."

***

"You can't be serious right now, are you?" Hamza asked, as if not believing his ears.

Kalila paused.

"How can you forget about dad so fast?"

"I didn't forget about your father."

"Then why *that* guy?"

"The change will be good for all of us. You, me, even Melvin," Kalila purposely included Melvin's name hoping to score some points.

Hamza paused, confused. "What do you mean, even for Melvin?"

"For one, I won't need to work outside the house, so I'll be around more." Kalila waited to let that thought take root. "And if Melvin decides to stay with us, he'll need an adult around to help supervise. That's a reality. Secondly, we no longer have to move. Brother Qasim promised to make sure we can stay in our home."

Hamza leaned forward in his chair, resting both elbows on his knees as he rubbed his temples.

Undeterred, Kalila continued. "It's okay to be confused by all of this. It's a lot to take in at once."

Hamza tilted his head. "I'm not confused at all," he said disparagingly. "I just can't believe you'd replace dad *with him*."

"Nobody is replacing anybody."

Not the way your father did to me, anyway.

"Forget him," shouted Hamza. "We can sell the house and move someplace else. Get three bedrooms—one for Melvin."

"Hamza—"

"I don't care if you have to work. I'm not a baby. I can take care of myself."

"Hamza, please—"

"I can even get a part-time job to help out. We'll be fine."

"You don't understand—"

Hamza stopped talking and glared at his mother. "I understand," he said, whipping his long bangs away from his face.

"But I don't think you do."

"Do whatever you want," Hamza yelled, his voice booming across the room. "But don't expect me to call him dad."

"Nobody expects that."

"And he can't live here. Not in Dad's house."

At this, Kalila's ire kicked in. "Look, let's get something straight. I'm not asking you to love Qasim or call him dad or even to like him, but I am asking you to at least treat him with respect.

The same respect you'd give to, let's say, a teacher at your school, or—"

"—or like the respect between you and sister Amara?" Hamza's razor-edged tongue never took a vacation.

Kalila continued to talk over him, reluctant to get into a tit-for-tat. "I'm doing this for us."

Hamza deadpanned her.

"This will all work out. Just give it time," Kalila implored. "I promise," she said, misreading his silence. Kalila tenderly added, "I love you. I will always love you. I know it will be hard to see me with someone else, but I have room in my heart for the both of you."

Hamza's head jerked up. Without warning, he let out a viciously cold, cackling laugh so haunting that it sent goosebumps down Kalila's arms.

Kalila snapped. "Do you know how hard things have been since your father died? Do you? Of course, you don't, and you want to know why? Because I have protected you from it. Me. Not your dead father—not Melvin—not your friends—not your teachers—me!" she yelled, pointing at her chest. "I put the food on the table. I pay for the roof over your bratty head. I buy the clothes on your back. And what do I get in return? A thank you? Some appreciation? No. I get your snotty attitude and disrespect, and I've had it." Shame colored her cheeks.

Hamza guffawed loudly; proudly flaunting his causticity like a crown.

Kalila leaped to her feet. "Oh, so now you think this is funny?" she screamed, close to slapping him.

Gripping the arms of the chair, Hamza recoiled, bracing himself for impact, but without warning, his mother took her vengeance out on the table with her fist instead.

"What-do-you-want-from-me?" she yelled, punctuating each syllable with a subsequent thump. "What?"

Hamza lifted his chin, deliberately defiant.

Kalila's heart sank realizing she had pushed him away yet again.

Damn it.

"I'm sorry, okay?" she cried, her shoulders quaking. "I didn't mean it. I'm just tired." Her words tumbled out into a choppy, sloppy mess. "You don't know how hard things have been for me lately–"

Hamza's expression never changed, glaring at his mother with dead, vacant eyes.

"I'm sorry, Okay? I'm sorry about what happened to your father, but the accident wasn't my fault. I begged him not to go out that night, but he wouldn't listen. You were sleeping, and we'd been," she searched for the right way to say it, "arguing." Kalila reached out to touch Hamza's shoulder, but he flinched and jerked away.

"Damn it, Hamza. You have to stop blaming me for everything. You think I wanted any of this to happen? If you only knew what he did you'd—" The words stuck in her throat. She'd almost slipped about Alexa and the baby. "Look, I'm sorry if I've disappointed you," she sputtered, beaten. No one had the power to destroy her like this child.

Hamza's mouth twisted into a cruel and vicious scowl. "You don't have to worry about me, Ma," he said flippantly; his voice bursting with sarcasm. "You didn't disappoint me because I never gave you that much credit to begin with."

Kalila's entire body stiffened. The brutal putdown sliced deep. "Fine. Have it your way."

Like father, like son.

"Not that you care, but we're getting married on Monday. We've decided to put the honeymoon off until later, so I'll be home by the time you need to get picked up at school."

"I'm back on the bus Monday."

"Oh, well, that works out fine then. You can let yourself in, and I'll be home shortly after."

"Can I go now?" he asked standing up.

Kalila lost it. "No! I'm not done. Sit yourself back down in that chair and don't get up until I say so."

Without warning, Hamza sprung from his chair and bolted upstairs, but this time Kalila remained in her seat; powerless to give chase. She hung her head and wept.

Later that evening, after hours of tossing in bed unable to sleep, Kalila decided to check on Hamza. She found him curled up, fast asleep with a pillow tucked under his chest. Kalila leaned in, half tempted to kiss him, but changed her mind and drew away. Watching him sleep now brought back a flood of memories when he was a baby. How she had loved rubbing his tiny soft brow or cooing sweet nothings into his perfectly shaped ears. His little chest would rise and fall with the sweetest even breaths.

It had been ages since Hamza had allowed Kalila close enough to touch him, no less kiss his cheek. Tiptoeing back to the door, she pulled it softly closed so as not to awaken him.

This is all my fault. If I hadn't been so desperate for Hamza's forgiveness.

Nothing she did worked. Nothing she said could penetrate the barrier Hamza had built around his heart. The impenetrable divider locking him in and blocking her out.

Maybe I should tell Qasim to forget about it—

A dire sense of hopelessness almost propelled her to abandon her plan and cancel the wedding, but if she had even the slightest chance of a new life, she'd have to stay the course. Kalila weighed her limited options.

No, I'll see this through. InshaAllah Hamza will come around over time. He'll realize I did this out of love.

CHAPTER 28

Kiss Me

Qasim

QASIM PERCHED UNEASILY ON the edge of the hotel bed, repetitively buttoning and unbuttoning his shirt sleeve, overcome with a sense of dread, worried that he wouldn't be able to please another woman...especially one as gorgeous as Kalila. Not sure whether to wait or disrobe. The sound of the bathroom faucet being turned off caused his heart to race with expectation. Qasim kicked off his shoes and peeled off his socks.

As he waited, Qasim thought about how glad he was when Kalila suggested they marry at a small *masjid* out of town where nobody knew either one of them. And as anticipated, the *nikkah* had been quick and to the point. The Imam there said a few words, had them sign their contracts and sent them off on their merry way. Had they married in their community, Qasim was certain Imam Abdullah would have made a big production out of it. Asking them a bunch of questions and demanding that Amara be told first. At least for now, they could be alone without anyone else's interference.

Damn, I don't even know what color her hair is.

He closed his eyes picturing long soft waves of hair cascading down her delicate, slender back. He became excited anticipating the silky texture of her skin next to his. It had been so long since he felt like this, and prayed he'd last long enough to enjoy her slowly, passionately, to taste her…to bring her to a—

"Qasim?"

Qasim's eyes snapped open. Standing barefoot before him was the most gorgeous woman, his wife, wearing nothing but a silky babydoll and thong. The outline of her nipples pressed against her creamy pale skin invited him to explore.

As Kalila seductively strode closer, a shoulder strap slipped alluringly down her arm. Reaching up, she unclasped the negligée from the front, allowing the silky fabric to slide off and flutter to the floor.

"Should I take this off," she whispered, running her thumb back and forth in rhythmic movements under the string of her lace thong; a tease intended to make most men cream.

"You're beautiful," Qasim murmured, pressing his face between Kalila's firm breasts; inhaling her alluring scent. Drawing her body in closer, his hands impatiently cupped each hip, pulling her hungrily into him.

"Let me help you take these off," Kalila purred, indicating his pants, while already busy unbuttoning his shirt.

"I want to admire you first," he said, grateful Kalila decided to leave a small, single lamp on to illuminate the room. With Amara, all the lights had to be turned off before she'd agree to strip, not that he cared to look at her anyway. Their connection had become so distant that Qasim barely bothered with foreplay—grateful when Amara had given up expecting it.

"Don't move," Qasim whispered. "Just stand right there. I want to take you all in." With jagged, sharp breaths, his hands clung to the curvature of her ass now nestled in the palms of his large hands.

Kalila used her tongue to explore his lips.

"I need you," he begged.

Kalila slipped him inside, tenderly running her fingers through his beard.

About to lose all control, Qasim began thrusting, grinding hard—*quicker*, but Kalila shut him down, squeezing him to a halt.

"Let me ride you," she cooed, seemingly determined to rock his world.

Qasim's hands caressed the soft curve of Kalila's back, bracing her hips over his.

"So, beautiful," he panted through heavy breaths, his lips buried into the nape of her neck.

Arching her back, Kalila teased Qasim, luring him onward, but then, without warning, torturously pulled herself away, making him beg for more.

"I can't," he groaned, no longer able to resist, but Kalila continued to ply her trade, refusing to concede.

"*I can't*," Qasim mumbled, deliriously lost in the cadence of her body, grabbing her hips, ravenously pulling apart her thighs, pushing, thrusting, his heart racing.

"Kalila," Qasim begged, imploring her for relief.

"Now," she commanded, a bead of sweat sliding down her neck.

Qasim squeezed Kalila hard causing her to gasp, but to his relief, she neither protested nor pulled back. Instead, she relaxed her body, welcoming him to indulge.

Waves of pure ecstasy washed over him. Eyes closed tight and powerless to stop, Qasim squeezed her close and—

He held her close until he drifted off to sleep. About an hour later, he felt Kalila begin to stir.

"I hate to cut this short," she whispered, caressing his chest with her fingertip, "but I promised Hamza I'd be home when he got back from school."

Qasim gently brushed a wisp of Kalila's hair away from her cheek. "No problem. I need to speak to Amara before the boys get home anyway."

"Sounds like a plan," agreed Kalila.

The two dressed quickly and left, each going their separate ways.

***

Outside the day had grown dark and gloomy. Gusts of wind carried trails of fallen crisp leaves, propelling them across the road…sure signs of an impending storm.

Pulling into the driveway, Qasim noticed Amara's van, but inside the lights were off. That should have been his first sign to run.

Opening the door, he called out his *salaams* but heard no reply. Leaving his keys on the hook, he gradually removed each shoe, dreading what would happen next. He had decided to tell Amara straight out and let the chips fall where they may, but Kalila cautioned him to be kind.

"You have to understand how hard this is for a woman to hear," she had told him, holding his hand. "Amara has a strong personality—"

"That's an understatement."

"Yes, but you need to consider that she's still the mother of your children and your other wife. She has rights over you." Kalila demurely lowered her gaze. "You need to deliver our news as gently and as kindly as possible."

Qasim sat back in his chair. "You're full of surprises, you know that?" he said smiling. Marveling at how perceptive and caring Kalila continued to be, despite how Amara had treated her over the years.

Kalila kissed Qasim's cheek. "She's going to be hurt. That's only natural. This is a big change for all of us. I wouldn't be surprised if she lashes out again."

Qasim guffawed. "Should I wear body armor?"

"Not a bad idea," said Kalila stifling a laugh. "Let Amara say whatever she needs to. Remember, at the end of the day, there's not a thing she can do to keep us from being together."

***

Qasim unlaced his shoes, peering up just in time to duck before almost being clipped by a candy dish.

"What the hell are you doing!" he shouted, jumping out of the way just as it hit the wall and shattered.

"You bastard!" seethed Amara, lunging for him again. "You had to do it," she screamed, slapping him on the side of his neck.

"If you'd just calm down a minute, we can discuss it."

"Now you want to talk? Oh, that's rich," Amara snarled. "Is this a pre-or-post-fuck chat, because guaranteed, what I use to talk with will change depending on that answer," she threatened, brandishing a vase over her head with one hand, and waving the other in a fist in the air.

"You're crazy."

"I'm not crazy, you two-timing, cheating son of a bitch, I'm mad as hell." Amara hurled the vase at his head. But instead of breaking, it merely rolled under the living room table. Rather than pick it up, Amara grabbed for the nearest coaster.

"Put that down!" Qasim yelled.

Amara swung her arm clipping the side of his shoulder; hurting her hand more than him. "Ouch," she cried.

"Just stop it. I didn't come home to fight with you."

"Then why did you come home? All fucked-out? Too tired to get it up again? Oh, I know, her boyfriend showed up and ruined all the fun." Amara lifted a large, heavy book off the coffee table and hurled it at him; only managing to throw it far enough for it to land by his feet.

Qasim hopped out of the way. "Can't we just sit down and talk about this without you throwing stuff?"

Amara stepped forward and lifted her arm in the air, ready to take another swing.

"How did you find out anyway?" he asked, surprised the news had gotten to her this quickly.

Amara stopped mid-air. "Find out about what?"

Now Qasim looked confused. He thought for sure Amara had found out about the marriage. "What are you talking about?" he asked, not exactly willing to jump the gun and put himself out there unnecessarily.

Amara stood her ground. "What the hell are *you* talking about?" she shrieked, eyes bulging, hands planted on hips.

Cornered, and no longer able to move out of the way, Qasim leaned on the wall, crossing his arms over his chest, projecting a presumption of calm that he certainly didn't feel. "I thought that if I waited to tell you face-to-face, we could discuss it like adults."

Confused, Amara tilted her head. "Discuss what like adults?" she asked, not sure what he was alluding to. "You're talking in circles."

Qasim leaned back to access the situation, thoroughly enjoying having the upper hand for once. He planned to use it to his advantage.

"I didn't cheat on you," he said.

"Liar!" yelled Amara.

"I'm not lying. I did not cheat," he repeated, barely masking the self-satisfaction creeping into every syllable.

"Be a man, Qasim. At least have the balls to tell me the truth. You fucked that ho, and you know it! I can smell her vile stench on you."

Qasim snickered. "Oh, I absolutely fucked her."

Amara gripped her throat. "I knew it," she growled, wildly clawing at him.

He grabbed her wrists and pulled Amara's red, angry face close to his, making damn sure she heard every last word he had to say.

"I didn't just fuck her, Amara. I-married-her."

Amara gasped. "You did what?"

"You heard me. I married her. Then I fucked her. And in every which way imaginable." He felt Amara's fight slipping. "No, no," he told her. "Stand up. You can't crumble now. Not when I have so much more to share with you."

"You're hurting me." Amara began bawling.

"Stand up."

"Ouch…stop it, Qasim," she moaned, twisting and squirming, trying to get free. "Why are you being so cruel to me?"

"You're the one who accused me of being an adulterer, which I gotta tell you, is a hell of a charge coming from a sneaky, despicable, bitch like you. Always in people's business and telling everyone how to live their lives. You've got some nerve."

"How could you do this," Amara whimpered, barely able to breathe. Her words caught in her throat as she tried to speak. "How could you do this?"

"You made it easy," he said, releasing his grip and letting her collapse to the floor. "I mean, just look at you. What man in his right mind wouldn't have married a gorgeous woman like Kalila when all he's had to come home to is a fat, sloppy mess like you?" Qasim crouched down to look into Amara's wet, weepy face. "She's my wife, Amara. You got that? My wife—and your co-wife. Not my girlfriend. Not a whore or a bitch, or whatever other demeaning names you've called her," he said, jabbing her shoulder with his finger. "And don't let me hear you say another bad word about Kalila or I will divorce you. I'll take the boys, this house, and the shirt of your flabby back. I'll leave you with nothing. Nothing!"

Amara gripped her stomach, rocking back and forth, crying hysterically. Qasim, bereft of sympathy and not willing to show her even an ounce of compassion, stepped over her and headed to the kitchen feeling triumphant. "When you're done blubbering, clean up this mess."

CHAPTER 29

And Then There Were None

FOR WEEKS, AMARA HAD barely left her house except to drop off or to pick up her sons at the bus stop, and even then, nobody remembered seeing her get out of the car.

"I feel like we should say something to her," said Walaa stealing glances in Amara's direction while waiting for the afternoon bus to arrive. "I know she's not the nicest person, but still, she didn't deserve this."

"Leave it alone," advised Nafiza, still steamed about having the riot act read to her by Abdullah for her part in the infamous *masjid* fiasco. He hadn't precisely yelled, which in the long run would have been better than feeling his disappointment. It hurt Nafiza to know that it would be a long time before Abdullah trusted her judgment again.

"She looks distraught," said Walaa, squinting. "Like she's ready to cry or something."

"Are you kidding me right now?" Nafiza hissed, practically losing her temper. "After the scene she caused, she should be ashamed. Amara made a damn fool out of herself and all of us!"

"Well, to be fair," said Walaa, somewhat contritely, "Qasim and Kalila did get married behind her back. Maybe that's why she lost it the way she did."

"Ugh!" Nafiza stomped her foot. "I love you, Walaa. I really do, but sometimes your gullibility drives me nuts."

"How am I gullible? Don't you think Amara's got a right to be upset after what those two pulled?"

Nafiza sighed. "Look, we both know Amara is immature. She's never made it a secret that she's out for herself. Thinks nothing of manipulating a situation and is a control freak. Over the years, she has disrespected, backbitten, and belittled more people than you and I can keep track of—and you've seen firsthand what happens when anybody dares fight back or decides to ignore her foolishness; then she totally loses her shit and plays the victim."

Walaa went to speak—

"No-no-no, let me finish. I get that she's our Muslim sister and all, but enough is enough. It's because of her insecurities, her self-loathing, her victim complex, and her jealousy, and let's not forget about her incessant need to be the center of attention; all of these things make those around her who genuinely care about her feel small and stupid. The minute she hears something she doesn't agree with or like, she goes on the attack. She's the same person who demands loyalty and the first person to name call and publicly shame a sister. Not only that, but she won't hesitate for even a baby's breath to throw someone under the bus—and publicly—because if she thinks she's right, she doesn't-give-a-damn. And you know why? It's because Amara's got it in her head that only she gets to decide what constitutes what being a real friend is or isn't. Only her feelings and opinions count." Nafiza lowered her voice so nobody else but Walaa could hear her. "Remember that time she cursed you out?" reminded Nafiza. "And all because you didn't call her about something. And after that—didn't she leave you a bunch of offensive messages on your phone…if I'm remembering correctly."

Walaa's head drooped, and her shoulders slumped.

"And lest you forget, Walaa, let me be the one to remind you; Amara's the same person who has no issue ignoring even basic boundaries when it comes to friendship, but becomes unhinged when people who have tried to befriend her decide they've had enough and leave because they can't take her nonsense anymore. And can you blame them? I sure can't because they're probably trying to protect their own sanity!"

"I know but—"

"No. Uh-uh. I'm still not finished," said Nafiza, on a roll. "Amara enjoys prying into other people's business and then holds whatever she finds out about them over their heads. That's called 'emotional blackmail' and that's some evil stuff."

"True, but—"

"Wait. Still not done. Allah talks about that…and after the way she treated her husband in public. *Man*, I can only imagine the humiliation and embarrassment he's had to put up with from her privately over the years."

"Enough. You've made your point."

"Good."

"But Kalila's no innocent in this."

"Not at all."

"I'm also mad at her."

"Yes. Good. Be mad," celebrated Nafiza, arms up in the air. "Be furious if you have to; you're supposed to be."

Eyes watery, Walaa shot Nafiza a glare. "Kalila's been hurt in the past as well. Maybe that's why she married Qasim—"

"You're not listening again, and you're still making excuses for people's piss poor behavior and choices."

"I don't know what you expect me to do, Nafiza—"

"I expect you to protect yourself for once. To put your emotional safety ahead of other people's drama." Nafiza lowered her voice even more. "You think I care why Kalila and Qasim decided to get married?"

"Well, do you?"

"I don't. Not one bit. Matter-of-fact, I don't care if those two decide to hump and bump at the top of the Empire State Building. I really don't. —Amara, Kalila, Qasim—their whole wives of the Poconos' dysfunction club-thing they've got going on—it's been nothing but a pain in my—"

"Fine!" Walla shouted. "I understand. I'm just having a hard time processing that Kalila did this."

"But she did."

"I *know* that, Nafiza. I *hear* you, but she was my friend, or at least I thought she was. Now?" Walaa shrugged. "I just can't imagine how I would feel if this happened to me."

"*Ya Allah,*" Nafiza yelled, imploring help from the heavens, flapping her arms while twirling in a circle. "But it isn't happening to you, and you have to stop projecting. For once, can you just stay out of it? I beg of you. Protect your health, your heart—*your baby.* Let crazy and company work things out for themselves, but without you."

Walaa frowned.

Nafiza tempered her tone. "Walaa, you seriously need to trust me about this. I know you and Kalila were tight but getting involved any further with her or Amara will only come back to haunt you."

"What Kalila pulled was still wrong."

"What Kalila pulled was some lowdown utter bullshit, but it's not my problem—or yours. I'm done with her. I'm done with Amara. You should be also. If either one of them gives the *salaams*, fine, wish them well. Heck, pray for them if you are so inclined, and then run in the opposite direction as fast as your legs will take you, *unless*—"

"Unless what?" asked Walaa warily.

"*Unless* you want the next husband Kalila goes after to be yours."

Walaa's eyes practically popped out of her head. "Okay. You win. I'm done."

"Now, that's what I'm talkin' about."

***

Kalila

Kalila stretched out her fingers to admire the gorgeous, two-karat diamond in a princess setting. Another expensive gift from Qasim.

"This is too much," she had cooed, watching Qasim slip the ring on her finger. "You surprise me."

"Do I?"

"How did you even know my size?" she asked, marveling how the diamond sparkled no matter what angle the light hit it.

"It's not too much," he told her, lifting Kalila's hand to his lips. "And in regard to size? Well, let's just say I'll never disclose my trade secrets," he teased, basking in Kalila's adoration.

Kalila wrapped her arms around Qasim's neck and kissed him passionately. "These last few months have been wonderful," she said. And they had been. She was no longer stressed out by work or clients, or how to pay her bills. She had even started sleeping and eating better. Kalila's relationship with Hamza, while not necessarily amiable, had been far less confrontational, especially since Melvin agreed to move in. Qasim had even promised to have his attorneys handle the remainder of Melvin's paperwork, and the sale of Felicia's home promised to provide Melvin with a nice-sized nest egg when the time came. Life's broken pieces were finally falling into place.

Qasim held Kalila tightly around the waist. "You've made me so happy," he whispered.

Kalila smiled. Admittedly, she did everything in her power in and out of bed to make Qasim feel appreciated and desired, and in return, he had showered her generously with gifts and adoration. She could only imagine how jealous Amara felt.

"Listen, this week is going to be busy," he said. "I have a ton of work to catch up on, and tomorrow I've got an important client coming in. I've been courting this arrogant SOB for a while. Hopefully, my efforts will pay off with a big contract."

Kalila lifted her face to his, nibbling his bottom lip.

"You're not making this any easier," Qasim moaned, pulling her in closer.

Kalila undid his belt buckle

"I…won't…be-home…for dinner, *oh man*, for the rest of the week," he said, panting through short escaping breaths.

"I understand." The stakes were high, and Kalila knew how to play her part as the dutiful, forever accommodating wife to perfection. Running her tongue teasingly down his neck, she dropped to her knees. "At least permit me to start your week off with a bang."

***

Kalila hung up the phone with Ruth. They'd been speaking daily about Felicia's declining health.

"She's not doing well," said Ruth, sounding exhausted. "I think she'll be heading to the hospice by the beginning of next week."

"Why so long?" asked Kalila, surprised Felicia hadn't been brought there already. For days now, her breathing had been labored and intense.

"No bed open. I've been calling every day, sometimes twice a day. I think they're getting a bit tired of me bothering them."

"I'm sure they understand."

"Who knows or cares?" Ruth paused. "I hate to say it, but the sooner, the better. Felicia needs more help than I can provide."

"How's her pain level been?"

"Increasing and hard to manage."

"And Melvin? He must be so scared."

"Melvin's taking it all surprisingly in stride. Don't get me wrong, he understands his mother is ill, and it frightens him, but now that he knows he'll be living with you and Hamza, his spirits have lifted. I can't thank you both enough. I know Felicia feels the same way."

"Please, don't thank me," Kalila said. "Melvin's very special to us."

"He's a doll," agreed Ruth. "By the way, Felicia's been asking for you."

"I'll try to get over for a visit tomorrow if she's up to it."

"Sounds great. Oh, and she mentioned needing you to sign some legal papers concerning the house."

"I understand," said Kalila.

***

Later that afternoon, Kalila began sifting through the wide selection of food stuffed in her overly filled refrigerator when she remembered Qasim wouldn't be coming home for dinner. Some meeting with an important client.

"Hmmm." Kalila had an idea. Qasim had mentioned a craving for baked ziti. Poking around, she took stock of her ingredients.

Chopped meat—check, salad veggies—check...tomato sauce? Yes. And mozzarella cheese? She pulled out one of the drawers. *I do-I do.*

Kalila moved a few jars around searching for ricotta. "Ah ha!" She found a medium sized container hiding on the second shelf.

Kalila had heard Qasim complain enough about Amara's cooking to know that he didn't eat anything made in a crockpot, referring to it as "Crock crap." Kalila had laughed at the time, although in all honesty, she didn't find most of Qasim's humor the least bit amusing.

Well, since he can't be here, I'll surprise him.

She placed the ingredients on the counter.

A surprise picnic basket dinner at the job would be perfect.

Kalila smiled, proud of herself for coming up with the idea.

"Ma! Do you know where I put my gym bag?" yelled Hamza from upstairs.

"Where'd you leave it last?" she hollered back.

"In the hall by the shoe shelf."

"Did you check the hall closet?"

She heard him clamor down the stairs. "Got it, thank you."

Kalila joined him in the hall.

"I'll be back later," he said, lacing up his sneakers. Hamza had been tending to Felicia's lawn, wanting it to look perfect for her when she left for the very last time, especially the tulip bed.

"I'm making baked ziti tonight. I'll leave it on the stove. You can warm it up when you're ready."

As the house filled with the comforting aroma of baked ziti bubbling in the oven, Kalila got ready, selecting a traditional navy blue *abaya* to match her beautiful French Mani-Pedi. Underneath her garment, she wore a new navy-blue lace panty and bra set just in case her husband decided he wanted dessert.

After wrapping a large enough portion of ziti for Qasim's dinner and packing it in the basket along with all the extra trimmings, Kalila slipped on her kitten heels and headed out.

Shoot! I better get the mail before the mail lady decides to have another impromptu visit again.

Kalila made a sharp turn to park in front of the community's mailboxes. Before she had a chance to step out, another car pulled in right after.

Nafiza.

The two women hadn't spoken since the *masjid* spectacle.

Kalila opened her mailbox to find four days' worth stuffed inside. She peered casually to her left, as if just suddenly noticing Nafiza, but they both knew that not to be true.

"*As salaamu alaikum.*"

"*Wa alaikum salaam,*" answered Nafiza flatly.

The door of friendship had closed, but Nafiza hadn't been the only cold shoulder Kalila had received since marrying Qasim. Quite a few women from the community had let their feelings be known, all except Walaa, of course. The ultimate do-gooder's do-gooder, who, while not overly pleasant, hadn't gone out of her way to snub Kalila either. Playing by the same rulebook, Kalila never gave any of them a second glance.

Kalila locked her mailbox. She turned under Nafiza's insufferable glare and walked away, refusing to spend an ounce of energy seeking anyone's approval. She'd already wasted enough of her life people pleasing and look how far that had gotten her.

The ride downtown went smoothly enough, although never having been to Qasim's building before, Kalila wouldn't have known about the private parking assigned for VIPs toward the private side entrance. She found a space almost parallel from the main entrance; she didn't much care.

Gathering up the basket and her pocketbook, she headed inside.

"Good afternoon," greeted the friendly doorman sitting behind the reception desk.

"Hello," said Kalila.

"Who are you here to see?" he asked, folding his newspaper in half and placing it into a drawer.

Kalila placed her basket by her feet. "My husband. Qasim Zubairi."

"Welcome, Mrs. Zubairi." The doorman's expression never changed. Either he never met Amara, or he was one hell of an actor. "Would you like me to call your husband down?"

"No, I'd rather go up to his office. I've planned a little surprise for him," Kalila said indicating the basket by her feet.

"Very good then. Please sign the visitor's log." He slid a clipboard in her direction, then handed her a pen.

Kalila obliged, signing Qasim's last name next to hers for the first time.

"Thank you," he said, accepting the clipboard back. "Floor one. You'll find the elevators at the far end to the right."

"Thank you." Struggling to lift her basket, she toddled in short, clipped steps towards the elevator, determined to avoid sliding on the highly-polished lobby floor.

I should have worn my flats.

"Have a nice day," called the doorman after her, already comfortable in his chair with his newspaper spread wide open.

Kalila pushed the button. The basket, while not large, had started to feel heavy.

The elevator doors opened, and she stepped inside. Kalila had no problem finding Qasim's office, slightly left of the elevators. Opening the door just a crack, she peered in and called out a soft hello. The room appeared empty; no one staffing the reception desk, although she could distinctly hear two male voices behind the main door.

Kalila stepped inside to wait, not wishing to interrupt Qasim's meeting. She recalled how emphatic he had been about how vital landing this particular contract would be to the growth of the company.

After a few minutes, Kalila decided it would be best to just leave the basket for Qasim to find on his own time. Reaching over and behind the fancy marble reception counter, she swiped a pen and a single sheet of paper to write Qasim a little note.

Loud laughter emanated from inside. A few seconds later, the voices sounded done for the night. Kalila heard one man;

presumably, the client's, say something about meeting again to finalize the paperwork and would Thursday work?

Kalila rushed to finish her note. Just as she got ready to tuck it under the basket's latch, the inner office door opened and out walked the client.

"Oh," said the man, stopping short, startled. "I'm sorry. I didn't realize anybody was here—wait. Marie? Is that you?" asked Roger, grinning from ear to ear.

For once, Kalila wished she'd taken up wearing the face veil.

"*It is you.* Wow, I hardly recognized you in that getup. Who are you supposed to be? The Queen of Sheba?"

Kalila waved her hands, to shush him. "Be quiet," she snapped, a bit more hotly than intended.

"What are you shushing me about?" Roger asked, twisting his neck to look around the empty office.

Kalila's eyes darted to the door. "Please," she whispered. "Lower your voice."

Roger's brow furrowed. "Why are we whispering?" he asked. "And what are you doing here?" And then the dim light went on. "—OH!" Roger exclaimed, almost laughing, "Is he one of your clients?" he asked, jutting his chin towards Qasim's office door. "Now ain't that a heck of a coincidence. No worries. My hungry lips are sealed."

"Shut the hell up!"

"Hey now, that's no way to talk to an old friend," Roger reached out to tap Kalila on her ass.

Kalila slapped Roger's lecherous hand away. "Knock it off. I mean it."

Not one to easily take no for an answer, Roger grabbed for Kalila's hand but missed. "Listen, once you're done with the old guy, why don't you hit me up? I'll make it worth your while," he said, rubbing his fingers together in the universal sign for money.

Kalila stepped back, terrified Qasim would walk out any moment. She bolted for the door, forgetting the note on the counter. Once in the hall, she kept pressing the elevator button as if that would speed its arrival.

"Come on, Marie. Cut me some slack, would ya? I won't ruin your gig. I'm not like that," Roger patted his chest like big daddy. "Not after all the fun we've had," he said solicitously.

"Roger," Kalila implored. "I need you to stop talking. Just pretend like you never saw me. Can you do that?"

"I guess, sure, but what do I get in return?"

"Ugh!" The elevator door opened, and Kalila leaped inside. Roger trailed behind her, but she shoved him back out. "Oh no," she pointed at him sternly. "You'll wait for the next one, and do not follow me," Kalila commanded. "I mean it."

But Roger took Kalila's threat as merely flirtatious and chuckled. "Gosh Marie, you know how much I love a woman who plays hard to get."

And with that, the elevator doors closed.

However, listening from the other side of the office door stood Qasim, seething. Betrayed. Angrier than he had ever felt before.

CHAPTER 30

Unleashed

HAVING FINISHED THE RAKING, Hamza and Melvin relaxed on the Vines' back porch, downing a bottle of water each.

"I gotta do my lawn next," said Hamza taking a swig. "Ah…" He wiped the beads of sweat off his forehead with the back of his flannel sleeve. "Mom's been hounding me to get ours done since last week."

"I will help you, Hamza," replied Melvin, taking a big gulp from his bottle. As he swallowed, he made sure to provide a suitably loud enough "Ah" to make Hamza proud.

Hamza chuckled. "I'm starving. Hey, my mother made baked ziti for dinner. You wanna come over to eat? She made a gigantic tray of the stuff."

"I like baked ziti," said Melvin.

"Me, too."

"I like garlic bread," said Melvin.

"We can make some if you want."

Melvin nodded enthusiastically. "I like garlic bread."

The guys had just finished drinking when Kalila's car tore into the driveway. They watched her sprint up the steps and bolt straight into the house; her blue *abaya* and *hijab* billowing as she ran.

"Why's she all dressed up?" Hamza voiced.

Melvin grinned. "Like a princess."

Hamza shot Melvin a playful side eye. "That's one old princess, dude."

"I like garlic bread."

"Yeah, I know already. Gosh. You want me to ask the princess to make it for you?"

A few minutes later, Qasim's Mercedes screeched into the driveway next door, parking directly behind Kalila's car.

Hamza got to his feet to stretch his cramped, tired legs. "Hail! The frog-prince has arrived on his trusty steed."

Apparently also in a rush, Qasim slammed his car door and sprinted up the walkway, barreling through the front door.

"Shoot. I thought he wasn't coming home tonight," griped Hamza, disappointed. "He always ruins everything."

"Always ruins everything," repeated Melvin, head tilted and eyebrows furrowed. "Always ruins everything," he mumbled for the second time, unable to control his fingers twitching on the empty water bottle or his knees from bouncing.

***

Kalila

Kalila quickly changed, throwing on a pair of sweatpants and tank top; she piled her hair into a messy bun on top of her head. Back down in the kitchen, head bowed, she leaned over the kitchen sink, unable to wrap her head around bumping into Roger, of all people, and at Qasim's office. She inhaled long deep breaths to the count of ten—anything to quell the anxiety playing havoc with her insides.

That could have been a full-fledged disaster.

What happens if Qasim saw me?

What if Roger opened his stupid big mouth after all?

I'm so stupid. If I hadn't left the basket with the note, there'd be no proof that I'd been there at all.

Grabbing a mug from the cupboard, she dumped a tea bag inside.

Damn it. I'm screwed anyway. I signed in at the lobby!

Kalila moaned, slamming her fist on the counter.

Kalila switched on the oven. Out of habit, she pulled on a pair of oven mitts to lift a cold tray of baked ziti, only to shove it into the equally as cold oven. Slamming the door shut with her knee, she groaned. "I *had* to play Suzy Homemaker. Always 'The Hostess with The Mostest.'"

The front door opened. "Hamza?" she called, setting the timer for thirty minutes. "I'm warming up the ziti. Go get washed up. It should be ready by the time you're out of the shower." She placed a cutting board on the counter.

No answer.

A sudden rush of heavy footsteps barreled from behind her. "Hamza?" Kalila spun towards the noise, expecting to see her son. "Qasim? Why are you—" A backhand slap so ferocious, so menacing, struck the side of her face. The impact sent Kalila whirling sideways, head first into the refrigerator.

A thin trickle of blood from her split lip ran down her red, stinging face. Terrified, she tried to stagger away. With one eye, locked on Qasim, Kalila flailed her arms wildly backward, blindly rifling for anything to use to defend herself. "Please—don't," she begged. A surge of dizziness caused her to drop to her knees.

"Get up," Qasim snarled, snatching Kalila by the arm and dragging her across the cold tile. "You lied to me," he shouted, slapping her again, this time causing her to bite her tongue. "You made me look like a fool," he yelled, raising his open hand in the air.

WHACK—

Kalila's head snapped back into the cabinet. The bitter coppery taste of blood made her nauseous. "Leave me alone!" she screeched, cowering behind her crossed arms as best as she could. More blood trickled down her chin onto her tee-shirt; tiny droplets landed on the floor.

Qasim lunged for Kalila again, this time managing to land another substantial blow to her already swollen jaw. A sharp, stinging pain pulsated between her eyes.

Kalila lunged for the knife drawer, but Qasim quickly blocked her with his body.

"You're going to pay for what you've done," he threatened, slamming the drawer shut. Recoiling his fist up to his ear, he landed another strike, then another…and another. Hitting Kalila anywhere her hands weren't fast enough to protect.

"Leave me alone," she shrieked, letting out a blood-chilling scream, clumsily tumbling to the floor on bruised arms and legs. Kalila curled her body into a tight ball, wrapping her head in her hands defensively to cushion the impact of each subsequent blow.

Qasim punted Kalila in the back, then her shoulder, causing her to scream in pain.

"Get up!" he ordered, dragging her to her feet.

Kalila slapped the floor, stretching her arms to swipe at anything to stop Qasim from pulling her, but he was stronger.

Lifting her to her feet, face forward, Qasim forced Kalila to look him in the eyes. "I fell in love with you," he said, eyes burning with fury, "I would have given you the world."

Kalila winced, bracing for the next slap or punch.

"And this is how you repay me?" he snarled.

She could smell his hot, foul breath.

"By making me a laughing stock?" Qasim shook her by the shoulders. "You must have enjoyed making me look like a fool—" he spat out, half-crazed. "Laughing at me…pretending to be my wife." His eyes narrowed. "What a joke. You. A wife! You're nothing but a fucking whore."

Broken, incapable of defending herself, and powerless to flee, Kalila gave in to the agony attacking every nerve ending in her wounded body. Weak and unable to support her weight, she dropped to her knees. Her head lobbed feebly side to side. No longer resilient enough to brace against the momentum of Qasim's assault, Kalila began to plead for mercy. "Please," she begged, moaning through a severely bruised jaw.

But Qasim's over the top rage and hunger for retribution wasn't through with her just yet. Heaving Kalila back to her feet, he bolstered her wracked body on the kitchen counter ledge into barely a standing position. Bloody mouth open, eyes rolling to the back of her head, Kalila beckoned death to take her.

"Shut up," he yelled, yanking her by the hair. "I mean it."

"*Let-me-expla–*" she gasped, gulping in ragged, clipped breaths. Her battered fingers clawed feebly at his hands.

"*Please,*" she begged him, trying to pry his fingers apart, but her waning strength against his wrath couldn't stop the room from weaving in and out. Eyes fluttering, she teetered on the edge of consciousness.

"Not yet you don't." Qasim curled his fingers tighter around Kalila's throat. "And to think—Amara was right about you all along." Enraged, he pressed and closed, pressed and closed, wanting her to suffer, wanting her to beg. "I watched Bashir die," Qasim viciously taunted her, his face contorted and manically crazed; his hatred curdling and rising to the top. "And now I'm going to enjoy watching you."

Rasping, fighting for each breath, Kalila scratched and clawed at Qasim, but without enough air, she could no longer support her weight. Legs buckling, she crumpled, but Qasim wouldn't stop clutching Kalila's neck until the blood vessels in her eyes appeared ready to rupture—

"Leave her alone," Hamza cried, bursting through the back door, lunging straight for Qasim's waist, but his child's strength was no match for Qasim, who was running on pure rage-filled adrenaline. Qasim snatched Hamza, lifting him easily into the air with one arm, and unceremoniously tossing him clear across the room. The child flew, crashing headfirst into the table, and then toppled helplessly over a heavy wooden chair, landing on the floor like a rag doll.

"Not nice!" Melvin roared, his face scrunched up in a contorted scowl, his nostrils flaring. "Stop bad man!" yelled Melvin, stomping his feet and waving his arms in uncontrollable fury.

Small gurgling breaths escaped Kalila's lips while her inflamed, red eyes strained to see. Barely able to focus, she pointed in the direction of Hamza with her one crooked, bruised and bloody finger.

Melvin saw Hamza on the floor, curled up in a ball, moaning in pain. Teeth gritted, Melvin tilted his head forward, snarling.

"And what do you think you're gonna do?" Qasim laughed. "Huh, retard?"

Melvin hunched his back like a bull, aiming for Qasim's torso, but Qasim, anticipating the move released his grip on Kalila's throat with enough time to move out of the way of Melvin's stampede.

"You-stupid-moron," Qasim taunted, spinning around to continue to gloat, when he lost his footing, causing him to lose his balance and tumble rearward. First, thwacking the back of his head hard against the corner of the counter, and then finishing with a final head-thumping on the solid, ceramic tiles.

A pool of blood swelled and oozed from behind Qasim's head. With his eyes wide open, his mouth gaping, and his arms spread-eagled to his side, he resembled the recently martyred dead.

Determined not to let him get up, Melvin raised his boot in the air, prepared to stomp Qasim's head when Kalila, swaying on all fours, swiped the cuff of his pants and tugged. Choking, she managed to garble out a raspy, "Don't. Help Hamza."

Fear turned instantly into panic. Melvin moaned, raking his fingers through his sweat-drenched hair.

"Phone…get-me-phone," slurred Kalila.

Melvin's head spun around. "Phone, phone, phone, phone," he kept mumbling, not sure what to do next.

"Counter," moaned Kalila, writhing in pain. "Police."

Melvin frantically searched the counter. By the time he found it, Kalila had already collapsed unconscious.

Melvin wailed and paced. Then he stopped moving when he remembered what his mother taught him.

"Now don't forget, Melvin, even if a phone is locked, you can always push 911 if you need help. Here, let me show you."

When the police and ambulance arrived, they found Kalila propped up against the counter, limply nursing her red and discolored face and neck with a bag of frozen corn. An inflamed handprint gracing her one swollen cheek had already begun to turn a garish black and blue.

Hamza had come around, complaining of a severe headache. Probably a concussion, said one of the emergency techs busy working on him.

Hearing sirens blasting through the small neighborhood's peaceful existence, Ruth rushed to glance out the front door. A stream of ambulances and police cars careened to a stop in front of Kalila's house.

"Oh, my God!" Ruth shrieked. "What the heck is going on over there?"

Felicia had heard the noise also. "Ruth? Ruth?" she called from her bed utterly panicked. "What's going on? Where's Melvin?"

"Not sure. The last time I saw him, he was running next door with Hamza." Ruth grabbed her sweater. "I'll go find out what's going on. Don't worry. I'll be right back," or so she thought.

"Ma'am," barked the officer standing guard on Kalila's front stoop." You can't go inside."

"I'm looking for—" Ruth hesitated. "My charge," she said, craning her neck to see around the man.

"Name?" he asked, pad in his hand.

"Melvin Vine."

"I mean yours, ma'am."

"Oh, right. Sorry. Ruth. My name is Ruth Epstein. I'm Melvin's custodian," she said for expediency, hoping that would convince him to let her inside. "I take care of Melvin's mother. Look, is he in there? Is he hurt?"

Ruth heard a familiar moan coming from within the house. "I gotta get in there. You don't understand," she snapped, losing her patience.

Just then, another police officer stepped out. "I'm Sergeant Sebulsky," said the heavy-set man, easily in his mid-forties, sporting a well-established five o'clock shadow. "What's going on?" he asked the officer, eyes locked on Ruth.

"I need to get inside," interjected Ruth. "I'm Melvin's—oh forget it. Can I get in there or what?"

"She's his custodian, sir," answered the officer.

Sebulsky looked Ruth up and down. "Follow me," he said begrudgingly, "but only to where I say and not a single step further."

Ruth nodded, half-listening, anxious to get inside to Melvin.

"He's over there. And remember," cautioned Sebulsky, "stay out of the way."

Once inside, Ruth found Melvin seated hunched over on the couch, mumbling and rocking back and forth; obviously scared to death and stressed.

"Oh, Melvin." Ruth rushed to his side. "You poor thing." Ruth kept a small space of distance between them, careful not to touch or startle him any more than he already seemed. "Are you all right, Melvin?"

"Bad man. Bad man," Melvin kept repeating. "Not nice."

"Bad man?" Ruth asked, giving Melvin a good once over, and relieved beyond belief to see that besides his shirt looking a bit mangled, he appeared physically unscathed.

"He's fine," confirmed the tech without being prodded. "Shook up, but physically we didn't find anything wrong with him."

"Thank you," she said to the EMT. To Melvin, she whispered, "Who are you talking about? Who's the bad man?"

"Bad man," repeated Melvin, tapping his foot.

A stretcher manned by two other EMTs wheeled past the pair. Melvin tapped his foot faster, becoming more agitated by the second.

Melvin leaped to his feet. "Bad man, bad man," he yelled, ready to bolt.

One quick glance at the stretcher confirmed the identity of the unconscious "bad man": Qasim Zubairi.

"It's okay," said Ruth, trying to calm him down. "I'm here. He can't hurt you anymore."

"Demon," growled Melvin.

"What did you say?" asked Ruth shocked, unsure she heard Melvin correctly.

"Keep him straight," hollered one of the EMTs as he lifted the stretcher, locking the wheels.

"Got it."

"Two steps are coming up behind you."

"Yup. See it." He said, peeking over his shoulder. "I'm lifting the front end. Are you ready?" asked the tech forcing the weight of the stretcher on the back wheels, then by the front as the rear end got lifted up.

Everyone moved out of the way to let the men do their jobs.

Inside the dining room off the kitchen sat Hamza, being seen to by a paramedic. Kalila had been placed on a stretcher, the next one getting ready for transport.

The kitchen floor had splattered blood everywhere. Two chairs had been knocked over as well. A bloody rag still remained in the middle of the floor, as the detectives milled about asking questions to assess the situation.

Kalila tried sitting up. "Ouch," she moaned, falling back, grabbing her upper arm.

"Here, let me see that," said the other paramedic. "Don't try to move until we get you all checked out.

"Is she able to answer a few questions?" inquired Sebulsky.

"She's got a major concussion." The EMT lowered her voice. "And Lord knows what else." She bent over to clip something to Kalila's wrist. "We're gonna need to transport her and the kid to General asap."

"Mrs. Zubairi," Sebulsky leaned in closer. "Can you tell me what happened here?"

It hurt to talk, so she whispered.

"I was cooking when my—my husband came in upset." She wasn't ready to give details until she could think clearly. "Started attacking me—choking me." Kalila drew in a haggard, breath. "My son, he tried to stop him, but Qasim attacked him too.

"And Melvin Vine?"

"Melvin tried to help but—" she shook her head no.

"Then what?"

"Is he dead?"

Sebulsky wasn't prepared to answer questions—only ask them. "You mentioned that your husband pushed his son out of the way?"

"Hamza's not his son." Kalila coughed mid-sentence. Her red, inflamed eyes were watering nonstop.

"Stay still." The EMT gave her something for the pain. "That'll do the trick," she said kindly.

Within seconds, Kalila's words began to slur, but she felt compelled to keep telling her side of the story. "Qasim laughed…slipped…on floor." Her eyes fluttered. "Banged…he banged head…"

"Where? Do you remember?"

"Counter," she murmured, practically lifeless. "Head bang…on…floor."

The officer checked his notebook. "And who's he?" He asked the other police officer, jutting his chin in Melvin's direction.

"Name's Melvin Vine. He's her neighbor."

"What's his story?"

"On the spectrum."

"On the what?"

"He's autistic."

Sebulsky shot him a dirty look. "For Christ's sake, Hippenstiel. For once, can you get your head out of your books? This is real life."

The tech tending to Kalila interjected. "We need to move her now." Crouching over Kalila. "Okay, sweetie. We're going to take you and your son to the hospital for observation. I'm just going to strap you in for the ride. We can't have you bouncing all over the place, can we?" she smiled. "Pete? Give me a hand."

The other crew member went to her side and clipped the belt. "Ready," he said. "Pull up the rail on your side."

Both officers moved out of the way.

Sebulsky walked around taking in the place, writing down some notes. From what he could tell, the scene seemed to support the wife's version of events. However, Sebulsky still had a few lingering questions, so he moseyed over to where Ruth and Melvin were seated.

"Hi, Melvin. My name's Officer Sebulsky. This is Officer Hippenstiel. Can I ask you a few questions?" he asked, his voice calm and friendly.

"Can't you see he's distraught?" accused Ruth.

"Yes ma'am, I can, but I'd just like to clear up a few points. I promise not to trouble Melvin more than absolutely necessary."

"Then I'm staying with him," Ruth said defiantly.

"That's fine." With fifteen years on the force, Sebulsky knew when to push and when to pull back. "Melvin? Hey Melvin, can you look at me?" Sebulsky reviewed Hippenstiel's notes, then structured his questions in the same sequence as Melvin initially recounted.

"I heard you were very brave back there. I gotta tell you, I'm pretty impressed," said Sebulsky, looking to build a rapport.

Melvin continued to rock and moan.

"You told Officer Hippenstiel that Mr. Zubairi hurt Mrs. Zubairi; is that right?"

"That is right. That is right," repeated Melvin, copying the last phrase he heard.

Sebulsky looked to Ruth for clarification.

"He's not mocking you. Melvin understands what you're saying, but his communication skills become stilted when agitated," she explained.

Sebulsky nodded. "Melvin, this is really important, okay? I need you to think back carefully." A siren went off outside. Melvin clutched his ears, swaying violently back and forth.

"Tell them I said to shut that damn thing off," ordered Sebulsky. "Now!"

"Yes sir," said Hippenstiel, rushing outside to relay the order.

Melvin's anxiousness appeared to subside as he peered down at his lap, twirling his hands.

"Melvin?" prodded Sebulsky, but Melvin remained silent, giving a slight nod.

"Terrific. That's really terrific." When Sebulsky pulled out his pen and paper, Melvin's eyes latched onto them.

"Melvin's an excellent artist," said Ruth, indicating that he should be given the pen and paper to draw his answers.

"Oh, right," said Sebulsky. "Here you go, Melvin. Can you draw me what you saw Mr. Zubairi doing to Mrs. Zubairi? Can you do that?"

"Pencil," said Melvin.

"He only draws in pencil," clarified Ruth.

Sebulsky asked around until he came up with a pencil and handed it to Melvin. "Better?" he asked.

"Better." Melvin accepted the pencil and paper and got busy. Fifteen minutes later, Ruth handed the finished product over.

Sebulsky whistled. "Well, I'll be damned. Ain't this something––Hippenstiel, come here a minute and look at this." Hippenstiel stared down at the drawing equally as impressed.

Melvin's foot tapped the floor rapidly. "Bad man. No! Stop hitting! Not nice!"

"I'd like to take him home now," said Ruth.

"One more question, please," implored Sebulsky. "Melvin, I know you tried to help Hamza and his Mom, and you were very brave, but I gotta ask anyways. Did you hit the bad man? Maybe push him over or make him fall?"

Ruth bolted to her feet. "Are you trying to blame Melvin?" she asked, incensed.

"No, not at all. That's the last thing I'd do. I'm just trying to understand what happened."

Ruth sat back down. "Then keep all questions clear and simple. Short sentences are best."

Melvin began rocking back and forth.

"What's he doing now?" asked Sebulsky.

"Self-soothing," answered Ruth curtly.

"Melvin? Did you hit Mr. Zubairi?"

"No, no, no, no," repeated Melvin, rocking faster.

"You didn't hit Mr. Zubairi?"

Melvin shook his head rapidly back and forth. "Hitting not nice. No hitting, Melvin."

"Look, quipped Ruth. "You got your answer. Melvin had nothing to do with this. Can I take him home?" she pleaded. "His mother is very ill, and she's worried."

Sebulsky had everything he needed for now. "Give Officer Hippenstiel your address and a number where you and Melvin here can be reached."

Hippenstiel handed Ruth his pen and pad. She scribbled the information they wanted down and handed the officer back his stuff.

"Let's go, Melvin," Ruth ordered.

Melvin stood hunched over, timidly staring down at the floor.

"Thank you, Melvin," said Officer Sebulsky. "I mean it. You've been a great help."

Ruth moved past Sebulsky, then gently guided Melvin outside.

Standing at the window, Sebulsky observed Melvin through the curtain, moaning and twitching his entire way home.

CHAPTER 31

General Hospital

Amara

"NEVER?" AMARA COULDN'T BELIEVE it. "Are you kidding me right now?"

"Mrs. Zubairi, please. No yelling. We keep the ICU quiet, so the patients don't get upset."

"Upset? The man's unconscious." Amara shook her head, flummoxed by the doctor's apparent stupidity.

"He's comatose, and although not talking, we believe your husband can hear what you say. I strongly advise that you never speak in front of him as if he can't hear you."

Amara glared, reasonably chastised.

"Any unnecessary stimulation can agitate and raise his blood pressure—something we don't want to happen. Why don't we step outside?" said Doctor Carlisle, the hospital's neurointensivist, holding the door open for Amara to step through. After closing the door behind them, the doctor wrote something down on his clipboard.

"Well?" asked Amara, unused to being censured.

"Mrs. Zubairi. Your husband has suffered a severe TBI," Doctor Carlisle explained.

"A what?"

"A Traumatic Brain Injury, so we will be closely monitoring him."

"That's what all those machines are about?"

Doctor Carlisle stuck the clipboard under his arm. "We're keeping him on a ventilator to provide him with oxygen to assist his breathing, since your husband's not opening his eyes even with stimulation, and because his loss of consciousness has lasted far more than six hours. We inserted a probe called the ICP–intracranial pressure monitor to drain excess fluid. We also placed him on the EEG machine."

"What does that do?"

"The electroencephalography machine records your husband's brain activity. It lets us know if he's having a seizure, the effects of the sedation, as well as if his brain functions are worsening."

"How long will he be on them?"

"It's entirely too soon to tell, but this is extremely serious. He'll be monitored closely for the next twenty-four to seventy-two hours; maybe longer."

"Will he wake up?"

The doctor had to tread carefully. "Again, we don't know the extent of his injuries. Not all head wounds behave the same."

"What's that supposed to mean?"

"It means that your husband will recover at his own pace. To what degree? We don't know yet."

"How long could this last? Him being like this?"

"If you are referring to his recovery, that could take weeks, months, even years."

"Could this be permanent?"

"Again, we don't have enough information to make that call right now. Let's hold tight and see what transpires within the next twenty-four to seventy-two hours." The doctor rattled off the remaining information as if by rote.

Amara cringed every time the doctor said "we" as if this horror—this nightmare—was some sort of a conjugal experience.

"What about surgery?" she asked, hoarsely.

"Surgery is sometimes necessary. I think there may have been multiple skull fractures, but we need to wait until some of the swelling goes down before taking any further steps unless of course, something else arises before then."

"Something such as—" Amara's thoughts and emotions crashed.

Ya Allah, how will I survive this?

"Such as a bleeding vessel for example, or a hematoma, or high intracranial pressure. Any of those could bring your husband to surgery, but I don't want you to worry about that. For now, he's stable and under excellent care."

Amara's legs trembled. The walls started to spin. "Could he die?"

"Not if I can help it."

The shock and enormity of Qasim's injuries smothered her sensibilities. "I-I don't know what to do," she whimpered, breathless.

Doctor Carlisle clipped his pen to his pocket. "I'm sorry," he offered in his kindest, trained doctor voice. "Is there somebody we can call for you?"

There it was again…that incessant 'we'—

This time, however, instead of snarling or losing her temper, Amara turned her face to the wall. She pressed her body against its coolness, covered her eyes with the palms of her hands and wept.

***

One week later…
Kalila

"Ready?" Ruth asked Kalila, still heavily bandaged and bruised, but anxious to leave the hospital. Ruth stepped behind the wheelchair holding it steady while Kalila gradually lowered herself down.

"Where's Hamza?" Kalila asked, as she inched her way down into the chair. Every part of her body throbbed, stung or hurt, aching in places she didn't know existed.

"Already in the lobby. He's got his nurse and Melvin to keep him company," said Ruth. "And they loaded him up with goodies. The nurses on his floor fell in love with your son. Spoiled him rotten."

Kalila heard Ruth. It warmed her heart to know that Hamza had been given such good care, but at the moment, the agony of being alive surpassed her ability to deal with more than one thing at a time. And for now, her total focus remained on getting the hell out of here. "I can walk," she said. While the doctor informed Kalila her ribs were, shockingly not fractured, it still hurt like bloody hell to breathe in deeply.

"Hospital policy," informed the nurse, busy gathering up Kalila's paperwork. "Here's everything we discussed. Your follow-up appointment is on Thursday. Until then, follow the instructions," she said pointing to the highlighted yellow paragraph. "And if you have any concerns or questions, don't hesitate to give us a ring."

"Thank you," nodded Kalila, paperwork in hand.

"Okay, let's hit the road." Ruth grabbed the handles and started to push. "I don't like leaving Melvin for long. He's not a big fan of hospitals."

Kalila's face broke out into a sardonic smile. "Who can blame him…"

Kalila's mood darkened on the car ride home, still shaken after the visit from Officer Sebulsky and his trusty sidekick, Hippenstiel.

"How're you doing?" Sebulsky had bellowed when he came uninvited into her hospital room, acting as if he and Kalila were two old friends catching up after a bout of hard luck.

"Better," Kalila answered groggily. The pain medication made her mind fuzzy, slowing her ability to think.

"We won't be staying long," Sebulsky said. "Just wanted to stop by; go over a few points so we can wrap this report up and have you sign off on it. Sound good to you?" he asked. His piercing trained eyes never left her face. Hippenstiel, presumably the official note taker, moved closer to the door, remaining quiet, but affable. The nice guy. The kind you'd take home to mother.

Head throbbing, Kalila closed her eyes. "Sure." She hoped the darkness would help her to work through the cobwebs currently annexing her brain. "Ask away."

"First question: has your husband ever hit you before?" Sebulsky asked expressionless.

"No."

"Never?" His raised eyebrows indicated her answer surprised him.

"Never," answered Kalila resolutely.

"What set him off?"

What could she say? That she married him out of revenge? Out of necessity? "I don't know. I'm not sure. He just barged into the house, furious."

"Then what?" Sebulsky asked.

"Then he started calling me names."

"What kind of names?"

"I can't remember."

"I need you to try."

"I don't remember."

"Not even one name? That's hard for me to believe."

"Ask him. I'm sure he remembers every last detail."

Sebulsky lowered his head as if in deep thought. "Well, you see, Mrs. Zubairi, here's where we have a major *problemo* because we can't exactly do that," he said, cagily.

Kalila's eyes popped open. "What do you mean?" She felt her heart rapidly pounding in her throat. "Oh, my God…he's not—"

"No. Not dead, but unconscious. His wife—*the other one*—what's her name?" he asked Hippenstiel.

"Amara Zubairi," answered Hippenstiel promptly.

"Ah, yes," he said with a snap of his fingers. "Amara. Well, funny enough, she said she didn't know either."

Kalila shrugged and turned her face away from the men.

"However, she did make a point of telling us that in her experience, Mr. Zubairi's not the—how'd she put it?"

Hippenstiel read off his notes. "Not the type to get upset or mad for no reason."

"Ah! And there you go," said Sebulsky, throwing his hands in the air. "And as a matter of fact, the other Mrs. Zubairi said that your mutual husband is just the opposite. How did the other Mrs. describe him again?" he asked Hippenstiel. "In her own words."

Hippenstiel flipped back a few pages in his notebook. "Kind and patient. Loving and considerate. Upright. Never loses his temper easily."

"She said that?" asked Kalila, incapable of masking the disbelief from her voice.

That lying b—

"Yep. She most certainly did. "So," shrugged the congenial good old boy, just doing his job, cop. "You can see our dilemma, right?" Sebulsky slid the visitors' chair closer to Kalila's bed and without bothering to take off his coat, sat down, making himself at home. Hippenstiel remained standing.

Kalila stared at the ceiling, weighing her options. Either she could end this and tell the whole embarrassing, sleazy story—Roger included, *or* let the chips lie wherever they will and allow Amara's bullshit version to stand. Either way, Kalila knew she wouldn't come out looking good.

As if a savant who could read minds, Sebulsky leaned in, mellifluously enunciating each word. "Look, bottom line; whatever his reasons, whatever set your husband off—it didn't give him the right to do this to you or to your son. Whatever you tell us stays with us. I just want to nail the bastard."

Kalila didn't know whether to trust him or not, but what choice did she have? "I don't want anyone in my business, especially Amara. I will need time to get my son and I away without having to deal with all that." She attempted to shift her position, but the pain stopped her. "I need to speak to my husband's doctor first."

"Fair enough. But I want you to remember, it's your husband who's being charged, not you."

"But it's my word against his."

"This is true," Sebulsky said, casually leaning back in his chair. "But he's not talkin'."

"Not or won't?" she asked guardedly, refusing to be bullshitted.

"More like can't. You should probably also know, from what the doctors are saying, he may never regain his speech again." Sebulsky crossed his leg over his thick thigh, never once taking his eyes off Kalila's face. "He took one hell of a blow to the skull, which is why we're here. We need to make certain—*from you*—that he slipped. That this was just a terrible accident and not anything more dubious." Sebulsky waited a moment before slapping his knees to stand. "Right then! Hippenstiel, get the nurse for me. Tell her Mrs. Zubairi needs to speak with her husband's doctor asap."

"Yes, sir." Hippenstiel promptly left the room.

Once the door closed, Sebulsky turned to face Kalila, no longer playing the nice guy. "Look, Mrs. Zubairi, I'm no rookie. I don't blush easily, and I've heard it all before so don't jerk my chain. Whatever dysfunction you and the other Mrs. got going on, I couldn't care less. Anything you may have had going on the side, doesn't faze me in the slightest. Are you getting my drift?"

Kalila nodded.

"Good. So, do us both a favor. Stop your deceptive bullshit and come clean so I can close this case and call it a day."

***

Ruth

Ruth drove home extra slow, mindful not to make any unnecessary sharp turns or stops.

She noticed how uncomfortable Kalila looked sitting in the front seat, probably wishing she was already home and in bed.

"Would you mind if I cracked the window? I need a little air." Kalila's cheeks looked pale behind the bruises.

"Of course." Ruth adjusted the window from her side. "Any better?"

"Yes." Kalila closed her eyes to rest. "Thanks."

From the back seat, while Melvin hummed, Hamza remained stoically quiet, lost in his own world.

Once in Kalila's driveway, Melvin headed home. "Bye, Hamza," he said.

Hamza barely nodded. To Ruth, the boy seemed scared, as if not entirely sure about what he would find once inside.

"I hope you don't mind, but I straightened up a bit last night. I didn't want you both coming home to that—mess." Ruth glanced away. Her voice trailed off, uncertain.

"Thank you," said Kalila, relieved. "That was kind." The place looked spotless.

"I'm going to bed," mumbled Hamza, climbing the stairs slower than usual.

"Wait. Aren't you hungry?" asked Kalila, barely able to stand on her feet.

"Nonsense," said Ruth. "Don't you worry about that. I'll put something together for the both of you and bring it up."

"But what about Felicia?" asked Kalila. "I don't want her to be alone."

"She's not. I have someone covering for me."

Kalila gave Ruth a halfhearted smile.

Ruth waited close by, watching Kalila struggle on the first two steps. "Are you sure you can make it up by yourself or do you need some help?"

"I thought I could do it. I honestly don't remember these stairs being this steep." Kalila gripped the banister. "I guess I could use an extra hand."

Ruth held Kalila firmly by the elbow. "Take your time. There's no need to rush."

Kalila nodded. "I couldn't agree more."

CHAPTER 32

Full Circle

Four months later…

"HAMZA!" YELLED KALILA. "YOU and Melvin grab the boxes from the hall and put them in my trunk. I think that's it." She scanned the room for stragglers. "Looks like everything else is already loaded up in the truck."

"All right."

"I'll meet you out front. Give me a sec." Kalila's eyes swept the vacant spaces around her. The click of her heels echoed against the floor amidst the vast, hollowed emptiness. She thought this day would never come and when it finally had, she could have never anticipated the deep foreboding sorrow it would cause. It saddened her to think about all the time she wasted trying to convince herself to leave…to learn to let go of everything that had transpired throughout the past year; raw, painful emotions kept safely hidden until she saw fit to drag them back out for dissection and a proper burial.

She needed this moment alone. To walk around and give the home she had once shared with the man she thought she'd grow old with, one last regrettable, but final goodbye.

The mantel above the fireplace now stood unadorned, once jam-packed with trinkets and baubles collected from family trips. Running her hand on the front doorknob, Kalila thought about the first time they both stepped inside. How happy she and Bashir had been, full of vivacity and expectation. Eager to begin the next exciting chapter of their lives together. Or was that also a lie? A projection? In hindsight, had Kalila only known then what lingered around the corner, she would have never agreed to move here.

"Ma," yelled Hamza. "Come on! The truck guys want to get going," he said, indicating the moving company crew.

"I'm coming," she shouted back, tugging the front door shut and locking it for the last time. Pocketing the key, she marched to her car, determined not to look back.

So much had changed in the last few months. Felicia's passing and funeral. Melvin's coming to live with them. The sale of not only her house but Felicia's home as well; a profitable endeavor which had provided the capital to start over elsewhere, but far from here.

"Where's Melvin?" Kalila asked Hamza, already standing next to their car.

Hamza pointed across the street where Melvin sat digging up a nice-sized patch of tulip bulbs; dropping each unearthed prize in an oversized plastic bag.

"Shit," moaned Kalila.

"Yup," agreed Hamza, stifling a laugh.

"Why?" said Kalila, throwing her head back and stomping her foot.

"They were his mother's favorite flower."

The driver in the truck tooted his horn to grab her attention. He rolled down his window, leaned out and yelled. "Ready to hit the road?"

"Just give us a few more minutes. I have, um," Kalila stammered. "My—" Unable to come up with anything that made sense, she settled on pointing next door to where Melvin continued on his quest. "He won't be much longer."

The driver and the two other guys in the front seat looked where Kalila had pointed and nodded.

"I shouldn't be letting him do that," said Kalila, shaking her head. "The new owners are going to lose their minds when they see those holes."

Hamza nodded. "Probably, but I'm not gonna be the one to stop him. Are you?"

"Nope. Not me. We'll let him finish." Kalila got an idea. "You know what? Why don't you go over there and nudge him along? While there, see if you can move the dirt around a bit, so it's not as obvious the place has been pilfered."

"Okay." Hamza jogged away.

Kalila avoided glancing across the street at Amara's house. The place still managed to give her the shakes. While not an ugly house per se, it had always been rather bland on the outside, if not gloomy. But now it appeared tattered and unkempt. Not surprising considering…

A rapid movement behind one of the curtains caught Kalila's attention, so she stared back, assuming the beady eyes belonged to Amara.

I'm just as thrilled to be leaving as you are to see me gone.

The two women hadn't exchanged a single word since the night of the attack.

Hamza and Melvin trudged their way towards the car.

Finally—

Apparently, they were discussing something that had Hamza cracking up.

Kalila watched the two and smiled.

Despite it all, Melvin's been a godsend to this family.

Kalila felt grateful to see that Melvin's magic seemed to be rubbing off on all of them.

"Okay guys, in the car," instructed Kalila, anxious to leave. "Melvin, there's room in the back seat for your bag. Hamza, take the front seat."

Without complaint, Melvin got in the back, strapping in and holding his bag of treasured bulbs securely on his lap. Hamza scooted in the front, ready to leave. Kalila leaned on her open door and waved at the guys in the truck. "Follow me," she yelled. They still had a long day ahead of them.

The very instant the truck revved up its engine, the front door across the street flew open and out stomped Amara, wearing a pair of men's flip-flops and a black overgarment that looked more like a muumuu.

Oh no. Not this again.

Kalila had hoped to be long gone before Amara had the opportunity to start her next round of drama.

Amara lumbered to the edge of her property, her hands cupped around her mouth. "You can run, Kalila, but you can't hide. What you did to me, to *my* husband, and *my* family—trust and believe, it's all going to come out. Every last nasty detail." Amara flipped Kalila the bird.

Kalila slid into the car. "Lunatic."

"You can bet your ass this isn't over," shouted Amara through the glass. "Not by a long shot."

Kalila started the engine.

"You home wrecking whore," yelled Amara at the top of her lungs. "They should've sent you to jail for what you did."

Hamza went to unroll his window to respond, but Kalila seized his arm. "Don't!" she snapped. "Don't give that crazy woman the satisfaction."

From the back seat, Melvin hugged his collection of tulip bulbs close to his heart and began to rock and moan.

"Are you okay back there, Melvin?" Kalila asked, once safely off their block and far away from Amara's taunts.

Melvin didn't reply, but his groaning and rocking simmered down. Head tilted to the side, he clicked his tongue three times.

Hamza winked. "Yeah. He's fine, Ma."

***

Their newly acquired three-bedroom home was substantially smaller than what they had all once enjoyed, but for all its lack of square footage, it felt safe. Contained. Away from the stress and painful memories left behind. For once, Kalila felt genuinely at peace.

Without missing a beat, Hamza asserted ownership of the bedroom facing the front yard. Kalila offered Melvin the master bedroom since it was considerably larger, and he needed the extra space for all his bookshelves with the possibility of a few more shortly. Kalila didn't need the space. She was more than content to lay claim to the smallest bedroom; more of an office since it didn't have a physical closet, but she didn't care. She'd make do. She just wanted peace and quiet. A place to think. A place to heal. A place to rebuild and a place to forget.

***

Kalila

On any other night, Kalila would have made the guys take their own folded clothes upstairs, but tonight being Friday meant movie night, so she decided to cut them some slack. With the laundry basket in hand, she headed upstairs, beaming with pride at the two of them snuggled on the couch sharing a bowl of popcorn. Melvin held the bowl on his lap while Hamza giggled and pointed to the screen, shouting, "This is the funny part." Domestic bliss never felt so good.

As expected, Hamza's room looked as if a tornado had hit it. Sports equipment on the floor, a desk piled high with books and papers. Even the night table had been lost under the strangest collection of junk and wrappers. Kalila grudgingly left Hamza's nicely folded clean clothes on the bed, wondering if they'd ever actually make it into the drawers.

Melvin's room, on the other hand, was the complete opposite. Clean, orderly, logical. Nothing randomly left on the floor. Bed made to precision. Even his bookshelves were dust-free and tidy.

His bookshelf.

Kalila fingered the spines of the sketchpads lined up in chronological order.

Hmmm...I wonder what he draws?

Kalila glimpsed over her shoulder making sure she was alone. She placed the laundry basket down on the floor quietly, wary of getting caught prying. For no reason in particular, she selected the fourth book toward the end on the last shelf, closest to Melvin's desk and began casually thumbing through the pages.

Wow…he's talented.

Kalila turned the pages, quite impressed until her eyes and brain registered precisely what—*and who*—she was looking at.

Oh—my God.

Kalila's fingers trembled as she held the sketchpad. Drawing after drawing depicted in meticulous, painful detail the life she labored to conceal, the life she tried to leave behind. "I'll be damned." That old all-too-familiar dreaded feeling of being exposed was now resurrected and taking control.

Melvin missed nothing. Kalila standing outside of the hotel, Roger's car parked next to hers.

Wait—

Kalila peered closer.

Holy crap—had Amara been there as well?

Watching?

No! Spying!

"*Astaghfirullah.*"

In a frenzy, Kalila flipped through page after page, one image more revealing than the next. The fights, the sorrows, Bashir's last night before…

She choked back sobs.

The funeral…

Alexa?

Glancing back at the door, Kalila's thumbs moved a brisk mile a minute; skimming through the endless pages. "*What the—*?" In some, Melvin had seen fit to draw angelic halos above her head, but she didn't have time to figure out that one.

In a panic, Kalila wanted to snatch every last one of Melvin's books and destroy them. One by one, ripping out every page.

Stay calm.

Think, damn it—think.

However, as crazed with fright and as out of control as she felt, Kalila knew that, in the long run, destroying Melvin's pictures wouldn't accomplish a thing. Nor would it stop him from drawing. Melvin, with a mind like a time warp filled with memories stuck in a perpetual, compulsive loop, would undoubtedly feel compelled to draw those awful pictures again.

After every agonizing passing minute, another, more corrosive wave of dread hit as she grasped the enormity of this new problem. She'd be screwed if Hamza found out what secrets lurked within those anything but innocuous pages. Scared to death, Kalila pressed the book to her chest, gasping, and unable to control the rapid pulse of her heart racing in her throat.

What do I do now?

She'd have to be careful. Nothing would get past Melvin. He'd be watching her day and night, and logging into that brain of his her every movement. Kalila knew it wasn't his fault. He couldn't keep from drawing any more than he could stop breathing.

Kalila let out a feeble, frustrated whimper.

What a sick irony. Just when I thought all my problems were behind me. And now this.

"Damn it."

All this time she believed Melvin had been a gift, but in reality, he'd been her punishment. His presence under her roof was akin to inviting the earthly-breathing version of the *Umm al-Kitab,* the Mother of all Books, where all of Allah*'s* knowledge of the existent and nonexistent resides; the tally of each person's deserved blessings and earned sins.

She could hear the guys talking loudly downstairs. Their movie must have run its course. Kalila forced herself to return Melvin's book to the shelf, moving listlessly like the perpetually condemned. She carefully placed the sketchpad back exactly where and how she found it while ignoring the overwhelming impulse pounding in her head to tear the incendiary pages apart with her bare hands.

Kalila laid Melvin's folded clothes on his bed and stole one last fleeting peek around the room, making doubly sure she hadn't disturbed anything else before closing the light and slipping out.

Hamza and Melvin were still downstairs. From the noise they were making, it sounded like they were straightening up before calling it a night.

Panic-stricken, she leaned on the wall and closed her eyes, scarcely able to breathe, no less think clearly. Unable to fathom how all her efforts to sever the connections from her tainted history had been for naught. And to think, after everything she'd been through, she had done nothing but replace one suffocating physical wall for a new, more complicated prison. With Melvin's damning drawings lurking about, she'd forever be a prisoner of her past.

Kalila exhaled, beaten.

What had Amara yelled? I can run but not hide?

She'd been right about that.

Pulse racing, she bent over and clasped her knees, struggling to inhale through her mouth to fight back the wave of nausea ready to consume her.

"Ya Allah," she pleaded in a soft, yet urgent supplication. "Tell me what to do now...*Please,* Allah, don't let Hamza find out what I've done. He'll never forgive me."

Footsteps.

Kalila quickly fixed herself. "All finished for the night, guys?" she asked from the top step, watching them climb upstairs, pretending as though nothing in the world was wrong.

"Yeah," said Hamza yawning. "I'm beat."

"What about you, Melvin?" she asked, unable to stop leering at him, second-guessing her every move. Before speaking, Kalila had to intentionally assuage the curt inflection determined to seep into her voice. "Ready for bed?"

Before Melvin could respond, his foot somehow wedged behind the other, causing him to stumble backward, gripping the railing in the nick of time.

"Careful!" she shouted, reaching out to steady him, but as soon as the declaration left her lips—in that tiny, infinitesimal, micro-second of time, a compilation of muddled, ugly, beyond evil thoughts careened through Kalila all at once.

"Damn, dude, take your time," said Hamza, helping his mother to steady him.

"Take your time, dude" Melvin repeated, completely unfazed.

Somehow, someway, Kalila would have to make sure Melvin's fastidiously penciled, capsulated pictures charting her past transgressions would never see the light of day. She'd have to figure out something. If not, her future, her relationship with her son—everything depended on the destruction of those drawings.

"Careful, Melvin." Kalila cautioned. "We wouldn't want anything to happen to you."

***

Qasim

Amara shut the bedroom door and turned up the heat. From their master bathroom, she filled two basins halfway with warm water, one without soap. She dipped her elbow repeatedly under the faucet to check it wasn't becoming excessively hot. By the bed, she spread one large, clean towel under Qasim's motionless body to keep the mattress dry and used another cloth to keep him warm.

"All ready for your bath?" she asked.

Eyes wide open, Qasim stared stonily at the ceiling, incapable of responding, but that never dampened Amara's incessant need to chatter. In fact, he believed she rather enjoyed keeping up a one-sided, uninterrupted conversation; basking in her element.

Dipping the washcloth in the warm water, Amara wiped Qasim's eyelid from the inner corner—out. "Now doesn't that feel nice?" She patted his eyelid dry, ready to repeat on the other side. A thin line of drool slid down the side of Qasim's stubbled chin and along his neck.

"Oh, no. Look at the mess you're making." She wrung out the washcloth, and dipped it back in the soapy water to bathe his face and neck, roughly tackling his ears last.

Qasim released a raspy—gurgling, asphyxiated sound. Amara leaned over, her face close to his as if attempting to decipher what her husband just tried to say.

So far, the prognosis for a full recovery looked grim but not completely ruled out yet. "Miracles do happen," reminded Qasim's chipper doctor at each visit. Still, therapy had done nothing thus far to help him regain his speech or movement.

"Now, now. No complaints from you," she murmured, rinsing the film of soap off his freshly scrubbed face, neck and ears. Amara then carefully folded the towel in half over Qasim's body, exposing his torso. The muscles around his hair follicles contracted, encasing his chest and arms in goosebumps.

"Aw, you're cold," she said, continuing to take her time washing the rest of his body from head to toe, one side, then the other, placing the towel back over him when finished.

"I need to change this dirty bath water before washing your privates."

Qasim heard her tromp into the bathroom. With every heavy-footed step, he cursed her; calling her a barrage of bitter, vicious names, all rattling around in his head, but refusing to pass his lips.

"I'm back." She plopped down at the edge of the bed causing it to dip and creak. Since his accident, Amara had put on more weight, eating everything in sight, apparently no longer concerned with what Qasim thought.

She squeezed out the soapy rag, then rolled him to his side. Leaning in closer, she checked his back for sores or areas of irritation.

"You've always had such a cute butt, Qasim," she goaded, running a washcloth repeatedly between his chilled, chafed cheeks. Once done, she rolled him onto his backside, and grabbed another clean rag, and plunged it in the foamy water. "Okay, you. Now for the fun part."

Wet cloth in hand, Amara massage-cleaned Qasim's penis, pulling the foreskin back and forth until he involuntarily became erect. Since leaving the confines and safety of the hospital, Amara had gone out of the way to deride and disparage Qasim at every opportunity.

"Oh my," she mocked. "Look at you." Her hand slid intentionally slow up and down his shaft. "I have to tell you, I'm always amazed it still works."

Qasim twitched; his strained breaths came out in short, clipped pants.

"Stop it!" she yelled, her flushed round face contorting into an ugly amalgamation of power and cruel disdain. And then in a split second, her features calmed, forming a half, wicked smile.

"Time to refresh this," she said, indicating the water. "I'll be back in a jiffy." Amara waddled to the bathroom, water sloshing and spilling from the washbasin with each heavy footstep.

Over the past few months, Qasim had come to dread the sound of running water.

Moments later Amara returned. "Ready, sweetheart?" she asked standing over him. Using two hands, she lifted the heavy, soaked washrag out of the plastic basin and began twisting every last drop of icy-cold water over his nether regions, causing him to jerk, shrivel up, and grunt out in agony.

"Now, now," goaded Amara, cackling. "Don't be mad, silly. I couldn't let you stay all stiff like that, could I? Why—that would be cruel." She reached across the bed for another cloth. "Time to clean up," she said, positioning a wet, icy towel across his bare chest.

Utterly helpless and cold, Qasim could do nothing but moan.

Amara bent over him, seething. "You should have left that bitch alone. And now look at you." She tossed a couple of the used towels across the room. "It's not like I didn't warn you, but did you listen?"

His lower lip protruded downward. A single, angry tear slid down the side of his cheek.

Amara gathered up Qasim's soiled laundry on the way to the bathroom. "By the way, big shot. Your fuck buddy and her bratty kid left this morning."

Qasim did know. In fact, he committed *everything* Amara said or let slip out to memory. Dark, damaging secrets he longed to one day reveal and use against them all.

"They moved out today. Needed one of them big trucks. I watched them fill it with all the nice stuff you and her idiot dead husband bought for her." Amara emptied the water from the basin into the tub and yelled. "And get this—she took that retard, Melvin, with them. One big happy family, minus you of course."

Robbed of his ability to respond, Qasim subsisted purely on the hate and venom locked deep inside his head, unable to break free.

If I ever regain control over my body, I'll make you pay, Amara—I'll make you sorry you were ever born—you evil, sadistic bitch.

I'll hunt you down.

You first.

Then Kalila.

I'll destroy you both.

ACKNOWLEDGMENTS

Books need a home and somebody to love and cherish them. They also need folks who think that the words contained inside books are worth reading and sharing. In a forever changing publishing world, I want to sincerely thank my incredible publisher and the entire DKP team for the continued support and care given to each one of my book babies. *You rock~Alhamdulillah!*

To my talented cover designer, Patrick Knowles: Thank you for investing the time and energy to create a cover that speaks so powerfully to the story. *Now, about those elves…* <— I win.

To my friend and fellow book addict, Dr. Jen Bradly: thank you for your valuable insights. Your suggestions and guidance required me to dig deeper, work harder, which made for a more dynamic read and highly complex characters. You are a blessing.

To my dear friend, Susan Moore Jordan: Where do I start? Thank you from the bottom of my heart for reading, and re-reading, and checking, and correcting my many comma disasters and *Saharisms*. I have, and continue to learn so much from you. xo.

To my kind, generous, and super-talented friend, J.C. Wing. Thank you for proofing my book baby before we set her free into the world. I can't thank you enough. xo.

To my incredible, brilliant, early readers: Harriet Van Houten, Anne Quirindongo, Catherine Schratt, Belinda M. Gordon, Kelly Jensen, and Diane Bukoski. Thank you, my friends, for hanging in there with me, believing in me, encouraging me, listening to me whine. I am so blessed to call you my friends.

To my family: You have never made me feel guilty for the long hours I spend behind my computer. Instead, you ply me with food, tea, snacks and endless amounts of hugs. Equally as amazing, you guard my writing time sometimes better than I do, and that means the world to me.

I must admit, however, that I adore how you all get just as excited as I do when that first box of new books arrives, or when we glimpse one displayed on someone's bookshelf or spoken about online. Your trust is energizing. Your faith is motivating. Your love for me is life. *My life.* My blessed life—filled with those I deeply love and forever cherish.

GLOSSARY OF TERMS

Abaya: A long sleeve dress. It could also be a full length outer-garment.

Allah: The One and only God

Allahu alim: Allah knows best

Abi: My father

Adhan: Call to prayer or *salat*

Afwan: You are welcome

Akhi: Our/my brother in Islam

Alhamdulillah: All praise is due to Allah

Allahu Akbar: Allah [God] is Great

Ameen: Agreement with Allah's truth

Aqiqah: A welcoming celebration of a newborn baby, naming ceremony.

As salaamu alaikum: May peace be upon you. It is used when greeting someone.

ASA: Acronym for *As salaamu alaikum*

Astaghfirullah: I seek forgiveness from Allah

Bint: Daughter of

Bismillah: In the Name of Allah

Deen: Way of life

Dua: Invocation; an act of supplication.

Fitna: Trial, distress, affliction; temptation or civil strife

Hadith: A collection of traditions containing sayings of the Prophet Muhammad ﷺ which, with accounts of his daily practices.

Halal: Permissible

Haram: Not permissible

Hijab: Scarf or head covering

Hijabi: Slang term for a woman or girl who wears the Islamic head covering called *hijab*, respectfully.

Iddah: The period of time a woman must observe after either the death of her husband or after a divorce, during which she may not marry another man.

Imam: Islamic leadership position, leader, the head of the Muslim community

InshaAllah: God Willing. If Allah wills.

Jumah: Friday prayer, congregational prayer

Kafir: Unbeliever, disbeliever or infidel

Khula: When a woman initiates a divorce it is called khula.

Khutbah: Sermon

MashaAllah: God has willed it. The exact meaning of *MashaAllah* is "what Allah wanted has happened." It is used to say something good has happened in the past tense. Some Muslims believe it wards off the evil eye.

Masjid: Another term used for mosque, place of prayer

Muslimah: Muslim woman

Nafs: The ego. Desires.

Quran: The word of Allah. The Guide and holy Book for Muslims.

Sadaqah: Charity or voluntary giving

Salat: Prayer [s]
The specific names and general times of the five prayers are:
- **Fajr**. This prayer is made before sunrise.
- **Dhuhr**. This prayer is made just after midday.
- **Asr**. This prayer is made in the late afternoon.
- **Maghrib**. This prayer is made just after sunset.
- **Isha**. This prayer is made in the late evening.

Shaitan: The Devil or Iblis

Shukran: Thank you

SubhanaAllah: Glory be to God. Glorious is God.

Subhanahu wa ta ala: The Most Glorified, the Most High.

Sunnah: A way of life, teachings and practices from the Prophet Muhammad ﷺ.

Thobe: A traditional Arabian garment worn by men, usually long-sleeved.

Umm/Umi: Mother, my mother

Wa alaikum salaam: And upon you peace

Wallahi: I swear to God or Allah

Wudu: Ablutions; washing the body to prepare for prayer.

Zawjah: Wife

BOOK CLUB DISCUSSION QUESTIONS

—with added author commentary

The Gatekeeper's Notebook brings attention to a myriad of sensitive and uncomfortable subjects, including mental health, which is all too often skewed or glossed over. The characters in the story are flawed, intense, and sometimes even twisted.

"I unapologetically write about subjects most would rather ignore or pretend don't exist. In doing so, I hope to challenge readers to question their misconceptions, preconceived notions, and fragilities." — Sahar Abdulaziz

1. What was your initial reaction to the book? Did it hook you immediately, or take some time to get into?

2. What made the setting unique or important? Could this story have taken place anywhere?

The Gatekeeper's Notebook is about a young woman named Kalila, who swore she'd found the man of her dreams when she married Bashir Rahim. After many heated arguments, Bashir finally comes clean and informs Kalila that he plans on taking a second wife. Furious, she kicks him out of the house and tells him to "never come back."

3. Do you think Kalila would have gone through with the divorce or would she have eventually accepted having a co-wife? What about Kalila's personality leads you to either estimation?

To make ends meet and to keep a roof over her and Hamza's head, Kalila returns to prostitution.

4. Did the admission that a Muslim woman could both profess her allegiance to Islam and still sell her body for money, shock you? How did that revelation make you feel and why?

5. Amara became Muslim when she met Qasim in college. Did you find Amara's relationship with Islam to be genuine or did you see her as disingenuous? Sanctimonious? Judgmental? Moreover, if so, in what ways?

6. Bashir had been seeing Alexa behind Kalila's back for quite some time. Do you think he handled the situation correctly with either Kalila or his new wife? Why or why not? What could he have done better? Kinder?

Amara Zubairi, Kalila's neighbor from hell, decides to snoop hoping to gather enough dirt to "out" Kalila in front of the entire Muslim community and expose her as a fraud to her husband.

7. Amara disliked Kalila profusely, but why? Jealousy? Religiosity? Protectiveness? Self-hate? Alternatively, pure evilness?

8. Amara's world implodes when she finds out that the woman she hates is now her co-wife. Even worse, her husband makes it clear that his love and affection lie solely with his new and beautiful spouse. Did that in any way impact how you felt about or for Amara, and if so, why?

9. Nafiza and Walaa were both in healthy marriages. How do you feel about the way they tried to make Amara and Kalila be friends? Should they have minded their business, or did they do the right thing?

While Melvin has difficulty verbally expressing himself, his incredible and exacting artwork speaks volumes. He is able to record through drawings everything he observes within his gated community in his sketchbooks.

10. What Melvin saw, he drew, yet most everyone overlooked his presence, repeatedly disregarding his talent. Do you think the same could be said if Melvin's drawings had been made known? And if so, would that have placed Melvin in danger and by whom?

11. Kalila took her *shahadah* after meeting Bashir, but do you think she ever really connected to Islam or was it more because of her relationship with Bashir? It is also important to note that Bashir's second wife was also not Muslim when they met. Why do you think that is?

12. How did the characters change throughout the story? How did your opinion of them change?

For a split second, Kalila contemplates letting Melvin fall when Melvin accidentally trips and almost falls down the stairs. The realization that her dark past and secrets are only as safe from exposure as Melvin's next drawing suffocates her.

13. In the end, the reader is left wondering Melvin's fate. Do you think Kalila will find some way to destroy Melvin or his books to hide her secrets or will her conscience take over? What would you have done in Kalila's place?

14. How did you feel about the ending? What did you like, what did you not like, and what do you wish had been different?

15. Which character did you relate to the most, and what was it about them that you connected with?

16. If the book were being adapted into a movie, who would you want to see play what parts?

17. Lastly, did *The Gatekeeper's Notebook* change your opinion or perspective about anything? Do you feel differently now than you did before you read it?